Moonlight:
the big bad wolf
THE CHRONICLES OF BLACK SWAN 4

by Victoria Danann

Discover other titles by Victoria Danann and
read more about this author and upcoming
works at   www.VictoriaDanann.com

This is a work of fiction.

***

VICTORIA DANANN

This is a serial saga intended to be read in order.

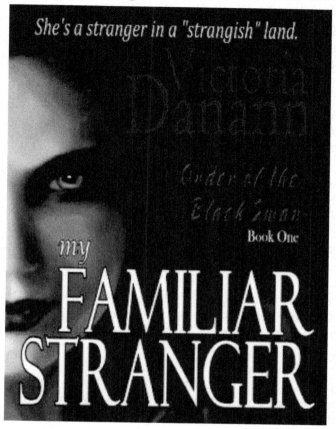

She's a stranger in a "strangish" land.

Victoria Danann

Order of the Black Swan

Book One

my FAMILIAR STRANGER

Praise for *My Familiar Stranger*, BLACK SWAN 1

"This book was a ride!)." - *Between the Bind.*

"I could write like this I would never do anything else… " - *Books, Books, and More Books*

"... shades of Lara Adrian's *Breed* books and shades of J R Ward's *Black Dagger* books. ... given time (she) will elbow them out of the way with the rich storytelling and deep emotional core." - *Musings of a Bookworm*

"This book is not the usual paranormal story that I am used to reading. It is way better." - *The Paranormal Romance Guild*

"...wonderfully engrossing paranormal romance with just a dash of science fiction that grabbed me from page one and didn't let go!" - *Bitten by Paranormal Romance*

"...wonderfully intriguing romance with its own twist on the paranormal world and I loved every page." - *Bitten by Love Reviews*

"...beautiful and heartwarming. ...laugh-out-loud moments, as well as several nail biting, edge-of-your-seat moments." -*TOP PICK Night Owl Reviews*

"...devoured the book in less than two days!" - *Book Nympho*

"... emotional, sweet, moving, funny, heart-wrenching, action-packed and totally enthralled me from the get go! - *Emily Guido, author of the Lightbearer Series*

"...get ready to dive into a new dimension with horrors, villains and true love that will keep the pages turning." - *Addicted to Reading*

VICTORIA DANANN

Praise for *The Witch's Dream: BLACK SWAN 2*

"...dramatically fun, sexy, and addictive." - *Between the Bind*

"...an awesome follow-up to *My Familiar Stranger*." - *Book Maven*

"A must read for all fans fans of the romance, paranormal and magickal genre." - *Cozie Corner Book Reviews*

"...a sweet and sexy good time." - *Bitten by Paranormal Romance*

"...an intriguing sequel that surpasses *My Familiar Stranger*." - *Ramblings of Coffee Addicted Writer Blog*

"You will be turning pages as you need to get to the end - and then re-reading as you await book 3." - *Booked and Loaded*

"...plenty of blazing hot romance, as well as plenty of adventure..." - TOP PICK Night Owl Reviews

A SUMMONER'S TALE

Order of the Black Swan 3

Praise for *A Summoner's Tale: BLACK SWAN 3*

"Let me just say SQUEEEEEE!" - *Reviewing in Chaos*

"As multiple stories are seemingly unrelated, each brings with it a new dimension that begins to form a pattern that slowly leads all players to one key game, one final showdown." - *Booked and Loaded*

"Danann is really onto something with this spicy, entertaining and exciting series!" - *Vampire Romance Books.com*

"Each time I read another book by Ms. Danann, I always say it's my favorite of hers, but really, ***this*** one is!" - *Between the Bind*

"What can I say, other than the series has it all." - *The Paranormal Romance Guild.*

"Fast paced, action packed, amazing characters - do not miss this series." - *The Wormhole*

"A titillating and quite heart-warming ride." - *Simplistik.Org*

"Just when you think things can't get any better a new twist forms." - *Bitten by Paranormal Romance*

"Victoria does it again. ... she makes you feel you are right there." - *Cozie Corner Book Reviews*

"...a great mixture of science and humanity – much like reality." - *The Reading Cafe*

"She does a great job of creating a world that we will never see but where anything may seem possible." - *Urban Girl Reader*

Praise for *Moonlight: BLACK SWAN 4*

Listopia #1 BEST BOOKS OF MAY 2013.

"...like a pitcher of Margaritas with a plate of jalapeños, like a guaranteed multiple orgasm with no mess or fuss, like designer shoes at a pre-season 90% off sale..." - *Fangs, Wands, and Fairy Dust*

"...a series that you must read, you'll thank me later!" - *Faerie Tale Books*

"You sink into the story and are swept away by the emotions." - *The Wormhole*

"Danann's witty and humorous style of writing creates laugh-out-loud moments." - *Sun Mountain Reviews*

"... a story that both demands to be read and leaves fans on the edge of their seats." - *Booked and Loaded*

"Demon-dads and romps with wolves, drunk vampires and star-crossed lovers collide..." - *Between the Bind*

"...after reading Moonlight I am ready to dive into the other stories." - *TeenBlurb.org*

"...plenty of romance, sex, adventure and suspense, what more could you ask for?" - *The Paranormal Romance Guild*

Special THANK YOU'S...

Thank you to Kelly Danann who gave me the confidence to publish the first book.

Thank you to Julie Roberts, world's best editor.

Thank you to my friend and bridge partner, Michele Murphy. I'm so lucky to have a native French speaker to trust with my outrageous translations.

Victoria is a big fan of the Black Swan A Team.

Anna-Marie Coomber
Ashley Logan
Brandy Ralston
Christine Merritt
Cristi Riquelme
Dawn Dow
Dee Bowerman
Diane Nix
Elizabeth Quincy Nix
Holly Collins
Joanette Fountain
JoBeth Sexton
Judy Fox
Kelli McDonald Young
Kim Staley Schommer

Leah Barbush
Leslie Miner
Lisa Jon Jung
Lovena Stover-Stump
Maggie Nolan
Mark Reeves
Megan Root
Nelta Baldwin Mathias
Pam James
Patricia Smith
Preksha Thaker Lakhia
Rochelle Taves
Sherry Evans Botelho
Tabitha Schneider
Talisa Martin
Teri Zuwala
Ticia Morton Hall
Tifinnie Henry
Tracie Runge

author's note...

One of the questions that I'm most often asked is, "What inspired this story?" Or, "How do you create your characters?"

For the first three books I was stumped for answer. The reason why I never knew how to answer these questions is because it doesn't *feel* like I *created* a story or characters. It feels like I'm just reporting events, chronicling the lives of certain "people" along with their friends, families, or associates.

Readers tell me they get the sense that the characters and world are so real that you might find them just around the next corner. I love hearing that because it's a reflection of my own perspective. I confess to entertaining the idea that I am reporting in fact on a world that is every bit as real as this - in a similar, but alternate dimension.

My best,
Victoria

PROLOGUE

This series is also a serial saga in the sense that each book begins where the previous book ended. **READING IN ORDER IS STRONGLY RECOMMENDED AND ENCOURAGED** in order to fully enjoy the rich complexities of this tapestry in book form.

There is a very old and secret society of paranormal investigators and protectors known as The Order of the Black Swan. In modern times, in a dimension similar to our own, they continue to operate, as they always have, to keep the human population safe. For centuries they have relied on a formula that outlines recruitment of certain second sons, in their early, post-pubescent youth, who match a narrow and highly specialized psychological profile. Those who agree to forego the ordinary pleasures and freedoms of adolescence receive the best education available anywhere along with the training and discipline necessary for a possible future as active operatives in the Hunters Division. In recognition of the personal sacrifice and inherent danger, The Order bestows knighthoods on those who accept.

BOOK ONE. The elite B Team of Jefferson Unit in New York, also known as Bad Company, was devastated by the loss of one of its four members in a battle with vampire. A few days later Elora Laiken, an accidental pilgrim from another dimension, literally landed at their feet so physically damaged by the journey they weren't even sure of her species. After a lengthy recovery, they discovered that she had gained amazing speed and strength through the cross-dimension translation. She earned the trust and respect of the knights of B Team and eventually replaced the fourth member, who had been killed in the line of duty.

She was also forced to choose between three suitors: Istvan Baka, a devastatingly seductive six-hundred-year-old vampire, who worked as a consultant to neutralize an epidemic of vampire abductions, Engel Storm, the noble and stalwart leader of B Team who saved her life twice; and Rammel Hawking, the elf who persuaded her that she was destined to be his alone.

BOOK TWO. Ten months later everyone was gathered at Rammel's home in Derry, Ireland. B Team had been temporarily assigned to The Order's Headquarters office in Edinburgh, but they had been given leave for a week to celebrate an elftale handfasting for Ram and Elora, who were expecting.

Ram's younger sister, Aelsong, went to Edinburgh with B Team after being recruited for her exceptional psychic skills. Shortly after arriving, Kay's fiancé was abducted by a demon with a vendetta, who slipped her to a dimension out of reach. Their only hope to locate Katrina and retrieve her was Litha Brandywine, the witch tracker, who had fallen in love with Storm at first sight.

Storm was assigned to escort the witch, who slowly penetrated the ice that had formed around his heart when he lost Elora to Ram. Litha tracked the demon and took Katrina's place as hostage after learning that he, Deliverance, was her biological father. The story ended with all members of B Team happily married and retired from active duty.

BOOK THREE. Istvan Baka was captured by vampire in the Edinburgh underground and reinfected with the vampire virus. His assistant, Heaven McBride, was found to be a "summoner", a person who can compel others to come to them when they play the flute. She also turned out to be the reincarnation of the young wife who was Baka's first victim as a new vampire six hundred years before.

Elora Laiken was studying a pack of wolves hoping to get puppies for her new breed of dog. While Rammel was overseeing the renovation of their new home, she and Blackie are caught in a snowstorm in the New Forest. At the same time assassins from her world, agents of the clan who massacred her family, found her isolated in a remote location without the ability to communicate. She gave birth to her baby alone except for the company of her dog, Blackie, and the wolf pack.

Heaven was instrumental in calling vampire to her so that they could be intercepted and given the curative vaccine. Baka was found, restored, and given the opportunity for a "do over" with the wife who had waited for many lifetimes to spend just one with him.

CHAPTER_1

"What do you know about my sister and that prancin' prick of a fairy prince?"

Elora blinked, but in the space of that flutter he learned all he needed to know. He had found out the first time Storm brought her to poker night, back at Jefferson Unit, that her very expressive face telegraphed even the tiniest nuance or feeling or thought. By now he knew her so well that she was as transparent as air.

She was caught off guard because she hadn't expected that question while Ram was cooking a leisurely Sunday breakfast. She recovered and tried to cover.

"Say that three times fast?"

"No' goin' to work this time. Stay on topic."

"You just don't like him because he can stand toe to toe with you and not be cowed by the H.O.H. elfster."

"ELFSTER!? What in Paddy's Name, Elora? And what is H.O.H.?"

"Hall of Heroes."

Ram turned away from frying bacon and gave her a look. It probably didn't have the effect he intended. He was wearing jeans, a long sleeve black tee that stretched across his chest enticingly, and a black Jack Daniels apron tied around his waist. She thought perhaps nothing was sexier than watching Ram's muscles ripple while cooking her breakfast.

"Do no' try to deflect. 'Tis I. And Paddy knows I

can tell when you're hidin' somethin'." Ram looked determined.

"Speaking of hiding. You're going to have to do something about all these guys overrunning our property. *Our home* - the one that was intended to be our *very own*, *very private* property. Please, Ram. Make them go away."

His expression softened a little as he decided to allow himself to be temporarily derailed.

"Sol, Simon, and every one of your friends agree that we can no' leave you and Helm vulnerable after the threat those alien buggers left hangin' in the air. That goes especially for your friend, Sir Storm."

"*My* friend, Sir Storm?"

"Aye. *Your* friend. The bloody wanker suggested that I'm no' responsible enough to be entrusted with lookin' out for you. Said, 'You're no' takin' good care of my namesake's mother. I'll be forced to give the job to someone else if you do no' shape up and begin takin' it seriously'."

Elora laughed. "He said that?"

"Aye. As if 'twas all my doin' that you ended up givin' birth alone in a freezin' wolf cave. With. No. Phone."

"Well..."

Ram narrowed his eyes at her. "Think very carefully about what you are about to say before you say it."

Elora smiled brightly. "I was going to say that no one in his right mind could fault you."

Ram nodded and resumed turning the bacon. "Exactly. I should have reminded him what happened when *he* was in charge of the Baka interview at Unit Drac. He pouted for hours after learnin' first hand that the Lady Laiken does as she fuck-well pleases."

Elora concurred by nodding vigorously. "It's a burden, but you bear it well, my love."

"All kiddin' aside, I do. I really do." He began setting strips of cooked bacon out to drain the grease.

"Well, Sir Storm is going to be plenty busy with his own burdens."

"What's your meanin'?"

"They're expecting."

"Expectin' a baby?"

"No. They're expecting Publishers Clearing House to pay for their villa renovation."

Ram gave her a look. "You know, I'm thinkin' there's only enough of this lovely bacon for one and, since I cooked, I really should be keepin' it for myself."

"Yes! They're expecting a baby. Litha thinks it's a girl."

"A girl!" Ram practically whooped. "Paddy's Great Balls Afire. I can no' wait to see Storm try to be da to a girl." He laughed enjoying that idea, and then grew serious. "As for the buggers who violated my grandda's forest, I'll no' be givin' 'em a second chance at my family."

"Rammel. I hear you and I understand you."

"I do no' suppose the next sentence will be 'and I obey you'?"

Elora smirked while she snagged a piece of bacon. "Have I ever mentioned you make great bacon?" She nuzzled his ear on the way back to her stool. "Almost as good as chocolate."

Ram pointed a spatula at her. "I swear to Paddy you have that thin'... that ADDD."

"ADHD?"

"Aye."

Elora started laughing. "Pot."

When his brows drew together she smiled, because Helm looked at her with that same expression several times a day. They made him accidentally in a snow-covered cottage, but he was made with love and now he was a little bit her and a little bit him. A miracle indeed.

"You can no' concentrate 'cause you've been smokin' dope?"

"No! 'Pot' as in 'you're the pot calling the kettle black'."

Ram stared at her for a few beats, finally shook his head and said, "No idea."

"You don't have an expression here about the pot calling the kettle black?"

"We do no' that I know of, but I think I begin to follow your point. You're tryin' to say that I should no' be accusin' you of short attention because mine is even shorter?"

Of their own accord, his eyes drifted down to the cleavage showing between the henley buttons she'd left undone.

She chuckled. "See?"

"See what?"

She did a little shimmy and he grinned sheepishly. "Guilty." He put an orange juice in front of her. "And be careful of the sexy dancin'. You'll be gettin' Helm's milk all over your clothes again."

Elora rolled her eyes. "He gets enough. Have you seen how chubby his little face is getting?"

"Well, blood will tell."

Elora narrowed her eyes to slits. "Rammel. Paddy help you if you're saying what I think you're saying."

"All I'm sayin' is that chubby cheeks do no' run on my side of the family." When she took a mock threatening step toward him, he laughed. "Just teasin', darlin' girl. Just teasin'. You know I would no' change a hair on your head. Or his."

"Okay. All *I'm* sayin' is that insanity doesn't run on *my* side of the family." A look of horror slowly covered her face as she realized what she'd just said. She hadn't yet personally confronted what the assassin in the woods had said about the Laiwynn clan, but if it was true, it meant that cruelty and despotic behavior might run in her family.

Ram put his utensils down, wiped his hand on his apron, and offered himself for a hug. She stepped into the comfort of his arms.

"What I was trying to tell you earlier is that I've never made any secret of the fact that I won't give up my freedom to live a restricted life, no matter how luxurious or comfortable. Not for anything."

"No' even for Helm? And me?"

"That's not fighting fair and you know it."

"When it comes to your safety - and our son's - you think I care about fightin' fair? 'Tis the very *last* of my concerns."

"Let me put it this way. You need to come up with a more agreeable Plan B and you need to do it while I'm still in a listening mood."

"Any ideas?"

She looked down at her pretty Holland china plate, part of the set they got as a wedding present from Kay and Katrina. She had a picture of how good life was going to be there in their new home. Had the Ralengclan assassins spoiled her vision of the future to the point of ruin? Was it time to confront that possibility?

"No." When she looked back up, Ram thought he might have seen her look just a little worn. Like her aura hadn't been buffed in a while. Sometimes he caught her looking off into space and he suspected that she was thinking about what she'd been told by the Ralengclan assassin, wondering if the massacre of her family was really a coup d'état." Armed people guarding the house. Hardly what I pictured."

"I know." Ram sat down next to her and took her hand in his. "We'll figure it out. Monq's workin' on it." He pulled up like he had an idea. The change was so subtle that no one besides Elora would have even noticed it.

"What?"

"He's workin' on detectin' interdimensional activity - identifyin' the source and location. He says 'tis a logical first step toward the defense system we're goin' to be needin'."

"Yeah. I heard."

"Well..." She knew she was in trouble when he turned on that look that he had given her the first night they had met, the puppy dog plea that was so irresistible she could be manipulated out of her socks with full knowledge and complicity. She hated that. It was... manipulation by consent.

"Stop that right now!"

"Was just thinkin' that, for the time bein', just while we're sortin' this out, maybe we should move back into Jefferson Unit. You and Helm would be safe there. I know 'tis no' ideal, but there is the courtpark, food, and babysittin' on demand. 'Tis no' this." He looked around the room and gave a little sigh. He had put a lot of himself into renovating the property and somewhere along the way had come to understand why she loved it and pictured their little family living happily ever after there. "But we were happy at Jefferson too. We could even help Monq. Maybe speedin' thin's along a bit?"

"I'm expecting puppies."

"I truly hope no one is recordin' this conversation." Ram's mouth softened at the corners making him look so beautifully kissable that she had to lean in and remind herself if those kisses were as good as she remembered. He didn't seem to mind complying with her wish. When she pulled back, he said, "We could get Glen to keep an eye on that. The wolf pups I mean."

"This is not just some ruse that's going to get us sucked back into active duty?"

Ram cocked his head like he was having trouble with that question. "Why would I go to so much trouble to keep you safe only so I could risk gettin' you killed?"

Elora stared at Ram for a few seconds. "I'm not the only knight in the room and we both know how persuasive Sol can be when he wants something. Before I even consider this proposal, I need some reassurance that none of us, not you, not me, not the baby - none of us - are going to end up on any field assignment. Not in *any* capacity."

Ram nodded. "Deal."

"Okay."

"Okay you approve of my answer or okay we're packin' for Fort Dixon?"

"Fort Dixon, but that's all of us. Blackie too. And we need an apartment big enough for the four of us."

"Thank Paddy. I'm goin' to get a good night's sleep for a change."

She hadn't realized just how much stress the fear of assassination had caused Ram until she saw his facial muscles relax. Yeah. It was a good plan. A good choice, everything considered.

"*And*, let's outline what would have to happen to make it possible for us to come back here and proceed to live life the way it should be lived. By ourselves. Speaking of which, I'm also not giving up the pleasure of a weekend at the cottage - just us - forever."

"Certainly. I'm no' unreasonable."

She smiled at him lovingly and indulgently. "Of course not. You're my hero."

Glen was giving Blackie a goodbye rough and tumble.

"Not in my living room," Elora said on her way past with her arms full of stuff the baby might need on the plane. She set the load down by the front door, looked around nervously, and pulled Glen aside looking like a woman with conspiracy on her mind. She spoke in a tone that was barely above a whisper. "I need you to do something for me on the down low."

"The down low?"

"Um. Yes. What do they call it here when you're off the record?"

"Off the record."

Elora let out a breath. "Okay. Off the record..."

"Which record are we off?"

"Let's start over. Between you and me..."

"Okay."

"Glen. Shut up." He chuckled. "You're messing with me, aren't you?" He grinned.

"Enough. Limited time here." He nodded.

"I need you to find out everything you can about the elf/fae war."

"Why?"

"Great Paddy, Glen."

"Okay. What exactly are you after?"

"How it started. See if you can find a reliable source - either a primary reference or an authority who knows for sure."

"You got it, boss."

"What has he got?" Ram came in carrying another load of stuff the baby might need on the plane, wearing his damn extra-sensitive elf ears.

"Just getting Glen to keep an eye on my puppies. Like we talked about."

Ram nodded, opened the front door, and started carrying Helm's busload of necessities to the Range Rover.

"Scary," Glen whispered to Elora.

"What?"

"How easily you lied to him and how genuine it sounded."

"Yeah, well, keep that in mind if you ever get married."

"I'm starting to recognize the appeal of bachelorhood."

Elora pinned him with a look. "Seriously, I would never lie to him if it wasn't to protect someone."

"You're protecting somebody?"

"Yes. I'm protecting them. I'm protecting him. And I'm protecting them from him."

"I'll find out what you want to know."

Elora gave him her high beam smile. "You're the best."

"Is payment involved?"

"Yes. Here it is." She kissed him on the cheek just as Ram came back through the front door.

"Catch! Stop cruisin' my wife and help me move the entire inventory of Babes R Us to the armored tank."

Prince Duff Torquil's family was having a small reception to celebrate his mid-winter graduation from law school from The University of Strathclyde at Glasgow. There was a tradition among the fae monarchy that those who were likely to rule should study history, with an emphasis on Fae history, and go on to law school, the logic being that the law was best administered by those who knew and understood it. The royal family, currently in residence at Holyrood Palace in Edinburgh, considered eight hundred guests a small reception. At that, there were sure to be at least two thousand more who would be in a snit and consider their lack of an invitation a snub.

When Elora received her invitation, she had written to the prince and explained that she and her husband had taken temporary quarters in the States. She added that she hoped it would not be presumptuous of her to ask that her good friend, Istvan Baka, and his bride, both employed by the same organization, take their place. Of course she knew it *was* presumptuous. After all, she had a background in the gentility of social arts, but she hoped he would grasp the code of her next sentence, which was this:

"You are certain to enjoy Baka's company and that of his new bride, who is popular among the entry level associates where she works. I'm certain you would make a loyal ally for life should you be kind enough to offer an extra invitation for her to bring a friend."

On the off chance that people were smarter than they appeared to be, Duff reread the note twice before tossing it on the glowing embers of the fireplace in his north wing office. He stabbed at the coals with the poker until the paper caught. After watching it burn to ash, he opened the door and stepped out to speak to his secretary. No matter how many times it occurred, the man always appeared startled when the prince leaned out and spoke to him. It seemed the palace staff would never get used to Duff's inappropriately modern and decidedly boorish behavior.

At first it had annoyed Duff that Grieve jumped in his chair whenever Duff opened the door to the outer offices and spoke to him. Grieve had been appointed by his father without giving the prince any say in the matter. Whatsoever. As usual. But eventually he came to terms with the fact that there was an odd little bespectacled man sitting just outside the entrance to his suite of rooms. He managed this internal resolution largely by appreciating the humor of the thing.

Grieve's display of shock had become part of Duff's day to day reality and one that he'd come to look forward to. In fact, he imagined that, should Grieve develop nerves of steel, he, Duff Torquil, Prince of the Scotia Fae and heir to the throne, would be forced to devise ways to deliberately create surprises, simply for the pleasure of seeing Grieve jump, gasp, and clutch his chest.

With that thought, Duff lowered his chin into his chest and chuckled while Grieve got himself together.

"Grieve," Duff repeated.

"Aye, your highness."

"Please send an additional reception invitation to an Istvan Baka at the Black Swan Charitable Corporation offices, Charlotte Square."

"But, sir, there are no odd invitations left to offer."

"Are you goin'?"

Grieve pushed his glasses higher on his nose. "Oh, aye. My presence is expected."

"Do you want to go?"

Grieve hesitated, mouth open, while trying to decide whether it would be in his interest to speak plainly or not. "I, ah..."

"The truth, man."

"No' particularly."

"There you have it then. Problem solved." Duff ducked his head back into his rooms and began to close the door.

"But, sir, your father..."

The prince opened the door and reappeared, but without his customary affable and approachable expression. He was clearly not pleased and might even have been scowling, although it could be hard to tell on such a beautifully smooth and youthful face.

"Who do you work for, Grieve?"

"You, sir?"

"Is that a question or an answer?"

"An answer, sir?"

"Hmmm. Well. I understand that my father hired you."

"Aye, sir."

"But he is no' in a position to oversee the minutia of my affairs every day. Do you no' agree?"

Grieve nodded. "Aye, sir?"

"Well, then it seems you must make a choice. Is your loyalty to the one who appointed you or to the one whom you serve?"

Grieve paused for only a moment before standing and pulling his shoulders back. "My loyalty is to you, sir. You can rely on me."

Truly, Duff was half joking and had not expected the equivalent of a chivalric vow of service, but seeing that the little man was serious, the prince was touched and decided not to dismiss it as a jest.

"Thank you, Grieve. I will treasure your declaration and count on it, from this day forward."

Looking like he had just experienced the best moment of his life, Grieve smiled like he'd just been knighted.

Duff withdrew and closed the door, but stowed away in his heart the knowledge that allies could be made from something so small as a little respect and recognition.

Baka would have loved to skip the prince's reception, but Elora had asked him to go and take Aelsong. So he was standing in front of the bathroom mirror in a blindingly white pleated shirt, trying to tie his black tie. He was just glad his tux came with pants instead of the kilt that most of the male guests would be wearing beneath their formal jackets.

Fresh from the bath, Heaven came up behind him with a towel wrapped around her. She pressed into his back and rose to her tip toes to peek over his shoulder at his reflection in the mirror.

"Hmmm. Handsome."

Baka gave her his best debonair smile. "Bond. James Bond."

She giggled. "Here." She urged him to turn around so that she could finish the tie. He could have used a clip-on, but the extra trouble paid off. While she was doing that, he casually unfastened her towel and let it drop to the floor. He pulled her closer with one hand while the other found delightfully wicked things to do to occupy itself.

Baka loved the way her chest heaved when she sucked in a surprised breath. "You don't *really* want this tied, do you, James?" Her voice had taken on a sultry undertone.

He laughed softly. "Not as much as I want to touch the valet. In fact..." Grabbing her waist, he lifted, turned and set her on the edge of the bathroom counter and stepped between her legs. "...what if we just...?" He froze in place when the door chime rang.

Heaven pushed him back and wiggled down from her perch making him groan as she slid down his body to the floor. "That's Song. Go get the door and entertain her for a few minutes while I finish getting ready."

He acquiesced with a big indulgent sigh and a look that was as good as a promise about what would take place when they were alone again later that night.

Baka pulled open the door and gestured for her to enter. "Song. You look lovely." His baritone had a velvety quality that made compliments sound smooth and sincere as vintage malt.

She hoped "lovely" was an understatement. She was going for good-as-it-gets and had pulled out all the stops.

"Thank you, Baka." She stepped in, looking him up and down. "No one would ever guess there's a dirty old vampire lurking underneath those pretty clothes. And I *do* mean old."

He chuckled good-naturedly. "My lurking days are over."

Nodding toward the bedroom, he added, "She's almost ready. I think. Something to drink while we wait?" He pointed to a bar that had been cleverly hidden in an antique French secretary.

"No. No' drinkin', breathin' nor sittin' down in this dress or 'twill crease and look a fright."

"Okay. We'll stand up together." The conversation dipped into a lag. "So. What's the mystery behind why the Lady Laiken wanted you to attend this party?"

Aelsong Hawking had the sort of expressive face that revealed every emotion, no matter how small, no matter how fleeting. That was doubly so when the observer was someone who had lived as long as Baka. She might choose not to tell him what it was about, but it was clear that something was up.

"Other than the fact that my sister-in-law seems to like seein' me happy, I do no' have a clue."

Baka knew she was lying. Aelsong knew that he knew she was lying, but he arched a brow and let it go. That was the best that could be expected.

The bedroom door opened and Heaven walked into the living room in very high heels and a shortened, tightened version of the blood-red dress she got married in. She was stunning. Stunning and delighted that Baka was speechless. His face said he liked this version of that dress even better. Her responding smile was like a starburst.

"Great Paddy, Heaven! You can no' go with me lookin' like that. 'Tis a crime for old married women to go sashayin' about the countryside drawin' all the attention for themselves. You should stay home with your old stodgy husband."

"Song. Those are the nicest things anybody's ever said to me. Thank you."

The "old stodgy husband" wasn't as pleased. "Well, it's not the nicest thing anybody's ever said to me! I am the furthest thing from stodgy and you know it."

Her gaze flew wide-eyed to Baka as soon as he said it, which alerted Heaven to the fact that there was something in that statement that alarmed Aelsong. Baka wasn't the only person who could read Song easily.

Song had learned enough about humans to know that Heaven would sever the friendship if she knew that Song had shared a memorable night with Baka, one that was wild even by elf standards, and she knew Heaven wouldn't care that it was before she'd met Baka. At least in that lifetime.

"What's going on?" Heaven looked directly at Baka. "What do you mean 'and you know it'?"

"Um. I met Aelsong in Ireland when Ram and Elora were getting married." *True.* "Didn't I tell you?" *No.* "I stayed drunk most of the weekend." *Also true.* "And I kept company with some of the attendees of feminine persuasion." *True again, if somewhat understated and a masterfully executed dodge.*

"Oh." Heaven looked uncertain, like the conversation had taken an unfortunate turn down a blind alley. She didn't know how to backtrack and recover the mood. Fortunately Baka did.

He gathered her in his arms with a devilishly intimate and reassuring grin. "You are absolutely the most ravishing, beguiling woman in this dimension or any other. And I haven't given another female a thought since the day Director Tvelgar introduced us."

The tension eased when she responded with a crooked little smile. "Introduced us? That's what we're calling it?"

"Works for me."

"Me, too." Song opened the door. "Let's get this party started. The royal family of Scotia awaits."

Baka stepped into the hallway and offered both arms to the lovely ladies on either side of him as the three dazzled their way toward the elevator.

The palace was an easy walk in walking shoes and a marathon in high heels. The doorman had a car and driver waiting, as promised. The women were having such a good time being dressed to kill that Baka was glad about going after all.

Aelsong insisted on an old-fashioned London-style cab so that she could half-stand in the car and try to keep from creasing her dress. "Just a warnin'. Tonight I'm along to listen, no' to talk. If I speak they'll know I'm elf and the ground might open up and swallow us all."

Heaven seemed to mull that over. "You mean the only difference between fae and elves is dialect?"

Song screwed up her face. "Can no' say for sure.

But 'tis a tip off. That I can say for sure. You will have to give me cover. Worse comin' to worse, just say I'm mute." When Heaven laughed, Song didn't like the impish look in her eye. "You would no'."

"Would not what?" Heaven batted her eyelashes and feigned innocence.

"You would no' deliberately say thin's, knowin' I can no' respond, that would make me either want to explode or want to squeeze your neck until that pretty amber necklace is permanently embedded!"

Baka was always surprised when reminded just how young his wife really was. "Come now. Nobody is choking anybody else. Heaven will behave."

Heaven looked out the window. "You can behave if you wish, stodgy old man. I will do what seems most fun at the time."

That threat miffed Song enough to make her forget about creasing the peau de soie dress. She sat unceremoniously and tried to reach over Baka to pinch Heaven. Baka blocked her with a stiff forearm while Heaven laughed with the impunity of a lady being protected by a powerful husband.

Baka stood on the fringe of the ballroom talking quietly with Simon Tvelgar. Both men were more interested in using their evening to discuss business than to engage in painfully inane small talk, chatting up people they would probably not see again, if they were lucky. Baka actually saw it as a momentous opportunity, because Simon's hectic schedule left him pressed for time and difficult to see. It was a bit of a challenge to manage verbal code so that nothing said between them would seem extraordinary if overheard.

Now and then Baka's eyes were drawn to his spouse's heavenly body moving through the room in her scarlet dress and her fuck-me shoes. So far as he was concerned all her shoes were fuck-me shoes, but the heels she wore that night screamed naughty by anybody's standards. There could be no doubt that she was having a marvelous time pulling the other beauty along, introducing Song to everyone as her very pretty, but tragically mute friend.

At one point Song leaned into Heaven with a big grin and spoke next to her ear without moving her lips. "I will get you for this if I have to spend years waitin' for the right moment."

Without looking at her companion, Heaven smiled and said, to no one in particular, but within Song's earshot, "Shaking in my knickers, darling. Oh, look, there's someone you haven't met." She grabbed Song to drag her in the direction pointed out by Heaven's beautifully manicured and scandalously red fingernail.

Song gave her a look so evil it would curdle milk. "Years," was all she said.

Baka suspected Heaven was having fun at Song's expense, but it would have been impossible not to appreciate the essence of life and liveliness in that sort of youthful mischief.

Turning back to Simon, with one hand in his pants pocket, the other holding a heavy crystal tumbler of Scotch etched with the monarchy's coat of arms, Baka did look as if he could pass for James Bond.

"One thing is clear. It isn't going to be as easy as we had hoped. So far it's been Myrtle's Law regarding getting the Inversion kick-started. Everything that

could go wrong *has* gone wrong."

"And you couldn't be more *wrong* about that," Simon replied.

"How so?"

"The worst thing that could have happened would be for the head of the task force to be reinfected with the virus, thereby becoming part of the problem instead of part of the solution."

Baka opened his mouth to respond, but his attention was redirected by a small fanfare.

The prince was being introduced and making a grand entrance.

Heaven leaned toward Song. "Do not tell my husband I said this, but oh, my, my."

Duff's eyes found Song like heat-seeking missiles. It was uncanny. Only a lifetime of pressure cooker discipline enabled him to tear his gaze away. But not before Heaven caught it. "Uh oh."

Song looked at Heaven and shook her head with such a tiny movement that it would have been missed by anyone not staring at her. That, coupled with the pleading look in Song's eyes, told Heaven all she needed to know.

"Let me take back that 'uh oh'." She glanced at the prince. "Bloody buggin' bags full of shite is what I should have said."

A guest standing nearby turned and gave Heaven a look of censure to indicate her severe disapproval of the word choice. Heaven just smiled and bowed her head gracefully like she was a courtier in a Renaissance play. The polite vocabulary enforcer seemed to accept that and moved on.

Heaven turned back to ask Song what the plaintive look was about, but she was gone. While

Heaven had been posturing for a stranger who needed some business of her own to mind, Song had noticed a little fae with glasses motioning her toward an alcove. Excited by the intrigue and the idea of possibly speaking to the prince, she ducked off to the side. He placed a handwritten note in her hand surreptitiously.

Her heart was beating a little faster as she opened it and read the words, *Meet me. -D.* She experienced one of those rare, surreal moments when her intuition worked on herself. And she knew her life was going to be permanently divided into everything that had come before that moment and everything that happened after she'd read the note she was crushing in her gloved hand.

Concealing the note in the palm of her hand, she slipped it into her little bag then looked squarely into the face of the messenger.

"Come with me?" The verbal question mark at the end of that phrase left no doubt that it was not a command, but her choice. She nodded her assent. The time for considering was over. Her course had been set before she'd accepted the invitation to attend the prince's party.

Looking back over her shoulder to be sure no one was paying attention, she slipped away doing her best to look nonchalant and no one saw her leave. No one except a double ex vampire who had been asked to take her to the party *and* see to her safety while out and about in "fairyland". He had no intention of explaining to the Lady Laiken after the fact of whatever was afoot that he'd been too busy to pay attention to Song's comings and goings.

Baka set his glass on a sterling silver tray as it

was carried past, excused himself from his conversation with Simon and followed Song with enough stealth to make a shadow envious.

Grieve led her down several deserted and dimly lit hallways, up a half tower of stairs then turned down a tiny curving hall that seemed to branch off and double back. He stopped next to another set of stairs leading higher.

"Down there." He pointed to the ground.

She stared at the stone steps beneath their feet. "Down where?"

"Fae Gods! You be elf!" he practically hissed.

She narrowed her eyes thinking it amazing that he had discerned that as the result of the utterance of two words. "Aye."

He stared for a moment, pressed his lips together, then shook his head. "Down. There!"

She looked closer at where he seemed to be pointing at the ground. At shin level there was an opening in the wall behind the steps. Her eyes jerked up at him. "'Tis a joke?" she hissed. "You can no' be serious! 'Tis your idea or his?"

"Have no fear, elf. You will fit. I assure you. I'm very good at spatial relationships."

"Spatial relationships," she repeated in a dry tone. "By that you would be meanin' the relationship between the flare of my hips and the width of that openin'."

He blushed a little and looked down, not meeting her eye. "Oh, aye."

"You're thinkin' I will be agreein' to acrobatics on a dusty stair? In this dress?" He continued to look at the ground, but said nothing more.

Song bent at the waist to take a closer look

thinking that she could not believe she was considering it for even a millisecond. There did appear to be a room beyond the little opening, but it was too dark to make out what was in there. She looked at Grieve. "You'll be gettin' the dry cleanin' bill and 'twon't be cheap. I can promise you that."

With two fearless older brothers, Aelsong wasn't big on shrinking from challenges. She gripped her little beaded evening bag with her teeth so that she could hold onto the banister with both hands and lowered herself part way, feet first, before letting go. Her hips brushed against old stone steps as her lower body let gravity do most of the work.

She let go of the railing, expecting to drop, but squeaked in surprise when strong hands gripped her waist. She knew that scent. Duff Torquil. He chuckled, preening with male satisfaction as he slowly lowered her down the front of his body. Aelsong, who was anything but inexperienced sexually, caught her breath and decided that, fully clothed and in the near dark, it was still easily the single most erotic moment of her life.

There was just enough light in the room to see the extraordinary shine in the prince's eyes. Every cell of their bodies caught the fire of mating excitation as the ancient and mysterious magnetism did its work. He pulled her closer for a sweet and tender kiss that heated to flash boiling. Since neither of them had ever felt mating frenzy, they were both surprised by the intensity and immediacy of the passion.

Duff took hold of her shoulders and forced himself to break the kiss. Taking a step back, he managed to whisper, "H'lo beautiful," even though his breathing was uneven. "You came."

"No' yet." Ram's sister she simply couldn't let that opening slide.

She tore her eyes away long enough to look around. The room under the stairs was where the palace staff kept the royal family's collection of pewter plates, trays, goblets, tankards and pitchers. There was a large rectangular table in the middle of the room laden with gun-metal gray objects and every wall was lined with crowded shelves.

"Where are we?" she whispered.

He glanced around. "Pewter Room."

"How did you know about this?" She waved at the opening between the steps.

"I used to play hide and go seek with other kids whose parents worked here. I never lost and nobody ever figured it out. The hard part was stayin' in here by myself and bein' quiet until they gave up."

"Shows patience."

"Aye. I'm almost out where you're concerned."

They looked at each other in the semi-darkness for a few seconds before throwing themselves into kisses and clutches with renewed fervor. Independently, each was thinking they had never experienced anything in life half as good as the feel of each other and each was thinking they never wanted to stop or let go. Again, Duff pushed away.

"What are we goin' to do?" Song's whispered question was couched in between breaths that were coming fast. She was almost panting.

He reached out for one of her blonde curls and rubbed it between his fingers. His eyes met and searched hers. "Run away?"

She stared into his darkened eyes for a few seconds then grinned. "I will if you will."

He laughed softly. "Let's do and say we did no'."

She nodded enthusiastically while he gave her a crooked little sexy grin. Her features went smooth and he knew the moment she became serious. "Are we kiddin'?"

He searched her face before moving to cup her cheeks in his hands. "I do no' have a better plan. I wish I did." He placed a tender kiss on her forehead and then jerked back. "Do you have a phone in that little purse of yours?" She looked down, opened the clasp, pulled out her phone and handed it to him.

He took it and started adding his contact. "This is a private number. My private number. The ID is 'Yam'." He pulled his own phone from the inner pocket of his jacket and handed it to her. "Give me yours. You can call me anytime, but I will only answer when I can. Do no' leave voice message or text. I will see that you called and call you back when I'm alone."

"YAM?"

He smiled. "You are mine."

Her lips moved as she repeated the words silently. She tore her gaze away from his handsome face long enough to enter her number in his phone.

He looked at the contact. "IAY?"

"Aye. I am yours."

Duff opened his mouth to say something, but heard Grieve's hushed voice above their heads. "Sir. Someone's comin'."

Duff grabbed Song and kissed her like he thought he had one minute to live then, placing his forehead against hers, he said one word. "Soon."

He left through the room's actual door on the other side from where she'd dropped in. She heard

Grieve speaking to someone above her head and knew she needed to remain as quiet and still as possible. Still feeling the warmth and tingle of his kiss on her mouth, she pressed her lips together and closed her eyes. Her mind was racing, imagining a hundred different scenarios of the future. The only thing they all had in common was a big comfy bed with a big and naked dark fae prince in it. *Soon.*

She smiled into the shadow-filled room, partly because of the idea of a lifetime with Duff Torquil and partly because it occurred to her that she might actually beat her older brother out of the position of family black sheep. Running off with a fae? She could see her father's face turning reddish-purple. She could see her mother's face pinched with disappointment and worry while hurrying away to oversee composition of a press release. Both her brothers would be turning the air blue enough to change the tint of the sky before vowing to hunt Duff down and skewer him.

At least she wasn't the heir. As difficult as it would be for her, she couldn't begin to imagine what Duff would be up against with his family. She let out a whispered laugh. She never asked to be mated to a fae, but there was no point trying to deny it. Life was strange.

CHAPTER_2

Litha sat at the end of a long conference table and watched the head of the Metaphysics and Mysticism Department tong a couple of ice cubes into her glass before he refilled it with water. For the hundredth time that day she wished that she and Storm had never confided to The Order that she was able to slip dimensions because of her something more than half demon heritage.

Sure. She could be the key to answering thousands of questions. From the perspective of paranormal investigators, she was a walking treasure trove. She was also witnessing the signs of her worst nightmare unfolding. They were starting to treat her like property of The Order.

There wasn't much that was less fun than being stuck in a room full of academics in Edinburgh while Storm was half a world away. He'd been summoned to Jefferson Unit. Well, he hadn't actually been summoned, but when his old boss asked to see him, it amounted to the same thing.

She had dropped him off at the New Jersey facility that morning. He had joked that her unusual abilities lent a whole new meaning to the question, "Can I get a ride?"

Storm had suggested that they use the opportunity to take a well-needed break, that she should join him as soon as she finished the current inquiry. Or "inquisition" as she called it. He said they could have a weekend in New York, then go home to the vineyard and regroup. She smiled, remembering that he had leaned into her ear and added, "... in bed," in a breathy whisper that never failed to give her visible shivers and make her nipples bead.

"Mrs. Storm?"

Her thoughts came back to the room, where seven faces were staring and waiting for a reply. "I'm sorry. Could you please repeat the question?"

"Of course. When you said you visited one dimension where they've been doing organic hybrid experiments for so long that there are no full humans..."

"Yes?"

"We're wondering what kind of hybrids have been developed?"

"Animal-human hybrids." It took every bit of patience she could muster to keep from shouting, "Duh!" at the end of that answer.

She glanced at her watch, as she was starting to wonder what she was getting out of her work with The Order. Their pay-off was obvious, but she was beginning to question her role. A quick assessment told her that she was beginning to feel less like an employee or associate and more like a victim. Something needed to change.

Another hour and she'd be gone. What a shame. She used to love her work. As far as she was concerned she was not only done with the questions and answers. She was *well* done and well on the way to being burned to a crisp.

When Litha had dropped Storm at Jefferson Unit that morning, she took him to Sol's office, partly to keep from causing a stir by materializing in the middle of some high-traffic area like the hub, and partly because one of the best things about emerging from a pass near a Black Swan facility was startling the codgers: Sol and Simon.

It was a joke that just couldn't be repeated so often that it wasn't funny anymore. Litha stayed long enough to make sure Sol hadn't had a heart attack, left her gorgeous husband with a big smile on his face, and vanished.

Storm turned to Sol, who was a little miffed about spilling room temperature coffee all over the front of his gray slacks in a pattern that would raise eyebrows. Sol scowled at the still-chuckling Storm, while dabbing his thighs with paper towels.

The very hour that Storm had announced his retirement - in person - the character of his relationship with the Sovereign had changed and transformed to friendship. On one level it felt like the most natural thing in the world to interact with Sol like he was a peer. Just two veteran knights sharing a coffee. On the other hand, it felt like the strangest thing in the world to have his recruiter, mentor, and former boss relax his demeanor and treat Storm like a peer.

When Sol decided that he had done as much as could be done with the pants, short of sending them to dry cleaning, he motioned for Storm to sit.

"Coffee?"

For a moment Storm wondered if that was a trick question. If he said yes, would he end up with room temperature coffee all over his lap? He decided that Sol was far too staid and mature for that sort of petty payback. And he was right.

"Sure."

Sol picked up the phone and asked for a coffee service for two to be served in the conference room, then moved the meeting next door. He recognized that sitting behind his desk skewed the dynamic in a direction that wouldn't be conducive to his purpose, part of which was to relax his guest. Talking to Storm from the authority side of a desk would suggest an unnecessary formality that would remind them both that, until relatively recently, Storm had had no choice but to do whatever Sol commanded. At least in theory.

Next door in the conference room, Sol motioned to two tufted leather club chairs that sat opposite the wall of windows with a small table between.

When they were seated, he asked, "So. How have you been?"

The inquiry was innocuous, but it gave Storm pause. In fifteen years, Sol had never asked how he was or how he'd been. It took a moment to absorb the oddity of the experience and, in the process, raised a hint of suspicion regarding the Sovereign's motives.

"No complaints. How about you?" Sol nodded without looking up from his coffee, acknowledging Storm's answer, but saying nothing more. After a lag that was starting to feel awkward, Storm ventured further. "Sooooo. You asked to see me?"

Sol brought his eyes up to look Storm in the face. Actually look was probably not the right word. Sol more scrutinized people than looked at them.

"I did. I want to run something past you and I suppose the easiest way is straight ahead."

"Always a good policy."

"Actually there are two things I'd like to scoot past."

"Okay. Shoot."

"Well, first, I do have some news." His face smoothed out into a goofy little smile that was so out of character all Storm could do was stare. Sol might have even looked a little embarrassed. "I'm getting married."

Storm was so grateful that the coffee hadn't arrived because, had he been in mid swallow he would have spewed right before half-choking to death. If he'd ever heard anything more shocking, he'd be hard pressed to remember what it was. After his brain freeze began to abate, when he was once again able to form a coherent and appropriate thought, he said, "Congratulations. Who's the lucky, um, woman?"

"Farnsworth." Sol smiled. "From Operations."

Storm smiled, but with a little squinting of his eyes. "You call your fiancée by her last name?"

Sol shrugged. "It seems to fit. And it's not like she minds."

Storm laughed out loud. "You don't know anything about women, do you?"

Sol frowned. "What's that supposed to mean?"

"Never mind. You'll find out soon enough."

"And what is *that* supposed to mean?"

Storm just continued to smile and shook his head. "So you want to retire. Good for you. You deserve it."

"I want you to take my place."

Storm's smile vanished as the color quickly drained from his face. Sol didn't have time to notice the reaction because he had turned away and risen to respond to a polite and well-timed knock on the door. He showed the trainee where he wanted the coffee service set up. Storm silently gave the rookie points for how hard he tried to pretend that he didn't notice the wet stain on Sol's pants. When they were alone again, Sol fixed his coffee and noticed Storm hadn't moved.

"What do you like in yours?"

"Oh." Storm's eyes seem to clear as he refocused on Sol and the coffee tray. "Black. One sugar. Thank you."

Sol stirred Storm's coffee, set it on the table next to him, and sat looking at the younger man expectantly.

"I told her I would give it up in two years which would give me time to tie up loose ends and groom somebody for the position." He wagged his head back and forth slightly. "She wants enough time to have some fun while we're still young."

Among other things Storm was trying to imagine referring to himself as "young" when he reached Sol's age.

Since Storm wasn't responding, Sol decided to continue.

"Let's face it, kiddo. I'm just an old vampire hunter witnessing the end of an era and the turning of the page. It's an historic moment for The Order. The Hunters Division is going to need to be reconceived and refitted. The old challenges are on the way out. The new challenges..." He blew out a long exhale. "I don't know. Defense against interdimensional breach?" He looked at Storm. "I'm thinking exit stage left."

Storm was toying with the possibility that Litha had dropped him in the wrong dimension. A Sol who was getting married and using theatrical references? Couldn't possibly be *his* Sol.

The imposter grinned at him and said, "There is one incomparable perk. You can behave like you invented asshole and the worst that your superiors will do is say, 'Good job'." He laughed. Storm stared, remembering some of the times Sol's asshole impersonation had been aimed at him. Personally.

Replace Sol Nemamiah as Sovereign of Jefferson Unit? There was no fucking chance in the whole of the fucking universe that Storm would consider that fucking job. But he liked and respected Sol too much to not at least give the impression of considering the offer. It was, after all, intended as an honor. A great honor.

"It'll be a loss to The Order, but you deserve to have some fun with your girl."

"My girl." Sol repeated that with a little smile, like he was trying it on for size. "Yeah."

"I need to give this some serious thought and talk it over with Litha." The truth of the matter was that Storm needed some time to figure out how to let Sol down easy.

"Oh. That reminds me! About the second thing I wanted to ask you." Sol set his cup in its saucer and put it down on the table between them. "I need to prevail upon Litha to get her father to come to dinner."

"Her father?"

"Yes. The Council wants me to find out if he might be a potential Friend of The Order."

For a few uncomfortable seconds Storm couldn't decide on how to respond. He finally gave in to impulse and laughed out loud.

Sol cocked his head. "What is so funny about that?"

Storm took a deep breath. "Waking Woden. Where do I start? Well, first, he can't come to dinner because he doesn't eat food."

Sol looked interested. "What does he eat?"

"He eats energy. Incubus demon?" Storm had his eyebrows raised like he thought Sol was missing something he should have picked up on. "The best he could do, on a good day, would be to sit at a place setting and watch you chew."

Sol's blank look was gradually replaced with understanding. "Oh."

"I will ask Litha to ask, but don't set the table. I'm telling you right now that my father-in-law is the very essence of unexpected. You cannot imagine a personality more unmanageable. He marches to the beat of his own whistle."

"You mean the beat of his own drum."

"No. That would be way too predictable for Deliverance. I will ask, but I'm not making any promises." Storm looked at his watch. "My wife is picking me up in twenty minutes. I want to go say a quick hello to Ram and Elora and see how they're treating my namesake before she gets here."

"Sure. They're on the sixth floor, east end. We had to reconfigure an apartment and an adjoining rec room, but I think it's going to work until Monq gets this thing figured out."

"Alright. Talk to you soon." They shook hands. "Congratulations about Farnsworth. Happy for you. I don't know about her."

Sol laughed. "Yeah. I hope to get a ring on her before she realizes the enormity of her mistake."

Storm and Litha checked into a suite at the Stanhope Hotel with a nice view of the park. They had a late dinner at a place that was rich in atmosphere, service, and gourmet fare. It was one of those places that showed four dollar signs in the price column of the restaurant guides. Then they returned to their suite and made love like honeymooners on crisp high count Egyptian cotton sheets. They ordered champagne, cheese and chocolate-covered strawberries for breakfast and Litha sighed with contentment. She never wanted to leave.

When Storm got around to recreating his conversation with Sol, she opened her mouth to protest, but he stopped her by holding up a hand and shaking his head.

"Don't worry. I wouldn't take that job even if I'd never met you. I just have to figure out how to tell him so that it doesn't seem like an outright rejection of him or his life's work."

Litha nodded, but looked concerned.

When he reached the part about agreeing to get Litha to request her father's presence at dinner, she laughed harder than he had.

"Dinner?"

"I know," Storm smiled.

"They don't know what he 'eats'?" Litha sounded mystified.

"Sol does. Now."

She stared at Storm for a minute before saying, "Okay. I'll ask him and I almost hope he accepts." She leaned over smiling and while she pressed her lips to his, she said, "It could be fun."

"I know." Storm narrowed his eyes a little and looked thoughtful. "I think maybe you're a bad influence on me."

"Sounds sexy."

He snorted. "Everything sounds sexy to you. You're a sex demon."

"Half sex demon."

"Whatever." He started to pull her onto his lap but she lost her balance and they both ended up on the floor giggling.

CHAPTER_3

Stalkson trotted across the ridge, silhouetted by the moon three days past full. There was a light dusting of snow that would melt off shortly after the sun rose the next day.

The borders of Elk Mountain touched the national preserve in northeast Washington and the wilderness of Canada. The reservation was over two million acres of pristine Rocky Mountain panhandle, but sometimes it didn't seem nearly big enough to satisfy his need. Schee-Chu-Umsh had lived for thousands of years in his territory before they made room for Stalkson's tribe.

It was big enough for them.

Wolves didn't typically seek solitude, but now and then he needed it for little stretches of time. He did his best thinking when he ran by himself. Whoever said, "It's good to be king", had obviously never been one.

He was restless. Most of his tribe was asleep - the lucky ones curled up with their mates, feeling as content as creatures can be. Werewolves got a surge of energy at the full moon - their blood waxing, responding to the magnetic pull in the same way as the tides. Their bodies and spirits responded to the call to hunt and mate. By the third day, they were usually exhausted. The unmated were exhausted from running. The mated were exhausted from fucking. And hunting. And more fucking.

It should feel good. It used to feel good, roaming alone, sorting things out. Sometimes he thought he could think better in wolf form. The brain equipment was different, but that was a good thing. It gave him a fresh perspective. His wolf simply processed information from another point of view.

Hot tonight. It's never hot. How could it feel hot on a December night? As cool air drifted across the warmer water of Coeur d'Alene Lake, the ghostly mist below would soon rise and give cover to even the most inept predators. At such times, even bumblers could be successful as hunters.

There was no one to see him trot past, but if there had been, they probably would have said he was a beautiful sight. Nothing says "wild" like a lone wolf on a full moon night. The combination of the snow and the white birch bark made his dark fur stand out on moonlit nights like that one.

Maybe it wasn't the weather. Maybe it was him, heat coming from the inside. Stalkson wasn't big on introspection. It had no practical application that he could see, and a thing that lacked practical application was, as his father used to say, useless as tits on a boar hog. The leader of one of the thirteen remaining tribes of werewolves had no time or use for introspection, especially not with something as catastrophic as extinction looming.

The thought of the extinction of the wolf people under his care was weighing him down. Sometimes it even made him feel short of breath. His mind was in such turmoil as he ran along that he almost missed the movement, but his peripheral vision was sharp and his reflexes were quick. He froze with one paw lifted in the graceful pose of a bird dog on point. Just ahead was a twelve point buck, weighing in at about four hundred pounds.

Stalkson realized he was upwind. The big boy

must have smelled wolf and been startled out of his nocturnal cover.

For just a second, just one crazy second, Stalkson felt an impulse urge him to attempt pulling the great horned monster down alone. Just a little surge of adrenaline... In his youth he might have tried it. *And might have barely limped his stupid, young self home, too.*

No. He wasn't going to challenge the other magnificent male, no matter how appealing the idea seemed. They stared at each other barely breathing, neither blinking nor moving a muscle. Stalkson knew the big elk would never turn his back on him. As predator on the scene, he was the one who would have to break the stalemate.

Deciding to make it quick and painless, he wheeled on his haunches and ran in the opposite direction for a few yards before slowing his pace to resume an easy trot. All too soon his thoughts drifted back to the ever present troubles.

These days his mind was always crowded with problems. And maybe fear. Fear of what could be coming if they didn't solve the problem.

He thought about the carefree days of his youth when there was beauty and balance in the world. The tribe was blessed with a new crop of pups every spring, half male, half female. The birth of a male pup was a joyful occasion because there was no question that he would find a mate when his time came.

Stalkson stopped long enough to look at the moonlit landscape. Beautiful. Still beautiful. But the balance was gone. Not just in the diminishing number of females, but also in the signs of spoilage. The part of his personality that was wolf would wax poetic with some romantic inanity, like "evil on the wind".

He wished it was. It would be easier to engage in spiritual battle than fight the ravages of technology fallout. Twilights were too pink and orange. It would be a watercolor dream if it didn't mean the choking air pollution from Los Angeles to Beijing had started to drift and hang in the air over the natural refuges set aside by Teddy Roosevelt and others. There was no such thing as natural refuge from bad air.

His ears pricked when he heard a distant howl on the wind. He would have sniggered if wolf lips worked that way. If only humans knew how bad they were at attempting to mimic animal language, he supposed they would stop trying. He turned and headed in the direction of the fake howl. Might as well investigate.

BlueClaw tossed a dry branch on the fire and waited. He felt a pair of eyes on him and looked in the direction of the sensation just in time to see a dark wolf emerge from the darker forest and shift into a man mid-stride. He smiled. "Brother Wolf. I thought you might be out and about on this fine moonlit night."

"ShuShu." Stalkson squatted down by the fire. The night might feel warm to fur, but it was chill to bare skin. The sensitive nerve endings of his balls reacted to the brush of dry grass beneath him. "You called?"

BlueClaw grinned. "I thought you might be out tonight." The gleam in Stalkson's eye was more than reflected firelight. There was teasing there as well. "I know. You think my wolf howl sucks."

Stalkson shrugged and smiled at his old friend. "What's troubling you?"

"Like most old men, I can't sleep. And, I suspect, like most old men I was thinking about love."

Stalkson couldn't have been more surprised if the old man had said he was thinking about becoming an investment banker. "You think the minds of old men are preoccupied with love? What about it?"

"I think that, when people near the end of their lives, we begin to review. Thoughts turn to what we did experience and what we didn't experience. Reliving our stories... Well, that's healthy. Dwelling on what might have happened and didn't? If we think about it too long, demons of disappointment turn those thoughts into regrets. Once that happens, it can be hard to think about anything else."

Stalkson arched an eyebrow. "Demons?"

"It's a metaphor. Are you paying attention?"

"You know you're going out of your way to be vague."

BlueClaw laughed softly. "So it seems."

"For once, why don't you just come at it straight and say what's on your mind?"

"You are such an alpha!" Stalkson had no reaction to that whatsoever. "Okay. I'll try."

"Go for it."

"I liked my wife. We lived together for nearly forty years before she passed over. We had a nice life, a nice partnership, a nice mutual understanding." When BlueClaw paused, Stalkson encouraged him to continue with a crisp nod. "The key word there is nice."

"Well... that's nice."

"Funny."

"I thought so. Look, I'm not being dismissive, exactly, I just don't see the problem. Do you regret having a nice relationship with your wife?"

"No. What I regret is that I didn't find *that* woman."

Stalkson looked confused. "What woman?"

"You know. *That* woman. The one who stirs the kind of passion that would make you run into the fire for her."

The fire drew Stalkson's gaze. "Why would you want a relationship with a woman who would ask you to run into fire? And what a waste of time it would be to consider such a silly proposition."

BlueClaw stared at him. "I don't think I ever realized before just how literal you are."

"Okay."

"I would have liked to have experienced love that was so powerful it was all-consuming. It's the one thing I'll be sorry to have missed. I think I would trade everything else to have had that."

The werewolf stared at the old ShuShu for a few seconds then threw his head back and laughed hard and deep. It was good. It was purging. He couldn't remember the last time he had laughed like that.

"BlueClaw. You're a powerful man. Everyone in your tribe envies you, wants to be you, and you... what? Wish you had thrown all that away for an idea that's very likely a myth?"

BlueClaw just smiled and sighed. "It gives me peace to know I told you."

Stalkson snorted and stood to leave. "Peace, huh? Next time you call me you'd better have something *real* to say."

"Well, what do I know? I'm just an old man."

"Yeah? You keep saying that, but you talk more like an old woman."

BlueClaw smiled wider. "Word to the wise."

"Right now I'm thinking you wouldn't know wise if it bit you in the ass."

Stalkson collapsed into his wolf form with an economy of energy and motion. He looked at the gray-haired figure sitting on the ground, shook his head, and sneezed once before he turned and trotted away.

After a few minutes he was again standing near the drop off to the lake below. His massive wolf chest heaved a big sigh and he resumed trotting along the ridge. Every heart in the tribe, from youngest to oldest, looked to him for answers. He was supposed to lead the way, supposed to know the way to lead. The position of alpha didn't come with a shroud of sagacity. It meant strength and will and fearlessness, not wisdom. He was failing the people who depended on him. He saw it in the eyes of every young blood, that unmistakable look of emptiness and longing that showed in the expression of a werewolf without a mate. Hopelessness was hard to look at.

They were going to die off and it seemed there was nothing he could do about it. No enemy to kill. No threat to scare away. The keyword was no. As he trotted along the ridgeline path that word rang in his mind over and over, increasing in volume. No. No. No. Until finally it rang out loud and true and clear. *No! I will not accept this!*

If the purported miracle worker, Monq, would not come to Elk Mountain, the king of Elk Mountain would go to Monq.

CHAPTER_4

Ram and Elora had left a trail of "firsts" in the wake of their turbulent and torrid relationship. For the most part, they took pioneering in stride. So becoming the first family to be quartered in a Black Swan Unit with an active Hunters Division didn't seem all that out of the ordinary - for them. Possibly because, until fairly recently, they had been hunters themselves.

After remodeling one of the extra large sixth floor corner apartments and annexing the adjoining rec room to their overall square footage, it wasn't that bad. At least not to Ram. He wasn't just mouthing words when he said he could be happy anywhere so long as Elora and Helm were with him. He was completely sincere.

Elora worked at hiding a dash of melancholy. She felt like she had come so close to her fantasy of a small Irish farm/kennel only to have it slip from her grasp when she had barely gotten a taste. Still, she knew there were far worse scenarios than sharing smallish quarters with the two boys who put stars in her heaven. Several hundred times a day she told herself that it wasn't that steep a price for Helm's safety and Ram's peace of mind.

Sol had asked her to resume her hand to hand classes for active and in-training hunters in exchange for free room and board and she was glad to do it. It kept her skills tight, kept her in good shape, and, more importantly, something one of the knights learned from her might save a life someday. It's rare that an opportunity with *no* downside comes along.

Ram had been right about having a legion of in-house babysitters. Helm was precious, magnetic, and fun. Put that together and it meant there was never a shortage of hands ready to grab for him. In other words, there was no question about the baby's paternity.

One nurse, who was hired after Elora left Jefferson Unit, said she didn't want to offend, but that she worried that the chemicals used in dying the baby's hair that color might not be good for him.

Sir Hawking, Black Swan Knight, Retired, quickly grew tired of nothing to do. He commandeered a couple of classrooms not in use and established a new music department. He used one to teach music as an extracurricular to the trainees who were interested. The other was being outfitted as rehearsal space for the band he was forming with some of the kids who played instruments.

He told Elora that he had never forgotten what she'd said about warriors in her world being required to also write poetry or play musical instruments so that they would be balanced.

"Rammel." She laughed at him. "I was talking about pan pipes. You don't balance warrior energy by plugging into heavy metal. That kind of music makes angst simmer like lava that's always threatening to erupt."

"There you have it then. 'Twill be a great release for the boys."

She just shook her head and smiled.

Ram thought it would be romantic to retrace the steps of their first date, even though it hadn't been officially called a date at the time. When the anniversary of that occasion came around Manhattan was, once again, decked out in all her glory for Yule. They left Helm with Elsbeth, the nurse who had become Elora's first female friend in Loti Dimension, and Sir Finnemore, who had been spending a lot of time hanging around Elsbeth lately.

On the way out Ram said, "Remember that you two are supposed to be babysittin'. Bottles in the refrigerator and, tonight, the only 'uck' word you're interested in is suck."

The babysitters stared at him like they weren't sure he'd been listening to himself speak. Finally Elsbeth laughed. "Sure thing, Ram. We'll concentrate on sucking until you get back."

Finnemore blushed.

Elora pinched Ram, who said, "Ow. What?"

They got a picture of the two of them taken in front of the tree at Rockefeller Center as a pair who was an official couple.

What a difference a year had made. The mission of Black Swan knights to eradicate vampire had transformed from kill to cure. They had retired, had a mating-wedding-handfasting, and a baby. They had bought an Irish farm and renovated the house then been forced to flee back to Jefferson Unit where it all started. As they smiled for the photo, Elora was thinking. *Here we are. Full circle.*

On the way to Bloomingdale's they passed by the little storefront where the gypsy fortune teller had so accurately predicted Elora's future. It was empty and dark. No sign or indication that the space was occupied. She had planned to stop and insisted they scour a four block area just to be sure they hadn't misremembered the location. Elora looked disappointed. It wasn't really logical, because her own sister-in-law was probably much more talented as a seer. She could go to Song anytime, but it wouldn't be the same.

Ram pulled her away from passersby and gave her his best little sexy crooked smile. He linked her arm under his. "Come now, my darlin' girl. Stay close. Warm me up and take me to shopaholic heaven. The future is ours to make and we're goin' to make the most of it. Startin' right now."

There was an unmistakable light in her eyes when she looked up at him. She pressed her body into his side as she nestled her cold nose into the crook of his warm neck. "I love you, Ram."

Just something about the way those words were put together never failed to make him smile. He didn't think he would ever get enough of hearing that. "Thin's change, Elora. Gypsies come and go, but by Paddy, there's one thin' that will no' change."

She stopped him right there on the city sidewalk and gave him the kiss he deserved.

It was just after midnight when they opened the door to their newly renovated living space. They would have been back ten minutes sooner, but Elora had pulled Ram close just outside their door. She intended to give him a "thank you" kiss for planning such a romantic, sentimental, and memorable first date anniversary, but Ram caught the sparks she was throwing off and they had gotten lost in heavy breathing and groping in the hallway.

When Sir Clivemoor whistled as he came down the hall, Ram pulled back and whispered, "Inside 'tis a very comfortable place where we can be naked and horizontal in private."

Elora concurred.

Elsbeth and Finnemore were sitting on the sofa talking. They were close together and holding hands, but everyone was dressed. Ram and Elora, on the other hand, stumbled in looking flushed as teenagers getting caught making out. They thanked Elsbeth and Finn, checked on Helm, and fell into bed laughing quietly so as not to disturb their sleeping baby.

The next morning, they were having breakfast in the solarium. As always, Helm caused a stir. Ram and Elora took turns grabbing bites and chewing between graciously thanking people for saying Helm was gorgeous. Helm loved the attention. He flirted with everyone, returning coos and giggles on cue.

Blackie sat by the baby carriage and watched the goings on with keen interest. He really didn't care for so many people coming so close to his baby. He tolerated the women with an aloof disinterest befitting his position as "most magnificent dog in the world". He tolerated the men so long as they kept their hands to themselves. Reaching toward Helm earned them a concentrated focus and a low growl. If pressed, he would put his nose on an outstretched hand and bump, which was an overt display of aggression. The guys who were smart changed their minds about touching Helm's cheek and took a prudent step back, especially the ones who had been at Jefferson Unit long enough to remember how Blackie behaved before he was adopted by the Lady Laiken.

During a break in Helm's fan base action, Elora turned to Ram and said, "Our baby pulls women in like a magnet. And it worries me."

Ram cocked his head and looked completely

mystified. "Why?"

Elora gave him a half smirk. "Because I don't want him to end up being a slut like his father."

He stared for a minute until he realized she was being serious. Then he laughed so hard he had to hold his side where she had once - accidentally - broken two ribs.

"Elora, you're soundin' like a human. We do no' see prematin' sex as a bad thin'." He leaned into her ear. "Surely 'tis better to have a mate with skills to please you." He punctuated that by nibbling on her ear before he pulled back.

"*Surely* there's something in between a little healthy experience and being a total man whore."

Ram responded with an ear to ear smile that left no question he was unrepentant about his past. "You can no' possibly be jealous of the ghosts of single, nameless encounters!"

She thought about it. "Actually. Yes. I think I am."

"In that case, just let me finish these bangers. Then I will stand up on this chair and ask who might be up for babysittin' for a couple of hours while I take the milf beside me back to bed and remind her why she has no' a thin' to be jealous about."

Elora tried to contain a smile, but it bubbled up anyway. "The milf?"

"Hmmm." Ram nuzzled her neck right there in front of the entire morning coffee crowd.

"Stop, Ram." She pushed at him. "It's not dignified for someone in your position to put on public spectacles."

"Dignified? You did no' seriously use that word in a sentence describin' me."

"Yes. I did. Hoh. Hoh. Hoh."

He pulled back. "You know you're makin' me wish I'd never heard of the fuckin' Hall of Heroes."

"Lady Laiken?"

Ram and Elora looked up to find one of the young trainees.

"Yes?"

"Dr. Monq sent me to ask if you could come to his study."

"I guess. Did he say why?"

"No, ma'am."

"Okay. Five minutes." She turned to Ram. "You got this?"

Her eyes slid to Helm sucking on his fingers and kicking his feet like he was trying for all the world to dance an Irish jig.

"You're no' afraid to leave us unsupervised with all the females prowlin' the premises?"

"Very funny," she shot back, but her smirk quickly turned to a frown. "You're right. You two need to come with me."

"Great Paddy, Elora. You know I would no' be touched by another hand."

She beamed at him. "Yes. I do know that. I was just kidding, but I never get tired of hearing you say you're *all* mine." Elora leaned over the table and gave him a kiss to remember. "And don't forget it. I'm insecure and need constant reassurance."

She put her hand on Helm's chest and wiggled it just enough to make him laugh. "Later."

Ram sighed with contentment as she walked away. He never got tired of watching her go or seeing her come.

When Sol received a memo that the king of the Elk Mountain werewolves was coming to Jefferson Unit for a visit with Monq, he had called around to ask who had met the reclusive werewolf alpha and knew something about him. The trail quickly ended with Simon Tvelgar in Edinburgh, who reported that, so far as he knew, the only person Stalkson Grey respected was Elora Laiken.

As she approached Monq's offices, he emerged from his study. "Hello, my dear." He gave her a welcoming peck on the cheek. "We're entertaining a guest who says he knows you."

"Oh?"

Monq opened the door to his study and gestured for Elora to proceed. Stalkson rose when she entered and gave her a slight bow. The movement made the natural blond streaks in his beautiful head of hair catch the light.

"Mrs. Hawking."

He looked her in the eye with a self-confident and slightly arrogant gleam, but she didn't see an outright challenge this time, other than trying to push buttons by calling her Mrs. Hawking when he knew that was not her preference. Or her name. She decided to ignore it. This time.

"Stalkson Grey! What a surprise! Are you here to pick up a stray?"

He managed to laugh without compromising his smug, arrogant manner in the least. "Not this time."

"Well, how is Harry?"

"He's... well, he's Harry."

"Oddly enough I think I know what you mean."

Monq motioned for Elora to sit in one of the stuffed chairs by the warmth of the gas fire. "I'm going to put a couple of people on looking into the problem of too many boys and too few girls. I understand that seeking me out was your suggestion."

Elora looked over at Grey and nodded. "I did say that, if anybody could help, it would be you. I may have gone so far as to call you a miracle worker."

"Schmoozing me, Lady Laiken?"

"I *sincerely* hope you can get to the bottom of it."

"We're going to try." Monq sat in the chair behind his desk. "Our guest will be here for at least a day. I'm afraid we're grilling him with questions, trying to eliminate as many dead ends as possible. I thought that, since the two of you are already acquainted, you might like to give the king a tour of the non-classified areas."

Elora looked between the two men. "Of course. Just say when."

Stalkson crossed his arms over his chest and looked amused.

"I was thinking now?" Monq gave Elora a pleading look. "We need to analyze some data before compiling another round of questions. Should take a couple of hours or so. If you would be so kind as to show him around the facility and take him to lunch, we should be ready to resume by then."

"Alright. I was just going to come down and see if I could do something to help the IBD team."

Monq glanced at Grey and decided it couldn't hurt to clarify that. "We've just formed a new team to develop an Interdimensional Breach Defense System. It's a project that's very personal to the Lady Laiken."

Grey looked at Elora with open curiosity.

She pulled a phone from her pocket. "Let me make a quick call to see if Ram wants to have lunch with us later."

Stalkson nodded. While Elora was talking quietly with Ram, he turned to Monq. "Any idea yet how long you'll need me here?"

Monq pursed his lips. "Probably just through the day."

"Will you be sending people?"

Monq looked at him closely and detected the worry and anxiety that was barely disguised by pride.

"Let's get through the afternoon and then we'll see."

Elora closed her phone and turned to Grey. "Okay. Tour bus leaving. All aboard."

Grey looked confused. "What?"

She grinned. "Never mind. I guess I just experienced a flash back to my own tour of Jefferson Unit. The guide had a sense of humor. He told me that he *would* accept a tip, thinking he was being funny, and then was sorry he'd brought it up because he had to spend a half hour explaining tipping to me." She chuckled. "I'm still not an expert on the subject."

Elora walked Grey around the facility showing him the workout facilities, the classrooms for trainees, the fabulous state-of-the-art medical clinic, and the courtpark. She explained the ins and outs of eating at Jefferson Unit including which baristas made the best hot chocolate and what time of day was best to ask for a club sandwich.

Last, she took him to her own apartment to show him their temporary quarters and the absolute best thing on the whole premises - her baby boy.

As they walked along the hall, he said, "You seem to be rather proud of this place, almost like it was your home."

Elora smiled and looked down for a minute before she slid her eyes back to his. "You're very observant for a werewolf."

He looked at her sideways. "How many werewolves do you know?"

She laughed. "Busted. I know a total of two.

"In an odd way, at the end of a very long story, this place really is like home to me."

"Does it have something to do with the Interdimensional Something Defense Thing?"

"Do you have security clearance?"

"Five."

"Okay. Consider it just between friends and off the record for now. Here's the nutshell version. I came from another dimension very similar to this one, which is why I'm strong enough to put you down without breaking a nail. I arrived here, at Jefferson Unit, as alone as a person can be. I went from prisoner of interest to Black Swan knight, which is why my name is *Lady Laiken*. I made friends who are my family. I fell in love and mated. And it all started here. So it does feel like home base. I guess it always will."

Arriving at her temporary quarters, Elora looked back at Stalkson and grinned. "Beyond this door lies the center of the universe." He cocked his head slightly to one side then looked past her when the door swung open.

Elora waved at Ram. "I brought Stalkson to see Helm."

Ram nodded at Grey and waved a hand toward where the crib was sitting in front of the window. When Helm saw his mother come into his field of vision, he pumped his little arms and legs like he was training for an Iron Man and gurgled excitedly. She laughed at him and he cooed at her adorably.

When Stalkson came into his field of vision, Helm grew still and studied the newcomer with intense interest and the suggestion of a scowl on his brow. Then he took a deep breath and gave Grey the longest, most perfect raspberry Elora had even seen rendered.

Grey blinked a couple of times like he was trying to decide if that had actually happened. Then he laughed openly, seeming to enjoy the baby's rebuke immensely. "The center of the universe has spoken." He looked at Elora and smiled. "I sense problems with authority. No doubt he's your boy."

Ram used his hand to wipe the laugh off of his own face. Elora gave Ram a cool look.

"On the contrary, problems with authority, should they develop, will be laid squarely at the feet of the elfling's father."

Grey smiled. "Whatever you say."

Counterintuitive as it may have seemed, Litha and Storm returned from their New York weekend loose, relaxed and prepared to thoroughly enjoy time together alone at the vineyard. It was Litha's turn to clean up after dinner. She was just finishing and planning to join her husband by the fire for a glass of sweet red when her cell played a few bars of "Devil Inside".

She looked at the caller ID. *Unknown caller.*

"Don't answer it," Storm yelled from the living room right on cue, like he had seen the caller ID.

She considered letting it go, but she had a strong suspicion that the caller, who'd prompted the mysterious ring tone that she did *not* have on her phone, was the furthest thing from unknown.

"Dad. How did you program a ring tone into my phone?"

"You noticed! Did you like it?"

"I haven't gotten that far. Answer the question."

"Magic."

"Really."

"I have to get off this plane."

"Okay. First, why are you calling me on a phone when you could just show up here if you have something to say and, second, why are you on a plane when you could just ride the passes?"

"Okay. First, I'm calling because the last two times I popped in I got in heap big trouble because you were boinking. Remember? Because you're shy about that. Remember?"

"Yes. Thanks for reminding me and for using such delicate phrasing."

"Second. I'm not on *a* plane. I'm talking about *the* plane, as in this limited version of reality."

She laughed. "Limited? Your options are practically infinite. What are you talking about?"

He sighed. "I'm bored."

"Well, maybe demons weren't meant to live for so long."

"That's your idea of sympathy? Feeling sorry for my grandchildren already." Instead of the indignant protest he was expecting, his daughter made no reply. "Hello? Can you hear me now? Where did I lose you?" He appeared in front of her on the other side of the kitchen island. He watched her reaction closely while he said, "Never mind," into the phone and then shoved it into the pocket of soft faux doeskin pants.

Litha set her phone on the counter next to her.

"I wasn't serious about thinking you'll be a bad mama jama." He flashed his most charming smile just as his eyes were pulled downward. "Ohhhhh." He grinned. "So all kidding aside, my little girl is *really* gonna be somebody's mama, which means..."

"Don't say it."

"I'm gonna be a grandemon!" He hadn't been this animated since, well, she'd never seen him so excited. "Forget what I said about being tired of this plane. This is just... It's just... I can't even think of a word to describe it. Transcendent! Yes! It's a transcendent experience. I can already tell."

"And when did you become interested in transcendence?"

Storm walked into the kitchen before the demon answered. When Storm heard voices in the kitchen, he knew it was his father-in-law and thought about hiding for a split second. He didn't, but suspected he would regret that decision before the visit was over. Deliverance almost knocked him over with a very big and, decidedly unwelcome, shirtless hug.

"The proud papa, I presume." He laughed and patted Storm on the back before turning back to Litha. "Have you named him?"

"He came with a name. It's Storm."

"Cute."

"What makes you think our baby is a him?" Storm asked.

Litha watched her father's face soften into something that looked like adoration. "It's a girl?" It was a whispered question that melted Litha's heart.

One thing that could be said about her dad was that you could never guess which way he would jump.

Deliverance pulled Litha into an embrace and hugged her tenderly, rocking her back and forth. Litha met Storm's gaze over her father's shoulder. That beguiling twinkle she loved was fixed in her husband's black eyes.

"This is the best thing that's ever happened to me." He pulled back and looked his daughter in the face. "Next to you," he said softly.

"You trying to make me cry, demon?"

Storm spoke up. "He's making me cry. I had a nice, quiet, relaxing, *private* evening planned with my wife."

Deliverance shot his son-in-law a dirty look that as much as said, "I could burn you to a crisp where you stand."

Storm replied with a sneer that as much as said, "Maybe so, but like it or not, she's mine."

They both thought they were clever, but Litha was always aware of their wordless communications.

"Ratchet it down a notch." She grabbed her father's chin and forced him to look at her instead of her husband. "I need a favor."

"Anything within my power."

"Storm's old boss is throwing a small dinner party. I've been asked to bring you along."

Deliverance's pupils could narrow to slits when his suspicion was roused. "Why?"

"What happened to 'anything'?"

"I didn't say no. I said, 'Why?'"

Litha sighed. "I think they want to ask you to help with some matters that require extra-human abilities such as yours."

Deliverance stared for a couple of beats. "What kind of women are they serving?"

Litha smiled.

Storm said, "I asked about that. Maybe you could snack..." He put the word "snack" in air quotes. "...beforehand and then go out for all-you-can-eat in New York afterward."

The demon moved his head back and forth like he was either thinking about it or responding to a dance tune that only he could hear.

"I'm saying yes to dinner." He giggled like the notion was ludicrous. Which it was. "Nothing else."

CHAPTER_5

Sol was certain there was no one in the known world better prepared to stage a dinner party than his fiancé, Farnsworth. He had left all the arrangements to her and damn if she hadn't done a bang up job. She had commandeered a private room on the far side of the mess that was large enough to feel elegant, and small enough to be intimate. The room looked onto a garden courtyard with ambient lighting, but was also located conveniently near the kitchen.

Sol had requested a round table for six to eliminate questions about the hidden meanings behind seating assignments. Some of the tufted red leather club chairs had been brought in from the lounge and set around the table. The hostess in absentia used white linens to contrast with the dark red floral design in the carpet. The table was set with the unit's fine china, crystal, and silver, but the pièce de résistance was a three foot high blown glass flute topped with a fountain spray of calla lilies garnished with sprigs of delicate orchids cascading down the sides, but not far enough to obscure eye contact between the diners.

The room was bare except for the table and chairs, a long side serving board, and two Black Swan flags proudly displayed in corner stands. Jefferson Unit considered itself sovereign territory and did not acknowledge any law or governing body other than The Order.

Sol had received a message from Storm in the afternoon saying that he was bringing Litha, Deliverance, *and* another unnamed guest. Counting Ram, Elora and himself, that would be seven. Not six.

Sol considered himself a lucky man. He knew his wife-to-be wasn't easily nonplussed. She would add a seventh person without breaking her stride.

Everyone was assembled except for Litha. Storm introduced his father-in-law and mystery guest, Glendennon Catch, to Sol.

Although Glen had been a trainee at Jefferson Unit for six years and undoubtedly knew the Sovereign on sight, Sol made it a point to avoid getting to know trainees. If an honored guest happened to bring one of them to dinner, he supposed he would have to make an exception. Sol raised an eyebrow when appraising Glen's piercings, tattoos, and chunks style hair and made no attempt to disguise his disapproval.

The six who had arrived were enjoying cocktails. More accurately, four were enjoying cocktails. Glen's drink request had been changed from Whiskey Sour to Virgin Daiquiri by Storm and Deliverance opted for drinking in Elora's curves, currently enhanced by nursing. She was telling the group about the raspberry Helm had given the Elk Mountain king.

Litha knew she was late. She'd been detained by a talkative researcher from the Department of Records of Extraordinary Occurrences. She was rushing through the haze of the passes with nothing in mind but her destination, when she brushed up against another rider. The fellow traveler grabbed her elbows and easily pulled her to a standstill, a thing she hadn't even known was possible.

She looked around to see who had brought her to a dead stop. Her captor was an attractive male with sandy blonde hair and eyes the color of sienna. His generous lips were spread into a grin that would have also been attractive were it not for the fact that it showed off fangs that were white as veneers and chillingly sharp. *Vampire.* His four companions watched her with varying degrees of interest ranging from mild curiosity to outright leering.

The vamp who was forcibly detaining her said something she didn't understand. Verbal communication seemed unlikely and, since she didn't relish the notion of either being late for a dinner with her husband's friends or gang raped by vampire, she muttered, "Screw this", and threw off enough heat to give the restraining hands instant second degree burns. For good or bad, the resulting yowls were rather satisfying to her ears. She didn't have time for an internal debate about whether or not that made her a bad person. She hurt him. He deserved it. She liked hurting him. So what?

As soon as he released her to snatch his burned fingers away and assess his damage, she resumed the journey post haste. She didn't see or hear them behind her, but felt, with every magical and demonic sense she possessed, that they were chasing her. *Fine*, she thought. *Follow me. It just so happens that my destination will lead you right into a cluster of decorated vampire slayers. If that wasn't enough, there's also a demon who's not going to be happy about the fact that his little girl was accosted on the way to dinner.*

There was a slight atmospheric pop just before Litha materialized running straight into Storm's arms, overturning his Whiskey Sour, and yelling, "Vampire incoming."

Reacting with pure reflex and veteran instinct, Ram pulled one of the flagpoles from its stand and rushed toward Litha. When the first vamp materialized, he was there at the ready to shove the end of the blunt, stake substitute through the intruder's heart. The four who popped in right behind him made no aggressive move. They looked curious, but not concerned.

The staked vampire couldn't have looked more shocked or more offended. Litha's pursuer didn't look like someone who had just been mortally wounded. His expression read closer to that of someone who'd had his feelings hurt.

He looked from the pole sticking out of his chest to Ram. "Hey, t'es baise' toi, ça fait mal." He grabbed the dowel with both hands and pulled it free.

It made a suction noise that caused Elora to wince. When Litha had first uttered the word vampire, Elora had grabbed Glen and put him behind her, which he resented, of course. After all, he'd spent the entirety of his adolescence training for a potential knighthood for cripes sake.

Looking down at the damage the vampire said, "Et j'aimais cette chemise."

As he rubbed his fist into his chest he glanced around the room for the first time. His eyes immediately lit on Elora and he grinned. "Ca va? Je m'appelle Javier. Quel est à vous ?"

The sound of male interest is unmistakable in any language.

Without taking her eyes away from him, Elora said, "Is that French? Who speaks French?"

"I do," Glen said from behind her. He stepped out to Elora's side. "The dialect is old-fashioned, like they're speaking medieval French or something, provincial at that." Glen looked at Ram. "Basically he said, 'Ow! What the fuck, man? That hurts.' Then he said, 'And I liked this shirt'."

Glen turned to Elora. "To you he said, 'How's it going? I'm Javier. What's your name?'"

Elora stared at Javier and let her eyes roam over his four friends. "Great Paddy." She leaned toward Ram, who had moved to stand near her. "Their eyes aren't pale and they're not acting very vamp-like."

Ram shook his head no in agreement.

"Nonetheless," Deliverance said nonchalantly, "they *are* vampire. Real vampire. Not the watered-down, diluted version of walking disease that humans call vampire. They're the source of the virus."

At that everybody temporarily forgot everything to gape at the demon.

Litha managed to ask, "You mean you knew about this?"

"Sure."

"What do you mean, 'Sure'? Your only child is married to a vampire slayer and you didn't think that would be good information to share?"

He looked around at the others like he was trying to decide whether or not they should be given clearance to hear his answer. He shrugged. "We have a non-interference policy."

"Okay, first, who is 'we'? And, second, what are you not interfering with? Exactly?"

"We, meaning the races of species who can travel between dimensions unassisted. We're not supposed to interfere with what the low..." He caught himself and thought better of continuing that phrase. "...um... *other* species are doing. Of course the fucking angels are always breaking the rules because they're such attention whores and The Council is too lazy to enforce their own laws, so in a way I guess that means that everything is really just a guideline. Still, some of us who are old school make an honest effort to comply with tradition even if it ends up being nothing more than a series of empty, meaningless gestures."

Everybody stared in silence for a long time. Finally Litha shook her head and said, "I don't even know where to start."

Deliverance grinned. "How about the Metropolitan Museum? Tonight at midnight there's a fundraiser in the Egyptian wing. Beautiful socialites. Dark corners."

"Stop! I meant I don't know where to start with questions!"

"Questions?" The demon scowled. "No. I'm hungry."

"Wait..." Litha yelled, but broke off, her hand in mid air, and growled with exasperation at the spot where her father had stood before he disappeared.

Litha looked at Storm. "Be right back."

He gave her a slight nod still not taking his eyes off the vampire.

She grasped her black diamond pendant and stepped into the passes. The pendant contained demon magic, or advanced tracking technology, depending on your paradigm. In a flash she was standing in the back recesses of the Temple of Dendur that were restricted to patrons of the Metropolitan Museum, roped off and hidden from view.

Deliverance was licking the neck of a woman he had pressed up against a wall. The first item on the midnight buffet was wearing long dangling earrings and a slinky black dress that probably cost thousands. She was moaning like she was in mid coitus, not foreplay. The incubus had taken advantage of the slit up the side of her dress and had her bare leg hitched over his waist.

Litha walked up to them and began talking as if they were having pie at the diner. The lady yelped her surprise.

Deliverance said, "Shhhh," and the woman instantly quieted.

He was clearly irritated when he turned to Litha. "Two things. I'm gone. And I'm busy."

Litha was just as irritated. "You're not gone. I'm talking to you and I have unanswered questions."

He scowled and narrowed his eyes. "You can have three questions now. If you have more they'll have to wait until after snack time."

Litha did a quick mental inventory trying to figure out which three questions would be considered most important if she had asked the dinner guests for a consensus.

"Was I actually chased by a gang of French vampire? From France?"

"Is that two of your three questions?"

"Yes. No. Wait." She willed herself to be calm and rethink the question. "Are they from a version of France in another dimension? That's one."

"Yes."

"How big a danger are they to us? That's two."

He snickered. "Dangerous? No. You might say they're lovers, not fighters. They never take enough blood to hurt anyone and the women they encounter are *happy* to give, if you take my meaning." He wiggled his eyebrows.

"Yeah. Very subtle." In a fine demonstration of nature over nurture, Litha waggled her head exactly like her father did in moments of cognitive dissonance. He pressed his lips together impatiently. "Come on, sweet. Daddy's losing patience."

"If they're not a danger, how did we end up with a plague of vampire virus?"

He shrugged. "Accident of biological chemistry. It's an anomaly that only affects the human residents of Loti Dimension, so far as I know. That's three. You can either take off or stay for the show. Your choice. You're the bashful one." He smiled in challenge, daring her to stay and watch.

"Thank you. More questions for you later." She gave him a quick peck on the cheek, and disappeared.

The remaining eleven humanoids eyed each other.

Sol calmly took out his phone and speed dialed a number. "You're needed in private dining now."

Litha popped back in next to Storm. He jumped a little less than usual and thought, in another fifty years or so, he might start getting used to that. "Litha?"

"Hmmm?"

"You want to tell us how you managed to pick up five French-speaking vampire who have normal-colored eyes and are unaffected by a flagpole through the heart?"

Glen laughed. "Lucy! You got some 'splainin to do." Everyone was silent. "Well, I thought it was funny."

She pointed to the one who had grabbed her,

whose fingers no longer showed signs of having been burned. "I was on my way here when that one grabbed me."

The idea of one of these vampire putting their hands on his wife infuriated Storm. He wanted to pick up the flagpole that had been tossed aside and put it through his chest again. Even if it didn't do anything more than further damage to the vamp's favorite shirt, it might make Storm feel a little better.

"Okay. Please don't take this wrong, but how did you get away?"

"Singed him. He's lucky I didn't turn him into a crispy critter 'cause I kind of felt like doing it."

"Would that work?" Ram asked.

"I don't know. I burned his hands, but they look okay now."

"Do you know anything else about them? Other than the somewhat sketchy facts the damn demon left behind?"

There was a brief knock on the door. Crisp swept in, made a slight bow and said, "Dinner is served."

Everyone in the room who wasn't a vampire simultaneously said, "No!"

The mess maître'd opened his mouth to say something, but decided against it. He backed away and would have closed the door except that Monq was entering.

Monq took a look around, briefly wondered who the five newcomers might be, and let his eyes come to rest on Sol who said, "To sum up, these five vampire are - according to Litha's demon..."

She interrupted. "He's not my demon. He's my father."

"...according to Litha's father, they're the *real*

deal and not the - and this is a quote - watered-down, diluted diseased version we think of as vampire. They chased Litha here, presumably from another dimension. Ram rammed a flagpole into that one's chest which resulted in the vamp saying, 'Ow. That hurt'. He proceeded to pull the stake out then attempted to flirt with Elora."

Ram targeted Javier with a murderous glare. The vampire noticed. His eyes widened as he splayed his hands toward Ram and said something.

Glen said, "He says, 'What?'"

"My dad was busy, but he gave me three questions." Everybody turned to stare at Litha. "Basically they're from a version of France in another dimension. He didn't say which one. They're not a danger to us. At all. The virus is the result of a chemical reaction that is specific to this dimension."

There was silence for a few minutes while everyone absorbed that.

Sol broke the silence by clearing his throat. "Suggestions?" He threw the question out to the room in general, but was looking at Monq when he said it.

Monq pursed his lips. "So *now* I get an invitation to your party?" He glanced at the vamps. "Well, obviously we need to keep them and get information."

"Ideas on how we *keep* vamps who can take a railroad tie through the chest and just complain that you ruined their shirt?"

"Glen..." Elora began.

"Yes ma'am?"

"Would you please translate for me?"

"Yes ma'am."

"Which one of you is in charge?"

Glen repeated the question in French. The

vampire who was standing off to the side who appeared to be taking life more seriously raised his index finger.

"Okay. Talk to him." Elora looked at the one who had claimed leadership as she spoke. "Please tell him that our reality has been plagued for at least six hundred years by a virus that mimics vampirism." Glen talked to them quietly. "The infected lose themselves to the disease and become dead to themselves and their loved ones. They commit gruesome murders when they feed. It is a plague that has ravaged our kind, creating centuries of fear and sorrow." Glen spoke quietly again. "And, apparently, you were the source."

When Glen concluded with an accusation of culpability, the five vampires' looks of shock were replaced by scowls. Everyone except the self-identified leader began shaking their heads in adamant denial.

"Tell them it's true, that we don't blame them, because they couldn't have known that our chemistry reacts differently to contact with their fluids, but intentional or not, their kind were the cause. We think the least they can do is agree to stay long enough to help clean up the mess.

"After that we'll be asking for a promise of treaty that their kind will declare this world off limits."

Glen translated. The five went into a huddle and talked animatedly for several minutes. Then the self-identified leader said something to Glen. Glen looked over his shoulder at Elora. "They agree. They will consider it a mission of diplomatic goodwill to the human people of Loti."

Sol looked at Monq. "So what now?"

"I guess we need a place for them to stay and some guidelines about blood."

Monq turned to the vampire and spoke in French. At one point they all laughed. Then Glen translated for the others.

"Monq thanked them for their commitment and said we are going to arrange quarters for them. He said the human population of this world is unaware that vampire exist. They laughed about that. And he said we're going to have to ask them to conform to a few ground rules.

"They said, 'Like what?'

"He said that they need to stay on the premises unless accompanied and that they are to eat the blood substitute - you know, the one we developed for Baka's confinement. And that they are not to interact with the people of this world, for obvious reasons."

One of the vampire said something in reply, but was grinning at Elora as he said it. Glen translated. "He says they do no harm, that women love them. They have a little nip, spread a little seed..."

Javier smiled at Elora seductively and spoke directly to her, saying, "Si je te mords, tu promets de couiner pour moi, mon amour."

Glen paled a little when he looked at Elora. She frowned and said, "Go on. What did he say?"

Glen turned an interesting shade of red and clearly didn't want to repeat it. "He said, 'If I bite you, will you promise to squeal for me, my love?'"

Rammel went straight over the delicately set table en route to a spectacular mid air dive at the vamp who had been looking at his mate while suggesting biting and squealing in the same sentence. When Ram got his hands around the throat of the surprised vamp, it took the combined effort of Storm, Glen, and Elora to pull him away.

Javier was unharmed, but flushed and looking angry, no doubt shocked about what he thought was an unprovoked attack. He didn't quite shout, but did give a small speech in an offended tone.

When Ram had regained a semblance of control, Monq turned to the knights. "I won't repeat that verbatim, but basically he said, 'What's your problem? First, you ruined my blouse and now you come for my throat as well?'"

Glen let go of Ram and walked toward Javier. He said a couple of things while pointing at Elora. Javier looked at Elora then at Ram. Considerably calmer, he straightened his clothes, looked at Ram and said something that was punctuated by a semi-sincere bow of his head.

Glen was clearly working hard at stifling laughter. He directed his attention to Ram and translated the last exchange. "He wants you to know that he meant no offense, that he did not know the lady was your property."

Elora gasped while jerking a wide-eyed and indignant gaze to the vamp. Javier looked thoroughly confused. He shook his head, threw up his hands, and muttered something.

Glen translated. "He said, 'Jeanne's Voices, what now?'"

The best idea they could come up with on short notice was to commandeer the trainees' rec room and turn it into a large temporary dorm. Sol called operations with instructions. When he hung up he said, "They can have it ready in forty-five minutes."

Everyone simultaneously turned and looked at the five vampire who reacted by raising eyebrows and shoulders in a universal gesture to indicate, "What?"

Monq explained that temporary quarters were being arranged and invited them to sit. The vampire said something among themselves and then cautiously advanced to pull five of the chairs toward a corner of the room. The Order personnel remained in a huddle on the other side of the room. The two groups eyed each other, except that what Ram was doing with Javier could better be described as glaring. No one on either side could miss that Javier was the target of a warning still in effect.

Elora turned to her little group of reluctant hosts and looked between Monq and Sol. "We need to get Baka here right away. He should take lead on this project. I wouldn't be surprised to learn that he speaks French. In fact I'd bet on it."

"What do you mean lead?" Monq seemed agitated. "He's not a scientist."

"No. He's not, but what does that have to do with it?"

"Well, obviously, the study of these creatures falls under my purview as head of science."

"Monq. Their principal value to us is not...

"You're actually thinking they've just volunteered to sit still and be your lab rats?" Elora shook her head. "When I got them to agree to stay and help clean up the mess, I meant that they need to actually *clean up* the mess. They need to be helping Baka's people find the infected and administer the vaccine until the last one is cured."

"What?" Monq was starting to look as petulant as a child being threatened with having a new toy confiscated. He looked at Sol for support. "Tell her she's off on a tangent. These vampire are mine."

Storm jumped in. "No. She's right. She's absolutely right. We don't need them for a vaccine. We already have it." He glanced at Elora. "Thanks to her.

"If they're willing to help, they could make short work of this because the va... the infected can't hurt them. They're naturally immune and, I'm guessing, just as quick and strong." He glanced over at the vampire who were practically huddled together. "They've already shown us 'hard to kill' with a demonstration that was sort of disturbing. To me at least, speaking in my capacity as hunter retired."

Monq narrowed his eyes at Storm. "You know your opinion loses all value when speaking on behalf of a former teammate."

"And why is that?"

Monq looked from Storm to Ram to Elora and back again before snorting. "Who in the known world doesn't know that you're going to back each other? *Always.* No matter what."

"That's crazy. Why do you think that?" Storm was calm, but baffled.

Sol stepped in on Monq's defense. "I can answer that. Name one time when one member of B Team has failed to back up another member."

Storm and Ram stared at each other for a minute and then smiled like they were sharing a treasure trove of private jokes. Ram grinned at Elora, put his arm over her shoulder, and pulled her toward him so that he could kiss her on the temple.

Storm turned back to Monq looking unperturbed, like a person on the higher ground of an argument. "I can't think of an example offhand, but that doesn't mean she's not in the right."

Monq opened his mouth to speak, but Sol held up his hand to stop him. Staring down at the floor, he crossed his arms then pressed his thumb into the indent below his lower lip as he so often did when he was contemplating a decision. Everyone knew when he was decided because he transmitted strong visual cues. He dropped his arms, straightened, and looked at Elora like he was about to give an order.

"You call Baka. I'll call Simon and get him to prioritize transport."

Monq threw up his hands in exasperation.

Sol tried to placate him by saying, "You can have them for brief periods when they're not needed elsewhere, but only on a volunteer basis. You are to do *nothing* that might endanger this association. They're doing us a favor and we're not going to forget that. Don't start thinking of them as captives. These aliens can go anywhere, anytime, and can't be confined."

Monq ran his gaze over the little group. "That's the point and none of you seem to be getting it. I don't need them because they're vampire. Like you said, we already have a vaccine. I need them because I'm trying to develop an Interdimensional Breach Defense System." His voice was getting louder and higher as he spoke, but it seemed to go with the shade of lavender he was wearing on his face. "And this, *dear friends*, was a very fine demonstration of Interdimensional Breach. It puts an exclamation point on why this work has become crucial.

"How nice for us that they happen to be friendly - even helpful - THIS TIME. What if they weren't?"

Again, everybody in the group looked over at the vampire. Again the vamps raised their eyebrows because the fact that they were being discussed was undeniable.

Sol woke Simon to talk to him. At the same time, Elora talked to Baka, who had also been sound asleep.

"It's a breakthrough for you. Well, for all of us, but you're in charge of the Inversion. You've got to get here soon as you can. Sol's talking to Simon right now about getting you on a plane. If you want to bring Heaven, he'll get it cleared."

"Of course I want to bring her, but she's neck deep in recategorizing dead case files as possible Interdimensional Breach Events. If it pans out and we need her, she'll figure out a way to extricate herself from the project. Count on just me for now."

"Your call. Either way, tell her I said hello. See you soon. And hurry."

Elora walked over to Ram who was still glaring at Javier. She pressed her body into his side and put her lips on one of his perfectly shaped elven ears. "You wrecked the table, hero. I'll have to protect you from Farnsworth because she's going to want to blister your gorgeous behind. And nobody gets to touch your gorgeous behind except me." She nibbled on his ear as he smiled at Javier with eyes burning like embers with pride of possession. *She's all mine.* It's not easy to maintain a glare while smiling, but Ram managed it brilliantly.

When Sol got the call that the room was ready, he instructed Glen to invite the little band of merry vampire to accompany them. Sol and Glen led the

way. The vamps were followed by Storm, Ram, and
Elora with Monq and Litha trailing behind more in
the capacity of observers than anything else.

As they walked down the long hall past the mess,
across the hub, to the elevator bank, the vampire
flirted with every woman they passed, using a range
of techniques from gestures to cat calls to body
movements that could only be described as obscene.
Elora thought Ram had cured her of blushing, but she
felt it coming on and hated herself for not being able
to control it. Black Swan knights should be above
blushing, even in the presence of live porn.

Every single woman responded to the antics,
some with giggles, some with blatant sexual interest.
When Elora realized that Ram was enjoying the effect
they were having on women more than he should, she
said, "Great Paddy," under her breath and rolled her
eyes at no one in particular.

"What was that?" he asked.

"Your days of charismatic seduction are over."

"To be certain. I'm just enjoyin' watchin' the
goin's on from the other side of satisfied."

"Very smooth, Ram."

The newly established alien vampire barracks
was large enough to accommodate five single beds
without disturbing the TV-centric lounge seating or
the pair of pool tables. The trainees were more than
okay with the arrangement because they were given
permission to use one of the entertainment centers
normally reserved for active duty knights.

The refrigerator was stocked with blood
substitute and Glen showed them how to use the
microwave if they preferred it warm. He also showed
them how to request on demand video with French

subtitles. The video feed had been programmed for trainees, which meant no porn.

The vampire stood idly by and watched with curiosity as the beds were made up with comfortable linens. Their curiosity made Glen wonder out loud about their sleeping habits. They confirmed that they did not sleep, ever. Glen then asked if they would like the beds to stay or go. The vampire seemed amused and Glen understood three of them to turn to each other and say, "There is more than one use for a bed, oui?"

Glen didn't bother trying to correct the misimpression of a future that included anything other than sleeping taking place in those beds. That was simply beyond his present pay grade.

Word spread like wildfire through Jefferson Unit that there were five pure vampire, unknowing authors of the plague and aliens from another dimension, being temporarily housed in the trainees' rec room. Naturally everyone wanted a glimpse, but access was restricted for the time being. It was fortunate that the room was down a short hallway, easily blocked off. One of the former teams of vampire hunters was assigned guard duty - not for the purpose of keeping the vampire in, because that would be impossible, but for the purpose of keeping curiosity seekers out.

It was late when the original dinner guests turned to leave.

"Does it no' matter to anyone else that we did no' get dinner?"

Storm grasped Ram by the shoulder affectionately. "Let's go to the lounge and see if they can rustle something up."

Everybody more or less fell in line behind them. Litha asked Elora about the baby.

"You can't leave without coming to see him. Are you staying tonight?"

"No. We'll pop home after dinner."

Elora smiled. "I keep forgetting. The ability to be anywhere almost instantly... Well, why ever sleep somewhere that's not your own bed?"

Litha leaned close and whispered conspiratorily, "Do you really have to ask that?"

Elora laughed loudly enough that Ram and Storm both turned around to see what their wives were finding so amusing. Elora gave them a too-precious look of innocence and hammed it up with a couple of big blinks. Litha wore an expression that said, "It's a complete mystery why she spontaneously breaks into hysteria at times."

When Ram and Storm turned around, Elora grasped Litha's forearm and made a motion with her head, signaling that they should let the others pass by. When they had lagged far behind the rest of the diners interruptus, Elora whispered, "You're showing!"

"I know."

"How is that possible?"

Litha shrugged. "Our baby has a unique heritage. We don't really know what to expect. My grandmother told me that, after my dad was born, he became an adult incubus in three days, complete with the sum of both parents' experiences stored in his memory. In detail." She chuckled under her breath. "Three years from now we could be taking her to preschool or planning a wedding."

Elora's brain seemed to stop working when she

tried to grasp that. "Wow."

"I know. So. I guess we have to be flexible." She frowned a little. "And I'm not sure that's Storm's strong suit. The pregnancy is going a lot faster than... You know the only doctor they'll let me see is that quack they had treating you."

Elora nodded. "You can't just walk into any OB/GYN and say, 'Hey. This might be a little outside typical.'" She paused and Litha sighed. "It could turn out to be good. Shorter pregnancy preferable to longer pregnancy? Anytime."

"I guess so."

"What are you going to tell Storm's family? And the monks?"

"The monks are no problem because their sect is basically mystic. They'll be cool about it. Storm's family? I don't know. He said we're going to have to buy a story from Ram, that, 'Rammel is king at making shit up'."

"Okay. I'm going to choose to not think about that too hard, but I feel fairly certain that, for Storm, he would make shit up for free."

Litha gave Elora a full-throated, sexy laugh she'd never heard before. Over time, she'd grown more and more fond of Litha. She admired her poise and the serene calm she wore so naturally, not to mention that she was as multifaceted as a prism. She was a perfect match for somebody as complicated as Storm and, most importantly, she loved him the way he deserved to be loved.

"So moving on to a normal question. How's married life?"

Litha simply smiled like a person who was happy with her choices.

"That good?" Elora laughed softly. "Just what I wanted to hear. He looks happy." She glanced at Litha and smiled. "You, too."

"The vineyard is heavenly. Married life is heavenly. But Edinburgh is starting to feel like quicksand. Choking me, trying to drag me under. If they had their way, I'd be working for them round the clock like a robot."

Elora stopped and turned to face Litha with a look of concern. "Does Simon know you feel that way?"

Litha shook her head. "No. I haven't said anything."

Elora searched her face. "It's not selfish to want a life, Litha. You need to take a lesson from the boys on this one. They would say that if you don't stand up for yourself, then you get what you get, and that's the way it should be. Figure out your boundaries and then fight for them."

"Oh. Look who's talking. You have three of the strongest men in this world who would run, not walk, but run to stand up for you."

Elora's eyes sparkled. "I know it looks that way now, but I did have to stand up for myself in the beginning."

"What's goin' on?"

The women both jumped like they'd been caught doing something wrong. They'd been so lost in the conversation they hadn't noticed their husbands approaching.

Storm angled his head toward Ram. "What do you suppose they were up to that would make them jump like that?"

"Do no' know, but it will definitely be keepin' me

awake."

"We're jumpy because we've spent an entire evening being stared at by vampire in an overtly sexual way," Elora lied smoothly. Litha didn't dare look at her or she'd give that away for sure.

"I see," said Ram. To Storm he said, "You might think that women who'd been made skittish by wicked horny biters would want to stick close to their males."

Storm slid his eyes to Rammel. "You would think so." As he looked back at Litha his face broke into a grin. "Fortunately for us these women are not like *any* others."

Ram grabbed Elora and pulled her in tight while bathing her in the light of one of his signature sexy smiles. "The talk about horny biters is downright arousin'. How 'bout skippin' dinner?"

"Come on. We'll eat fast."

Elora made a point of calling Litha almost every day after that because she was concerned about the pregnancy and knew that Litha, whose relatives consisted of an incubus and seven monks, had no women to confide in. Storm's girl was a new case study for The Order's annals and the delivery of a mostly demon hybrid was an event. Elora didn't want the woman to get lost in the shuffle.

With each passing day that she called to ask for a report, she felt closer to Litha, and as she became more fond, she realized how much she'd missed female companionship - her cousin, Madelayne, and even her younger sisters. Litha managed to couch her concerns and physical complaints in an entertaining dry wit so that Elora was never sure which of them benefitted most from their talks.

CHAPTER _6

The next morning Elora woke to her phone buzzing on the bedside table. She looked around. Ram must have gotten up with the baby. She heard voices in the next room and knew that nanny had already arrived. She tilted the phone to look at the caller ID. *Love Bites.* He'd changed it from *White Fang* when he was cured. The first time.

"Hey. Did you get a plane?"

"I did."

"Good. When will you be here?"

"Two minutes. I'm stepping off the sixth floor elevator and coming down your hallway."

Elora sat straight up. "I haven't brushed my teeth yet."

Baka chuckled. "Well, in that case, I guess I'll just have to find something to occupy myself until your breath smells good enough to give me a briefing. Something like say, I don't know, holding a baby?"

"If I keep letting you near him, he might get the idea that I think you're okay. By the way, thank you for taking Song to the reception and looking out for her."

"You're welcome."

"And whatever you do, please, *please*, don't tell Ram."

"Elora..."

"Thanks. Love you." She hung up before he could finish his thought and peeked out the bedroom door. "Ram. Baka will be at the door in one minute. I told him he could hold Helm while I get ready, then we'll take him to breakfast and do a briefing."

"He'd better have his briefs on already."

She laughed at him and shook her head, not because that was funny, but because Ram was of the opinion that, if a joke was good once, it grew better with age and would kill on the hundredth telling.

When Ram opened the door for Baka, Blackie growled and showed how big he was by making his ruff stand straight up.

Baka chuckled. "Still not a fan, I see."

Blackie whined in protest when Ram confined him to the bedroom with his mistress. Before they left the apartment Elora called Sol. "Just keeping you in the loop. Baka's here. We were thinking we'd do a breakfast briefing downstairs. Do you want to join us?"

"You know what I know. Spell it out then stop by my office before you take him to meet the vamps."

"Okay. See you later."

Next she texted Glen. *where are you?*

visiting vamps.

?? ok taking baka to breakfast brief then coming there

TEXT me when ur on the way

ok why?

There was no reply.

Over an "Eggie Spinach Benedictine" skillet for two, Ram and Elora relayed every detail they could remember about the events of the previous night which were extraordinary even by The Order's standards. Baka was quiet as he took it all in. It was easy to see his mind was busy processing through the logical ramifications of what such a fortuitous development could mean for the success of his Vampire Inversion project.

"If they're willing to help, it could shorten the time-table. By years. Possibly." He appeared calm, but Elora could tell that Baka could barely contain his excitement.

"I thought you'd be pleased and I'll bet you're eager to get a look at them. If you're ready, Sol wanted us to stop by his office on the way down to meeting your new recruits."

"Recruits? Let's don't get ahead of ourselves."

"Positive thinking. Never hurts."

"No indeed."

Sol's welcome to Baka was as warm as it ever got with him. The Sovereign said hello and shook hands, then instructed Baka to let him know if the Lady Laiken wasn't seeing to his needs. Ram, Elora, and Baka each had their own internal reaction to the way that thought was phrased. It never seemed to cross Sol's mind that innuendo might be inferred so they ignored it.

On the way to the former trainees' rec room, at the last minute, Elora remembered that Glen had asked her to text.

Almost there.

Just as they were at the door Glen came rushing out and held his arms across the entrance with the door to his back, blocking their way.

"Hold on. There's something I have to tell you."

"Move aside, Catch." Ram stepped forward with his authority face on.

"You sure? 'Cause it's horror night at the frat house in there."

Elora frowned. It was out of character for Glen to hesitate when Ram gave him an order. Odd behavior and an even odder thing to say. Horror night at the frat house?

"Now." Ram said it quietly and firmly.

Glen moved out of the way.

When the door swung open, Ram, Elora, and Baka stood in place staring with mouths open.

Finally Ram said, "Great Paddy."

Elora turned on Glen like it was his fault. "Glendennon. What the...?"

Glen held his hands up, palms outward, like he was fending off an attack. "Tried to tell you."

The place looked like it had been hit by a hurricane. The pool table balls had apparently been used for high velocity dodge ball. Some of them were lodged in the plaster amid scores of holes that had been gouged in the walls. The extra large TV monitor and the wall on which it was hung were untouched and pristine. The vampire had, apparently, carefully avoided interfering with the entertainment unit which was currently playing *Animal House* at a near-deafening volume.

Javier and two of the other vamps had pulled white sheets off their beds and fashioned togas, which they were now wearing over what appeared to be well-proportioned, but entirely naked bodies.

One of them, who was jumping up and down on one of the cots stopped long enough to throw his head back and wail, "Now. Waiiiiiiit a minute," at the ceiling. The fact that he delivered a pitch perfect imitation of the memorable lyric from "Shout" made the moment either more surreal or less appalling. Elora couldn't decide which.

The one who had seemed quiet and serious was mostly draped over the pool table on his back with one leg hanging off, snoring loudly. He looked like he'd just collapsed there. Someone had found a red marker and written something on his forehead.

When Baka gave Elora something akin to a dirty look, she realized that she had never seen him angry before.

"Recruits? I left my work and my wife and a warm, comfy bed to fly all night for..." He threw his hand out at the mess. "...this? Refugees from drinking games?"

Elora turned her attention back to Glen. "*What* was it that you were trying to tell us, Glen?"

"That it looks like the blood substitute makes them drunk."

"Drunk?" Her eyes ran over the scene and came to rest on Ram, who had his chin pressed against his chest laughing silently, but so hard his face was red and his entire upper body was shaking. On impulse she put her hand on his bicep and gave him a shove. Thankfully she remembered at the last second to pull back or she could have done some serious damage to her baby daddy. Having to shift to regain his balance seemed to make him laugh even harder. He turned and faced the wall, propping his forearm at eye level so he could bury his face and not get into even more trouble with his wife.

Baka's jaw went slack when Glen's words registered and his anger dissipated quickly. "We're probably lucky it didn't kill them."

Ram had managed to regain enough composure to turn around, but he was still red-faced and looked on the verge of renewed eruption. When Baka turned to look at him, Rammel made a valiant attempt to keep it bottled up, but couldn't. When a new round of laughter came spitting out, Baka succumbed as well, covering his face with one hand and taking a step back to lean against a wall covered in billiard ball-sized craters.

Elora looked at the two of them, then at Glen who had been chuckling along with the two older men, but when her scowl fell on him, he straightened and almost managed to wipe the smile off his face. "Great Paddy," was all she said.

The room was so loud and full of pandemonium that she hadn't noticed one of the toga-wearing vamps coming up behind her until he was breathing on her neck. Out of reflex as much as revulsion, she threw him off. His body flew across the room, hit a wall, and slid down to the floor in a real life reenactment of cartoon violence. The onlookers stopped what they were doing to see if he was incapacitated. After a couple of seconds, he rolled over giggling, propped himself up on his elbows, and sang, "Now. Waiiiiiit a minute."

Everyone simultaneously resumed what they were doing and that included the elf and the ex-vamp who were then laughing so hard they were holding each other up.

Elora turned and walked out. When she got to the end of the hallway, she glared at the four knights who were supposed to be guarding. They scrunched their faces into comical masks trying not to laugh, but in the end, it was hopeless.

Feeling like the only adult left alive, she speed dialed Monq and he answered. "Has somebody reported the problem?"

"What problem?"

"Shit."

"Young lady."

"Don't you *dare* young lady me! You know I hate that shit!"

Monq sighed in response, but she didn't hear it due to the noise coming from down the hall. Composing herself, she said, "Okay. Sorry. Let me start over.

"Monq. We have an urgent problem with the vampire. Can you come quickly? Please."

"Much better. I'll be there shortly."

"NOW!"

He hung up.

Monq stood near the door surveying the damage and marveling that five aliens could demolish a room so quickly while leaving the TV and entertainment unit without a scratch. He was doing a mental inventory of the ingredients in the substitute blood and could not, for the life of him, figure out what could have this sort of effect. Of course they were aliens, which meant alien chemistry.

He motioned to Elora and Ram. They followed him from the room and the three of them drifted over to where Sol and Baka were talking.

"I can't begin to guess what it could be and, obviously, they're no good to anybody in this state."

Everyone nodded.

Sol said, "Suggestions?"

"Yes. You may not like it, but it's all I've got. We could try to get some of the female personnel to donate. We vaccinate them first. Wait for four hours..."

"...then feed them to the lions?" Elora gaped at him. "You cannot be serious. There are not more than, what, a thousand things that could go wrong with that?" She looked at Sol. "I must have been gone longer than I thought. Monq's been possessed by a maniac while I've been away."

Baka jumped in. "As much as I'd like to find a quick solution, I've got to agree with Elora."

"Oh, what a surprise!" Monq said sarcastically.

Baka pulled back a little and scowled like he was both puzzled and offended.

"Don't worry about it," Elora told him. "Monq thinks everyone is ganging up on him if he doesn't get his way."

Monq arched an eyebrow at her. "Got a better suggestion?"

She hesitated. "Yes. As a matter of fact I do. We'll test your plan on me. I'm the perfect test case. Immune and strong enough to keep things from taking an unfortunate turn. I'll give one lucky biter what I can spare. If all goes well and he behaves himself, then we can consider trusting them with humans. Of course, you still have to get volunteers and that might not be as easy as you think."

"No." Ram wasn't laughing anymore. Neither was Baka. Neither was Sol.

"No, it might not be as easy as you think?"

"No. You're no' goin' to do any such thin' and, frankly, 'tis inconceivable that you would suggest it."

"Ram, I..."

"No! 'Tis the end of it. You will no' be chew toy for one of those thin's."

Elora looked around the little group and said, "Excuse us." It was almost a whisper.

She asked her mate to walk with her to the other side of the room and spoke quietly. "Ram. What's scaring you about this?"

He looked back over his shoulder at the group they had left. "I do no' like it."

"I know. Me either. And what else?"

"You're talkin' about lettin' one of those thin's drink your blood."

"And that's bothering you because you think I'll be hurt or because you think it's an act that's intimate?"

Ram shoved his hand through his hair and looked exasperated. When he pinned her with those Hawking blue eyes, she could read everything in his heart.

"You're afraid I would enjoy it? A vamp taking my blood?" He searched her face and looked away. They were both remembering the last time she was bitten.

"Only if there's no other way and only if I'm there. Just so you know I can no' stand the idea."

Baka didn't feel any better about using Elora for an experiment than Ram did. They sat in an empty classroom a few doors down and argued, hashing out the logistics.

Which one?

How could they be sure it would just be one?

What if the other four got excited about the prospect of real blood?

Was she strong enough to protect herself from five of them?

The whole thing seemed crazy risky.

"I need a break." Elora left them arguing and stepped out into the hallway. She took out her intelliphone and called Litha's number.

Soon after starting the story, Litha said, "Just a minute. I'm with Storm. I'm putting you on speaker."

When Elora summarized what had happened and what they were thinking, Storm simply said, "No."

"Yeah. It's not like I haven't heard that one before. I'm just trying to make sure we haven't overlooked some other option. I thought Litha might have an alternative. Or maybe Deliverance?"

There was silence for a few seconds before Litha said, "Stay right where you are and don't do anything. Let me see if I can reach him. Maybe he knows something. I don't know."

Elora started to pace the hallway. She had a ten step path. Ten steps up. Ten steps back. After going back and forth a few times, she turned to start the other direction and nearly jumped out of her skin. Storm, Litha, and Deliverance stood in front of her. For once they didn't find startling somebody funny.

"Elora, my dad is going to take them to his place and keep them there until they sober up. At that point we can explain the situation to them and get their cooperation in finding a solution."

Elora nodded at Deliverance. "Thank you."

He stepped toward her, picked up a lock of red, pink, and blonde hair, looked into her eyes, and said, "You'll owe me."

Storm slapped the demon's hand away from his teammate. "Touch her again and there'll be trouble."

Deliverance smiled at his son-in-law, then vanished. When Elora reentered the classroom, she had Storm and Litha with her.

Storm looked around the room.

Baka raised his chin and smiled, genuinely glad

to see him. "Sir Storm."

"Problem solved. You should have called me in the first place."

Ram's brows drew together. "Problem solved?"

He looked to Elora for clarification, but Storm continued. "The demon took them home to his place to sober them up. When they come around, he'll talk to them about how we should handle the sustenance issue then bring them back. I hope he teaches them some Anglish while he's at it."

Ram was looking at Storm like he might leap at him with a big wet kiss.

That night Ram and Elora were crossing the hub on their way to dinner, pushing Helm in a stroller when they passed Stalkson carrying a small bag on his way to the elevator.

Elora stopped. "Going home?"

"Yes. Thank you for the tour." He sneaked an amused glance at Helm.

"Why don't you come to dinner with us?"

"I don't know if there's time."

"Let's find out." Elora called Farnsworth.

While she was talking, Ram said, "Did you make progress?"

Grey shook his head. "I don't know. This Monq fellow is tight-lipped. It's hard to tell, but doing something feels better than doing nothing."

Elora put her phone away. "She says you've got forty-five minutes and she'll call when she needs you on the roof. Come on. Go with us."

He smiled and nodded.

While they waited to be served, Elora put Helm on her shoulder and bobbed him up and down gently.

They had finally gotten the werewolf to open up and talk about the subject of his home terrain. He stopped mid sentence. "Looks like someone you know is coming this way."

Glen was approaching with a grin on his face. He went straight to Ram.

"Sir Hawking. Do you mind if I interrupt?" He looked at Elora. "I completely forgot to show you last night. I've got pictures of the puppies!"

Ram introduced him to their guest.

"Glendennon Catch. This is Stalkson Grey."

Glen's face registered surprise and his gaze jerked to Elora. "Stalkson Grey? Isn't that what you...?"

Elora shook her head at him, but it was too late.

She turned her attention to the photos on Glen's intelliphone and gave a delighted little gasp while he pulled up a chair.

"How did you get these?"

"High powered telescopic lens attachment."

"Wasn't that a little pricey for your practically non-existent pay grade?"

"I told Simon you were requisitioning it."

"You did what?" Ram was aghast.

Elora arched an eyebrow.

"Well, I knew you *would* have if you were there."

"Practical. And correct. What can I say? Except that it's really a *personal* expense. I'll find a way to funnel the money back into The Order's coffers without making a deal out of it.

"Thank you for taking care of my puppies and getting these pictures. They are *so* adorable! Oh, I wish I was there so I could feel their little paws and put kisses on their little noses and smell their brand new coats of fur."

"I just sent them to your phone, but I wanted to see your face when you saw them the first time. Look. These two are really black."

"I know!" She couldn't take her eyes away from the images.

He stood to leave. "Gotta go. Gotta date. Later." Turning to Grey. "Nice to meet you."   When he didn't leave, Ram finally said, "Elora, give the boy his phone. Did you no' hear him say he has a date?'

"What? Oh! Sorry." She handed the phone over. "You're the best, Glen. Have fun tonight and don't forget that Black Swan knights in training are gentlemen."

"Yes, ma'am."

Food arrived and was being set in front of them as Glen walked away. Elora hoped that would be enough of a distraction, but no such luck.

"What was that about, Mrs. Hawking?"

Ram laughed. "You call her Mrs. Hawking?"

"He does it just to irritate me."

"I'm not a very progressive type werewolf."

"In other words, you're a crusty old has-been."

"No. I'm the elegant Old Guard."

"Hmmm. How's the trout?"

"Very nice. A little overcooked maybe. So what was the youngster's reference to my name?"

Elora sat back and sighed. "Okay. Busted."

Just then Helm started fussing so that she had to jiggle with a little more enthusiasm.

"Allow me," Ram said. "My wife became very attached to a pack of wolves in my grandfather's forest. 'Tis a nature preserve in Northern Ireland. 'Tis uncertain who adopted who, but I suspect the wolves would say they adopted Elora and her dog. To make a long story short, they gave her refuge and protection. She gave them names."

Grey looked amused and turned to Elora. "And you named one of them after me?" She nodded. "Well. It was very nice of you to be thinking of me. Was he alpha?"

Elora's smile was blinding. "He was. Is." Her smile faltered and clouded over as memories flitted across her face. Her eyes started to brim.

Stalkson Grey frowned. "What happened?"

Elora blinked rapidly and sniffed. "He saved my life." She looked down at the baby. "And Helm's. Just a few hours before he was born. But... Don't ask me to retell the story. Please. Some of the wolves..."

Ram interjected, "Some of the wolves were killed that day and she feels responsible because they were tryin' to protect her." Stalkson looked at Elora with renewed interest. "Glen, the kid who was just here... He and I gave them a very fine funeral."

"Here." Elora brightened and jostled Helm so that she could get to her phone. "Look at my puppies. My dog, Blackie, is the father."

Grey looked at the photos, but his amusement had been replaced with a look of displeasure.

"These little ones are half dog?" He was incredulous, a little horrified, not being able to believe that someone would deliberately weaken wolf genetics.

Hearing the prejudice in his tone, Elora was indignant on Blackie's behalf. "The bitch came in heat. There were rival wolves, but my dog won her fair and square."

The werewolf studied Elora's face for a few

seconds and then looked down at the photos again. "You do know those are not *your* puppies, don't you?"

"Oh yes. I just call them that. I'm not going to keep more than one or two."

"You..." He was going to tell her that she couldn't *own* wild creatures, not even half wild creatures, but Elora held her hand up to look at the phone. "That's Farnsworth. Whister's on the roof pad and waiting for you."

Grey hesitated and then rose to leave. He wasn't sure he could change her mind in under a minute. She seemed to have a strong point of view.

Ram asked if he knew the way and offered to escort him. The werewolf king more or less snorted at the suggestion that he didn't know where he was, after he'd been given a tour. He shook hands with Ram, nodded at Elora and drew a collective feminine sigh in the mess as he walked past.

The combination of his beautiful hair pulled back in a leather thong and his muscular athleticism, common to natural predators, gave him an air of danger and a graceful economy of movement that was irresistibly appealing. He turned heads but either didn't care or was oblivious.

Without a segue way that made sense to anyone except Elora, she turned back to Ram. "You know, I've been thinking the past couple of days about Litha and her interdimensional slippage."

"Storm says 'tis called 'ridin' the passes', whatever that means. But what about it?"

She handed Helm over to his dad who had finished eating so that she could try and eat, if not enjoy, wilted asparagus under cold Hollandaise sauce. "Well..." She looked up at him through thick reddish-brown lashes.

Ram's eyes widened a little and he started shaking his head. "No. No. No. No. No." She smiled. He shook his head again. "No. I mean it. No."

"I'm not saying now. Maybe after Helm is grown? I want... Maybe I kind of *need* to find out what happened with the Ralengclan, find out if any of my family survived." She trailed off.

Ram looked thoughtful. "After Helm is grown?" She nodded. "So, is he to be an only elfling then?"

Elora sighed deeply as she looked around. "Depends on what happens with the IBD I guess. I'm not bringing more babies into a life of captivity. Growing up in military secure quarters?" She pressed her lips together and shook her head. "The only difference between this and palace grounds is what you call it."

Ram looked crestfallen. As someone passed the table he looked up and smiled, but his focus came right back to Elora and the conversation at hand.

She continued. "If we were able to reclaim our vision, our stone house by the stream with elfren and puppies growing up outside walls... That would be different."

Ram felt like he'd let her down. He knew she was doing her utmost to be upbeat about their predicament, but sometimes, when she didn't know she was being watched, he observed her looking melancholy. On a winter night in an ancient New Forest hunting cottage, he had promised to make her dreams come true. Instead, he had pressured her into reliving her nightmare of strict confinement.

He felt a wave of guilt and helplessness wash over him, and helplessness didn't easily share space with a proactive male, especially not one who was accustomed to affecting outcomes by force of will.

There was not a thing he could do to protect his little family if they left Jefferson Unit. For Paddy's sake, he might not even be able to protect them *inside* Jefferson Unit. That became fairly evident when five French-speaking vampire from some random dimension just popped in for dinner. To be secure, Helm and Elora would have to sleep in the middle of a knights' barracks. If there was such a thing, which, of course, there was not.

The bottom line was that celebrated hero, Sir Rammel Aelshelm Hawking, didn't know how to keep his wife and baby safe. And he was hating every microsecond of it! Awake or asleep, he was going to resent every fucking minute until he could turn to his mate and say, "Get your stuff. We're goin' home."

Farnsworth had booked a commercial flight for Grey from Newark to Spokane and put him in first class as a diplomatic gesture of goodwill. Even so, nine hours of traveling high above the ground, disconnected, was a harrowing experience for a werewolf.

When he reached Spokane, he headed straight for the FedEx office. The last thing he needed was more time in a transport vehicle. So he crammed his boots and jacket into his travel bag and shipped his bag to the reservation border station. He knew he was taking a chance by leaving his travel ID and money in his bag, but the reward was going to far outweigh the risk. Naturally he got some double takes from people who noticed he was walking around barefoot in winter.

He jogged from the airport to the cover of trees, feeling joyful to be on the ground and away from the noises and smells of tightly packed crowds of humans. It was just twenty eight miles to the western border of the reservation - an easy run for a wolf still in his prime. Stripping out of the remaining clothes, he collapsed into wolf form then stretched his neck and limbs. He allowed himself a whine of pure pleasure in the feeling of freedom as he headed toward the first climb.

When he reached the reservation overlook, he whined again. *Home.* So good to be home.

He was coming back with a heart that was a little less heavy. Certainly the scientist had made no promises other than to send people to investigate, but that was progress because it was *something,* where there was nothing before.

When he reached the edge of the community made up of log buildings and lodges that blended with the environment so well as to be almost invisible by satellite, he shifted into human form. Some of the young ones in wolf form came bounding to meet him with happy yapping, ears down, rear ends wiggling pretending to challenge him in play. He laughed and gave each one a little tumble.

So good to be home.

CHAPTER_7

Two days later Storm and Litha met Sol in the knights' lounge for a late coffee by the fire. Well, it was late for Sol on east coast time, but just after dinner for the Californians.

Storm told the server to add Baileys for all three.

"Baileys? Is there a reason why you think my edge needs to be smoothed out tonight?" Sol asked.

"Matter of fact, there is." Sol arched a brow as he took a sip of Irish coffee. "I've been thinking about what you said about wanting to retire." Sol sat up straighter, thinking a favorable announcement was coming next. "It's a once-in-a-lifetime opportunity and a great honor to be considered." Sol brightened, looking even more pleased, which just made it harder for Storm to say what had to be said. "I'm not the right man for the job."

Sol seemed to visibly wilt at that. He sat back allowing the plush cushions of the chair to mold around him like a comforting hug. He nodded slightly and brought his cup to his lips looking thoughtful.

"But I do want to recommend someone."

A tiny bit of the tension in the furrows between Sol's brows smoothed out. "Really? Someone I know?"

"Sort of. Someone you just met. Glendennon Catch. He translated for the, um, vampire the other night."

Sol gaped openly before laughing out loud. "That baby? He's not even at the age of declaration. Not to mention that he can't keep his pants up around his waist where they belong. Does he really think the rest of us care to know that he's wearing Cameron tartan boxers?"

Storm cocked his head and looked amused. "I didn't know you were an expert on plaids."

Nemamiah's ears turned pink. "There's a lot about me you don't know."

Storm quietly studied his mentor. "No doubt. Likewise, there's a lot you don't know about him." Sol responded with an abbreviated snort. Storm leaned forward and put his forearms on his knees. "Do you remember when I buzzed my hair and bleached it platinum blonde?"

"You didn't!" Litha sounded part horrified and part intrigued. Storm cut his eyes at her, noting the sudden interest.

A slow smile spread across Sol's face and grew into a chuckle. "You looked ridiculous."

"Okay." Storm nodded agreeably. "How do I look now?"

Sol's expression returned to his characteristic sobriety. "Point taken. Make your case."

Storm set his coffee cup down carefully. "Alright. You said it yourself. It's a new world. Or should I say worlds? New challenges are going to put some strain on The Order. The only way it survives is by revising perspectives and goals, then reorganizing. That kind of overhaul is for the young.

"The kid is unique. Brilliant and so multi-talented that nobody wants to put him in a box. There's simply nothing he *can't* do. He masters everything he tries. Effortlessly."

"And you think he can manage the wild bunch?" Sol's gaze wandered over the other people occupying the lounge, his eyes resting on various active duty knights here and there. "They won't just follow because somebody says, 'I lead'. Add that he's just a kid..."

"He's impressive, Sol. In every way you can think of.

"Simon gave him lead on the rescue operation when Elora was missing. He was put in charge of the snooty head of medical who's a pretentious asswipe, and a veteran Whister pilot with enough hubris for a squadron. And he did okay." That was high praise coming from Storm. The two people sitting with him both knew him well enough to recognize that.

"That pilot..." A grin flashed over Storm's face as he seemed to be remembering. "He told me that the kid thing is just a weird choice of disguise; that Glen's balls are big and hard like the ones they use in croquet."

Sol looked unconvinced. "Okay. I get it. You think he's a gift to Black Swan from the gods. I still don't like the way he dresses."

"We don't have a dress code though, do we?"

"No. We don't," Sol admitted, adding, "as demonstrated by Z Team."

The gleam that instantly flamed into life behind Sol's eyes when he mentioned Z Team might as well have been a banded news ticker running across his face announcing what he was thinking.

Storm started shaking his head emphatically. "No. You're not turning Fuck Up Team loose on my protégé."

Sol's smile was slow to form and disturbingly sardonic. "So now he's your protégé is he? If he's everything you say, he should be able to pass a little test."

"A little test." Storm's intonation was flat and dry as dust.

"He'll fit right in with the..."

"Fuck ups."

"Come on. All second sons are fuck ups, to one degree or another."

"Thanks. Thanks a lot."

"Don't forget that I'm including myself in that assessment. Before I was your lord and master, I was a trainee and then a knight. I started out as a second son just like most. I was going to say that he'll fit right in with the team that sets the standard for, ah, color."

Storm groaned.

Z Team had been stuck in Marrakesh because Marrakesh was such a mess that The Order simply didn't care if they left a trail of chaos behind them. Who would notice? Known as "back door land", nobody in Morocco would build a structure without a back door because they knew there was always a chance that, at some point in the future, they might need it themselves.

The reason Marrakesh was a big draw for vampire was because it had become a famous pleasure destination - permanent, year round spring break, with a big streak of danger that was curiously appealing to a certain personality type. It was the sort of place that brought "s" words to mind: skanky, seedy, sleazy, shitty, shaggy, shifty, and sodding.

Owning an I-survived-vacation-in-Marrakesh tee shirt was good for permanent water cooler creds. People knew when they bought a ticket to the capital of decadence that lots of people with round trip tickets never showed up for a return flight. In an inexplicable quirk of human psychology, that seemed to be part of the draw - at least for a percentage of the very young demographic who were old enough to travel, but not old enough to realize when they were being reckless or stupid or both.

Regarding Sol's reference to Z Team's appearance, they rocked bad boy in ways that left little to the imagination. Their tastes ran toward colorful tats and hair streaked with color du jour. They avoided piercings that might compromise them in a fight. Giving an opponent something metal in your skin to grab and rip was even dumber than people who chose Marrakesh as a vacation spot. Although there was a rumor that at least one of them had a piercing in his pants that was designed to pleasure the little ladies.

Z Team took the usual second son rebellious nature to a new level. The idea of calling them knights went against every pressed crease in Sol's wardrobe.

He would have loved to tell them where to get off while planning to give them a push a minute before they got there. Unfortunately, these guys not only fit the profile well enough to be recruited, but they had excelled in certain areas of field duty, repeatedly demonstrating extra keen instincts and hunter talent that just couldn't be denied or overlooked. They were high maintenance, but far too valuable to waste.

"I call fair, Sir Storm. You want me to challenge myself to consider grooming an untried trainee, not yet old enough to vote, for the job of Sovereign of the most powerful hunter unit in Black Swan? I return the challenge by saying he needs to give me some reason to think he could be up to the job in two years.

"I'll send him to Marrakesh in some capacity of authority over Z Team and see how he fares."

Sol had to chuckle at the shocked look on Storm's face, which may have even paled a little. "Authority over Z Team? Even *I* wouldn't walk into that. Even *you* wouldn't walk into that."

Recovering his characteristic serious expression, Sol said, "That's exactly the point. I *would* walk into that. And anybody planning to take my place is going to have to be prepared to do what needs to be done." Sol's gaze flicked to Litha and back. "Have you asked the boy if he's interested in administrating Hunter? Do you know for a fact that he wants the job?"

"No. I thought it would be pointless to bring it up without talking to you first."

Litha had been very quiet throughout this exchange, but she was a good listener and, being something more than half demon, she was also exceptionally good at negotiating.

"Maybe a compromise?"

The way both men looked at her made her think she'd been transported to another time when little women were supposed to be seen, but not heard. For a second she wondered if she was going to be patted on the head and sent for more coffee with indulgent smiles and a wink between the two men. Seeing her surprise and the tiniest suggestion of offense, Storm recovered first.

"Of course, Litha. What do you think?"

"It strikes me that, if it's a *real* test, and not just a patronizing way to dismiss, or sabotage, the prospect..." Sol raised an eyebrow at that, "...that it needs to be controlled to the extent possible. That would mean bringing this Z Team here."

She directed her attention to Sol. "You'd be able to monitor your test and you wouldn't be taking a chance that you might have regrets later about throwing a lamb to wolves and walking away.

"You'd be able to observe Glen's actions and reactions first hand, his mental processes and coping skills, ultimately - his success or failure."

Both men frowned, but both were clearly considering the suggestion. Compromise was never fun. Naturally everyone wanted to have one hundred percent of their way one hundred percent of the time.

After a few seconds, Storm said, "Would it be possible to shift some teams around and keep Marrakesh covered?"

Sol absently ran his thumb over the design on his china cup. "Z Team here? Why don't we just gather up a dozen Rhinocerotidae and turn them loose in the hub? Less chaos and less destruction."

Storm's intense gaze slowly became a wickedly hot smile. "But much less entertaining."

Sol stared. "You think that much of this kid. Really?"

"It's not just me. Call Simon and ask what the Edinburgh crusties think of him. If you want people to vouch for his dog walking and babysitting skills, call Ram or Elora. And, I'm not sure you want to know this, but I hear there are a lot of young ladies in Scotia who would be sorry to see him go."

Sol couldn't believe he was considering shuffling some teams around for an experiment that was a recipe for catastrophe. He could kick himself for having started down that road.

"I might agree, on the following condition. Since

you're the one who put him up for the job, you're the one who needs to supervise for, eight weeks?"

Storm couldn't believe he'd set himself up to be out-manipulated by Sol. Again. He looked at Litha who shrugged.

Storm gave Sol a look that could kill. "I'm having a baby. Litha is my first priority. My second priority is the health and well-being of our vineyard. I can check on him by phone and in person sometimes, but I'm not going to live here. And, if something happens to Glen because of Z Team, I am going to hold you responsible."

"Is that a threat, Storm?"

"Did it sound like a threat?"

"Yes."

"Well, then, there you go."

Sol laughed and shook his head. Scratch the surface of Black Swan's quintessential knight and you find a kid with his third finger at the ready.

On the way back to his office, Sol was thinking that he'd catch up on some paperwork for a couple of hours and then call Simon, who should be up and about in Edinburgh by then.

Director Tvelgar was having breakfast in his office when Sol called.

"Glendennon Catch? As recommendations go, there just aren't words. The kid is a phenomenon all in himself. There doesn't seem to be anything he can't do. *Everybody* here wanted him in their department or on their team. Somebody floated the idea of making him a floater." Simon stopped to chuckle at his own word play. "And I was considering it.

"To top off the package, he's well-liked. Got one of those easy going, affable personalities that draws people in."

"According to his file, decision time is coming up. Did he give any indication where his interests lie?"

"Bollocks. Now that you mention it, I'm not sure he was ever asked."

"Hmmm."

"You wouldn't want to tell me why you're asking. You're not thinking about trying to snatch him away for yourself."

"It looks like he's my protégé's protégé."

Simon laughed. "He's your grand protégé?"

"Funny. I'm asking because I'm getting married in June and retiring in two years. I wanted Storm to step in here. He said no, but put this kid up for the job. Have you ever heard anything more outrageous than a trainee being considered as my replacement?"

"It's... different. Congratulations by the way."

"Thank you. So a test has been proposed. We're thinking about bringing Z Team here and putting him in charge of them." There was silence on Simon's end for a few beats before he started laughing. Sol sighed. "Yeah. If it was happening to you, I'd be laughing, too."

The second attempt at holding an exploratory dinner for Deliverance was less eventful. The guests arrived on time and were seated at the same round table. This time they were seven plus one. Baka was invited because he had a stake in what happened with the French vampire and Deliverance had them.

Litha and Elora had decided together that they would turn it into an occasion and dress up. Both wore after-five dresses. Elora's was an off the shoulder red that revealed a generous swath of near-flawless skin. Litha's was a black, empire cut, with vertical rows of sparkly beading. Although the style was designed to conceal, Elora couldn't help but be a little alarmed at the fact that Litha's pregnancy was noticeably more apparent in just four days.

When she had first turned to see Litha approaching, she had started to smile then her eyes had been drawn downward to Litha's stomach. She tried to jerk her gaze back upward to Litha's face and hide her surprise. Storm, standing next to his wife, had caught every nuance of Elora's reaction. He shook his head almost imperceptibly.

Litha was unfazed, clearly relaxed, content with her condition and not missing a thing. She laughed at Elora. "Don't look so worried. Everything's fine."

Elora smiled and nodded, but Litha's reassurance failed to reassure. Of course there was cause for concern and it was expanding rapidly.

The dinner presentation was the same except for the centerpiece flowers. Instead of calla lilies and trailing Epidendrum, Farnsworth had chosen huge ivory colored chrysanthemums and trailing stems of Paphiopedilum, Lady Slipper orchid. Showy and elegant at the same time. She had also replaced the plates and stems that Ram had broken. If he was still on payroll, she would have taken it out of his plus column.

Crisp sent the bar attendant and the sommelier in for drink choices.

Deliverance was asked about the vampire.

"When the effects of the spiked fake blood wore off, we talked about the best way for them to help you without causing any more trouble. When you get them back, they're going to be able to speak Anglish well enough to talk for themselves. They've been alternating between language programs and movies. Their favorites are *American Pie* and *Alien from L.A.*"

Elora mouthed, "*American Pie* movies" to Ram with a look of horror. Ram was clearly enjoying the déjà vu. As much as Elora objected to the vulgarity of thirteen-year-old-boy humor, she remembered watching every video in that genre with Ram while his ribs - that she had broken - healed. Somehow he overcame the basic offense of that and she'd accepted him as her mate in spite of one indignant blush after another. When her eyes came back into focus, she saw that he was watching her with a sexy little crooked smile, looking like he knew exactly what she was thinking.

Deliverance was still talking. "Since the artificial blood isn't going to work, it seems like there are only two other options. Either they can come and go and take care of their own needs as needed or you can provide them with local volunteers. Since there's no way to tell what contact with the vaccine will do to them, they prefer the first option. They will live here, if you wish, until the situation is resolved, but will pop out for meals."

The other seven guests looked at Deliverance like they thought he was going to say more. He didn't.

"When do you expect them to return?" Baka asked.

"After dinner?"

Elora turned to Sol. "Have repairs to the trainees' rec been completed?"

Sol nodded. "It probably still smells like paint,

but, yes."

Anyone who looked at Baka could see he was excited. "So. Does that work then?"

Sol looked around the table. "Objections?" No one spoke. "Suggestions?" No one spoke. "Corrections? Additions? Amendments?" Silence. "Very well. A bona fide miracle has officially transpired. Consensus has been reached by The Order's version of motley crew. Let it be entered into the annals."

Everybody laughed. Baka raised a glass. "To Motley Crew."

That was repeated joyfully while everyone clinked, smiled, and drank to the end of the worst plague in human history. The dinner guests had started to relax in earnest with another round of clinking, smiling, and sipping.

Sol had instructed Crisp to be discreet about the service since they would be discussing matters for top level clearance personnel. Crisp agreed to peek in and get an okay before delivering and clearing between courses.

Farnsworth had planned the menu around the guests. She knew the women probably wouldn't want to eat a rack of ribs with grease running down their hands and she also knew that the men wouldn't be satisfied with watercress, particularly not Sol, Storm, and Ram. They didn't hold themselves to the punishing regimen of conditioning that active duty knights kept, but the habit of working out was so ingrained that all three still burned a lot of calories and ate more than most.

They were served a colorful salad with endive, arugula, spinach, romaine, strawberry slivers, and feta cheese with a raspberry ranch dressing. After the servers left the room, Sol turned to Deliverance.

"We want to thank you for coming. Again. And for taking care of the vampire."

"No prob," said the demon as he stared at the salad in front of him. He was thinking that it was quite a good joke of evolution that people would shove such things into their mouths and find it appealing.

"Now that you're practically in the family..."

Deliverance looked up at that and looked around the table as if to say, "Wait. What?"

"...we were wondering if we might be able to call on you from time to time for help with various issues relating to slipping dimensions."

The demon looked blank for a minute like he was trying to understand. Litha, who was sitting next to him, said quietly, "He means riding the passes."

"Oh." He nodded, looked around the table again with his gaze coming to rest on Sol. "Of course not."

A small laugh bubbled up from Litha. Her hand flew to her mouth to cover the fact that she had been in the middle of a bite of romaine. When she finished chewing, she said, "That's not how it works."

"I see." Sol shook his head. "No. I don't really. How does it work then?"

"He's a demon. If you want something, you have to give something in return." Deliverance sat up a little straighter and beamed at his daughter like she'd just won a spelling bee.

"Every transaction is a contract. You have to spell out what you want - exactly - and what you're willing to give." An expression crossed Litha's features that indicated she'd had an epiphany. She leaned toward Storm who was sitting on her other side. "Actually I could take something from that model. Maybe I should think about personally instituting that approach with Headquarters."

"But you helped with the vampire situation." Everyone heard the question in Baka's simple statement.

"Yes," said the demon whose eyes swiveled to Elora and remained there, smoldering with suggestion. "But she owes me."

"What?!?" Just in case he missed the challenge in the tone, Ram stood up and threw his napkin down like a gauntlet. "What did you demand of her?"

"He didn't demand anything," said Storm, who leaned over to glare at the demon. "And he's not going to either."

"I agree." Litha was also shooting daggers with her eyes.

"Alright. Alright. Unbunch the knickers everybody. Sometimes I make an exception to my rule and I just decided to except the beautiful elf with Stagsnare hair."

"Stagsnare hair?" Ram looked at Elora's hair and then at Litha. "What in Paddy's Name is he talkin' about?"

Litha answered. "It's the name of the dimension she's from. Her hair color is not unusual there."

Crisp opened the door and leaned in. "Is this a good time?"

Seven people turned toward the door and said, "NO!" Crisp closed the door so quickly it almost slammed shut.

Ram sat back down, but pulled his wife's chair closer to his.

The demon blithely changed the subject. "Properly executed contracts are not the only consideration. There's also the non-interference policy."

"You said that was more a guideline than a rule then added that it isn't enforced."

Deliverance slowly slid his gaze to his daughter and looked at her through impossibly thick, black eyelashes. The look he gave her said he wasn't at all happy. "Using my own words against me? So this is an ambush?"

The others sat in awkward silence while the demon and his daughter stared each other down. At length, Litha's mouth spread into a wicked smile. "Maaaaybe."

Deliverance looked at her for another couple of seconds and then both of them broke into laughter.

Elora leaned toward Baka who was sitting on her left. "I guess the apple really doesn't fall far from the tree." Baka nodded, just as fascinated by the odd behavior as everyone else.

When their mutual laughter ran its course, without taking her eyes away from the demon, Litha asked, "Sol. Would you like me to help you navigate a negotiation? Just until you get the hang of it?"

Deliverance's grin seemed to say, "As if."

"I'm not much of a diplomat," Sol began and Storm quickly stifled a snicker. "I would very much appreciate your tutelage."

"Certainly. First, you need to spell out what you want from him."

"Alright. As a point of clarification, are you saying that each request for service requires its own contract resulting from a unique negotiation? Even if the requests are similar?"

"Yes."

Sol seemed to slip into contemplation. After a few minutes the guests were engaged in typical dinner conversation with each other and the atmosphere was feeling more like a dinner party.

Sol rose, walked a few feet away from the table and made a brief phone call. When he reseated himself, everyone looked at him like they were expecting a profound announcement.

What he said was, "Main course on the way. Let's take a break from negotiating and enjoy our dinner."

Conversation picked up where it had left off. Storm took the opportunity to quietly turn to Glen, who was sitting on his left.

"Just curious. Have you given any thought to your declaration? It's coming up in, what, a few months?"

"Three weeks."

"That soon?"

"Yes. I've given it a lot of thought and have actually been decided since, um, since Helm was born."

"Well, I don't mean to pry."

Glen smiled and for the first time Storm noticed that the kid was not bad looking at all. Might even be a heartbreaker if it wasn't for his misguided sense of style. "S'okay. Somebody has to be the first one I tell."

"You've made up your mind then."

"Yep. Hunter Division. Like Sir Hawking and..." Glen turned a little pink and looked embarrassed, "...and you."

Storm smiled. "That's the worst excuse for an aspiration I ever heard. Where's your ambition? You have everything it takes to be so much better than Ram and me."

Glen beamed like he'd won the lottery. Ram, who was sitting on Glen's left, turned toward them. "Takin' my name in vain again, Sir Storm?"

Storm leaned forward a little. "The kid is declaring Hunter. Three weeks."

Ram looked at Glen like he was a proud father. "Nah. He's much too good for that." He reached out, intending to ruffle Glen's hair affectionately, but found that it had been concrete gelled into perfect spikes. Ram drew his hand back and looked at it like he needed to go wash.

Glen was over the moon, sitting in between his two idols and being praised by both.

When Ram turned back to the conversation between Baka and Elora, Storm spoke to Glen. "How long are you going to be here?"

"I think they were planning to send me back late tonight. Looks like I'm not going to be needed for more French translating after all."

"What do they have you doing in Edinburgh?"

Glen almost rolled his eyes. "Honestly I never know from hour to hour. They have me running all over." He glanced over at Elora and grinned. "And I have to keep an eye on Lady Laiken's puppies. But I was helping with recategorizing the dead case files, the ones that might have been interdimensional events. Also helping with getting The Order plugged in. We're only, like, decades behind in getting the files computerized and securely networked."

"If it's okay with you, I'm going to get Sol to

delay your return. Tomorrow I'd like to talk to you about your, um, career."

"Sure." Glen suddenly looked like a much older person. It was a transformation that was a little unsettling for Storm. One minute he'd been talking to a kid who wouldn't be out of his teens for another three weeks. Next minute he was looking into the eyes of somebody who was both mature and self-aware. "That's all you're going to tell me tonight, isn't it?" Storm nodded. Glen shrugged and smiled. "Okay then. I had a date tomorrow night, but I'm sure she'll understand."

Storm nodded, thinking he would place bets that the girl in question was not going to "understand".

Crisp knocked on the door and opened it part way to see if he'd be welcome. Walking like he had a wedgie, he led in a couple of servers pushing stainless steel carts and refused to look at any of the guests. Elora guessed that meant his pride had been stung. Twice.

As the servers began to serve plates of New York strip with lobster on top, garlic smash, and green beans almandine, Elora turned to Jefferson's theatrical, but capable maitre d'. "Crisp, this looks simply amazing."

He sniffed and refused to look at her. "There was a second course of cheese soufflé, but it was ruined and had to be thrown out."

"That's a shame. I know it would have been wonderful, but we just weren't at a good stopping place." She pushed her chair back, rose, and gave Crisp a hug. "Please forgive us. You've always taken such good care of us. We're so lucky to have you and we probably don't thank you nearly as often as we should."

Baka held his glass up. "Hear. Hear. To Crisp."

He glanced around the room, blinking rapidly, as the diners repeated the toast and clinked glasses. Elora grabbed Deliverance's unused wine goblet and poured a little then handed it to Crisp.

"Here. We insist you drink to yourself."

Unaccustomed to having all the attention on himself he looked both flushed and flustered, but was enjoying the moment nonetheless. He began to protest. "Madame, I..."

The diners cut him off by starting to chant his name like it was beer pong. He turned bright red, but downed the wine and held up the empty stem. Everyone cheered and clapped their way back into Crisp's affections.

Ram leaned over to Elora. "You're the best person I know." She smiled at him. "And the sexiest by far."

She gave him a lingering kiss on the cheek and somehow made it unbelievably hot and seductive just before she breathed into his ear, "Don't drink too much. I want you wide awake later."

His lip curled up in one of his smiles that was reserved just for her as he pushed the whiskey tumbler further away. Under the table, where no one was the wiser, he gingerly ran his fingers under the hem of her skirt and inched up her leg. When he reached the garter at mid thigh he froze and sucked air through his teeth before venturing just enough higher to confirm that she wasn't wearing panties. He groaned, murmuring, "Great Paddy, Mrs. You tryin' to find out if an elf's dick can rupture from internal pressure?"

Baka leaned out and said, "Pardon?"

"He just remembered something he needs to do later." Elora smiled and turned back to Ram.

"If your dick is in imminent danger, 'tis your own fault. No one forced you to put your hand up my dress, Sir Hawking."

He pulled back just enough to show her that his lids were heavy. "But you must have suspected that I might." His beautiful mouth twitched just a little. "Am I growin' predictable then?"

She leaned over and breathed in his ear. "Absolutely. I can *always* count on you to deliver." And with that she showed him that two can tease under cover of a white linen table cloth.

When she ran her hand slowly up his thigh, he caught her wrist before she reached her target and whispered in her ear, "You can spend the whole of the wee hours drivin' me past mad if you wish, but unless you're wantin' to branch into performance sex, I'm warnin' you. Do no' tease me more."

She withdrew her hand. "Just remember who started it."

He gave her the signature Rammel killer grin that oozed with promise. "We can discuss that later if you wish. I say you started it when you chose to come 'hello kitty'. With garters. Are they red?" The way he breathed the question into her ear made her eyes close as she gasped a little. It seemed to be a game with him to see if he could still make her blush.

They both realized things had gotten quiet and looked up to find everyone staring at them.

"Welcome back," Storm said.

There was more than one thing that could still make Elora blush.

When the servers were gone, Sol once again turned to Litha.

"Here's the thing. All this is so new to us. It's all uncharted territory. We probably can't even begin to guess the ways your father could be helpful at this point. Last Thursday I wouldn't have been able to guess in a hundred years that we were going to need his help with five French vampire from another dimension who got so drunk they destroyed their guest quarters."

Deliverance seemed to be enjoying Sol's quandary. At some point during the dinner, resistance to the idea of working with The Order had morphed into a game to him. He leaned toward Litha. "Ask him what are his three biggest concerns right now."

Litha looked at him. "You can ask him that yourself."

He pouted. "But I like having you moderate."

Litha shook her head a little, but asked. "What are your three biggest concerns? Right now?"

"Curing the vampire virus, but you may have accidentally brought us the means to do that quickly by picking up the Frenchies on the way to dinner."

Storm narrowed his eyes and a muscle in his jaw ticked. "She didn't pick them up."

"You know what I mean."

"Yes. You meant to say that my pregnant wife was terrorized by a gang of host monkey vampire who chased her here, with biting on their minds, at the *very* least."

Sol looked at Litha. "I meant no disrespect."

"None was taken, Sovereign. My husband can be very protective."

"Completely understandable."

Deliverance made a circular motion with his hand the way Sol sometimes did when he was losing patience. Sol found it infuriating to have his own abrupt and borderline rude mannerism turned back on him, but he smothered the bit of temper that threatened to erupt, knowing that a relationship with the demon would be a boon to Black Swan.

"The second matter of utmost importance is the proposed Interdimensional Breach Defense System that Monq is working on. The third is a matter of species survival. The werewolves have begun whelping males, almost exclusively. The king of one of the most powerful tribes was here a few days ago asking if there's something our science department could do.

"We can't really spare much time or attention for that, as tragic as it may be, because the defense system has become critical."

"Why?" Deliverance asked the question directly.

"Because there was an assassination attempt made on one of my knights by aliens from another dimension."

"How do you know?"

"Let's just say there was no question."

"What species were these aliens?"

"Elves."

Deliverance cocked his head to the side. "And how did they accomplish the intrusion?"

"Apparently by some sort of device designed for interdimensional transport."

Deliverance looked thoughtful. "Since that's against the rules, more or less, I might be able to help under a righting-a-wrong clause. I'll give it some thought. Meanwhile, I can help with the werewolves."

Sol was both shocked and captivated. "How?"

The demon smiled. "Like most non-human species, werewolves can survive riding the passes with someone such as myself. Most of their kind migrated to other dimensions hundreds of years ago when it became evident that humans breed like rabbits. That combined with the fact that they find difference distasteful made it an easy choice."

"Choice?"

"Yes. Some earth elementals gave them a choice between staying or migrating to human-free dimensional zones. Most left. A few stayed."

Everyone at the table was quiet while they absorbed that.

"So," Sol continued slowly, "you're saying that you are in a position to offer that same choice again. Stay or go to a place where immigrants would be welcome. A place where there are female wolves?"

"Um," Glen interjected. "Why don't they just choose human mates?"

Ram answered. "The Elk Mountain king told us that werewolves are seldom attracted to humans. Happens." Ram's look said, 'As you well know'. "But 'tis rare."

Glen searched Ram's face and looked a little angry. "He said that mixed progeny is looked down on, didn't he?"

Ram loved Glen. He didn't want to hurt his feelings and he really didn't want to embarrass him in front of the others. There were only two things that would be worse: not answering or not telling the truth.

"Aye."

Ram knew that Glen didn't have any family still alive. There was no one to give him a hug and assure him he was wanted, that he was special. No one except Ram and Elora, who had become an adopted family.

"To answer your question," Deliverance spoke to Sol. "Yes. I know where to find thriving werewolf colonies and societies. They would have to be asked if they would take in refugees, but wolves are more hospitable than some. I'm sure placement could be arranged. The question is, what would such a service be worth to you?"

"Dad." Deliverance jerked his eyes to Litha. She didn't call him Dad very often. "Could you really help with these two things?"

"Werewolves definitely. Defense? Maybe."

"Then would you do this for me? Please?"

The demon opened his mouth and seemed to be struggling with what was going to come out. "You know I need something in return."

"I'm going to give you something in return."

"What?" His expression was an odd cross between excitement and suspicion.

"Forgiveness."

"Forgiveness! For what?"

"Skinned knees, missed birthdays, missed holidays, missed prom pictures, missed graduations, missed..."

He held his hands up. "Stop!

"You forgive my debt for abandonment, neglect, and absence in exchange for helping your friends with these two problems. These two and only these two."

She grinned. "Yes! Twenty-six years wiped clean and you get grandemon privileges."

Just before clasping together, their right hands burst into flame. "Deal."

"Deal."

Sol looked at their hands. "I don't think I'm going to be able to manage that."

Deliverance laughed. "If you'll excuse me, I'm going to go get real dinner and let the vampire know you'd like them to report for duty."

"Thank you. Just one more question. It's a quick one - about your ability to move from one place to another."

"Riding the passes," Litha supplied.

"Yes. Who exactly can go along?"

"Elementals and ancients, vampire, elusives, and higher forms... We can navigate without assistance. Most humanoid species like elves and fae and most hybrids like werewolves can go piggyback - not literally, but you know what I mean. Most of the human variants can survive it, but not all. Transporting species that don't travel naturally is generally frowned upon, but as long as The Council keeps looking the other way..."

"By human variants you mean..."

"Humans from different dimensions have evolved differently and express different looks, strengths, weaknesses. Even here in this one dimension humans can be identified on sight as one of three categories that you call races. Imagine how many differences there are across dimensions."

"Are we a human, uh, variant that..."

"Can piggyback? Pure Loti Dimension humans?"

Litha interjected, "Loti is what travelers call this dimension."

Deliverance went on. "No. It's more pressure

than your bodies can stand. You wouldn't want to see what happens." The demon shuddered for theatrical effect and not because he was personally fazed.

Sol looked at Glen. "What about someone who was part human? Say, one quarter werewolf?"

Deliverance followed Sol's gaze to Glen and said, "Let's find out." Moving almost too fast to see, he grabbed Glen's arm, pulled him to his feet, and vanished. Ram knocked his chair over trying to get to Glen. Putting his hands up, he was shouting, "Wait!" at the demon. For all the good it did.

Everyone present was frozen in shock, staring at the spot where Glen had been a moment before. As Storm looked at Litha, his face clouded over with anger that matched his nickname, but before he could say anything he might regret, Deliverance reappeared. Glen was a little wide-eyed, but otherwise didn't seem worse for wear. The demon laughed and slapped the kid on the back. "Looks like you're good to go."

In a near-recreation of events from the first attempt at a dinner party, Ram dived through the air, tackled the demon, knocking him to the floor, straddled him, and began pummeling his flawless, arrogant face with his fists. Deliverance giggled hysterically. When Rammel paused, thrown by the odd reaction, the incubus smiled smugly and looked at him through heavy-lidded eyes.

"You can't hurt me, but I might be lured into a little boy-on-boy action." He let his eyes wander slowly down Ram's body and then winked.

Ram would be hard pressed to remember a time when he was more infuriated. In that moment he learned that the phrase "seeing red" was based on something that actually happens when anger crosses the border of madness.

Ram's ego was raw and bleeding from knowing he was powerless to protect Elora and Helm. Rubbing in his face that he couldn't protect this kid they had practically adopted, not even when he was twenty-four inches away, well, the whole thing was just too much. The whole dimension jumping, popping in and out, it was more than a reasonably well-balanced elf should be expected to manage.

Snarling loudly he drew back his fist to smash that smile again, but Elora grabbed his wrist. She leaned down and whispered in her mate's ear. "Stop, Ram. You can't hurt him. You're only hurting yourself. Come to me. Please." She pulled on his arm, urging him to stand up as she kissed the knuckles that were broken and bruising.

Deliverance continued to taunt him. "I've got no problem with you being on top, just kiss me first and let me turn over. Maybe you can work off your mate's debt."

Ram tried to lunge at him again, but Elora had a firm hold.

Litha came into the demon's field of vision and stood over him with her hands on her hips. "Enough! That's enough. There are people in this room who care about that boy and my husband is one of them. What if it had turned out that he *couldn't* survive the passes?"

He clearly didn't like being reprimanded by his daughter. "I was keeping an eye on him. If he couldn't breathe or started to crumple, I would have brought him right back. There's no other way to find out."

Litha considered that for a minute. "So you're claiming he was never in any danger?"

Elora pulled Ram away.

Deliverance did a showy kip-up to get to his feet before staring down his daughter. "He was never in any danger. What kind of demon do you take me for?" The demon smiled in a disconcerting way that left a question mark hanging in the air, and vanished.

Slowly, everybody drifted back to their chairs. After a few seconds of stunned silence, Glen said, "Hey. If he's not coming back, can I have his lobster?"

They were just finishing Bananas Foster when a small atmospheric change preceded five vampire coming to dinner. "Hello, again," said Javier in heavily French-accented Anglish.

"Mr. Baka," Sol said, "are you ready to get to know your team?"

Baka looked them over. Truthfully, he was overjoyed. They were gods sent.

Litha's upbringing dictated that she thank Sol for hosting a lovely dinner, but she knew there was no way to say that without it sounding sarcastic. So she and Storm simply said goodnight. Two minutes later they were standing in front of their fireplace in their own living room on the opposite coast. Litha flicked a small fireball and hearth flames jumped alight.

"You going back to Edinburgh tomorrow?"

"Yes. But I'm not going tonight," she said it suggestively. "*And*, I'm going with a new attitude regarding contracts and negotiation."

"Good for you." Storm smiled down at his wife and pulled her as close as her growing tummy would allow. "I was so proud of you tonight. What you did was a great thing. You saved a species and, if he ends up helping us with the defense system, you might get credit for saving the world." She brought her hands around to his chest and reached up to start untying his tie. "And have I mentioned how much I like having a wife who provides the coolest transportation in the world?"

She laughed. "That's exactly what you said when you thought my dowry was an Aston Martin."

He pulled her tighter against the growing evidence that she still thrilled him. "If you had come with a bus token, you'd still be the one."

She melted. Just like she always had when he said such things. Just like she always would.

CHAPTER_8

Storm texted Glen to meet him in the solarium at eleven and got confirmation. Litha dropped him off, brushed her lips over his, and promised to see him for dinner.

Glen was early and nursing a large Brazilia coffee.

"Join you?" Storm joked.

"Yes sir. Would you like me to get you a coffee?"

"No. It takes a few minutes for my stomach to come to grips with being inside my body after Litha gives me a ride." He glanced around to see who might be within hearing distance. Then he seemed to get lost in thought.

"You know I'm dying here."

"Hmmm?" Storm turned back to Glen. "Oh. Yeah. So, okay, I've got to have your word that this is confidential. Not a sound to anybody. Right now we're just talking."

Glen nodded.

"Sol's getting married."

Glen grinned. "Wow."

"And he plans to retire in two years."

"That's nice. He... deserves it."

"He asked me if I wanted the job."

Glen's eyes went wide. "Whoa. Really? That's... shooting pretty high. There's nobody in the organization more powerful except Council members. Right?"

Storm watched Glen's reaction carefully. "Pretty much."

"So you're going to be the new Sovereign of Jefferson Unit. And I *know* you! Can I have your autograph? Will I get special treatment because you know me?" The kid was grinning and seemed genuinely excited about the prospect of being personally acquainted with the incoming boss man.

Storm couldn't help but chuckle. "No. You can't have my autograph. And, no, I'm not going to be the new Sovereign of Jefferson Unit."

"You're not?" Glen's excitement died as his brows drew together. "Why not? How could you turn it down?"

"I'm not going to be the new Sov here because you are. And I'd better not ever find out that you're giving people special treatment 'because you know them'." Storm put that last phrase in air quotes.

"I don't know what you..." The kid's forehead smoothed out as his grin returned. That gave birth to a good-natured laugh. "Good one. Is there a camera?" Glen was looking around for evidence of being punked.

Storm shook his head. "No camera, kid. And no joke either."

"Okay. I don't get it. What are you *really* trying to say?"

"Sol offered me the job. I said no, but recommended you."

"Me?!? Why would you do that?" He made it sound more like an accusation than a question.

"Got a feeling that you're the right guy for the job. When I was a vampire slayer, I learned to rely on gut feelings. I give them credit for the reason why I'm standing here right now breathing in and out. They're more reliable than eyes and ears."

Glen frowned. "But I'm a trainee. Not even..."

"I know. Sounds crazy. But there it is. What do you say? You interested?" The boy looked dumbstruck. "Sol and I talked about it..."

"And he agrees with you?" Glen sounded incredulous.

"Not exactly, but for whatever reason, he thinks enough of me to be willing to give you a try. A... test of sorts. To see how you might handle yourself in different situations."

"So it's not like I'm being offered the job straight up. I'm being offered an opportunity to audition."

"Exactly. It's not a command performance. It's only if you want to.

"I don't want to give you the idea that the tests he has in mind are easy. In fact, I wouldn't lay odds on *anybody* else." Oddly enough, as Storm proceeded to make the prospect of occupying the Sovereign's chair sound more and more challenging, the more interested Glen became. "Have you ever heard of Z Team?"

"Z Team. No. Who are they?"

"Never mind. It's just as well. So you know, I should point out that the job is typically thankless and lonely and not nearly as glamorous as Hunter Division is cracked up to be."

"Yeah. Don't sugar coat or anything."

"Eyes wide open. Best policy and practice. Questions?"

"Well, when you say 'lonely'...?"

Storm shrugged. "That's the way Sol did it. I guess everybody who's ever held that job put his own stamp on it, sort of molded it to fit his personality. My understanding is that, as long as things run smoothly, the higher ups don't really care how you get it done.

"Sol's approach was to work 18/7." Glen winced at that. "I'm not saying it couldn't be done differently, but...

"Look, you probably don't know this. Sol recruited me."

"He did?"

"Yep. By the time I declared he was Sovereign of Jefferson Unit. My first active duty years were mostly in Europe. When I was assigned here, the place ran like he'd invented the job. Since I've never seen anybody else in that position, it's hard to say what could or couldn't be done.

"I can tell you for sure that there's one aspect that's constant and that's the ability to make quick decisions. Are you a person who can make quick decisions?"

"Yes sir."

"That's good because I need an answer right now. You interested?"

Glen was thinking about how to respond when he realized his head was nodding up and down. Oddly enough he *was* interested. He wasn't sure why. Maybe he had gut feelings, too.

Storm looked at his watch. "Meet me at the Sovereign's office at 1400. Dress warm and in layers. Grab a pack with snacks, water, hat, gloves and a few thermapacks for fingers and toes - just in case. Your first test is coming up and it's not a fake test or training exercise. It's an important assignment and an indication of just how much faith I have in you.

"You're leading a team of three, including yourself, to Elk Mountain to talk to the king about the demon's proposition. It's the position of The Order that, if we *can* do something to save a benign supernatural species from extinction, then we're obligated to help. Any questions?"

"How long will we be gone?"

"Probably a few hours."

Glen looked perplexed. "Hours? Isn't Elk Mountain in Idaho?"

"Yes."

"And aren't we in New Jersey?"

"Perceptive, Catch. We're hitching a ride with my wife and... my father-in-law."

"Oh." He nodded. "Am I moving back here?"

"Yes. I'll talk to Sol about retrieving your stuff from Edinburgh." Storm laughed softly. "Simon's probably going to be fit to be tied when he finds out we stole you right out from under him, but, technically, you were ours first and we never gave you up. We just loaned you out for an internship."

"You make it sound like Jefferson and Headquarters are rivals."

"I did make it sound that way, didn't I? Shame on me." Storm grinned.

"Thing is, if I'm leaving Scotia, there are a couple of people I should probably say goodbye to in person."

"Goodbye sex?" Storm was pretty matter of fact about the question and Glen wasn't expecting that. After all, Storm was an old married man. The best response he could come up with was blinking. Twice. "I'll take that as a yes. In a few days, we can see about letting you stow away on a flight with an extra seat."

Storm started to get up, then sat back down. "One more thing. This, considering you for this job... It's all kinds of record breaking. You should feel really good about yourself. *Mixed* progeny or not."

Storm's protégé put his lips together in the smallest suggestion of a smile. "Thank you, sir. And, just one more question. Who are the other two on my team?"

"Sir Hawking and myself. He's going because the king knows him. I'm going to observe and report on your strengths and weaknesses." Storm smiled. "No pressure though."

"Right." He tried not to sound sarcastic even though his brain had already gone into stress or steroids. They expected him to complete a portion of a performance interview in front of the two men he admired most in the world. And it was a real mission. Not a training exercise. He felt a lump in his throat and his palms were already starting to feel clammy. "Thank you, sir."

Walking away with his back to Glendennon Catch, Storm smiled to himself, thinking that the trainee was probably feeling a lump form in his throat just about then, followed by noticing that his palms were getting clammy. Good. The more pressure he felt to perform, the better. If he couldn't handle a friendly diplomatic outing with Ram and Storm, his two biggest supporters, then Z Team would shred his ass while having cookies and milk. They wouldn't break a sweat doing it. They wouldn't feel bad. And they wouldn't look back.

Glen needed to prove to Storm and himself that he could handle whatever was thrown his direction. And that was the only condition on which Storm would sign off on turning Z Team loose on him.

Glen was leaning against the wall with his pack on the floor at his feet, waiting in the vestibule that led to Sol's suite of offices. He heard the elevator ding at the end of the hall, coupled with the laughter of occupants exiting on the same floor. Of course he recognized the voices before he could see the faces. Sir Storm, Sir Hawking, Lady Laiken. With his slightly better than pure human hearing, he also picked up the much smaller sound of bubble blowing and gurgling that had to be Helm.

He grinned when they came into view.

Elora was carrying Helm. Glen leaned over to plant a kiss on the baby's flawless, smooth little rosy cheek then offered his finger which Helm grasped with a toothless smile and a little free-form jig.

"Glen," Elora's eyes looked misty, "I don't care if they put you in charge of this assignment because you're a quarter werewolf. I'm so proud of you." She sniffed and had to look away. Controlling tears was a constant struggle for her. She had learned that people were often uncomfortable with too much crying, but she was an emotional girl.

"Oh, for Paddy's sake, Elora. We'll probably be back in time for dinner." Ram chided her playfully.

"You know perfectly well that's not why I'm..."

"No' why you're what?" he teased.

"...feeling sentimental."

Looking at Glen, Ram said, "You could do worse than have such a creature as that on your side, you know."

Glen looked embarrassed. "I know."

Storm led them into the conference room and shut the door behind them. "Litha and her dad will be here in a minute. Elora, we probably don't need a full briefing, since Ram knows Grey, but is there anything you want to share with Glen that might be useful for him?"

Elora sat and adjusted Helm on her lap. "I don't know how much you know. His name is Stalkson Grey. According to the stray we retrieved in London, he's old school by werewolf standards. Here's the *Catch 22*." She grinned when she realized there was a connection to his name. "He will probably want to 'dominate' you..." She did a one-handed air quote on dominate. "...but won't give you his respect if he can. He does this weird staring thing that's some sort of whoever-looks-away-first game."

Glen, being very familiar with werewolf culture, looked down and quietly snorted in amusement at Elora's irreverent, outsider's perspective. He could see why it probably did seem both bizarre and stupid from her point of view.

"You probably have a better handle on werewolf politics than we do. The first time we met I called him a despot or a tyrant or something like that. After I put him down on the ground, he got over our differences and became, I don't know, amiable, maybe even charming. It was just an odd transformation. The hardest part is getting past the dominance ritual.

"When he was here a few days ago, it was evident that he's really worried about what's going to become of them. I wish you had time to learn more about the tribe, their society, history, and so on before you go, but..."

"No. That's okay. I have that covered. I hacked The Order's database a couple of hours ago and pulled what I need. Thank you."

Elora looked up at her team mates. Storm's

features were passive, but she knew he was duly impressed. Ram was wearing a little smile of unmistakable pride. He nodded at Elora as if to say, "That's our boy." She nodded back to him, smiling in complete agreement.

"Good. I talked to the king on the phone last night and told him The Order is sending emissaries with news. He's expecting you."

Litha and Deliverance appeared right next to Elora. Mother and baby both jumped. Helm cried loudly about being startled while Elora grasped at her chest like she was having a heart attack.

Litha was appropriately contrite. "Oh no. I'm *so* sorry," she told Elora. Looking at Helm, whose little face was almost as red as his hair, she said, "I've been a bad auntie." Still sniveling, Helm turned his face into his mother's breast and refused to look at Litha.

"Yes. You certainly have." Storm pulled her away and put his arms around her. "I'm thinking spanking."

Litha narrowed her eyes. When she hugged him back she let a little heat build up in her hands. "I'd like to see you try it." She arched an eyebrow while he laughed, sidling away from getting burned.

"Okay. So how does this work?" Glen asked.

"I guess that means you've taken command." Storm looked at Ram, who shrugged and smiled. "Well, we have two mules and three riders. You tell us."

"Only you could turn getting a ride in the passes around to make it sound like you're in control." Litha gave Storm a mock dirty look.

"You go with Litha. I'll go with the demon. Litha, will you please come back for Sir Hawking?"

She nodded.

Storm looked at Glen. "Okay. Since we're following you, we're giving you temporary permission to drop the formalities."

"Speak for yourself," Ram teased, winking at Glen.

"Will that be copasetic with you, um, Ram?" Truthfully, Ram's first name on Glen's tongue felt awkward and out of place.

"Aye, sir."

"Very well." Glen withdrew an old-fashioned paper map from his pack and showed it to Litha and Deliverance. He pointed to a marking he'd made in orange highlighter. "This is the south entrance to the Elk Mountain reservation. There's a lightly guarded border station there. We need to be dropped close, but not so close that we would alarm anyone." He glanced at Elora and the baby and his meaning was clear. "We have to be cleared by the security station to gain official admittance to the reservation. They might give us a ride or they might point to the road. We won't know until we get there.

"Either way, we'll be about twelve miles from the settlement. It's a short ride or a medium jog." Glen eyed the two old men who were already well on the other side of twenty-five. "You're both up to it?"

Ram looked at Storm. "He just insulted us, did he no'?"

Storm nodded. "I think we can manage."

Glen rolled up the map and stuck it back in his pack. "Let's go then."

Storm gave the kid points for knowing that it was always good to have a paper map back up. While small electronic devices were convenient, sometimes weather or atmosphere or concentrations of technology interfered with their operations and you had to be ready to go old school.

Storm and Glen were delivered to a location within visual range of the reservation entrance. Storm was glad he got to go first so his stomach had a minute to settle down.

So far he was impressed with everything about the way Glen had conducted himself. He had taken the initiative to do his own research in case the intelligence briefing missed something. He'd listened to Elora attentively and respectfully, while acknowledging deference to her rank and personal experience with the king. When deciding how they would travel he had, apparently, factored in Ram's dislike of Deliverance and arranged for him to go with Litha. And, last, he had adopted a practical approach to what he'd learned about werewolf tribal customs. The plan to arrive outside the guard station, but not so close as to alarm anyone, confirmed Storm's past impression that Glen had some innate talent for strategy and tactical application.

The kid was the whole package: brilliant, likable, and able to turn any situation into an equation to be solved by sorting through available data, and arranging various factors in order of importance. There were only two things Storm still needed to evaluate. How did he react to stress? And, did he have *it*? That mystic quality that science couldn't define or categorize. Women called it intuition. Men called it gut instinct. Naming it was irrelevant. Having it was crucial.

Storm jumped when Litha popped in with Ram.

It seemed that, even when you knew it was coming, it was still so unnatural that the body reacted independently of the brain.

"Sorry," she chuckled quietly. She leaned up and gave him a peck on the lips. "Have fun. See you later."

"I'm not here for fun, woman!" Storm protested with his brows furrowed.

"Right," she laughed and vanished.

"You were right," Glen said to Storm. "It's cold here."

It was a cloudy day threatening a big dump of snow. They looked around at the inch of recent snow on the ground. Not so much that rocks and twigs weren't visible, but the moisture in the air made it seem even colder than it was.

"Ready?"

Storm and Ram nodded and fell in behind him.

When the guard saw people approaching he stepped outside the hut with a silent, but open question hanging in the air.

Nearing the gate, Glen said, "Visitors to the king. We're expected."

The guard looked them up and down unapologetically as if he began every clearance encounter with an assumption that non-werewolves were up to no good. "Names?"

"Glendennon Catch. Rammel Hawking. Engel Storm."

He checked his list then picked up his cell phone, speed dialed a number, and repeated the names. "Do you need visual confirmation?" He grunted, touched his handheld device a couple of times, then held it up and panned across them to transmit video. He switched back to audio communication, grunted into the handheld and put it away.

"Do you have weapons in those packs?" All three said no. "Would you mind opening up and letting me take a look?" He rummaged through each pack so thoroughly that, at one point, Ram and Storm gave each other meaningful looks. The potential guests from Black Swan did have weapons, of course, but none that would be identifiable by sight, which was the most primitive method of security scan. When the werewolf guard was satisfied, he pointed at the dirt road behind him. "Twelve miles that way. Stay on the road. You can take that jeep. Keys are in it. When you see buildings, leave the jeep. The village is pedestrian only."

Glen thanked him and led the way toward a topless jeep that looked like it could have been a relic from World War II. He threw his pack in the rear and pulled himself up behind the wheel.

"You know how to drive manual?" Storm asked as he folded his long legs into the shotgun seat.

Glen just grinned as he started the engine and threw the gearshift into reverse. "You two should hold on. The lack of hydraulics in this model might be a little hard on old bones."

Storm looked behind him at Ram as if to say, "Can you believe this?" Being with someone who thought of them as old would take some getting used to. Glen was masterfully ambiguous which kept them guessing about whether or not he was kidding.

At almost exactly twelve miles they reached the edge of the settlement. They pulled off the path, parked, and shouldered their packs.

The center of Elk Mountain reservation so

perfectly blended into its surroundings that Frank Lloyd Wright would have called it a masterpiece of low impact architecture. The buildings varied in size, but used identical building materials. Wood logs that came from the local forest. Stone that came from the river nearby. Homes were situated in concentric circles around a community center which appeared to be a place of central meeting and a country store with basic provisions.

There was a lodge sitting on a rise at the edge of the village. Glen knew from his research that it was the alpha's home. It wasn't larger than most in square footage, but its height, both in terms of structure and how it was situated relative to other buildings, strongly suggested dominance. What he didn't know for certain was whether they should go to the center of activity or to the lodge. He headed toward the large meeting hall. If no one had been designated to greet them, he would ask someone there.

Storm and Ram fell back just a little behind him. Under his breath Storm said, "Don't interfere unless his life is in danger."

Ram gave Storm a questioning look and narrowed his eyes. "You sure? He's a rookie."

"Would you rather see him tested *without* us watching out for him? Gonna happen one way or the other."

Ram nodded and they picked up their pace until they were right behind him again.

Glen looked over his shoulder. "Secrets, gentlemen?"

"Storm's expectin' fatherhood and needin' advice from a more experienced family man."

Storm always marveled at how easily stories slid

out of Ram's imagination and onto his tongue.

A score of children had started following, laughing and running circles around them. Glen smiled at them, but didn't speak. Werewolf tribes were isolated. They didn't get many visitors and didn't readily trust people from the outside world. A handful of adults who could tolerate humans conducted business on behalf of the tribe. The rest of the population preferred to keep to their own territory.

Glen looked over his shoulder. "Don't say anything to them. Their parents may not want us to interact with them and make them feel comfortable about humans."

When they reached the settlement center, there were several young bloods hanging around the entrance, leaning against the wall. When the three strangers approached, they straightened. Glen offered a courtesy nod and started toward the door. They immediately closed ranks and blocked his path.

"We're here to see the king. And we're expected."

One of them repeated his words back to him in a high mocking voice while the largest stood right in front of his face and stared down at him. The one directly in front of him inhaled deeply, then made a face like he smelled something bad.

Glen narrowed his eyes, but didn't look away. The werewolf standing directly in front of him started to growl low in his throat. Glen responded by letting his pack drop off his shoulders onto the ground, but he didn't look away while he did it.

"Maybe I wasn't clear. Once again. We're here as the *king's* guests. We don't want any trouble. We're just trying to find out where to meet with him. So either take us to him or get out of the way so I can ask somebody else."

The wolf in Glen's face responded by showing his teeth. Without further warning or ritual threatening behavior, Glen unleashed a snarl so loud and menacing, and inhuman, that the werewolf in front of him stumbled backward and ended up on his ass with a shocked look on his face. The three friends behind him backed away quickly. Still growling, Glen leaned down toward the boy on the ground and waited for him to submit. When the other kid showed his throat, Glen looked at the others so they could see what alpha looked like on someone their age. That gave the young male on the ground time to scramble to his feet and retreat to a safe distance.

Storm and Ram both raised their eyebrows. A look passed between them just as the door opened. Stalkson Grey was standing behind it.

"Mr. Catch?"

"Yes."

"I apologize for that behavior. You were supposed to have been met and escorted here. By the time I heard the disturbance and realized that some of the young bloods were misbehaving, I saw that you were doing fine on your own. I saw what happened from the window."

Grey was looking at Glen with unexpected admiration. All three of his team were thinking that the potential ambush might have turned out to be the best thing for the success of the mission.

Glen offered his hand to the king. "Glendennon Catch. I'm here on behalf of Black Swan. I believe you've met Sir Hawking."

Grey stepped off the porch and greeted Ram with a handshake, then introduced himself to Storm.

"Since we're having a small get-together of a private nature, I thought we could talk at my house. The tribe's two elders are already there waiting."

Grey turned to Ram. "How was your flight?"

"Actually we used another method of transport. 'Tis related to what we came to discuss. Mr. Catch knows all the particulars, so I'll be lettin' him fill you in.

"'Tis a beautiful place you have here. A little cold maybe."

Stalkson Grey laughed at that. "It's funny to hear you say that because lately I often find myself feeling too warm."

"Aye. Well, 'tis probably the menopause."

Glen froze in his tracks and held his breath, wishing to all the gods, as much as he loved and admired him, that Rammel had stayed home.

Grey stopped moving. Then, seeing the twinkle in Ram's eye, he threw back his head and laughed. "You know, Sir Hawking, you and your mate are the only people I know who aren't afraid of me even a little. It's... refreshing." As they continued walking, Grey slapped Ram on the back. Then, in a more serious tone, he said, "You know I'm not experiencing the menopause."

Ram took another couple of steps before asking, "How do you know?"

There was a hitch of hesitation in Grey's stride, but he broke out in laughter all over again when he realized he'd been teased, not once but twice. And all in the same day.

Grey's lodge was stately in its own way. It was a tribute to Northwest Pacific art and architecture.

There was a comfortable conversation area by a large free-standing rock fireplace that could be seen from both the living area and the kitchen beyond. A small, cheery wood fire was burning and filling the house with the delicious aroma of green wood and sap.

Two old werewolves sat on either side of the fire like bookends. Grey introduced them as Drift and LongPaw and they rose without the effort normally expected with age. A tall woman with wholesome, natural good looks brought in a tray with six wooden mugs and set it down on the knee-high table. Each member of the impromptu Black Swan team looked at the liquid they were holding, but couldn't begin to tell what it was.

"I'm told this takes the chill away, Sir Hawking." Grey tipped his mug.

It was some sort of ale, warm and delicious.

"This is wonderful. Thank you." Glen offered his appreciation and accepted another mug from the nameless woman with a nod.

Grey nodded. "We hope you have some encouraging news for us."

Glen smiled. "We do."

In many ways Glen was the ideal Black Swan ambassador for that particular mission. He dealt with the dominance parrying by flicking his gaze away from the king every five beats or so. It was long enough to let Grey know that he was also an alpha personality who should be respected, but not long enough to be interpreted as a challenge to his authority or position. Although the king didn't say so, he appreciated The Order's astute choice of representative.

As the afternoon wore on, Glen explained about the windfall opportunity that had presented itself for the unmated to relocate. A few questions were asked about the nature of multiple dimensions. The old werewolves seemed to be blasé about it, as if they were already familiar with the concept.

As a picture of a possible future slowly took form in Stalkson Grey's mind, he began to realize he was feeling something he hadn't felt in such a very, very long time. So long he could hardly pair a name with the feeling.

Was it excitement? Maybe. Another question followed close on the heels of that conclusion. What did that mean?

Was he excited about the prospect of averting the catastrophe of extinction? Was it excitement about the prospect of seeing light and life come back into the eyes of his young male wolves? Then an unbidden thought entered his mind. He couldn't possibly be excited about the fact that somewhere out there were enough females for old wolves as well.

He pushed that thought away, but found himself looking at the elders and thinking that perhaps he wasn't *so* old. When he left the reservation, didn't the human women stare at him with something that looked like heat? Perhaps he could still be appealing to female wolves as well?

He realized that it was quiet. Everyone had been looking at him while his mind had wandered into the realm of smoke and fantasy. Dreams.

Turning to the elders, he said, "What do you think?"

Drift spoke first. "There are stories about wolf people who left our world long ago. It is good to know their journey was fruitful. They found a better place and survived.

"We should have a tribe meeting and decide which wolves will go. All the young males will say yes, but their families will be sad. Some might find mates who would be willing to come back to Elk Mountain, but I'm not convinced that would be the best thing. The world is changing. It becomes less friendly to the wolf people every day.

"It will be hard to see our young ones go away forever. It would mean many tears, but it is the best thing."

Stalkson looked at Drift without speaking for a long time. Then he looked into the fire for an equally long time before turning to the other elder. "LongPaw. What do you think?"

"I agree with the ancient one." Glen, Ram, and Storm simultaneously glanced over at the other elder being referenced as 'ancient'. To them, he looked the same age as the speaker. "For the young men who will keep the spirit of the wolf people alive, it will be a great and marvelous adventure to share with their great-great-grandchildren. For the mothers who say goodbye to their sons forever, it will be a source of sorrow.

"Still, it must be done. Every path is imperfect. You must choose the one that will keep the wolf people alive. Somewhere."

Stalkson studied his hands for a few minutes. "The descendants of old ones who left this world for a better life are proof that the legends are true.

"It occurs to me that you didn't mention restrictions. Has Black Swan stipulated that *only* young men can go?"

Glen shook his head. "No such restriction has been indicated at this point, but we also have nothing to offer you. The purpose of this conversation is to confirm interest. Once we have that, we will initiate a search. We can't move your people without first gaining permission from the tribes that currently occupy the territories under consideration. We can't make promises about what to expect, but we can promise to start searching for tribes open to integration or worlds with enough lands.

"In a perfect universe we would find a tribe somewhere with an abundance of females without mates."

Stalkson and the two elders laughed at that. Grey looked from Glen to Ram to Storm and back to Glen.

"It is decided then. If room can be found for us in a world that is good for our kind, we will explore this course of action. We'll call a meeting to determine interest."

Glen nodded. "As soon as we know whether we're trying to find a few brides or plan an exodus, we'll get started. But no decision will be made without your approval." He hurried to add that last part, not wanting any misunderstandings because of a misstep on protocol.

"Let me ask you one more thing." Glen looked straight into Grey's eyes without flinching or showing any sign of discomfort. "Would you want to personally accompany the, um, entity on scouting missions?"

Grey indicated no hesitation whatsoever. His answer was quick and forceful. "Yes, Mr. Catch. I would like that very much."

"Don't speak too soon. His personality is a bit

quirky and he can be, um, unpredictable."

The king looked amused that Glen was worried about... what? His feelings getting hurt?

"I'm sure we'll work it out."

They stood.

"The Elk Mountain Tribe thanks you and please thank those who sent you as well."

Grey shook hands with Ram last. He smiled with a little mischief in his steel blue eyes. "Please give Mrs. Hawking my fond regards."

Ram laughed in his face. "No' a chance. If you want to call her that, do it yourself."

Grey smiled in a way that indicated that he would do exactly that the next time he saw her.

The three were quiet on their way back to the guard station. The breeze in the open air jeep was cold on their faces and stung a little. Storm was thinking that Glen could not possibly have handled himself better. One of the things they needed to establish was whether or not he would be taken seriously by powerful personalities like the one they had just spent the afternoon with.

The demonstration of alpha traits had been a bonus, a surprise bonus. Storm almost chuckled to himself, but didn't want to have to explain to the kid that the show of dominance had been both entertaining and highly encouraging regarding his career prospects. Storm was feeling better by the minute about the possibility of Glen surviving Z Team. Maybe he would even accept Sol's wager.

In the backseat by himself, Ram was taking in the remarkable beauty of the scenery, the sights, the smells. Even the discomfort of a frozen face was good in its own way.

He thought, I wish Elora was here to share this. And that's when it hit him, what Elora had been trying to say all along. That life confined to a box, even if it was a big, functional box like Jefferson Unit or a big, luxurious box like the palace she grew up in, was a compromise of life's potential. To a species that craved freedom, it was a shadowy imitation of living. A punishment. Not a joy.

As he watched trees pass he began to contemplate deep-end philosophical questions of the sort that he usually avoided. Questions like whether it was better to live confined or die free. By the time the jeep came to a stop, he had decided that he needed to be a worse protector and a better listener.

They left the jeep where they had picked it up and waved to the guard on their way out.

When they'd walked until they were out of sight, Glen said to Storm, "How will you let them know we're ready to be picked up?"

Storm gave Glen a wry look followed by a smirk as he withdrew his cell phone from his glove pocket and held it up.

Baka asked Elora if she would like to accompany him for his official introduction to the five vampire that Glen had started calling Delta Kappa Fang. Having a known ally sit in on an initial meeting could never hurt.

They opened the door. Four of the vampire were lounging on and about the sofa facing the huge screen TV. They were watching reruns of "Buffy" with the volume turned up so loud that Baka and Elora almost missed hearing Javier shout, "Oui. Stake the ugly motherfucker."

Elora was thinking, *Wow. Everything really does sound better with a French accent.* The vamps seemed to have a talent for creating surreal moments. Watching the vampire watch Buffy, and watching the vampire root for Buffy to stake the ugly mofo, certainly qualified as surreal.

The vampire who always seemed to be more subdued had been sitting away from the others at a game table at the back of the room, quietly observing. His attention had shifted to Baka and Elora and he was watching them with open curiosity. Since the others hadn't even noted their presence, Elora headed in his direction and Baka followed.

The vampire stood when she came close enough to extend her hand.

"Hello. I'm Elora Laiken. This is Istvan Baka. He's actually head of the task force assigned to eradicate the vampire virus. You'll be working for him."

The vampire shook hands with first Elora, then Baka, and nodded to each respectively. "Jean Etienne. I am the garde d'enfants." Elora noticed Baka jerk his head toward the four who were watching TV.

"Garde d'enfants? I don't know what that is." She was asking Baka for a translation.

Jean Etienne motioned for them to sit as if he was the unquestionable host entertaining guests at his own home.

When they were seated, Baka turned toward Elora. "He said he's their babysitter."

The garde d'enfants frowned at the simplified

explanation. "Their families pay me to watch them, to keep them safe. And to keep them from being cause of harm so they grow up."

His Anglish was so heavily accented that Elora had to listen carefully.

"I see." She glanced at Baka. "You're saying they're children."

"Juvénile."

Baka asked for clarification in a brief conversation Elora didn't understand. He nodded then turned to her. "My best guess is that they're post-pubescent, the equivalent of fourteen or fifteen-year-olds." Elora's gaze wandered to the vampire watching TV, who looked more like early twenties. "They're mature physically - as you see, but their emotional development is slower. They're going to live for..." Baka turned to Jean Etienne. "How long will they live?"

"How long?"

"Yes."

He shrugged looking mystified by the question. "As long as they wish."

A stunning answer to be sure. So much so that it froze Baka and Elora while they tried to process the presence of virtual immortals.

"They've agreed to help us? And you can manage them?"

"Manage them? It is my job. Oui. They will be managed. If you do not try to poison us with more of your blood substitute.

"Have they agreed? They are not presented with a choice. They will help. Is good for them. Like your... ah... community service."

"Community service." Baka repeated it back in a

quiet monotone. He seemed to be processing, but each new revelation was more stunning than the last.

"Oui. For all we know your problem may have genesis by one of their own brothers. Or fathers."

Noticing that Baka was staring blankly, his eyes a little unfocused, Elora took over. "We have developed a cure for the condition. We call it a vaccine. It's a liquid that is packaged in a small vial. It enters the system when the skin is punctured, in much the same way that the disease was passed to the infected individual. Our biggest problem is that we need to be sure it doesn't get into your systems because we don't know what it would do to you."

Jean Etienne barked out a laugh. It was the first time he had smiled and, it turned out, that he had one of those faces that transformed into sardonically engaging with a large dollop of sexual suggestion.

"No." He shook his head. "That is not *our* biggest problem." He emphasized the word "our" in a way that could have been interpreted as sarcasm. "*Our* biggest problem is keeping their minds on the ugly vampire and not on the pretty femmes."

Elora looked at the TV screen. "Great Paddy."

Baka followed her gaze, then laughed and started shaking his head.

"No. The vampire we must... Let me start over. We are apparently not looking for vampire. We're looking for humans whose systems reacted very badly to certain chemical properties in your fluids. These sick humans don't look like the vampire on "Buffy"."

"No?" J.E.'s response was so nasally French and so comically delivered that Elora started giggling and couldn't stop. For the first time since these creatures had interrupted dinner by chasing Litha into the middle of the tightest security facility in the whole of Black Swan, the entire idea of immortal French, skirt-chasing vampire struck her as hilarious.

"Elora?" Baka ventured with caution. "Is something wrong?"

"They..." She waved a hand at Jean Etienne. "... are the reason why The Order exists. All this trouble... And it was a giant cosmic fucking joke accident." Baka reached out and let his hand curl around her shoulder. She searched his eyes, looking uncharacteristically vulnerable. "Do you know what they did to me?"

Baka swallowed hard and nodded. "You know I do. I was there. It was unspeakable. Do you know what they did to me?"

Her eyes seem to clear up a little and she whispered, "Yeah. There's nothing funny about vampire, huh?"

He smiled. "I once said something similar to Kay when we were in Ireland."

While Jean Etienne studied their exchange closely, they had all but forgotten he was there until he spoke. "So. You are lovers, no?"

They both looked at him like he was crazy and, in perfect unison, said, "No!"

He held up his hands, palms outward, as if to say, "Don't mind me. And don't shoot me either. I'm just an innocent immortal vampire with a French attitude."

Elora turned to Baka. "I'm going to check on Helm."

As she started toward the door, Javier noticed her and bounded into her path to intercept her. He smiled and cocked his head to the side. "Hello again. You never answered my question."

"What question?"

He stepped closer, his eyes drifting down to something about her neck that seemed to fascinate him. "If I bite you, will you squeal deliciously for me, my love?"

He reached out to touch her hair. At the moment she didn't have extra patience for vampire. She responded to his overture by lifting him above her head and hurling him into the opposite wall over twenty feet away. He grunted when he hit the wall, and sank to the floor. The other three boys, er, boy vamps, laughed so hard they couldn't make a sound. One slid off the couch and onto the floor so he could hold his ribs while rolling about. The other two leaned on each other.

When the one on the floor was able to speak, he pointed at Javier and said, "Dude! The chick slammed you into the box and set you on your can! Totally!"

Javier didn't bother to get up off the floor. He was laughing as hard as the others. It appeared that they didn't need any encouragement from artificially enhanced blood to have a good time.

Elora looked at Baka over her shoulder. "This Cirque de Dénouement used to be a perfectly respectable clandestine facility." Again, she turned toward the door, talking to herself under her breath. "So this is retirement." Closing the door behind her she heard one of the "boys" say, "Whipped, man." She had to wonder if Rammel had programmed their video feed.

Honestly, every single part of the day had made

Elora feel bone tired. Even the fact that Ram had been so uncharacteristically quiet and distant at dinner. It had just been one of those days when things seemed "off".

When Helm went down for the night, she withdrew to the cocoon sanctuary of a long, hot bath and even dozed off for a bit. When she woke, the water was still warm but no longer hot the way she liked it. She wrapped a bath sheet around herself and went to her closet to get a nightgown. She felt more than heard Ram come up behind her. When she reached for the gown his fingers closed around hers and interlaced.

There was no question that the male standing behind her was her mate. The aroma of musk and wild fern was strong in the enclosed space and nobody smelled like him. It was as intoxicating as ever. He stepped closer behind her, rested his hands lightly on her waist, and pressed his mouth to the nape of her neck.

The fatigue she had felt melted away and was replaced by a sudden desire to turn and encourage the silent seducer. She knew his feel and knew his smell so she was hardly surprised to find her mate when she turned to weave her arms around his neck, but she was surprised by the event.

Ram was a great lover. He should be. He'd certainly had enough practice, but sex with Ram was typically playful. He had a ritual pattern that included a series of leers and innuendos, usually during dinner, followed by signals of touch that throughout the evening gradually advanced to suggestions about outrageously acrobatic positions, or costumes, even laundry baskets.

This. This was something different.

There had been no verbal foreplay. No provocative ramp up. He just stole into her closet after her bath and silently put his arms around her while she was still warm, damp, and completely relaxed. When she had turned around to face him, one look at his face told her that he was not feeling playful.

He pulled back just far enough to grab the hem of his Nine Inch Nails tee shirt and pull it over his head. Normally he would take the time to smirk and enjoy watching her visually feast on his beautiful body. But that night, without taking his eyes away from her face, without the slightest hint of humor, he quickly divested himself of boots and jeans and boxers. The look of purpose and sexual intensity on his face caused her to feel suddenly shy, as uncertain as the day she'd waited for him in the New Forest cottage with her heart beating fast with the hope the beautiful elf would return to his childhood retreat and claim her.

When there was nothing left between them but the oversized bath towel, she realized that she was clutching it to her chest with a death grip. He didn't try to take it from her. He just began slowly backing toward their bed, pulling her with him as he went. It was a journey of a few feet that felt like miles to Elora.

Since the near totality of what she knew about sex had been learned from Ram, she didn't know how to respond or behave.

Rammel urged her onto the bed and lay down beside her, ducking his head to place a gentle kiss on her shoulder before his fingertips feathered down the side of her face and along her jaw. He was staring at her mouth like he'd never kissed her before. When he ran his thumb over her bottom lip with the lightest of touches, she drew in a small gasp that made his eyes jerk up to hers. He cocked his head slightly while he studied her face and her reaction. Likewise, she was desperately trying to read what she saw in his eyes, and failing.

He gently urged her to relinquish her hold on the towel she still clutched to her breast. Even when prying her fingers open, one at a time, she saw nothing of the usual lift of his beautiful mouth. No sexy smile of challenge. No cocky grin. No groan of approval.

When she gave up the towel and lay bare to his gaze, she felt like he was seeing her naked for the first time. The way his eyes ran up and down her body made her want to curl up and hide from his view, but she forced herself to remain passive. Feeling stripped of the role she'd grown comfortable playing, she drew in a ragged breath that, again, made Ram's eyes come back to her face like he was looking for something there.

He began a torturously slow path of kisses and touches, progressing down her body, avoiding her nipples because she was still nursing. His tongue slowly swirled in her navel and her clit jerked, probably more from the erotic sight than the sensation. She was squeezing her thighs together to ease her arousal, but he nudged her legs apart as he slid further down her body. It felt like he'd been teasing her for hours.

She alternated panting and moaning as he nuzzled and nibbled at the fiery red pubic curls. She had taken hold of handfuls of his silky hair and had just opened her mouth to beg when his tongue slid slowly up her slit and flicked across her swollen nub.

Breath was frozen in her lungs when the first wave of climax extinguished all thought. Rammel's demeanor and behavior were confusing. His careful and intense lovemaking had made her feel awkward and off balance, but it was also working her up to the point where it didn't take much encouragement to bring her to orgasm. She was ready.

Gently, but deliberately, Ram settled himself into the cradle of her thighs. Using his muscular arms to hold himself just above her breasts, he kissed her long and deep. She responded with a renewed series of moans that punctuated the slight arch of her body, pressing him closer in ancient feminine invitation. Of their own accord her legs drew up to encircle his waist and lock him in their embrace. At the same time she reached down with her hand to encircle the engorged evidence that he wanted to be inside her as much as she wanted him. When he felt her touch, he closed his eyes for a second and sucked in a shaky breath.

She guided him to the spot where she wanted him. He entered slowly like the sweetest torture, keeping his eyes locked on hers. The drawn-out friction of his first unhurried withdrawal made her hiss air between her teeth. That was followed by a powerful thrust that was so unexpected she cried out in surprise, then felt embarrassed about the sound she had made.

He knew her so well there was no hiding any part of herself from him. He placed his lips next to her ear. "Do no' be embarrassed with me. Ever. I'm the elf who loves you. All of you. Exactly as you are."

Elora's body betrayed her feelings about the pent up emotions and his declaration with an involuntary sob. As she felt the first tear run down her cheek and onto her pillow, her mate said again in a voice that was little more than a whisper, "I love you." Those three words were repeated with every advance of his body and every retreat from hers, winding her feelings tighter.

"I love you. I love you. I love you."

She cried openly, not having known that lovemaking could be so thorough that it was soul-baring. Feeling exposed to her core, she came harder and longer than she ever had known was possible. Ram's hands were still on either side of her, lifting his upper body so that he could watch her from that position. His release followed moments after, looking down at her with a flush that measured the heat of their coupling. She watched, mesmerized. As the powerful arms holding him up started to shake while he came, she reached up and cupped his face, just needing to complete the connection by touching him and feeling his feverish skin underneath her hands. His eyes, turned to their darkest blue, reflected the dim light so that they seemed to shine from within.

"I love you, Ram," she whispered back to him. He collapsed to the side of her with his face in the crook of her shoulder so that she wouldn't see his own eyes watering.

After a while he rolled them onto their sides so that they were facing each other. They lay quietly looking at each other. When Elora parted her lips to speak, Ram's eyes traveled down to her mouth and back up again.

"Tell me what this was about." She waited for the wisecrack. It never came.

Finally, still not smiling, he said, "You complainin'?"

"You know I'm not. That was..." She paused, trying to find the right thing to say.

"What?"

"It was more than making love, wasn't it?" She watched a parade of emotions flicker across his face.

"'Tis me feelin' shame for no' bein' a good mate to you." Elora opened her mouth to protest, but he put his fingertips against her lips. "When I said I wanted to leave our home and come here, you tried to tell me 'twas no' what you wanted. And I did no' listen.

"I was set on havin' my way, sure that no price is too much to pay to keep you safe. Today, when we were at the werewolf's home, I knew I made a mistake. I want to protect you." He cupped her face and brushed away a lingering tear trail with his thumb. "But I want you happy more. Do you want to go home?"

Her eyes threatened to spill again. "We just got here," she whispered.

"'Tis neither here nor there." She looked like she was trying to find an answer in his eyes. "Tell me what you want. You have my full attention and I'm listenin'."

She swallowed hard. "I don't want to put our baby in danger."

Ram nodded slowly.

"But I don't want him to grow up in captivity either."

"Captivity," he repeated. "Then 'tis settled? We're goin' home?"

Elora pulled in a rush of breath and blinked repeatedly to keep from breaking into sobs. She hadn't let herself feel either how much she hated the current arrangement or how much she wanted to be home. "Sir Hawking. I have never loved you more."

"I..." It sounded like Ram's voice was going to break. She nestled in closer, pressing her body into his to encourage him. "I'd never do anythin' to hurt you. When I think what might have happened on Helm's birthday... I can no' stand the idea of livin' without you."

She felt his fingers tighten on her skin like he was holding on for dear life and knew that it was subconscious.

"We're smart enough to figure this out, Ram. We know that life comes with risk. We just have to manage the level of risk that we can live with."

"What are you thinkin'?"

"Since we're here, I say we give Monq a chance. He's a genius, right? That justifies giving him a few months to make our miracle. I can make this work that long, especially since it seems to relieve your stress and worry. If it looks like it's going to drag out beyond that, we'll need to come up with a fall back plan.

"Meantime, I need to get trotted out more often. I want to go into the city and visit some of the other museums, spend time in the Soho galleries, check out clubs in Greenwich, go to plays and concerts. We're living so close to New York and, if all goes well, that's a temporary thing. Let's get the most out of it while we're here."

Elora's hair had grown several inches since she was on active duty. He reached up and pushed it back from her, face cupping her head with his hand. When he opened his mouth to speak, she cut him off. "And I have the most impressive secret weapon in the history of the world."

"Speak."

"Litha." Ram looked stumped. "If I call her, she can find me with the signal of my phone. If I can survive for thirty seconds, she can grab me and get me out."

"And what if she happened to be busy doin' her funky spells? Or seein' a movie? Or sleepin' or showerin' or fuckin'?"

"Then I'd be fucked."

"Funny."

"Life is risk." She gave him a small peck on the lips.

"But you can count on the way I feel about you."

He pulled her close so that their naked bodies were perfectly aligned, and reveled in the way she fit him like she was custom made. When it came to the scent and feel of this woman, her wry humor and unlikely talents, her constant faith that the best was yet to come, he would never get enough. And, since he knew he'd come close to losing her, he had vowed to treasure every second.

Since you've been snugglin' so close, and I'm no' complainin' mind you, but since so much of Helm's milk is runnin' free, I thought I might have a wee taste. Out of curiosity?"

She laughed. "Go ahead. It's not like you're not really a baby."

CHAPTER_9

The community building wasn't nearly large enough to hold everybody. It wasn't often an issue, since the entire tribe gathering together all at once was a rare occurrence. Except for those who volunteered to patrol the borders, all the wolf people were present, those who lived in the settlement and those who lived in the mountains. The meeting place was a dry canyon with naturally amplified sound. No microphones needed. The rock walls were also a shield from wind.

Large ground fires dotted the area and served the assembly in three ways. Visually, the collective clusters of flame lit the geological strafing in the rock face cliffs in a beautiful rendering of nature's random abstract art. Physically they provided warmth for those close by. They also alerted the psyche of each and every attending werewolf that it wasn't an ordinary night. It was an event.

Some of Stalkson Grey's strongest, and most trusted young males stood on promontories above the congregation. Their presence reassured everyone that the extended pack was safe and well-guarded. Grey stood on an outcropping raised a few feet above the heads of his people. The tribal elders sat on boulders on either side of him.

When the king faced forward, ready to speak, everyone grew quiet so that the only sounds were an occasional pop of sap coming in contact with flame.

"I've gathered the wolf people of Elk Mountain because we've come to a crossroads. The old ones sit to my left and to my right so that all know they guide me with their wisdom. The little ones are here so that they will bury the memory of this night deep in their hearts and carry it to future generations. The rest of us have a decision to make.

"It's a decision that begins with a story - the story of our ancestors who left this world for fairer hunting grounds, where game is plentiful and people of the wolf are free. You all know this story. You heard it many times in childhood and probably grew up to believe it was a legend. But we have learned that it was an actual, historical event."

A murmur rippled through the crowd.

"There came a time in the distant past when those like us were presented with a choice. They could stay and watch the world grow smaller around themselves and their young, or they could migrate to another world that is real, but hidden from our awareness, and start a new life there.

"Some stayed. We are evidence of that. But many chose to go.

"We find ourselves with a quandary. We do not have enough young females to replenish the tribe with a new generation. Our young males long to pair with mates according to the natural order of things, and bring young into the world. Parents long to be grandparents. But this cannot come to pass without life-bringers.

"This is a trying time, but fortune has been kind. Our friends at The Order of the Black Swan have sent emissaries. They have shown a light onto a path that was dark and hopeless. They have promised to help find a new home that is suitable to our needs and then provide us with a way to follow the tracks of the old ones.

"There are worlds where land and females are plentiful."

Another crescendo of murmurs rippled through the crowd. Stalkson paused and looked over his people.

"There are some unknowns, some questions still to be answered. I cannot promise that we will all be reunited elsewhere. Depending on how many want to go, we may need to assimilate into other tribes in different locations. Before we go, we will have an understanding with the wolf people who are scattered on the winds, and be welcomed into their tribes and onto their lands. Families will be kept together. For now, that is all I can promise.

"The choice is yours. There will be no objections if you wish to stay. Nor will anyone think less of you. But if you want to go, you must declare your intention. We will require names and ages and mating status. If you are part of a family group, we need the number who must stay together. If you are a young blood in need of a mate and you are willing to go alone, we need to note that for the record.

"Please go home and talk amongst yourselves. Tomorrow WhiteDawn will be in the community center to create a manifest list. Those who want to be included in this journey must go and enter your names. Those who want to stay need do nothing but go about your business.

"You may ask questions. If I have the answers I will tell you."

Silence persisted for only a heartbeat before the single young males began offering their pledges in loud excited voices, "I'm going."

"I'm going."

"Put my name down now."

The unmated laughed and gave each other shoulder nudges, pats on the back, fist bumps, and high fives. Stalkson felt a hint of optimistic joy seeing the flicker of hope renewed in the eyes of those who had come of age with no prospect of cultivating a family. They had looked far too resigned and sorrowful for far too long. An adult male without a mate was a shadow of the wolf he might have been.

Most of the young males had never had a heterosexual encounter, but the gleam in their eyes said they were overeager to experiment with mounting a female.

One of the women spoke up. No doubt she was mother to one of the unmated who had issued a public proclamation and was alarmed by how quickly their lives had been irrevocably altered.

"Forgive me for saying so, Alpha, but you're asking us to give up everything familiar without knowing our destination. Are we to follow blindly?"

Conversation broke out among the people and quickly became too loud for Grey to be heard above them. He let them talk to each other for a few more minutes then held up his hand. The power of his authority was absolute among the wolf people of his tribe. He expected their instant attention and silence and that is what they gave him.

Stalkson Grey was calm and composed, unmistakably commanding, immeasurably handsome. Those who were close enough could occasionally see firelight catch in the steel blue of his eyes as they listened, captivated by the authority of his manner and the rhythmic cadence of his speech.

"If I asked you to follow me blindly, I would

hope that you would." Another murmur moved through the crowd and many heads were nodding in assent. "But that is not your future or mine.

"I will personally accompany the Black Swan representative on a scouting mission to find new lands that are suited to the best interests of our people. While I'm away, my son, Windwalker, will be charged with fulfilling the duties of alpha. Your problems and concerns will still be my problems and concerns, but he will take care of you in my stead.

"When I return, I hope to have word for you on what awaits us in the new world. What I must carry with me, when I go, is a count. How many? Who?

"As you go to your respective homes tonight, consider this. The future of the wolf people has weighed heavy on my heart for many seasons. It is only a matter of time until humans become jealous of our land. Their numbers increase like cancer. They have no respect for the land or for other species.

"When the wind blows from the east we hear their voices and machinery at the edge of Elk Mountain reservation. They rape the land beneath our feet by horizontal drilling. When that is gone, they will find a way to break the Jefferson treaties. We do not want a war with the humans. We want to live in peace, to run, to hunt, to nuzzle our mates and keep our children safe.

"There is one more thing. Human technology makes it more and more difficult to keep our privacy and our secrets safe. They now carry cameras on their phones and many videos of wolf people shifting. They have been made public and can be seen on computers that are owned by many humans.

"Right now people assume that the pictures are

the result of technical magic, cleverly manipulated. The photographers are called liars and are laughed at. But the day will come when they begin to suspect that it is not a trick.

"We could stay and try to hide our ways and adapt by integrating into human society and keeping our natures secret."

The tribe reacted angrily to that idea, shaking heads, collectively saying, "No."

"Understand, then. We are living the twilight of this way of life in *this* world. We cannot be children or cowards and refuse to face the inevitable because it is unpleasant. The way I see this, we can either make a choice about our future or the future will make a choice for us that is far less agreeable."

One of the elders rose and said in a voice that seemed too loud and clear for his old body, "Spirits be with our alpha. Guide him on his path. Keep him safe and strong."

CHAPTER_10

Deliverance left Glen outside Sol's office as requested. Litha was only a microsecond behind with Rammel. In two minutes she had returned with Storm. He gave her a peck on the cheek and told her he would just be a couple of minutes if she wouldn't mind waiting.

"I'll see if Elora and the baby are free. Call me when you're ready." Litha walked a few steps down the hall and speed dialed Elora. Storm knocked on Sol's office door. When he looked back, Litha was gone. She could have taken the elevator like everybody else, but she had gotten very comfortable with saving time by getting where she wanted to go virtually instantly.

Sol swiveled around to greet Glen and his team and ask how it went. After a couple of seconds, Glen realized the question was being directed at him. That was going to take some getting used to.

"As well as could be expected, sir. The king was receptive to the idea of migration. He wants to leave it up to his people whether they want to go or stay. We told him he could go with Deliverance to scout possible situations."

"And he's okay with the fact that Deliverance is a demon?" Sol asked.

"Well, um, we... or, I should say, *I* didn't mention ethnicity."

"Ethnicity?" The question was dripping derision. "You didn't tell him."

"No, sir."

Sol steepled his fingers as he stared, or glared, at

Glen depending on interpretation. When Glen started to feel the tingle of self-consciousness under the Sovereign's intense inspection, he distributed his weight evenly so that he wouldn't embarrass himself by shifting back and forth, which according to the training would imply nerves or anxiety.

"Anything else to report?"

"He, the, uh, king, will advise when he knows how many of his people would like to be considered for possible migration."

Ram and Storm waited quietly at ease while Sol continued the uncomfortable, silent scrutiny that the two of them had been subject to *so* many times. The familiarity of shared experience made Ram look over at Storm to see if he was thinking the same thing. Catching the movement out of the corner of his eye, Storm responded with the tiniest nod and hint of a smile.

Finally Sol lowered his hands. "You're dismissed, Catch."

"Thank you, sir." When Glen turned around, he allowed himself a microsecond's glance at Storm and Ram and thought he saw a hint of amusement on their faces.

When he closed the door behind him, Storm and Ram both sank into chairs without asking for permission. Given their long history with Sol and the cob-in-the-ass way he'd treated them when they were active duty knights, it was kind of fun to just plop down and dare him to say anything about it. They grinned at each other like they had just shared a victory.

"Would you gentlemen care to report your evaluation of Catch's performance in the field?"

"Flawless," said Storm.

"Impeccable," said Ram.

Sol stared at them like it was their turn only they were no longer available for the silent treatment tactic. Storm saw no reason to prolong the pretense so he broke the silence barrier.

"Are we done? My wife is waiting to give me a ride home."

Ram looked at him thoughtfully. "You know 'tis way cool, right?"

Storm gave him a big smile. "I do know that." He looked back at Sol. "So? Anything else?"

"As a matter of fact, I have the paperwork prepared to put Z Team's transfer in motion." Ram sat up straighter and looked between Sol and Storm. "I didn't want to make it official before seeing that he was up to this somewhat minor task."

Ram had to ask. "You did no' want to make what official?"

Storm sighed. "Sol's getting married." Ram laughed with complete conviction that it was a joke. "No, really, he is. To Farnsworth."

Ram's gaze jerked to Sol. "Oh, em, congratulations. And I can no' wait to hear what that has to do with Z Team."

"He has promised her he'll retire in two years so that's how long he has to groom a replacement." Ram nodded. "He asked me. I said I'm not the right guy for the job." Ram nodded vigorously. "So I recommended Catch."

Ram looked like he was once again waiting for the punch line. When the other two continued to look perfectly serious, he gaped. "'Tis utter insanity! The boy is no' yet twenty. No' even declared. He's my dog walker for Paddy's sake!"

"It is unorthodox."

"Unorthodox," Ram repeated. "'Tis the understatement of the millennium. And..." Ram's expression went dark as his brows drew together. "And... what has this to do with Z Team?"

"Well, Sol wants to test him."

By the time Storm was halfway through that sentence Ram was on his feet. "You used to accuse me of bein' reckless. But I never came close to doin' anythin' as irresponsible as turnin' those miscreants loose on a nice kid like Glen."

Sol sounded so calm Ram wanted to punch him. "If he's Sovereign material, he'll be able to handle it. If he's not..."

Ram turned red in the face and loomed over Sol's desk. "He's. A. Kid."

Not one to shrink or cower, Sol rose slowly so that he was eye level with Ram and lowered his voice. "He's a kid who's been put up for my job."

Ram wheeled on Storm with accusation all over his face. "What are you no' tellin' me?"

Sol chuckled. "Given how much fondness you have for the boy, he's probably not telling you that we've made a wager on the outcome."

Ram looked at Storm like he'd been betrayed. Storm looked at Sol like he could kill him.

"Come now," Sol began, "it's all in fun."

"Does Glen know what you have in mind for him?" Storm looked away and shook his head. "I have no' put my fist in your face since we were younger than he is now. But if anythin' happens to that boy, we're revisitin' a proper beatin', you and I."

Ram stormed out of the office causing the door to

slam against the wall on his way out.

After a couple of seconds Sol said, "Not showing any signs of mellowing, I see."

"Actually, it *does* take a lot to get Ram going these days. His reputation as a hothead has pretty much been lived down, which is why that outburst is making me think this is probably a mistake. If Ram is the clear choice for grown-up in the room, it means we're on the wrong side of a thing."

Sol's eyebrows lifted in an expression that was downright triumphant. "In that case, I suggest you keep a close eye on that situation and make sure nothing irrevocable happens."

As soon as Storm saw that look he knew he'd been manipulated and outmaneuvered. "Shit."

"Don't slam the door on the way out. It would just enlarge the hole in the wall that Sir Hawking made and Farnsworth would be forced to invoice both of you for repair." Sol chuckled and seemed to be enjoying himself way too much.

"Shit."

"An education money couldn't buy and that's the extent of your vocabulary?"

Storm pinned Sol with a piercing look he never would have dared before he retired. "I know other words. Would you like to hear some of them?"

Storm stepped into the hall and called Litha. When she answered he could hear Elora in the background, probably talking to Helm. "Is this yellow cab?"

"Close enough. When would you like to be picked up?" She waved goodbye to Elora.

"Now."

He jumped when she appeared right next to him, and she sniggered. A couple of minutes later, when they were alone in their own kitchen with the lights turned on and the temperature regulated, he cornered her between the sink and the island. He reached down to run his hand over the tummy that was shockingly full and rounded as he searched her eyes.

"The word that keeps coming to mind is alarming."

She smiled. "If we were fully human, I think we should be alarmed. But I feel good and I think the baby is fine."

"How do you know?"

"I think so."

Storm narrowed his eyes. "When was the last time you saw the doc?"

If looking away wasn't a big enough clue that she was hiding something, the fact that she also looked sheepish would have raised the suspicions of even the least observant husband.

"Three weeks ago."

"Three weeks ago? Litha. Three weeks ago you were barely showing. Now you look like you're ready to pop."

"Pop? Great image. Very smooth."

"Don't deflect. This is weirder than a virgin birth."

She laughed. "It is *not* weirder than a virgin birth. *That's* impossible, whereas *this* is not. Obviously."

He pulled her as close as he could get which meant he had to angle toward her side. "Baby. We've got to find out what's going on. Seriously. I don't know if we need to finish the nursery or schedule an

SAT prep course. Let's go see Doc Lange. I'm going with you."

"You gonna hold my hand?"

"Damn right."

She looked at her watch. "It's 0315 in Edinburgh."

"Okay. We'll have a little dinner. Get a little restless sleep then go. Together."

"Are you insisting?"

"Damn right."

"I'm not sure I like it when you're demanding."

"Yeah. You're sure. You like everything about me."

He treated her to the boyish grin that was such an effective tool for manipulating Litha, and forced that smile in place, but on the inside his stomach was clenching with worry. In purely human terms, she would still be in her first trimester.

Storm was a thinker and a planner. As soon as he found out he was going to be somebody's dad, he researched pregnancy thoroughly. He knew that a first baby might not show until four months had passed. Litha was looking more like the last stages and not even three months had passed.

Of course he had no regrets. He knew the witchy demon's daughter wasn't the girl next door. Well, actually in his case, she was pretty close to the girl next door, since they grew up just a few miles away from each other. He knew when he chose her that life was probably going to present some out-of-the-ordinary issues and events.

He had no regrets, but that didn't keep him from sometimes stressing about what was on the next page.

"I don't like doctors."

"Nobody does."

"Yes. But other people are more used to them."

He cocked his head to the side. "What do you mean?"

"Before I got pregnant I'd never been to the doctor."

Storm just stared like he was trying to process that. "How is that even possible?"

"Well, I was home schooled so I didn't have to prove I'd had shots. I never got sick. And, since Cufay strongly suspected I was different somehow, I think he was afraid that exposing me to the medical community would be the first step toward a *captivating* career as a carnival exhibit."

"He was smart to be concerned about that. You know you were lucky to end up where you did. You landed on your feet."

"Yep."

"Never had a broken bone?" She shook her head. "No bike accidents requiring stitches?"

"No broken bones. I got cuts and scrapes sometimes, but Brother Mossbind was like an old kitchen witch. He had a cellar full of dried plants and was adept with potions and concoctions. There was always something to make me heal quickly and not scar." Storm seemed deep in thought. "What?"

"I was just thinking that, since this is virgin territory for everybody, you might want to have your Bro Mossbind take a look. It couldn't hurt. If you went from infancy to adulthood without ever seeing a doctor, I'd say that goes in the plus column of his resume."

Litha's eyes sparkled. "I can't believe you managed to talk about *this* pregnancy..." She ran her hand over the basketball shape under her tunic, "...and virgin territory in the same sentence. Between that and the virgin birth reference, it seems like you have virginity on your mind."

He lowered his dark head and pressed a kiss into her neck with a smile. "What I have on my mind is you, just you, always you."

They set the alarm for 0200 so that they'd be sure to catch the good doctor at his best when they arrived in Edinburgh. They weren't on his schedule, but on the other hand, what could he possibly have to do that would be more important than looking after the first human-demon-witch-demon hybrid pregnancy?

As anticipated, Doc Lange complained about "walk-ins". Storm pointed out that they didn't *walk* in. Litha laughed and the doctor grumbled some more.

He performed a fresh ultrasound while Storm held Litha's hand, as promised, and got misty-eyed looking at the baby.

"It's a girl, isn't it?" Storm asked, sounding like he was awestruck.

Doc just nodded. Litha couldn't be mad because she'd forgotten to remind the doc that she didn't want to know for sure. But truthfully, the confirmation was pure formality. She had known it was a girl as soon as her intuition told her she was expecting. The confirmation caused emotion to bubble up. To keep from crying she squeezed Storm's hand and clutched her black diamond pendulum tight with the other hand.

A naked demon appeared in the room looking a little curious and completely unabashed.

Doc Lance jumped and clutched his chest like he

was having a heart attack.

Storm didn't know whether to be more put out about the fact that his father-in-law had interrupted a private, family moment or about the fact that he was wearing nothing but the pendulum that matched Litha's. He quickly settled on the penis exhibition.

"For craps' sake. Would you cover it up? This is your daughter!"

Deliverance ignored the doctor and Storm. "What's going on?"

"What are you doing here?" Litha asked.

He seemed confused by the question. "You called me."

It was only then that she realized she had a vise grip on the pendulum he had given her. She had a fleeting thought that, maybe subconsciously, she had wanted him to share in the moment.

"Oh, sorry. Since you're here though, you might as well enjoy the human magic. Look at your granddaughter."

Since he was looking at the screen, Deliverance didn't see the folded, thin cotton hospital blanket that Storm threw at him until it hit him in the face. "Cover up *before* you look at my daughter."

"It's a dick, dude! Not a bomb." Deliverance unfolded the blanket and wrapped it around his waist like a sarong. "You need to think about getting therapy for your issues with prudity."

"I've told you before, don't call me 'dude'. And prudity is *not* a word."

The demon turned to Litha. "Seriously, how's your sex life?"

Storm made a strangled sound and tried to grab his father-in-law across the bed, since the doctor and the machinery was blocking the way around the end. Litha put her arm out and tried to restrain Storm from leaping the rest of the way across the bed to try and strangle he-who-could-not-be-strangled.

"Stop. Storm! It's none of his business."

Litha kept her hand on his chest until he seemed to calm. When he straightened and took a small step back, she dropped her hand and turned to her father. "Our sex life is fabulous in *every* possible way. Thank you for asking."

Storm simply gaped at her. He wasn't a visionary, but he did know for certain that life was never going to be boring. When he looked from Litha to his incubus-in-law, he found the demon staring at the screen, mesmerized by the baby's image. "Beautiful," he whispered.

Deliverance was exasperating in countless ways and was fast coming to feel like the price the Universe exacted from Storm for the gift of Litha. But if he was going to compliment and appreciate their daughter, he would be tolerated, within reasonable limits.

CHAPTER_11

About half of the Elk Mountain tribe put their names on the list. Undoubtedly each soul of an age to make their own decision had their own reasons for signing up. Conspicuously missing from the list was Stalkson Grey's only child, Windwalker.

Win was grown, of course. He was fortunate enough - and strong enough - to have won one of the few young females and was happily mated. They were expecting in late summer. Twins. He suspected that might have something to do with a decision to do the safe thing.

It could just be a simple matter of timing. Pregnant with two pups wasn't an optimum time to pull up stakes and start a new life.

Late that night Grey walked the settlement in human form thinking about the utter strangeness of life. Just a week before he had never given thought to whether or not there were other dimensions, much less the existence of other realities similar to his own. Realities where werewolves like himself congregated and lived.

As an afterthought, he decided to revise the comment about finding other werewolves like himself. Humility just wasn't a good fit with his personality.

The next day he was to meet a guide and make plans for a tour of some of those other worlds. He walked until he found himself near Drift's encampment. As he approached he amused himself with the thought that he had been walking aimlessly and had "drifted" there. The old wolf didn't care for human-style structures. He had never slept in a building for even one night of his long life. His home was teepee style, made of thick tanned buckskin fitted together like patchwork, then stitched with latigo lacing.

The tent flap was up in welcome. "Son of StalkingShadow, come. You are welcome in my home."

Stalkson smiled and crouched so that he could enter. He sat across the small fire from Drift, who was smoking a thin pipe. Age had drained the color from his eyes making them exceptionally pale and a little eerie looking.

Drift took the pipe from his mouth. "Have you decided what you're going to do?"

"About what?"

Drift laughed. "Going. Or staying."

The king didn't answer at first, but appeared to be concentrating on something in the blue flames. "I don't have the answer."

"Well, when you do, you will know."

Grey smirked at him. "Was that supposed to be profound or just your usual folksy bullshit?"

Drift laughed harder. "Let me know when you find out for sure."

"I didn't see *your* name on the list."

"Oddly, I was ready to pass in peace and reunite with my mate, but the prospect of this fine adventure has made me a little sad that I'm too old to start over."

Grey nodded. "And LongPaw? Does he also think he is too old?"

The old wolf had a curious look on his face. "You'd have to ask him." Stalkson rose to go. "Spirits with you, Alpha."

"I'm coming back, old one."

"See that you do."

He'd received very specific instructions from the youngster Glen Catch. By face phone, Glen had told him that his guide, named Deliverance, would arrive at 0900. Grey's initial reaction had been to think, "How bad could someone be with a name like Deliverance?"

As preparation, Grey had been told that Deliverance would transport him to Jefferson Unit by highly unusual means, that he would need to maintain physical contact during the trip, and that he should not let go under any circumstances. Highly irregular, but easy enough.

He hadn't asked Catch what to wear, but the kid had volunteered that he should dress for comfort. At 0830 he had wolfed down some venison flank steak and eggs with a little overcooked spinach mixed in, showered, dressed in jeans, pulled his hair back into a leather tie, and was waiting. At exactly 0900 there was a polite knock at the door.

When the king opened the door, the visitor became a guest for all of thirty seconds. Before Grey knew they were leaving, Deliverance had taken the wolf's forearm into his powerful grip and delivered him to the conference room next to Sol's office. The king wanted to take the occurrence in his stride, but there was a difference between entertaining a thought and processing an experience. The fact of being instantly transported across the country was a shock that took getting used to. And his stomach felt a little queasy.

He recognized Catch, Monq, and Elora Laiken, of course, but there was another man and woman he had not previously met.

Litha was closest to their point of arrival. Deliverance pulled her into an embrace and kissed her temple. "This is my daughter, Litha."

Litha beamed like a daddy's girl. "Hello."

The king noted that father and daughter appeared to be the same age, which meant they must age like werewolves.

Waving her hand toward Sol, Elora said, "This is Sovereign Nemamiah, your wolfiness."

Sol gave Elora a look of reprimand then offered his hand to Grey.

"I see you've met the demon."

Grey's head jerked toward Deliverance. "Demon?"

Deliverance shook his head and smiled, "A rose by any name..."

"S'okay, Grey. He's a semi-good guy." Elora tried to reassure him.

"Semi?" He scowled at Elora.

"You worry too much." She pointed to his forehead. "Those what-the-fuck lines between your eyebrows are just going to get deeper and deeper until they're frozen there even when you smile."

Sol stepped in. "Please forgive the Lady Laiken. She meant no insult."

"Actually," said the werewolf, "I'm used to being insulted by Mrs. Hawking."

Glen's eyes widened. "She lets you call her Mrs. Hawking?"

Grey laughed at him and just like that the tension over the demon in the room dissipated.

Ram came in, his blonde hair looking damp from the shower and darker than usual. He raked his wife with a look of sexual interest as he closed the door behind him. She responded with a promising smile. Observers probably wouldn't guess that they were married and had been sharing a bed together just a couple of hours earlier.

"Sorry for the tardy. Nanny was runnin' behind as usual." He nodded at the king. "Grey."

"Please, everybody. Sit." Sol took his usual place at the end of the table closest to the door. "There's a coffee and tea service... Can we get you something?"

"No. Thank you."

"Very well, then. Let's discuss what we came to discuss. As I understand it, the number one priority is finding a situation where there are available females for mating purposes." Even though that was a statement and not a question, Sol looked to Grey to confirm or deny.

"That is the priority, although about half my tribe has expressed an interest in migrating to a place more conducive to our way of life. To answer your point, would it be possible to look for mates in the, uh, same dimension our ancestors colonized?"

Sol looked to Deliverance to answer that question. He stared back at Sol until Litha said, "Dad. He wants you to field that question."

"Field the question?"

"Answer it."

"Okey-dokey." He looked at Grey. "I don't have to tell you that werewolves are typically territorial. Most of the time they wouldn't be welcoming off-world males come courting. They'd see it as poaching.

"However..." He stopped for a dramatic pause, "...I do know a dimension where male werewolves routinely mate with human women. The human male population dwindled because of war and male infant mortality, but the female population thrived. Their biology must be a little different because they breed without any problems and their offspring are werewolves - strong."

"Hybrid vigor," Monq said thoughtfully while stroking his chin like he had an invisible goatee and looking at Glen.

"An overpopulation of human women that are attractive to us. And they produce purebreds?" Grey sounded hopeful and dubious at the same time.

Deliverance grinned. "Oh, yeah. All you can eat pussy buffet."

"Dad!" Litha was stifling laughter while trying to appear scandalized for propriety's sake. The overall effect was a suggestion of rapid cycle bipolar. Truthfully, she knew from experience that it was better to laugh than to try to domesticate her sire 'cause that simply wasn't gonna happen. Others, however, were not always as tolerant of his antics.

"What?" The demon looked baffled as to why his daughter was doing that correcting thing she did.

Litha turned to Grey. "He's an incubus, which means his perspective on sex is very unorthodox, which means inappropriate comments are inevitable."

"Hellooooo. I'm in the room, you know." He rolled his eyes at Litha and continued. "We would still have to get clearance from the occupying species, but it's not an overpopulated dimension. There may be enough open space and available females so that neither would be an issue for them."

Ram and Elora had both seen Glen bristle when Stalkson Grey specified that he wanted offspring to be "purebred". Naturally they both felt defensive about their boy. Ram quietly excused himself, holding up his phone as if to say he needed to step out and make a call, but when he walked behind Grey, he flipped him off with a big grin for Glen who smiled in response and relaxed, knowing there were two retired knights who had his back and his feelings, too.

"We could establish a territory of our own?"

"I don't know everything about how wolf politics work. Could be tricky, but I can ask if the idea appeals to you."

"And you could cause interdimensional ill will that gets us banned from contact for generations." Litha turned to Sol. "Honestly. The idea of my father as diplomat is scarier than a French horror movie. When you asked if he could assist with Order business, it never occurred to me that you were going to try and make an ambassador out of him. The phrase 'lost cause' comes to mind."

Deliverance cocked his head and looked at her with interest. "So. What are you saying?"

Sol cleared his throat. "I understand your concern, Litha, but our demon is the only game in town."

Arching an eyebrow, Deliverance said, "*Our* demon???"

"Um, forgive the error. Definitely a misplaced pronoun." Sol looked at Litha. "I get it. Diplomacy is hard. One wrong word..."

"...has been known to start wars," Litha finished for him.

"Yeah."

Everybody was silent while they absorbed that. Ram was as inconspicuous as it was possible for Ram to be when he came back into the room. As he took his seat, Elora gave him a smile of approval for the well-placed bird and a silent high two.

"Well, if you won't be needing me further, I'll just slip away..."

"Sit down, Dad. We need you here. And stop looking like your feelings were hurt. That won't play either."

Litha got a perfectly demonic grin in response. She shook her head and rolled her eyes like a teenager.

Having been quiet for some time, Stalkson spoke directly to Deliverance. "It seems to me, if I'm understanding correctly, that you've been visiting these various worlds and mingling with their inhabitants off and on for a long time."

The demon nodded. "Eight hundred years. Give or take."

"How many wars have you started because you said the wrong thing?"

"None."

"In that case, on behalf of my people, I would like to ask that you do what you can for us. We will be obliged for whatever that is."

The demon said nothing, but offered his handshake in the custom of Loti Dimension humanoids. "Very well, wolf. You've got yourself a guide."

As they shook hands, several of the meeting attendees, who were there to ensure that an agreement was reached, were thinking that they should have stayed out of it and let the demon and the wolf handle it between themselves to begin with.

As Stalkson Grey, the werewolf king, and Deliverance, the Incubus, talked quietly, beginning to devise a plan, Sol said, "I think the rest of us are just in the way. We might as well go about our business and call this a success."

Sol was first out of the room. Litha waved to Elora and disappeared before Elora could ask how 'things' - meaning pregnancy issues - were going.

Glen filed out with Ram and Elora. "Thanks, Mom. Thanks Dad."

In a clear gesture of affection, Ram put his hand on Glen's shoulder. "'Tis Sir Hawking to you, rookie."

"Hey, you should give me some respect. In two years I could be running this place." Glen looked around like he was imagining it before turning back to face Ram and Elora. When he saw the smirks on their faces he laughed. "Yeah. I don't believe it either."

Three nights later Stalkson Grey was reading an Isaac Asimov treatise on alternate dimensions by his fire and getting drowsy enough to think about going to bed, when he heard a knock at the door. He stood and set the old-fashioned, paper book on the table next to his mug of mulled wine that had gone cold before he'd finished it.

The king opened the door to a shirtless demon. "Deliverance. Come in. You must be cold."

"No. Not at all."

Grey's brows drew together slightly. "Can I get you something? I can warm up some mulled wine."

"I only consume sex energy."

"I see. Well, not really. What do you mean?"

"Dude. Do you not know the meaning of incubus?" Grey looked like he might be struggling for the right words. "I don't eat or drink. I'm sustained by having sex." He held his arms out. "And, as you can see from the state of my vigorously thriving good health, I do alright. You could say I'm prosperous."

"Well, would you like to sit down then?"

The demon sat in a large, leather chair that was worn but generously sized and comfortable.

"I have some properties to show you that match your specifications."

"Properties?"

"I heard it on 'House Hunters'."

"Oh."

"Okay, seriously. I tried the dimension where most of your ancestors settled. When I explained the situation, they said their world can easily accommodate another tribe. They kept calling you cousins and they almost seemed to like the idea of assimilating you.

"Then there's the dimension I told you about that's been favored with an overabundance of feminine occupants who are human with the propensity to whelp werewolves. They're not really interested in immigrants, but they agreed to give your young males one month visas to look for mates. If in thirty days they find a bride and convince her to go, it will be with the blessing of the local authority.

"We can move everybody in your tribe who wants to go to Lunark, where your 'cousins' are. Your boys can go vie for brides in Shrifthet and then join the others on Lunark when they're mated. I can show you some uninhabited dimensions that would be suitable if you prefer a true frontier, but this seems like it might be the best fit."

"You think the Shrifthet females would be willing to leave their families?"

"Depends on incentive I guess. Are your boys attractive?"

Stalkson had to think about that. "I honestly don't know whether they'd be considered attractive to humans or not."

"Well, what have they got to offer? Are they skilled as lovers?"

"Actually, most of them, maybe even all of them will be new to sexual experience with a female."

Deliverance was abashed. His mouth worked for a few seconds without making sound. Finally he managed to whisper, "Great Balls of Fire."

"I assure you it's not that they aren't eager."

The demon's body shuddered involuntarily when he tried to imagine life without women. "Have you... given them instruction?"

"Me? No! Of course not. They'll figure things out. It's not that hard."

The demon snorted. "Not that hard? Maybe it's not that hard if you're a wolf mounting a female in heat, but human women? That's a whole other story. Their anatomy, along with their sexuality is far more complicated. It's not hard for me because I was born knowing what to do, but most men *never* 'figure things out' to the satisfaction of their mates.

"Somebody had better take them to school before they go shopping for wives. They're going to have to offer some powerful motivation to get girls to give up their friends and families and home world. A push in with a squirt just won't do it."

Grey winced at that. "What do you suggest?"

"I don't know. Training classes?"

Stalkson laughed out loud. "Training classes? Really?" He seemed to grow more serious the longer he thought about it. "Thank you for offering. I don't know how we can refuse."

"No. I didn't mean I would do it. I'm not a teacher. I'm an incubus."

"Well, I'm the spirit-damned Alpha of this tribe. You think it's my job to tell a gang of young bloods, 'Put this there'? No thank you very much. You're the one who's qualified."

Deliverance studied Grey for a minute. "I'll think about it. If I do it, you can come. I mean, you can attend."

"Let's not get too far ahead of ourselves. Can you show me what we're talking about before we get deeper into planning?"

"Sure. You ready to go?"

"Ah, I guess." Bed had been calling before the knock on the door, but Grey realized that he was fully awake. If he went to bed at that point, he wouldn't be able to sleep.

"First stop, Lunark Dimension. I wore a belt for you to hang onto. Take hold and don't let go until we get there. And, wolf, it would be very bad if you let go."

Grey nodded and prepared himself for that unpleasant sinking of his stomach that felt like an elevator dropping too fast. The trip took a couple of minutes longer than it had taken to get to Jefferson Unit in New Jersey. One minute they were in halls of gray fog, then, without warning, they emerged onto a pink granite mesa overlooking a large settlement by a wide river with water so teal blue it didn't look real. It was early morning. The sun had barely cleared the horizon. The air was a little crisp but perfumed with a smell like ground thistle leaves.

"That's it." Deliverance pointed downward. "We'll walk from here. I've learned that it's not a good idea to startle people when you want something from them."

Stalkson turned in a circle. From that vantage point he could see that there was plenty of room in every direction for running and hunting. Temperate climate. Nature at her very best. He followed his guide down the path toward the village.

Everyone watched as the demon passed. The locals looked at the strange werewolf with curiosity, but not animosity. They were met by a delegation that included the tribe's Alpha, SilverRuff. She acknowledged Deliverance quickly and nodded toward Grey. "Is this one of them?"

"Yes, ma'am. This is Stalkson Grey." Grey was careful to avoid holding eye contact with her for too long, as it would be a sign of disrespect. "He is pleased with your generous offer of welcome to his tribe."

"Stalkson Grey. This world has enough resources to support many tribes for many generations to come. If there are tribes other than yours who wish to leave the human world, we will make room for them as well."

"Thank you, ma'am."

The demon looked into Ruff's rust-colored eyes. "Shrifthet Dimension authorities have agreed to give Grey's young males thirty days to find wives. Will your people accept human women?"

She frowned. "It would probably be easier on your tribe and mine if you establish your own territory. We know how much space we need for hunting and running and will not be greedy beyond that. We will welcome your people, offer friendship, and help you build, but it would be better for your tribe to stay intact and preserve its ways.

"To be sure we reserve enough for future generations, we will retain fifty sectares square for our tribe. There is a tribe to the east and another to the south, but you could make a claim on the lands to the west or north." Looking at Deliverance, she said, "Perhaps you could show the alpha his options so that he can make an informed decision."

Deliverance took Grey to the lands to the west and north.

"This is paradise for wolves."

Grey couldn't help but be elated. It was the first time he had felt optimism about the future since he was a very young wolf. He was reminded about how good it had once felt to have that blood-coursing tingle of aliveness.

He had raised a son without the benefit of a soft touch to his skin or a gentle breath near his ear. He had thought of nothing except his duty to his child and the welfare of his people. And, while he was busy being responsible, his heart had withered and dried up. Somewhere along the way he had become hard and cold and never realized it until that day.

"Yes." The demon looked around trying to view the landscape through the eyes of a wolf. "Paradise for wolves, but not for men. Your people have grown accustomed to human magic. You have vehicles on your reservation, electricity, communication equipment, some even have satellite TV."

Grey sighed and nodded. "It is true and something that I need to make my people aware of before they make a final decision."

"Good. On to Shrifthet."

They visited Shrifthet briefly so that Grey could confirm the demon's claim of plentiful females. Deliverance said that he would need to know the exact number of young wolves interested, along with their names, so that he could procure visas and living arrangements.

"How much money will be required to pay for living arrangements?"

"None. The Order will pick up the tab."

Stalkson wasn't sure he liked that idea. "We can pay our way. We have... resources."

"Whatever you say. I need to make a short stop on the way back if you don't mind. Got something to drop off with my mother's sister."

"Alright."

"What is that look for?"

"I... just never thought of demons as having mothers, much less aunts."

"Well. I do."

"Okay."

The exchange seemed to bother Deliverance. "You knew I had a daughter."

"Yes."

"Well?"

"Well what?"

"Well, if you knew I have a daughter, then why does it come as such a surprise that I also have a mother and an aunt?"

"Why are you acting pissy?"

"I'm not."

"You are. And I'm not offering either an apology or a hug."

"Okay."

"Okay."

"You know, wolf, I've noticed that you're very partial to having the last word."

"Really?"

"Yes."

"Okay."

They walked out of the passes into a forest on the edge of a large park. "Wait here."

CHAPTER_12

Grey stood in the shadows on the periphery of a vast area of park gardens surrounded by a forested apron of pine trees that reached for the heavens. On the far side of the park he could see the spires of modern glass buildings rising higher even than the trees. A city. A densely populated city where humans lived and worked in buildings with glass outer walls in a variety of colors. One would never guess an urban area was nearby, based on the deserted appearance of the park. The hundred foot slash pines did an amazing job of quieting the noise of the city beyond.

Though the werewolf king was of the opinion that nature didn't need improving, he had to admit that the sophisticated design of botanical placement, fountains, walkways, berms, canals, and grassy areas was pleasing to the eye and soothing to the spirit. There were also large, dense patches of flowers that were red with an intensity that didn't occur in his world.

The centerpiece was a large white marble building similar to the style of the Parthenon except that each of the supporting columns was actually a giant statue of a young woman in Greco-Roman style dress and no two were alike. It was an imposing structure that dominated the parkland in such a way as to suggest that the park was there to serve the purpose of the building.

In his world it would be assumed to be some sort of temple, but there was no guessing what it might be on Throenark - a laundromat for all he knew. He noticed that there were seven smaller buildings at the rear connected by covered walkways resembling fingers.

He wished he hadn't been ordered to wait. First, he didn't like taking orders and found that it made his teeth grate together of their own accord. Second, he especially didn't care for *that* order since it contradicted his desire to give the building a closer inspection. That impulse, in itself, was curious because he wouldn't have described himself as someone who was interested in art. After a few seconds of deliberation, he decided to follow his own counsel about where he would wait out the demon's family errand.

Fascinated by the sculpted relief apron that wound around the top of the sculpture just under the roof, Grey walked toward the rear. The frieze was a mural, apparently depicting either folkloric or historical events of the local culture. It was hard to interpret their meaning without knowing more. A door to one of the annex buildings opened suddenly and immediately drew his eye.

A group of young women emerged wearing red silk the same color as the patches of those remarkable scarlet blooms. They seemed to be conversing happily as they made their way toward the central building. They wore long, hooded, sleeveless shifts with side slits to the knee, cinched at the waist with thin gold belts with serpent clasps. The fabric was thin enough to conform to their figures, but loose enough for ease of movement. A sudden breeze whipped up and blew the hood back from one of them. Laughing to the others, she caught it in the breeze and pulled it back over her dark auburn brown hair, but not before he had seen her face.

He saw her.

And he wanted her.

It was as simple as that.

It was as complicated as that.

The sensation of instant attraction was foreign to Grey. He didn't know if it was the surprise or the feeling that made him uncomfortable, but he wasn't at all sure he liked the feeling.

It was outside anything he'd ever experienced or prepared for. He was sexually stimulated by the smell of bitches in heat. When the bitch was his mate, he acted on the impulse to mount, preferably in wolf form. It was urgent. It was compelling. It was an activity that was as necessary to mammals, including werewolves, as eating and breathing, but it wasn't a goal.

Stalkson Grey had always been more or less disinterested in sex, outside the occasional copulation for procreation's sake. His preoccupation was that of typical alphas. His personal, professional, and recreational goals revolved around power and were fueled by the belly fire of ambition that had been bred into him by generations of alphas. Mating was about breeding and sometimes about companionship. It wasn't about sex for pleasure's sake.

The wolf side of his personality and the human side of his personality had always worked together in perfect harmony, each complimenting the other, making the whole stronger. At least that was true in regard to his single-minded pursuit of gaining and holding the position of alpha. If the human side of his personality had other ideas about interaction with females, it had never surfaced before.

She moved with a grace that suggested healthy muscle beneath the fluid movement of the silk over her body. He studied her with the concentrated focus of a born predator until she disappeared into the rear entrance set back from the porch formed by the monolithic statuary.

Deliverance appeared next to Grey. "I told you to wait."

Grey shrugged. "What do you call this place?"

Deliverance looked around. "Which place? The city, the dimension, what?"

"Let's start with the dimension."

"Throenark."

"Throenark," he repeated. "Do you come here often?"

The demon smiled. "As a matter of fact I do. A couple of times a week." With that, he took hold of Grey's wrist and they were back in the thick mists of the passes.

When they emerged, the king was looking at his own front door. "You want to come in?"

"No. I want to fuck." Grey turned to him with a stern expression, lines formed between his brows. When Deliverance saw his face, he couldn't help laughing. "Not you!" The demon looked him up and down. "You're pleasing enough to the eye, but too tough. I'll bet your skin feels like old leather."

"If it keeps me from being attractive to you, then it has just become my best feature, so far as I'm concerned. What is important is the plan. What happens next?"

"Running out of juice fast. Fuck first. Talk later." The demon disappeared. Stalkson sighed then went inside to light a fire and collapse in his big chair. It couldn't hurt to have a respite with his own thoughts. He made a sandwich piled high with meat seared on the outside and rare on the inside and ate in front of the fire with a cup of mulled wine.

He sat back feeling full and drowsy. Plans needed to be formed and finalized, but his thoughts turned to the vision of the Throenark woman. When he drifted to sleep in his chair, he dreamed of red silk floating around him, teasing his skin with light touches and pooling at his feet. Reaching to grab the fabric, he felt it move across his fingers and heard the sound of a woman laughing, a human woman laughing. And knocking.

As his eyelids were drifting open he realized that the knocking was coming from the front door. Deliverance stood on the mat, smiling.

"Feeling better I see."

"You wanted to talk plans?"

"Come in. I'd offer you something, but I don't have what you want."

"Truer words, wolf."

They sat by the hearth.

"Going back to what you said about my young bloods not having the courting skills they need..."

"Hmmm?'

"I was thinking about the classes you're going to teach."

Deliverance stared. "You're really serious about that?"

"Who's better qualified to teach sex ed than a sex demon?"

"You have a point."

"Well?"

"Well." Deliverance pulled his hair to the side

and occupied himself braiding it. He grinned. "Like a slide show presentation. Why not? It would be a first. Incubus tells all. It could be hysterical."

"I don't want it to be hysterical. It's a serious subject. I think a serious approach makes more sense. These are young, impressionable minds and I don't want to give them a tainted view of natural processes."

The demon narrowed his eyes. "Jumping Jehosophat. You don't know any more about pleasing a woman than they do!"

Grey kept his expression blank and gave away nothing. "I'm a widower. I had a mate." Deliverance just shrugged. "So you agree?"

"I don't know why, but I like you, wolf. I like you and I'm feeling generous so, yeah, you're going to get the crème de la crème of expert advice on how to make a woman scream your name and rut on your leg."

Stalkson sighed as he tried to not imagine the feel of red silk moving against his bare leg. He crouched in front of the fire and poked at it. "That place, the one we went to last..."

"Throenark."

"Yes. I'm curious about the... building."

"Oh. It's a temple. Cult of the Vergins. They've made a religion out of healing.

"They're sort of like a cross between doctors and priestesses. They work with the red vervain that grows on Throenark and nowhere else that I know of. It heals just about anything that ails. Of course the vervain that *they* grow in the temple greenhouses is a little different than the wild plants."

"So the women I saw..."

"Dressed in red? Those are the thirteen Vergins. Second daughters from aristocratic families who give them into sacred service when they're children in exchange for a blessing that accompanies the family for generations. When the girls turn twenty, they're either released from duty or chosen to serve as one of the thirteen for ten years.

"My Aunt Pandora has been their protector, the acting Grand Mother for two hundred years."

"And you visit her a couple of times a week?"

Deliverance laughed out loud. "Well, I'm not exactly visiting *her*. As a favor to her, I stop off a couple of times a week and service the Vergins. According to their sacred law, they are never to be touched by the hand of man." When the demon grinned demonically, Stalkson Grey knew what was coming. "But I'm not a man. So it's a win-win-win-win. Everybody's satisfied: my mother, her sister, the pretty little ladies, and moi."

The last thing Grey wanted was to form an image in his mind of Deliverance pleasuring the beauty with tints of mahogany in her hair, but there it was. And it made him seethe. His fists clenched involuntarily. Irrational as it was, he wanted to launch himself at Deliverance, changing form in flight. And he might have if the demon's elemental power was anything other than fire. But the lupine side of Grey's nature had a healthy respect for fire in general and a deathly fear of fire out of control.

"You treat them like a harem?" he growled.

The demon looked surprised by Grey's deep, gravelly tone. "Is that a problem? I assure you they enjoy my attentions. As always, satisfaction guaranteed."

Grey struggled for patience, trying to remember that the demon was the instrument of salvation for the continuation of his species. He told himself that, for the same reason you can't be mad at a woodpecker for pecking, you can't be mad at an incubus for fucking anything willing. At the same time, his imagination was reveling in the imagery of tearing the smarmy look off the demon's face with very long, sharp teeth.

In a dazzling display of self-control, instead of shifting to wolf form and ripping the demon's lips away from his head, Grey said, "Are you going again soon?"

"Day after tomorrow. Why?"

"Just curious," he lied. "I guess I... liked it there."

"So what are you saying? You want to go back and hang out in the trees while I get a fill up?"

"Maybe."

Deliverance laughed. "Sure. Whatever floats it."

CHAPTER_13

The stark truth was that Jefferson Unit had been quiet since Monq and Baka had sealed the tunnels. Most of New York's vamp population had grown fat and complacent living in the underground. The irony was that it was one of their own who had planned and executed the operation that turned the vampire version of the easy life into their tomb.

The event had done such a bang up job of extermination that there had been little to do since. Sol shared with Storm and Glen that he worried about the knights losing their edge. They still maintained a duty roster and patrolled, but no longer expected to find anything. It was making them sloppy - a very dangerous thing for a vampire slay..., uh, curer.

"In fact we haven't scored a single cure."

Sol placed his coffee cup in the saucer then leaned back, causing the leather desk chair to squeak and groan.

"It's decision time. And this is what I'm thinking." He paused before steepling his fingers. "Very strange asking other people what they think. I've been keeping my own counsel for a very long time." Glancing between Storm and Glen, he began to lay out his thought process.

"It seems several matters are converging here and need to be sorted out. We're stabling the top Black Swan knights and giving them virtually nothing to do but walk around and pretend to be busy. Likewise, we're hosting Baka and the new stars of his task force without giving them anything to do.

"At the same time we have the arrival of Z Team

looming."

"Looming?" Glen asked.

Sol glanced at Storm. "I say that because they're a spirited bunch who can be a handful."

Glen didn't look satisfied with that answer, but Sol forged ahead.

"We can't abandon this facility. For one thing, we need to protect Monq's research."

"And Elora," Storm interjected.

"Yes. And Elora. Not to mention that this is the largest training installation for recruits. It would be silly to uproot the research and training aspects of this complex, but I think we need to disperse the knights and medical personnel where they could better be used."

Storm nodded. "I'm betting you've already thought this through to its furthest logical ramifications. So let's hear the whole enchilada."

Glen perked up. "Mexican sounds good."

Storm smiled. Sol ignored him.

"Cleaning out the underground havens here and in Edinburgh pretty much means we can cross those two cities off the list." He turned to Glen. "If you were in my place and you were going to split up and relocate our complement of hunters, what units would be under consideration?"

Glen didn't hesitate to answer. "Without having access to the numbers, it's hard to say conclusively, but, working blind, I'm going to guess you'll send them to London, Paris, San Francisco, and Rome. Maybe Brasilia and Buenos Aires."

Sol looked at Storm. "He named the six units I was looking at *and* he named them in order. Quite remarkable." Sol studied Glen for a minute or so with such an intense scrutiny that even Storm was impressed that his protégé didn't squirm or seem nervous. He sat quietly relaxed, blinking slowly, belying the possibility that he would shoot from his chair if he heard the engine noise of a taco truck nearby.

"I'm thinking it might make the most sense to send Baka's new team to Paris. They've been trained on the use of the cure canister tranq guns, they speak the language, and, since they're not afraid of contracting the virus or being overpowered, they may bring a superior ability to clean out the sewers. So to speak."

Storm nodded. "Sound reasoning."

"That creates a surplus of knights in Paris, so we should disperse some of them to London or Rome depending on who speaks Anglish and who speaks Italian. The extra boys here should be split between San Francisco and Brasilia."

"You should try and keep teams together."

"Understood."

"So you're thinking about basically leaving a skeleton crew here."

"Well, that brings me to another point."

Storm looked at Sol for three seconds before saying, "Shit."

"Sir Storm. There is a child present."

Glen laughed, clearly entertained by being called a child and having someone object to the word 'shit' being spoken in front of him. He turned to Storm. "Yeah. Watch it!"

Storm wasn't deterred. "You're not leaving Jefferson to Z Team. I vote the biggest fucking no that has ever been cast anywhere, any time."

"Well, first, this is not a committee. And, second, Sir Hawking and Lady Laiken will still be here."

Storm gaped. "They. Are. Retired." Sol just smiled like a person keeping unsavory secrets. "Okay. You want to leave Team FuckUp in charge? I've got a better idea. Let's just evacuate and blow the place now. Baka's here and I don't know anybody better at demolition. Turn it over to him and put a 'gone fishing' sign on the door. It'll be cheaper and probably save everybody a lot of trouble."

"Exaggerating much?"

Storm turned to Glen. "What the man is saying is that, when his plan is in place and operational, the only thing that will be left standing between The Order's star installation and disaster, is you."

Glen looked from Storm to Sol, who smiled and shook his head. "You are overreacting. When did you get to be such a pu...wuss?"

"Right. And Marrakesh is the last stop before being immortalized in the Hall of Heroes." Storm turned to Glen. "It's the modern day equivalent of the French Foreign Legion."

Sol directed his attention to Glen. "He had a disagreement with Z Team years ago in... Was it Berlin?" Storm glared, but didn't confirm or deny. "I don't know what it was about, but Sir Storm doesn't think much of Zed Company."

"You wanted my input. Here it is. And mark my words. If you go through with implementing the plan you just outlined, you're going to regret it. Big time." Sol scowled and looked down at his coffee cup. "Plus. According to what you've just described as a plan for the new improved Jefferson Unit, you're not going to need someone with Glen's talent to act as your replacement. Any mid level bureaucrat would do."

Sol pinned Storm with an old familiar look of authority. "Flexibility is a qualification for the position. We may be downsizing here for the moment. But..." He flicked his gaze to Glen. "Could I have a moment alone with Sir Storm?"

Glen was nodding on his way up out of the chair. "Yes, sir."

When he closed the door, Sol continued. "You know I'm not a philosopher or a metaphysicist or a mystic or anything of the sort. It might even be argued that I'm not a particularly deep thinker. But one thing I pride myself on is my ability to keep my ear to the ground and know when to pay attention.

"There's a historical pattern of shifts in mass consciousness occurring in clusters, like an idea floating around in space that touches the minds of several people at the same time. People who are not connected by association or geography. It's particularly true in the area of advancing technologies."

Sol paused.

Storm shifted forward in his seat. "I've never known you to go off on irrelevant tangents before."

Sol looked up, but didn't smile. "I sincerely hope it does turn out to be irrelevant. Here's an example. Take almost any innovation or invention and you'll find an argument over who should get credit. That's because there were several people who did not know each other, in different locations, who seem to have come up with the same idea at the same time.

"Lots of stories about runs on the patent offices to record invention of a particular thing. The one who got it officially recorded first got historical bragging rights. That expression 'an idea whose time has come' has some basis in fact."

"I'm sure there must be a point and I'm just as sure you plan to get there someday."

"Elora Laiken plops out of the air right in front of us and lands on the floor as a pile of mush." The words and the resulting image made Storm wince visibly. "Fifteen months later she's attacked by people from her dimension who have perfected the same transport that tried to eat her alive. Two months after that we get proof that there are entities who can travel between dimensions at will.

"Fresh on the heels of that we're visited by a scout troop of *real* vampire on an interdimensional field trip. Add that to the fact that The Order's Psychic Department is warning about preparing for paranormal life as we know it to undergo an overhaul. We're on the interdimensional map now and we need to be preparing for everything from social mixers to invasions.

"We probably won't ever find a way to defend against visits from the species who slip dimensions naturally like demons and vampire, but we need to come up with some way fast to protect ourselves from the ones who use technology to slip dimensions."

Storm quietly absorbed that and then processed quickly, according to his typical modus operandi. "So the knight shuffle really is temporary while we gear up and re-outfit."

"Same page, Sir Storm. Took you long enough."

"Yeah. Well, you better make sure there's something left to come back to after you walk away and leave Z Team in the role of principal protectors."

Stalkson Grey attended the demon's workshop on seduction and intro to female anatomy. He waited until the classes were underway, then quietly slipped into the back. The young males seemed to be reacting with an interesting mix of anxiety, arousal, and impatience to get started looking for mates.

Deliverance was having such a good time teaching that he decided to also offer units on flirtation, male exhibitionism, multiple orgasms, and creative positions. His students were exemplary, perfectly attentive, and enthusiastically appreciative.

Stalkson was grateful to the demon for giving the young bloods a chance at finding happiness, but he wasn't crazy about the use of porn as visual aids. Having come to an agreement with Grey about what would be presented, the incubus had approval to demonstrate with videos that were explicit, but wholesome. The demon turned the sound off so that he could lecture alongside the imagery, and used a pen light to focus attention on details such as the proper laving of a nipple or stroking of a clitoris.

Every day was filled with the buzz of activity at Elk Mountain. The half of the tribe who were preparing to pioneer a new life were caught up in the excitement of adventure and transition. The other half tried to look happy for them while they were preparing to say painful goodbyes and see their way of life change forever.

The young males had their papers in order, along with instructions about how to behave in Shrifthet culture. The fact that the clock would start ticking down thirty days upon their arrival was surely a lot of pressure, but the demon had given them techniques to help manage and hide stress so that they always looked cool, confident, composed, and, most importantly, sexy.

Since Deliverance could take only one person at a time, the alpha was first transported so that he could be there and waiting for them at the other side of their first experience slipping dimensions. He personally greeted each one on Shrifthet and checked to make sure they had their visas and some walking-around money.

When all were assembled he went along to make sure they found their temporary living quarters. He wished each one good luck and assured them that he and the demon would be back every day to check on them. The king wasn't worried. He knew they had each other.

The plan to move all the tribe transplants was progressing as expected. The demon moved several families at a time, delivering them into the hands of the wolves who had volunteered to help them build and get settled on their own territory. Grey had chosen the land to the north and had run the boundaries of New Elk Mountain's fifty sectares as a wolf. To a werewolf it was glorious. Like something out of a dream.

The king and the demon returned to Shrifthet every day, as promised, to show support and hear reports. The suitors often had questions for Deliverance. The demon seemed to thrive on the attention and on the subject matter.

Afterward, on Tuesdays and Saturdays, the incubus stopped at Throenark to service the Vergins who desired a good body buffing. The first couple of times, Grey simply squatted in the shadows of the forest apron and watched, imitating stillness to perfection. Various women would emerge from the complex to walk or meditate alone or in pairs, or to tend the patches of red vervain.

On the third such occasion, the girl that haunted Grey's thoughts wandered through the garden pathways leisurely and alone. She was carrying a basket and a pair of garden shears. She stopped by one of the large patches of red vervain, snipped some stems, and placed them in her basket. He shadowed her, staying under cover of the forest, without ever making a sound. When she drifted close to the trees, he let her see him.

It was evident that she was startled, by the little jerk of tension in her body. She didn't squeak or squeal or even hiccup, but her copper-colored eyes did get wider. She took his measure quickly, but not so fast that he didn't notice the path of her gaze.

"What are you doing there?" She made it sound like an accusation.

"Looking at you." Stalkson had never practiced the art of seduction. He'd never been interested in a human so why would he have? But he wasn't worried. He knew there was always a basis of truth in myth and there had to be a good reason why wolves had an ancient and persistent reputation for seduction. He decided to relax and rely on what might be a dormant instinct.

"What's your name?" she demanded.

He smiled. She was haughty. He liked that. "Stalkson Grey. What's yours?"

She caught her breath when she saw the flames behind his eyes. They reached out and licked at her, singeing something inside in a deliciously pleasurable way. That look he was giving stirred feelings she'd never experienced. There was a nagging suspicion that the smart choice would be to run, but she ignored it and gave him her name instead.

"Rejuvenata."

"Mouthful." He was talking about her name, but as the word fell from his lips, his mind was replaying imagery from the demon's class on female anatomy.

"I was, ah, renamed when I was initiated." She had no idea why she was standing there talking to a strange man, no matter how fascinating he might be. The way his steely blue eyes caught light and shadow when he moved was mesmerizing and made it impossible to look away, much less run away.

"What was it before?"

"Luna."

The sound of that resonated to his very core. He said Luna with a little growl that sent a tremor up her body starting at her core and ending where her nipples beaded visibly against the red silk. His eyes flicked downward and back to her face.

"Luna what?"

"Just Luna. We give up family names when we enter into the service of vervain."

"Luna. Just Luna. Just perfect." He smiled. "I'm very partial to moonlight."

She had thought he was handsome before, but he had one of those sardonic smiles that transformed his face into a mask of wicked perfection promising delights beyond wildest dreams. Her certainty that she shouldn't be talking to this magnetic creature was growing stronger every minute.

When her eyes started to feel dry, she realized she hadn't blinked. Shaking her head a little she said,

"Did you tell me your name?"

He laughed and she felt it ripple down the front of her body, caressing everywhere it touched. "Stalkson Grey."

"Oh, yes. You did tell me. Well, it was nice to meet you, Stalkson Grey."

He took a step toward her and it alarmed her enough that she took two steps back. He could see that she was skittish so he held very still. "Wait. Luna. Will you meet me here and talk to me again?"

She stared without answering for a few heartbeats. It could go either way. "Why?"

The innocence and wariness in her question made the predator inside Grey grin. "I liked talking to you. I'm here on Tuesdays and Saturdays at about this time. Will you come?"

"Maybe."

He looked as pleased as if she had given him three wishes and for some reason that, in turn, pleased her. She turned and walked away. Knowing that he was watching made her super aware of the movement of her hips and she was disgusted with herself for being self-conscious. Temple Vergins were not temptresses! They were healers! Still, she walked slowly enough to feel a graceful roll from side to side. What would her sisters think of that?

It was one thing to indulge in regular, healthy sexual exercise with Grannie's nephew. After all, how could a sexually frustrated healer heal? But it was something else to engage in a clandestine conversation with a strange man. The tingling sensation she was feeling about seeing him again was the exact reason why such things were discouraged. Strongly discouraged. She was supposed to focus on her vocation and not be distracted by a rendezvous with an irresistibly attractive man. Had she just said irresistibly?

When she had said 'maybe' to his question about whether or not she would meet him, she had known it was a lie. There was never a moment's doubt in her heart that she would meet him the next time he came. They would have to bind her with chains to keep her away.

Three days later she emerged from the dormitory to the rear of the temple, eyes searching the forest shadows. The wolf part of Stalkson's personality was triumphant. The human part was ecstatic. Watching the way her body moved as she approached was erotic in a way he'd never experienced and he wanted to pleasure that body in the ways the demon's classes had outlined.

The air was still in the dense part of the forest. As she watched his eyes roam over her slowly, she felt a trickle of perspiration run between her breasts and down her torso. Her breath made the tiniest hiss that would have been inaudible to human ears and her thighs clenched.

Since Stalkson Grey's ears were not entirely human, he had no trouble hearing that tiny hiss. In response his nostrils spread as she neared. He inhaled deeply and smiled.

During the following two weeks, Rejuvenata the Vergin, also known as Luna, and Stalkson Grey, both together and separately thought about little else than the next appointed time of meeting. Luna's sisters wondered why she seemed distracted. She was preoccupied during her healing rotation and absent from sign up for a turn with Deliverance on Tuesday and Saturday afternoons. To say that the Vergins were rarely absent on Tuesday and Saturday afternoons would be an understatement. Some of them lived from one of the demon's visits to the next.

Her closest friend, Sirenata, thought Luna was wearing a curious luminescent glow, but why should being visibly happy raise suspicion? They were supposed to be joyful in service to the Cult.

When Luna and Stalkson were together, they walked in the cover of the forest and, even though they were technically in the heart of a city, it sometimes felt as if they were alone. Grey hadn't realized he was lonely. He was never alone, in fact. He couldn't step outside his front door without being approached by someone who wanted or needed something. Luna didn't want or need a thing, but seemed happy to spend time with him for its own sake.

He wanted to know as much about Luna as she would share. She told him about how her parents had given her to the temple when she was five years old. She told him about her work with the Herb of Grace, about how she used it to cure ulcers, fevers, headaches, and rheumatism.

"So you like your work?"

She shrugged. "I never thought about it. I like making people feel better of course. I mean, you would have to be an awful person to not like that." She looked up at him to see if he agreed, but he said nothing.

He looked around. "Why is there never anyone here?"

"Here in the park?"

"Yes."

"We have two days to rejuvenate. On Tuesday and Saturday the park is ours and visitors, such as yourself..." She looked at him pointedly, "...are considered trespassers. The other five days of the week the park is crowded with people who come in need of many different kinds of healing. Some can be helped just by walking in the gardens and need nothing else to be better."

"Tell me about your family."

"We don't have relationships with our former families because it would interfere with the work."

"You haven't seen them since you were five?"

She nodded, but didn't seem bothered by that fact. The reality of her strange existence had long ago become normal to her.

Grey said he had lived in a wilderness area all his life, that when he looked at the tall buildings of the skyline above the trees, that life struck him as the closest thing to the myth of an eternal pit of fire.

"Oh. I don't know," she said. "Maybe it wouldn't be so awful."

"Crammed together like socks in a drawer?"

She laughed. "Socks in a drawer?"

He looked down at her bare feet in sandals. She wore toe rings in gold and silver designs that curled like the Celtic art of his world. He thought that even her feet and toes were beautiful, smooth and well-proportioned.

"You don't have socks. Do you?"

She grinned and shook her head and they laughed together in a way that signaled an easy and effortless companionship. Once, she stumbled over a tree root. Grey reached out to steady her, but she jerked back her arm out of his reach and righted herself on her own.

"We're not to be touched by the hand of man."

He opened his mouth to tell her that he was not a man, but thought better of divulging that particular bit of information at that time. Luna always stayed until Grey looked at his watch and said he had to leave. She would say goodbye and confirm that she would come again with a smile so fetching it made his chest feel tight. Then he would pretend to leave, but watch her as she walked back alone.

Stalkson knew that Luna thought of the temple complex where she lived and worked as home. He, however, saw it as her prison where she'd been taken and enslaved as a baby. Every aspect of her life had been decided for her. Where she lived, what she did, when she did it, what she ate, what she wore, where she went, and whom she saw. She was able to read a limited selection of books from the library and watch preapproved television and movies about the lives of laypeople, but she wasn't given access to any other sort of communication technology.

He doubted that she would agree with the analysis that she was virtually imprisoned, but the wolf in him wanted to howl at her to break free.

Twenty-eight days, the exact length of a moon cycle, had passed since the young males had been left on Shrifthet. The king was extremely pleased, but a little astounded that they had all managed to find girls who fell in love with them and agreed to go to Lunark. Even Harefoot O'Moors. Grey kept his opinion about the value of Harry's potential contribution to the gene pool to himself and trusted that nature would work it out.

Love had to be powerful to persuade people to give up everything and everyone they had ever known - forever - and face the unknown. But the boys had done it. They'd made humans fall in love with them. For a fleeting moment Grey wondered if he had it in him to do the same.

No doubt they had been assisted by the serious imbalance in the ratio of males to females, but still, they had done it. The young bloods had mates who were going to happily bear young werewolves and snuggle close to them on cold winter nights.

Deliverance had moved all the Elk Mountain immigrants to Lunark and was taking the last of the newlyweds. After that there would be one more stop on Throenark. Grey's heart seized. His hand went to his chest out of reflex because, for a moment, he felt like he couldn't breathe. He couldn't imagine not seeing Luna again, not hearing her laugh, not seeing her form a question in those exotic copper eyes. But that was exactly what was going to happen at the end of their afternoon together.

"You seem sad today. What is it?" she asked.

He stopped walking and faced her. "Will you do something for me?"

He saw that old wariness flicker across her features. "If I can. What is it?"

"Will you let your hood down and let me see your hair?"

She searched his face for a second or two before reaching up and dropping the hood so that it fell to her back. She pulled thick waves of mahogany tresses free and let them fall around her face and shoulders, watching him with a question in her eyes. Suddenly she laughed and it was his turn to look at her with a question in his eyes.

"I was just thinking about how much this is like the fairytale. You know, Red Riding Hood."

"Fairytale?"

"You don't know the story?"

He shook his head. She proceeded to tell an abbreviated version of the story as they walked and didn't cover her hair again with her hood. She ended with, "...except you're not a wolf, of course." And then she laughed.

She noticed that Grey wasn't laughing. "About that..."

He glanced at his watch. He'd run out of time. Deliverance would be waiting to take him back to Elk Mountain. The king's gaze jerked to Luna's and she saw unmistakable panic there.

"Grey. What's wrong?"

His mouth tried to work. "I can't." He swallowed really hard. "I can't leave you."

"What do you mean?"

Stalkson Grey, the great alpha king of the wolf people of Elk Mountain, master of self-discipline and control, who had never done a single impulsive thing in his life, crouched down, bent the Vergin over his shoulder and began running with her. It was only thirty yards to where Deliverance would be waiting.

Luna was so deeply stunned she would have lost her breath even if the action of being jostled by the uneven pressure of Grey's shoulder didn't rob her of breath. But before they reached the demon, she had recovered enough voice and presence of mind to raise a ruckus. She was also pulling his long hair in a way that was so painful he finally slapped her on the most generous portion of the curve of her derriere, which stunned her into silence again for a few seconds.

It would be hard to say who was more shocked by the scene that unfolded, Deliverance or Luna.

"Take hold of my arm and take us to Elk Mountain now. Hurry."

Deliverance just gaped at Grey. "Wolf, have you lost your mind?"

Grey was breathing hard and talking fast in the maelstrom of Luna's flying fists and kicking feet. "I have not lost my mind. I have found my mind.

"I heard your daughter tell you to help me get what I need and this is what I need. Her." Deliverance still balked in indecision. "Demon, I'm going to use a word I have never used before. Ever. Not once in my life. *Please*."

Not being able to argue with that, the demon grasped Grey's wrist and rode them through the passes right into the king's living room. Stalkson set Luna down on her feet and with a scream of outrage she launched herself at him.

"Well," said Deliverance. "I'll leave you to it, but, just so you know, there are no werewolves on Shrifthet. She's not going to believe you when you try to tell her what you are."

Luna grabbed for the demon. "You will *not* leave me here you..." And he was gone.

She wheeled on Grey with murder in her eyes. He knew he should be ashamed of himself. He knew there was nothing funny about the situation. But having her there in his own house, even with her looking like she would kill him the first time he went to sleep, was more pleasurable than anything in memory.

There was nothing about his attraction to her that made sense. It might even be insane. But it felt *so* good that he couldn't find it in himself to be sorry. He didn't want to smile as he faced the infuriated beauty, but he couldn't help himself. Naturally, that infuriated her all the more.

"You kidnapped me!" She reached for a wooden totem figure and threw it at his head.

He ducked. "I prefer to think of it as a romantic abduction."

She gaped. "*Romantic!*" The fact that she was alone with Grey and, perhaps, at his mercy seemed to creep into her awareness and onto her expression. "Where is this?"

"Elk Mountain." He looked around. "This is my house."

"It's freaking cold here. Do you know that?"

He looked at her bare arms and the thin silk fabric and remembered that she came from a balmy climate.

"Here. Let me start a fire and I'll get you some warmer clothes."

When he started toward the fire, she dashed for the front door. He grabbed her before she got there and pulled her back into his body wrapping his arms around her waist. The feel of her body pressed close to him and the aroma of her hair almost brought him to his knees. It was exponentially better than any of the thousands of times he had tried to imagine how it would feel.

"Luna. Listen to me. You're not in your world anymore. You're in mine. The demon brought you here for me. There's no place for you to go and no one to go to.

"You know me. You know I won't hurt you. I'll take care of you and I'll... care for you."

Luna knew the appropriate reaction was fear, but, oddly enough, she wasn't afraid. Angry? Definitely. But not afraid. As much as she wanted to hate the feel of his warmth pressing against her, she relaxed a little, deciding to play nice and bide her time.

"The last thing I want is to restrain you. If I let go, will you let me light a fire and get you something warm to wear?"

She nodded. Not nearly ready to trust her, Grey backed toward the hearth without taking his eyes away from her.

He lit the fire and put a mug of mulled wine on the hearth to warm. She followed without resistance when he took her by the hand to go with him in search of clothes. He covered her upper body by pulling a denim shirt lined with soft flannel over her robe then covered her feet, sandals and all, with heavy wool socks. When she started to feel a little warmer, she began to calm, but her eyes were still wide and her pupils were dilated.

Grey bade her sit by the fire and handed her the warm mulled wine. Without taking her eyes off him she took a tiny sip. A moan of pleasure almost escaped her throat, but she strangled it with a swallow. Within a couple of minutes the wine was working its magic. She was feeling warm and more relaxed.

"Are you hungry?" asked the king.

She shook her head. "Why did you take me?" Luna watched the shadows of the flames dance on his cheek and reflect hypnotically in his eyes while he formulated an answer.

"Did you like me? Before I took you?"

She hesitated, but decided to tell the truth. "You know I did."

"Right before I grabbed you, if I had told you that I would never be coming back, that you'd never see me again, how would you have felt about that?"

"It... would have made me sad."

"Well, that is what was about to happen. And it made me more than sad. The idea of never seeing you again made me feel like I couldn't breathe. It made my heart hurt."

As much as she wanted to beat him with a stick, she felt her own heart soften at that. What sort of woman wouldn't respond to such an admission?

"I didn't plan it or think it through. Completely. I just knew I couldn't face the idea of waking up tomorrow morning knowing the separation was permanent."

She searched his eyes, but didn't want to reveal that her initial rage receded further with every word he spoke. "And I get no choice in the matter?"

"Do you remember telling me how you came to your vocation?"

She nodded, frowning. "Yes. What...?"

"Did you have a choice?" She narrowed her eyes and pursed her lips so prettily it caused an arousal to stir uncomfortably in the confines of his jeans. She was glaring in a way that challenged the part of him that was wolf to claim her so that she would know their joining was a fait accompli, not up for debate. "You came to embrace that life so that now you *do* choose it. You'll do the same with me."

"I won't."

"You will."

"I can't believe I thought I liked you."

His smile turned wolfish. "Luna. You *do* like me. Your body tells me so."

"That's nonsense and not at all true."

"Liar." He pointed to his nose. "Great sense of smell."

She stared blankly until she comprehended the reference. Then a blush colored her cheeks and looked so hot he didn't think he could suppress a low growl of interest.

"I don't like it here." She rubbed her arms like they were still bare. "It's cold."

He moved closer. "All the better to warm you."

"Stay away from me. Just take me back. I want to go home."

"Why?"

"Why?" She repeated it and then gaped as if she couldn't believe it would need further explanation.

"Why do you want to go back?"

"It's my home. It's my work. It's everything that feels comfortable and familiar. My sisters are my family." He nodded slowly like he understood, which only served to renew her fury. She wanted to say something that would erode his self-assuredness. "And then there was sex with Deliverance".

Luna felt the deepest wave of satisfaction wash over her as she watched the varying emotions play out on Grey's face. Something in her womanly instinct told her that a reference to intimacy with Deliverance would be a taunt that would make her captor go wild with jealousy. On some level she had also known it could be dangerous to provoke a man crazy enough to nab her from her own home in broad daylight.

Stalkson Grey felt a red hazed rage wash over him. He snarled and howled. The snarling terrified her. The howling sent her running for the door. He caught her easily and carried her back to the chair she'd left in spite of kicking, screaming, pinching, slapping, and, worst of all, hair pulling. When he dumped her in the chair, the unmistakable huff and look of warning on his face caused her to decide that she had pushed him as far as she wanted to push for the moment. She stilled and tried her best not to look as frightened as she felt.

She sat in the chair and watched, aghast, as he ripped pillows with his teeth. He picked up furniture and threw it against the wall in a way that suggested inhuman strength.

The front door flew open and revealed several faces crowded together on the porch. The man who entered without an invitation bore enough of a resemblance to Grey to be a brother. He looked around at the destruction with a wrinkled brow. Then he looked at Luna huddled with her body drawn up for protection. Last, he turned to his father with confusion all over his face.

"Dad! What are you doing? Have you completely lost your mind?"

Stalkson Grey stopped abruptly. "Maybe." He glanced at his son then went back to staring at Luna with his chest heaving and his eyes burning with anger. "But it's none of your business. Get out."

Windwalker didn't move. He jerked his head toward Luna. "Who is that?"

"This is none of your business, Win. The young lady and I are negotiating."

Win gaped.

Grey growled low in his throat in a way that made the hairs on the back of Luna's neck stand straight up. "Please don't make me tell you again."

Win backed out and closed the door. For a minute they heard voices outside and then everything was quiet.

Grey kicked one of the destroyed cushions out of the way as he stalked back to stoke the fire. He threw himself back into his chair. At least he had retained enough presence of mind to spare his favorite chair and the one on which Luna sat, looking terrified. He faced Luna, still breathing heavy. She looked around while he stared at her, afraid to meet his gaze.

When she heard his breathing even out to normal, she said, "There's another room with some stuff you didn't destroy yet." Grey took in a deep sigh and slumped further against his chair. "Why did that guy call you Dad? He's the same age as you."

The king took in a deep sigh. "He's not the same age. We look the same age because we're not human."

Luna was nonplussed. It was certainly not the reaction he'd expected. "Not human?" Her eyes wandered down his body. "Is that what the snarling was about? You know that tearing-things-up-with-your-teeth thing is not attractive. In fact it makes you look sort of crazy."

"I'm not crazy, Luna. I'm a werewolf."

She stared for a few beats before shaking her head. "No idea what that means."

"You never heard of werewolves?"

"Look, Grey, if there's something you want to say then say it. This welcome to your home hasn't really put me in the mood for games."

"I can shift between man and wolf."

"By shift, you mean you change into a wolf."

"Yes. Everybody here does."

"Everybody in your world?"

"No, everyone you will encounter near my home while you're here with me."

She noted the loophole. If he said "while you're here" then he wasn't planning to keep her forever. "And how long will that be?"

He hadn't thought far enough in advance to formulate an answer to that question. At length he said, "When you no longer want to leave, then you can go."

"Is that a riddle?"

"No. It's the truth."

"Okay, look, I said *no* games. If you're going to persist in this werewolf fantasy, which - by the way - is a weird choice, then I can only conclude you're not just a kidnapper, but a *crazed* kidnapper who's very good at fooling girls who go for innocent walks in the woods."

"It was not a kidnapping. It was a romantic abduction."

He got up and left the room. She heard some faint rustling followed by soft clicking on the hardwood floor. When a large black wolf with yellow gold eyes peeked around the side of her chair, she shrieked and jerked back. The wolf quickly moved in front of her and put his head in her lap while gazing at her with soft, imploring eyes.

The adrenaline sent pinpricks of unpleasant tingling through her nervous system, but the tension in her muscles relaxed. It was clear the wolf didn't intend to harm her.

"Stalkson Grey?" She said it quietly, wanting to get Grey's attention without alarming the beast. The wolf bumped her leg with his nose.

"Stalkson Grey?" she repeated just a little louder and, again, the wolf bumped her leg with his nose.

Her eyes grew big as she began to consider the possibility of the impossible.

"Is that you, Grey?" she whispered. He bumped her with his nose.

She would have liked to simply faint and give herself a ten minute break from consciousness, but, unfortunately, she remained wide awake and clear headed. So far as she could tell.

She looked into his eyes, not knowing that wolves usually don't like that. Even Grey thought it was odd that he didn't feel an adverse reaction.

"Werewolf."

He picked his big head up and looked at her intently with ears standing straight up like he understood exactly what was being said.

Then, as if she hadn't already had more than her quota of excitement for the day, he smoothly shifted in the form of a man. A beautiful man who also happened to be beautifully naked. His penis was exactly at face level with where Luna sat in the chair. She tried to drag her eyes upward to his face, but they had an agenda of their own and intended to stay put until they'd had their fill of admiring the utter perfection of his male equipment. His skin was evenly tanned, as if he'd actually been out in the sun without clothes. It was also smooth and hairless except for a dusting of light brown on his arms and legs and a slightly darker trail leading downward from his navel.

As she became vaguely aware that he was speaking, she finally managed to look up.

"So you're challenging me to satisfy you sexually as well as Deliverance did."

Shock registered on her face and she quickly began shaking her head. "No! That's NOT what I'm doing."

"That's what it sounded like to me. You'll have to tell me what to do, but one thing is certain. Whatever he does, I can do."

It took a minute for her brain to make sense of what was happening. She was aware of the fact that possessing a mind that adapts to new circumstances quickly was a survival trait, but she didn't think anyone could adapt to so much so fast. In the space of an hour she'd been kidnapped and taken to another dimension with no means of escape. She'd watched her captor demolish his own living quarters. She'd not only learned that there were supernatural creatures called werewolves, but that she'd been abducted by one. And now the werewolf, who was hung like a masterpiece, wanted to know how he could please her sexually.

Her assessment only concluded that the scenario was as improbable as a fantasy and comical in a way that it shouldn't be. She snorted with disbelief then laughed from deep in her throat. Luna didn't intend for her laugh to conjure images of wild nights, but that's the way it affected Grey. So much so that the sound of it made his balls pull tight.

It also made him angry. "Why are you laughing?"

She shook her head. "Honestly. This is all so bizarre I just don't know what else to do."

He knelt in front of her. Her eyes immediately

flicked to his mouth, which was generous and lush for a man old enough to have a grown son.

"You know the fact that you're not wearing clothes is, um, intimidating."

He seemed irritated by that. "Werewolves are comfortable with our bodies, Luna. We sort of have to be. I'm naked because I was just in my wolf form. Not because I'm trying to intimidate you."

"Are you married?"

"What?" The woman made his head spin. "No. I was..., uh, mated. She died twenty-three years ago."

She cocked her head. "You look like you're no older than thirty. At most. How old are you?"

"Older than you."

"Well, that cleared that up."

"Are you hungry?"

"No."

"Then let's go to bed."

"Bed?"

"Bed. A comfortable place to sleep or engage in other horizontally oriented pastimes. A piece of furniture, usually with a mattress and pillows."

"I know what a bed is. I don't want to go to sleep. I don't want to go to bed. I want to go home."

Grey stood up slowly. When her eyes locked on his manhood again, he smiled a wolfish smile. "Come to bed. Give me a chance to change your mind."

"No. I don't trust you." She was thinking that had to be the dumbest thing she'd ever said. Of course she didn't trust him. He was her kidnapper.

"Understandable. But you can distrust me just as easily sleeping in a bed as in chairs."

"I don't know that that's true. How many beds do you have?"

"One."

"Then I'm not going."

"Alright. I won't insist. We'll sit by the fire awhile longer." He stoked the fire and put another cup of mulled wine on the hearth to warm, giving Luna a long and leisurely view of his backside that was as taut and muscled as a wild animal. The way his hair fell around his shoulders made him seem all the more untamed.

He was the exact opposite of everything she'd known since she was a little girl. The Cult of Vervain maintained strict order and control. The Grand Mother often said that chaos in one's environment would create chaotic thought. The man... The werewolf wasn't concerned with law or rules or propriety. He did what he wanted. Fundamentally he was anarchy personified.

Clearly that appealed to Luna's body, based on the way it responded to him, but it seemed it also appealed to her spirit. Until the werewolf had shown up in the forest on the edge of the park, she had never considered doing anything outside the routine expected of the Vergins. Of course she had broken any one of a dozen rules just by repeatedly meeting and spending time with Stalkson Grey. She supposed that meant she deserved the punishment that she was now receiving. *Or the reward.*

She could have slapped her own brain for that last unwanted thought.

The king dipped his finger in the cup of mulled wine and held it out to her. "Here. See if that is warm to taste."

She parted her lip and sucked in the tip of his finger as far as the first knuckle. His abs tensed so suddenly it made his cock twitch. She heard the little hitch of his breath and saw his eyes darken as he stared at the finger she tasted.

The longer she was held captive by the king, the more certain was she that he wouldn't hurt her, and that knowledge emboldened her. Seeing his cock twitch right in front of her face was the most erotic thing that had ever happened to her. The impulse to reach out and touch was strong. After all, a few hours ago she had been walking and talking with this man and had been interested in him sexually. That hadn't changed.

There was a part of her that was naughty enough to wish that he would just pick her up and take her to bed and there was another part that was glad he wasn't the sort of male to force her - past taking her away from everything she knew. Forcibly.

Grey handed her the cup of wine she had just approved and sat down in his chair. As he expected, when things grew quiet so that the only noise was the soothing crackle of the fire and the only light were the flames from the hearth set a foot above the floor, the excitement of the day caught up with her and the warmth of the wine lulled her to sleep.

He carried her sleeping to his bed, lay beside her, and pulled the covers over them. She made the tiniest little snoring noise that was as inexplicably appealing as everything else about her. He lay on his side watching her sleep, smiling like a fool. If there were to be consequences for taking her, he didn't care. Everything about having her here felt so completely right. He would never regret his actions. He promised himself that, if he was ever tempted, he would remember that night, the feeling of peace that he had in that moment and he concentrated on burning it into his memory.

Luna woke to light filtering through the window. Early morning sunlight was filtered through the shadows of leaves dancing in the wind. It made patterns of movement on the walls and ceiling that were delightful. She realized that she was toasty warm, cuddled in fur. Her right hand grasped a handful of the soft stuff. She turned her head to the right and found herself staring into a pair of gold yellow eyes with very large pupils.

She gave a little gasp and started to scramble backward, but Stalkson Grey shifted into human form instantly and pulled her back toward him, laughing. Up close his face was even more handsome because she could see tiny lines. Rugged. Ruggedly handsome. He was masculinity expressed at its most glorious. He also wasn't human. She found herself asking whether she cared about that and, surprisingly, the answer was no.

"Why did you take me?" she whispered.

"I saw you and I wanted you. I want you now. I always will."

She searched his eyes for a second like she was looking for something, then suddenly began looking around. "Bathroom."

He brought a finger out from under the covers and pointed.

Grey couldn't stop smiling. Even though he'd awakened every time Luna had moved during the night, he had enjoyed the best sleep of his life. He didn't like having her in his bed. He *loved* having her in his bed. He loved her smell, the sound of her breathing, the warmth her body generated under the covers.

He left the heat of the bed to pull on jeans and a long sleeve gray tee shirt. He had just pulled the shirt down to his waist when he heard a knock at the front door. His gaze automatically went to the short hall. He heard running water and knew Luna was in the bathroom.

Someone was brave enough to knock a second time. He padded toward the front of the lodge without bothering to stop for footwear. He had to step around some of the destruction his tantrum from the night before had caused.

Drift was standing on the porch. He said nothing when the king opened the door.

"Did Win send you?"

"Yes, Alpha. Your son asked me to look in on you."

"Fine. You've looked in on me. Are we done?"

"You won't ask me in for a cup of coffee by your fire?"

Stalkson stared at him for a few seconds. "You can come in for one minute. *One.* No coffee. No fire." He stepped back and let the elder inside.

Drift looked around at the vandalism. "Who did this to your home, Alpha? This ruin is a desecration. Someone must be punished."

Grey was annoyed that the elder was playing games. He knew the king had trashed his own lodge in a rage and was trying to be crafty. Grey was a little ashamed, but he wasn't about to admit to that. "Don't be so dramatic, old one. I did it. It's my home to do with as I wish."

Drift looked at him strangely. "Certainly that is

true. I did not mean to question your judgment."

The alpha's stare bore down on his friend and counselor until Drift looked down. "I'm keeping her."

"That is your privilege, of course. May I ask, who is she? Windwalker said he believes she is human."

"It is not his business. Nor is it yours."

"Again, you speak the truth. Should the tribe be concerned that her people will be looking for her?"

Luna came into the room behind him. Drift looked at her and nodded. The old man noted the fact that she did not appear to be either afraid or in any kind of distress when she responded by saying hello.

"No one will be looking for her. She is from another world. We cannot go there unassisted. Neither can she. Neither can her people."

"I see. And she is to mate with you willingly?"

Drift saw surprise cross Luna's face when he used the word "mate". She came closer to the door. "What do you mean, mate?"

Grey turned toward her. "You're not a child, Luna. You may be a Cult Vergin, but you're not a virgin either. You know perfectly well what it means to mate."

A good night's sleep had renewed her capacity for lividness and she was also indignant about being spoken to like she was an idiot.

"For your information I was trying to establish whether the word was being used as a noun or a verb. Perhaps that's too fine a distinction of semantics for someone who behaves like a mindless beast." She gestured toward the room to put an exclamation point on her statement.

She turned toward Drift. "As to whether or not

I'm here willingly..." She cocked her hip, put her hand there, and used a bored monotone to say, "Help. I've been kidnapped by a werewolf and there's no escape."

Drift looked away as he tried to stifle a chuckle. "Forgive me for disturbing your morning, Alpha. I can see you have your hands full." He backed out of the door and closed it behind him, laughing softly which infuriated the king.

Once they were alone again, he wheeled on Luna with anger in his eyes. "You embarrassed me in front of one of my subjects!"

"One of your subjects. What is that supposed to mean?"

"I'm king!" he shouted.

"Okay, well, first you never mentioned that, not that it's either there or here."

"And?"

"And what?"

"You said first. I assume that means there's a second."

"Not necessarily."

She might have had a second thing in mind when she began speaking, but the soft gray knit shirt that pulled across the king's chest reminded her how well-defined his abs were and the color brought out the steely blue in his eyes. Really, anyone would forget what they were saying.

He hesitated, not really knowing where to go from there. "Are you hungry?"

She gave him a tentative, tiny smile. "Maybe."

He blinked and cocked his head slightly. "That's definitely a yes or no question."

"What do you have?"

He looked at the path of destruction between

where they stood at the front door and the kitchen, then picked her up to carry her there. She squealed and it made him smile because it was clearly more from surprise than protest. He walked slowly so he could savor having her in his arms for the first time. Willingly that is. Her arms had gone around his neck out of reflex and he knew she had surreptitiously tried to inhale his aroma.

When he set her down in the kitchen and backed away, she immediately regretted the loss of contact. She came up behind him when he opened the refrigerator and nudged him out of the way.

"What is this? Where is your food!?!"

Grey looked at her like she was insane. "This *is* my food. Meat, eggs, cheese, fish. And there might be a little spinach to boil."

She gaped at him. "I see that. But where is your food?"

"What do you eat, Luna?"

"Fruit, vegetables, nuts, bread. Sometimes I might eat a little cheese or eggs, but not every day."

"You don't eat meat?"

"No."

"How can a person survive without meat?"

She shrugged. He blinked and stared. At length he sighed.

"Perhaps you could eat cheese and eggs this morning? Then we can go get you clothes and... fruits, nuts, etc."

She brightened a little. "So you're not going to hold me prisoner in this house?"

He scowled. "Of course not." It occurred to him that she was taking all of this better than might be expected and that could be because she had always lived under conditions of repression and confinement. To her it was just a change of scenery.

That's when he made a bargain with himself. It took the young bloods less than twenty-eight days to win their mates. If he couldn't win Luna's heart in that amount of time, he probably never would. So he promised himself that he would get Deliverance to return her if he failed.

Twenty-eight days. One moon cycle.

"I'll have eggs and cheese, please."

Luna was hungrier than she thought. She ate the three egg omelet with Colby and was tempted to lick her plate. Watching Grey devour huge quantities of rare meat would take some getting used to.

"So what are you king of?"

"We're on a large piece of land reserved for the wolf people in my tribe. No one can come here unless invited. The land and the resources we need to live independently were given to us over two hundred years ago by an organization that promotes peace between humans and other species. We were given this in exchange for agreeing that we would live and hunt our own territory and leave the humans alone."

"So that man who came to the door is a..."

"...werewolf. Yes."

"How many of you are there?"

"Just in my tribe there were twelve hundred until a few weeks ago. Now there are half that many." He told her how they were threatened with extinction because of the lack of female births and how they had addressed the problem.

She listened intently and heard the passion he felt for taking care of his people and their problems. There was even more to Stalkson Grey than she had thought before. When he finished the story, she didn't respond right away.

When she spoke, she said, "Tuesdays and Saturdays." She nodded to herself like she had just put it together. "You were on Del's schedule. You came when he came."

"Yes." As he rose to take the dishes away, he realized for the first time that Luna had chosen him. Every time. She could have had her turn at being serviced by the demon and she chose the innocence of being with him instead. With his back to her, he rinsed the breakfast plates and smiled a wolfish smile. He would win her.

He opened the front door and called one of the pups who was playing nearby to come over. He instructed the young one to go to his daughter-in-law's house and borrow a pair of her pants and a hat and bring them back right away.

Fifteen minutes later the boy was back with a pair of faded jeans, soft from lots of wear. Luna had never in her life, since she was five, worn anything except a silk robe. White when she was a child. Yellow when she was an adolescent. Red while she was an acting Vergin. Everything about these clothes was foreign to her, but Grey convinced her that she would be cold and uncomfortable without them.

The jeans were a little bit loose in the thighs and derriere and a little bit short, but they would work as a stop gap measure. He gave her a knit cap and put her in one of his own jackets. It swallowed her.

"What is this?" she asked, running her hand over the jacket.

"Sheepskin."

She looked at him with genuine amusement. "So when you wear this, you're literally a wolf in sheep's clothing."

He grinned. "I want to show you around the reservation, but we need to go to town and get you clothes and food first. One thing about that, the townspeople are human and don't know that we're not. Will you promise not to say anything about werewolves? Although, truthfully, if you did, they'd probably either laugh at you or call for a pickup by the sanatorium.

"Likewise, if you try to accuse me of anything untoward publicly, I will just laugh and say you also believe in werewolves."

She narrowed her eyes at that. "Devious, Grey. I agree that I will not talk about werewolves and will not reveal that I have been kidnapped by one."

"Romantically abducted."

She raised her chin. "Seriously? This is really your idea of romance?"

He smiled his wolfish smile that stopped her breath. "I'd love to hear your ideas about romance, Luna."

Turning toward the door she was thinking that she was probably only minutes away from telling him her ideas about romance. He was weakening her defenses with lightning speed and she hated that she was melting with so little effort on his part.

"Shouldn't we clean up this mess?"

He guided her toward the door. "Don't worry. Somebody will do it."

CHAPTER_14

Storm knocked on Monq's office door.

"Come in," he called. "Sir Storm! How good to see you."

Storm lingered at the threshold. "I brought a nickel for the jar."

Monq's expression changed to more serious. "Very well. Join me." He motioned for Storm to take one of the two chairs that faced each other. "Would you care for some sherry?"

Storm shook his head.

"What's troubling you?"

"My wife is pregnant."

"I've noticed that."

"She shouldn't even be showing yet, but it's looking like we'll have a baby really soon."

"I see. And you're feeling..."

Storm scrunched up his face. "I'm feeling feelings that I'm not used to feeling."

"I see. Any chance of narrowing that down?"

Storm splayed his fingers over his lap. "I don't think I want to say it."

"I see. Do you want me to guess?"

Storm nodded. His right leg was bouncing with nervous energy. "Okay."

"Are you feeling a little anxiety about becoming a father?"

Storm nodded.

"Are you feeling a little anxiety about becoming a father sooner than expected."

Storm nodded.

"Are you worried about your wife?"

Storm nodded.

"Because things are not going to be 'normal'?" He put 'normal' in air quotes.

Storm nodded.

"If I tell you that what you're feeling is perfectly normal for first time fathers and it would be no different even if everything was perfectly 'normal', would you believe me?"

Storm grinned and shook his head. "No."

"Nonetheless, it's a fact. Have you chosen names?"

Storm nodded and smiled. "I've teased Litha a lot about naming her Elora because it never fails to get a reaction that's just the cutest thing, but we're naming her Liberty Rose.

"Can you really imagine me raising a girl? How many thousands of things could go wrong with that?"

"Not as many as you think. I know something you don't."

"What?"

"You've already had years of practice being a father figure to B Team." Storm frowned a little at that, but Monq just smiled in the annoyingly beatific way of wise men. "Liberty Rose. An excellent choice for a little girl who is certain to be beautiful as her name. You plan to call her Libby?" Monq noticed that Storm had stopped fidgeting and looked more relaxed.

"Rosie," Storm said shaking his head. "After Litha's mother."

"Well, my suggestion is that you spend as much time as you can with your wife. When Rosie enters the picture, your lives will never be the same again."

Storm nodded and stood. "Thank you." He reached in his pocket and pulled out a nickel. "Here you go."

"Just leave it in the jar."

Jefferson Unit was buzzing from top to bottom after announcements were made concerning temporary reassignments, but nothing was more gossip-worthy than the impending arrival of the infamous Z Team, a.k.a. Zed Company.

Sol wanted to be sure that most of the active duty knights had already been transferred ahead of time or trouble was sure to follow. Z boys and trouble were like bees and honey.

Even though they were anathema to people who appreciated some semblance of order, like Sol and Storm, the female personnel were eager to get a firsthand look and find out if they lived up to their reputation.

Ram had always said they weren't that bad. No one spent time wondering why he felt that way. Elora had never met them, but she'd heard enough to be okay with keeping the status quo.

The Order purchased and converted a hotel with a roof pad suitable for Whisters, installed the best security possible outside a no-fly zone, and moved the entire Paris unit and its personnel practically overnight. They outfitted a large, fully staffed med unit and prepared three entire floors to serve as halfway rehabilitation housing in the hope of finding and curing an unknown number of vampire virus victims.

Baka's offices and living quarters were furnished and ready for use when he arrived. On the same floor, lounge rooms were assigned to Jean Etienne and his boys, but they were free to come and go at will and probably wouldn't be around unless they appeared on the posted schedule.

The three teams of knights, who had been stationed in Paris before the new regime, were less than enthusiastic about the idea of working with host vampire. The three of those knights who were also Frenchmen were offended that the host vampire appeared to be *French* aliens. And spoiled at that.

Heaven had been reassigned to Baka's team. No one could possibly be more useful to vampire hunting than a person who could call them at will by playing a musical instrument. She was ecstatic to join Baka for a Parisian honeymoon, even if his mind was sometimes preoccupied with the search they were undertaking. When she left Edinburgh what she had in mind was romantic dinners, walks along the Seine, and the intense scratching of mutual itches.

There wasn't going to be as much of that as she would have liked, but she understood her new husband's level of commitment and the paramount importance of the work. There was no doubt in her mind that he was the best choice for the job. Who else could present a resume with a bullet point reading, "Double Ex-Vampire"?

The main thing was that there were times when she did have his undivided attention.

Baka spoke flawless French, as he should since he'd had centuries of intermittent practice. He could speak modern conversational French, as well as the provincial, medieval dialect spoken by the teenage immortals.

Heaven had been exposed to a smattering of French, but she lacked both an interest in the subject and an ear for languages. So the effort she made was a constant source of entertainment for Baka. He thoroughly enjoyed teasing her about ridiculous sentence construction and endless pronunciation goofs. She didn't resent the fact that he laughed openly and often at her expense. Her philosophy was that, if anyone in the world deserved a new collection of happy moments, it was her gorgeous husband. When she was privileged to be the source of that happiness, it gave her a natural high that would be worth billions if it could be bottled or reduced to a pill.

The young vampire on Baka's team continued to behave like college kids on Spring Break, but Jean Etienne took the mission very seriously and could corral them into focus for brief periods of time. Hopefully, that was all that would be necessary.

They had already mapped the underground, both modern and the historical unimproved, and had decided the best plan of attack would be to split the available assets into three groups. Each of the Parisian teams would be assigned two additional members. One would get Jean Etienne and the charge he thought least likely to be trusted on his own. One would get Baka and Javier. And the last would be assigned the remaining two vampire even though the prospect made Baka crazy trying to anticipate all the things that could go wrong with that.

Jean Etienne had assured him that he would regale the boys with sufficient lectures to ensure they behaved themselves even when he was out of sight. Baka hoped J.E. had as much respect and authority as he thought he did. Since the host vampire were not compelled to assist for any reason other than their own self-imposed sense of duty and responsibility, The Order was, in that instance, beggar and not chooser. In other words, they would take what they could get and be grateful for whatever it was.

In a decision that Storm thought was particularly sadistic and utterly uncalled for, Sol decided to begin Phase Two of Glen's test by dispatching him to tell Z Team, in person, that they were transferring to Jefferson Unit. Further, he was to escort them back.

The Fates must have been busier than usual because it happened that Z Team was not in Marrakesh. Torn's father had died, expectedly, and the entire team had been given a four day leave to go to Ireland with Torn.

The three other members of the team were Americans who had a history of raising Cain with Torn since they were teenagers. Undoubtedly the dynamic had a hand in shaping the path and personality of each of the four individuals who molded themselves into a group, or team, that could - when necessary - think and act as one.

Torrent Finngarick had escaped his old man and the tiny town of Dunkilly when he was recruited by Black Swan at thirteen. He was one of the rare exceptions to the second son rule. Circumstances had artificially created the environment necessary to instill the seeds of knighthood even though he was an only child. His da had been a widower who couldn't manage his whiskey or his strong-willed boy.

Torrent was dismissed by the community as being Mick Finn's ne'er-do-well kid. He was disliked by his teachers because he made their day harder and longer than it would have been otherwise. Neighbors would have said he was a list of undesirable traits. He was no good. He was a troublemaker. He was smarter than a person should be and, worst of all, he was a terrible influence. The other boys admired him, wanted to be like him, and would jump off a roof if he said they should.

Someone in Dunkilly might have come forward, taken an interest, and tried to channel all that raw talent and energy in the right direction. But no one did. Until Black Swan stepped in.

Anybody could see he had that one special thing that separated Black Swan knights. It was a quality that defied definition, but might best be described as fire. The entire world was a better place because kids like Torrent Finngarick, who found their way to Black Swan, sometimes grew up to be the kind of person who would willingly walk into the unknown, knowing he might not come back. The irony is that the sort of kid who may grow up to save the world often gets kicked to the curb early on.

As it turned out, Torn was hard to handle even for Order personnel who were trained in the care and development of Black Swan knights.

When the boy left the little fishing town, nobody grabbed a kerchief to dry a tear. Not even his father. Truthfully, the arrangement had worked out for the best for both of them. So Mick Finngarick's wake was not a solemn occasion. Not for his son or for anyone else.

Twelve years later, nobody in Dunkilly was surprised to see young Finngarick turn up with a nickname like "Torn" and friends who looked like hard-core biker mafia. They were, however, surprised that he arrived on a Whister that landed in a goat pasture. He stepped out with three boyos every bit as large, strange, and colorful as he, strapping duffels over their big shoulders and looking for all the world like they owned it. Dunkilly residents were surprised that Torn had enough money to buy the entire town drinks for three days and not miss any of it.

The proprietor of the pub that faced the harbor was happy to stage the wake there since the event's patron assumed responsibility for the tab. Torn paid some of the old women in the town to dress in black and watch over the body's soul at night so that it wouldn't be snatched away early by spirits. He brought in musicians from Donegal and Derry to give the wake a lively, celebratory atmosphere. He gave the funeral director enough money to get a suit for the body and gave the church an honorarium to bury him, buy a stone marker, and say some words.

Torn knew he didn't owe the fucker all that much for having contributed his sperm and his name, but when the three days were over, he would leave Dunkilly and return to Marrakesh. He would never be back and would never give the deceased another thought because he would know in his heart that he'd done more than he should.

He dragged the rest of Zed Company along with him not because he needed emotional support, but because he wouldn't want them to hear later that he had picked up the tab for a three day Irish Malt bender and hadn't included them. Besides, he knew they could use a change of scenery. Anything can get old after awhile. Even hash and belly dancing.

Planning Glen's travel wasn't much of a challenge for Farnsworth. She wouldn't even consider it a particularly complicated itinerary. Glen was dropped in the same goat pasture where Z Team had been dumped two days before. The idiot pilot, whom Glen had "worked with" on the Lady Laiken's rescue, pointed him toward the harbor as he silently lifted away.

Glen threaded his arms through straps, dropped the pack onto his back, and started toward town. By the time he got to the Land's End Pub his teeth were chattering uncontrollably. He had spent time in Northern Ireland before, but the wind that whipped up the Atlantic coast absorbed ocean moisture and went straight through clothes and skin and flesh, all the way to the bone.

Standing on the sidewalk in front of the pub, he could hear live music playing inside. The memory of standing in front of that door, wanting to simply open and step inside would stay with him forever. So close, but his fingers were too numbed to grasp the door pull. There was no choice but to wait in the biting cold with only the chattering of his teeth for company until someone was either headed in or out.

Finally the door opened and someone stumbled out singing and adjusting his wool cap. Glen wedged his knee into the door before it closed and stepped in. The chill was so thorough that the initial warming sensation stung his hands and face. He stood near the door, shivering and trying to keep his teeth quiet while he looked around.

It was crowded for early afternoon and visibility was compromised by thick smoke hanging in the air. He resisted the impulse to cough. There was an open casket in the middle of the room a few feet away from where the musicians were seated. His eyes rested on the body long enough to have the thought that at least that poor fellow was beyond caring about secondhand smoke.

Those who noticed him stared with open curiosity. Strangers in Dunkilly were as common as unicorns.

He caught the eye of the bartender who simply pointed toward a back corner. Glen couldn't see what the man pointed to, but he nodded and began making his way toward the rear.

He wound through a few layers of standing people who were holding glass mugs and talking loudly to be heard over the music, until he could see a corner snug in the back. It was close to a window so there was enough light to see, even with the smoke, that the bartender had been right in surmising that he was looking for Z Team.

There they were, the farthest thing from inconspicuous. Glen couldn't begin to guess how they had managed to be successful vampire slayers when everything about them drew attention and broadcasted vibes of this-is-your-last-chance-to-run. It was a message that floated around them like a diaphanous cloud of warning.

The four of them fit comfortably in a snug designed for eight. That was partly because of their sheer size and partly because they had a casual way of draping arms and legs so that they took up as much space as possible. It also communicated disdain for established notions of propriety. Glen knew instinctively that even the word "propriety" would make Black Swan's infamous misfits laugh out loud.

One of them was wearing a sleeveless shirt that had once been a denim jacket. His left arm had been transformed into a tattooed sleeve by an intricately inked mural of muted colors. It was odd to see bare biceps when it was brittle-dick cold outside, but Glen supposed that if he'd made *that* much of an investment in ink he might want to show it off too.

Glen's initial impression of the guy sitting next to Sleeve was that he should have the nickname, Dark, or Black. He wore black jeans, a black metal band shirt that was probably a collectable, and his spiky hair was so blue black it had to have been dyed that color. All that with eyes so pale he could almost get away with going undercover as a vamp. He wasn't wearing eyeliner, but the contrast between his ice-color irises and those thick ebony lashes made his eyes pop in a dramatic way that probably drew interest from a lot of babes. *The Black Knight.* Glen smiled a little to himself. He enjoyed his own company and his own offbeat sense of humor.

The third wore a plain gray long sleeve tee that covered his upper body, but Glen could see black ink climbing out of the neck of the guy's shirt, stopping just below his pronounced jaw line. Either tribal pattern or angel glyph. Hard to tell with just snake tails in view. He had a serious case of bed head going, probably by design, and one eyebrow that was raised and had been since he'd noticed Glen standing there watching them.

He said something to the others. Then the fourth, the one facing away with one long arm draped over the back of the snug, turned to look at Glen, revealing elfin ears. Those ears were outlined by light brown hair with titian streaks. Same curl as Sir Hawking. Had to be Torrent Finngarick.

They looked exactly the way Glen had expected them to look. Hard. Tough. And like they belonged together. He was thinking, *So they're Black Swan knights with a little bit of a nasty reputation. They put their pants on one leg at a time just like me. Right?*

It was an inadequate internal pep talk, but he just wasn't feeling it. He decided to go with Plan A, which was taking life straight ahead, one step at a time. Glen had a reputation of his own for being easy going, but he made an exception for passive aggressive nonsense. He didn't like it, didn't like people who habitually avoided the front door, and didn't mind letting his irritation with bullshit bubble over.

Plan A meant walking straight up to them, stating his business, hoping for the best, but being prepared for the worst. That was the thought bouncing around in his mind as he observed their reactions to seeing him approach the table.

When he was standing over them, he looked around the table and said, "I'm Glendennon Catch." Then he zeroed in on Torn. "Sorry for your loss, Sir Finngarick." He said "sir" quietly enough so that only they heard him, but they got the message. It was as good as a secret handshake. "The office sent me with a message from the HR department."

They left him standing there for a minute without saying anything or changing expression. It was a thinly disguised intimidation strategy to get him to reveal nervousness, timidity, or some other weakness that would register as a flaw in their eyes. That sort of thing didn't work on somebody who had inherited the dominant werewolf gene. He could stand there all day without flinching or looking away.

Finally, the big guy with the glyphs crawling up his neck grinned, showing dimples which seemed entirely out of place against the persona he'd so carefully crafted. "So go ahead and deliver your memo, Sweet Cheeks. We're waiting."

The other three chuckled softly without taking their eyes off of him. Glen laughed openly and good-naturedly, but let the sound trail off ending in a low level growl, incongruent with the smile on his face. The growl wasn't loud enough to draw attention from the wake-goers, but it was definitely heard by Z Team. They all sat up a little straighter and took another look at the kid. He had their interest, but that was worlds away from respect.

Looking at Glyphs, he said, "My briefing didn't mention that any of you are hard of hearing. If you want to call me by a name, it's Glen."

Finngarick's blue eyes twinkled in a way that brought Ram to mind while the other two laughed at Glyphs being put down by a kid who was years away from growing into his big frame.

"Long way to deliver a message. Would you no' have a pint with us then? Glen." He reached out with a long leg, put the toe of his scuffed boot through the leg brace of an unoccupied chair, pulled it up to the snug, and made a gesture of invitation. "You'll find we're no' much on formality. Call me Torn."

CHAPTER_15

Stalkson Grey walked Luna through the settlement to the livery garage. The people she saw all stared at her on the way past.

"Are all of these people really werewolves?"

He looked down at her and seemed amused. "Yes. I don't suppose you're going to make each and every one prove it. I warn you. Nudity will be involved."

When they reached the garage, he raised the door and pointed to the Range Rover.

"We're taking this one. Get in." She made no move toward the car. "What's the matter?"

"I don't know how."

"You don't know how to what?"

"I don't know how to get into this."

He looked at her like he was seeing her for the first time. "You've never been in a car?"

She shook her head and his expression softened.

He gestured for her to follow him to the passenger door and showed her how to use the handle to release the latch. She tried it a couple of times and was pleased about learning to do it by herself.

On the inside of the vehicle, he reached over her to get the seat belt and showed her how to fasten and release.

"Why do I need to wear a harness?"

"Because we're going to go very fast. Accidents are unusual, but, if we should be in one, the harness will keep you in place and you'll be surrounded by a big bag of air."

She gave him a look that implied she would have

none of that just before she released her seat belt, opened the door, and got out of the car. He easily caught up with her a few feet past the garage. Laughing, he grabbed her and turned her to face him then wrapped his arms around her securely.

"I must have made it sound worse than it is. Everyone here routinely rides in these contraptions. You'll like it. I'll go slower than usual and I'll be with you every minute."

Certainly it was bizarre that Luna was comforted and reassured by her captor. Somehow hearing him say he would be with her every minute made the gamble acceptable.

After a little more coaxing, she agreed to get back in the vehicle. He found that kissing was a great motivator. While standing there with her in his arms, he succumbed to the impulse to touch his lips to hers. He would have said the moment was magical even with the bulk of a sheepskin coat between them. She feigned outrage, but he knew she was pretending to take offense. He could smell that she responded with almost instantaneous arousal.

"Stop that!" she said. "You cannot just kiss me."

Never challenge an alpha in such a manner. He laughed and did it again just to prove he could.

"Either get in the car or prepare to be kissed senseless. Your choice."

When he leaned in to kiss her again, she agreed and he let her wiggle free. She stomped to the passenger side of the Range Rover, opened the door like a pro, fastened her seatbelt and crossed her arms in front of her in mock aggravation.

The moment when Grey realized that he was having fun was cathartic. He stopped and asked himself if he remembered ever having fun before and the shocking answer was, no, he didn't. When he slid into the driver's seat, he looked over at Luna. She was wearing a little petulant pout that almost undid him.

He smiled, started the engine and backed out. Luna's hands tried to grab onto parts of the car and they were only going three kilometers per hour.

Grey waved to the wolf at the guard station as he went by. Luna was quiet, but taking everything in. He reasoned that, if she'd never been in a vehicle, she'd probably never traveled very far from the Temple park where he'd been courting her.

"Did you travel away from the park where we met very often?"

"No. I never did."

"Then the scenery here is probably different from anything you've seen."

"Yes."

He was dying to ask if she liked it, but knew she might reply with a scornful or sarcastic answer just to spite him. So he remained quiet, deciding that he would handle her as one would small children or wild animals. He would encourage her to relax and feel comfortably confident around him and let her come to him when she was ready.

 Luna thought everything about Stalkson's world was beautiful, the mountains, the lakes, the evergreens and pines. When he turned onto the highway that would take them to Coeur d'Alene, he picked up speed. Traveling so fast terrified her speechless at first, but she amazed herself at how quickly she adapted.

It took less than twenty minutes to drive to Northwest Outfitters store. When they parked, he said, "Remember your promise."

She blinked twice then nodded.

Inside the store, the king told the saleswoman that he was entertaining a guest who didn't own any cold weather gear and that she needed to be outfitted with a native's wardrobe top to bottom.

"Of course," said the nice lady. "Outfitting is what we do just like the name says. What size do you wear?"

Luna looked at Grey for the answer. "We don't know. She was, um, home schooled."

"Oh. Alright then." The saleswoman looked down at the socks Luna was wearing before raising her eyes to the oversize jacket. "Why don't we get you out of this coat so that I can guess a starting point for sizing?"

Luna looked down at the buttons and began fumbling with them. Grey had fastened them for her because she was inexperienced with buttonholes. He reached in, quickly undid them and helped her out of the heavy sheepskin.

The sales woman looked at Grey again. "Top to bottom?"

"Whatever she needs to spend some time in this part of the world and be comfortable."

"Well, then, let's get started." She helped fit Luna for everything she needed from jeans to shirts to sweaters to footwear and socks and patiently taught her customer how to work buttons and zippers. After adding gloves, a down vest and an all-weather coat of modern lightweight material, Luna picked out a red hat.

When all was said and done, the woman leaned toward Grey so that she could discreetly mention that the Northwest Outfitters did not sell ladies' undergarments. He thanked her for her kindness and asked if she would like to suggest a store for such things.

Luna walked to the front of the store in her new clothes feeling warm and fashionable. She arrived just in time to witness the exchange of money for packages. When it came to the idea of trading currency for goods or services, Luna was as inexperienced as a child. She'd never handled money. Never made a purchase and didn't have the most rudimentary grasp of how economies flow.

When they were again seated in the car, she had questions about the transaction. "What did you give them?"

Grey looked confused. "You mean money? In order to get something of value from them, we needed to offer something of similar value. They sold us clothing for you. We gave them gold."

"I didn't see you give them gold."

"Let's go get your fruits and vegetables and I will explain it to you on the ride back to Elk Mountain."

Luna was amazed at the produce section of the supermarket. The process took longer than Grey could ever have imagined because there were so many fruits and vegetables she didn't recognize. They added nuts, bagels, and fresh artisan bread from the in store bakery. The werewolf would never have predicted that grocery shopping could be an amusement, but Luna's enthusiasm turned it into a memorable event. When they reached the check out, he noticed that she was paying careful attention to the cashier scanning each item and that a corresponding number appeared on the screen.

On the way out they passed the coffee stand and he asked Luna if she would like a hot drink for the ride home.

"Like the wine from last night?"

"No. Not like that. Like hot chocolate maybe. Or tea?"

"I've never had either one."

So he decided to take a chance on the cocoa. Even werewolves knew that human women liked chocolate. Handing her the paper cup, he instructed her to just sip it through the little hole in the side of the lid, then watched while her face lit up.

"I'm guessing that look means you like the hot chocolate."

"Hmmm." She smiled and looked so perfectly yummy in her red hat that it made him think the same thing. *Hmmm.*

On the ride back to the Elk Mountain reservation, Luna ate grapes and drank hot chocolate while the king tried to explain the value of precious metals and how they were stored in a central, secure facility while paper symbols were used to represent the actual gold. She wasn't sure she understood all the complexities of economics, but she liked hearing the soothing timbre of his voice and she liked the fact that he was patient about explaining things.

They parked the Range Rover. Grey carried the groceries. Luna carried the clothes. On the way back, the alpha told one of the pups to go get his daughter-in-law and have her come to the king's lodge. When NightCloud knocked at the door, Luna was trying to persuade Grey to try a variety of nuts.

"Cloud, this is Luna. She's going to be my guest for a time." Cloud and Luna exchanged hello's. Cloud was obviously curious and looked a little confused. Turning to NightCloud, Grey said, "Could I speak with you outside for a moment?"

They stepped out on the porch and the alpha closed the door quietly. Cloud looked up at him, waiting for the reason behind the singularly unusual request for her presence.

"This is a little bit of a delicate matter."

"Alright."

"Luna comes from a... situation that required a uniform. She's never worn ladies undergarments." Whereas the king would not be the least self-conscious about walking through the settlement at mid-day wearing no clothes, he seemed to be embarrassed and perhaps even flustered talking about lingerie.

Cloud pressed her lips together to keep from laughing at her father-in-law's discomfort with the subject matter. She was having way too much fun to let him off the hook. "What would you like me to do?"

"Ah. Explain about clothing customs here and secure these items for her. I will cover the expense, naturally."

"Naturally. Of course I will help. Um, Alpha?"

"Yes."

"People are wondering about your... guest. Who she is. Where she came from. Why she's here. And my mate is worried about you."

He looked away and sighed. "Until I've settled the question of whether she's to be a permanent resident, they're just going to have to wonder. As to Win, you should assure him that there's no cause for concern. My faculties are functioning perfectly. As you can see."

The look on his face indicated that the subject was closed so she wisely nodded and held her tongue.

When they reentered the house, Grey said, "Cloud, perhaps you could help Luna put her new things away?"

"Certainly. Where would you like them to go?" Of course Cloud knew the answer, but how often would she be in a position to mess with the alpha?

Grey noted the mischief in his daughter-in-law's eyes and knew that she was daring to play with him. He pinned her with a look that caused the smile to vanish from her pretty face. "In my room, Cloud. Where else?"

Grey sat in the living room and listened to the conversation coming from down the hall in the bedroom. He knew that, being human, Luna would have an illusion of privacy since she wouldn't know that he could easily hear conversation from that distance. Apparently Cloud had determined the easiest explanation would be by demonstration. So she showed Luna what bras looked like and what they did. She also showed her panties and explained why they were worn.

"Bras and panties come in a wide variety of styles. Everything from purely functional plain, white cotton to drool worthy."

"Drool worthy?"

That was exactly what Grey was thinking. *Drool worthy? Is that how females talk about us? Ridiculous.*

Cloud smiled and sat on the bed. "The wolf part of the male personality could care less about lingerie. But the human part sits up and takes notice when you wear something colorful or lacy or provocative."

Just as he'd been thinking the word "ridiculous", the alpha realized he was salivating.

Cloud was watching Luna carefully enough to see the little flare of her eyes at the suggestion that undergarments could tease.

"I'm going to gather up some things for your use. I'll bring two or three sizes to be sure you have a nice fit. What kinds of things would you like me to look for?"

"Thank you, Cloud. That's very kind of you."

"I'm happy to do what makes the king happy."

Luna blushed at the implication that lingerie would make Grey happy. "I like red. I don't know. What you have on now... is it drool worthy?"

Cloud laughed out loud. "No. I guess these things fall somewhere between functional and lacy. I will bring you a few things to choose from. If you stay, maybe we can shop together next time."

"If I stay? Did he tell you that I might not be staying?"

Cloud thought she may have seen disappointment flit across Luna's features, but she could have been wrong. She was worried that she may have said the wrong thing. It was never a smart idea to be on the wrong side of the alpha.

"No. He simply indicated that you hadn't made a definite decision."

"Oh." Cloud turned to leave, but Luna's voice stopped her. "He took me." In the other room, every muscle in Grey's body tensed. "I called it kidnapping, but he says it was a romantic abduction."

Cloud tried to reconcile using the term romantic in a conversation concerning the king and came up short. "And was it romantic?"

Luna seemed to be thinking that over. Grey had gotten up to pace over the sharp turn the dialogue in the other room had taken. He had stopped still, holding his breath while he waited for her answer to that question. And she was being slow to give it. He heard her shallow sigh.

"Maybe. I'm undecided." Luna laughed softly like she was embarrassed about that.

Cloud took Luna's laughter as a very good sign. "But you seem to like him."

"Before he took me, I liked him a lot."

"And now?"

"He has his moments."

In the other room Grey did a small, quiet version of a happy dance that would, in his mind, require his honor suicide had anyone witnessed it.

"Well, I've never seen him seem so... I don't know. I should go. I have shopping to do. I'm going to guess that you don't have toiletries either."

"Toiletries?"

"Toothpaste, shampoo, lotion, tampons..."

"No." She shook her head.

"I'll be back before dinner with booty."

"Booty?"

Cloud laughed. "Never mind."

She went straight to the king and held out her hand for money.

He gave her a credit card. "Don't get carried away. And I want that back." She smiled. When she opened the door to leave, he called her name and stopped her. "Cloud. Thank you."

She nodded her head like a little bow and smiled again. "Back soon."

When Cloud was gone, Luna stood in the living room looking at Grey expectantly, silently asking, "What's next?"

"Would you like to see the settlement?"

"Yes. Do I need my red hat?"

He laughed. "You cannot leave here without your red hat. The king commands it. I also recommend your gloves and your vest. Maybe even your coat."

They spent the afternoon walking around the settlement. He introduced her to everyone they saw. When the light began to fail, they returned to the lodge and prepared dinner. They sautéed vegetables for her and seared meat for him. As they sat at the table she tried to get him to try nuts and fruit. He tried to get her to gnaw on a rib.

After dinner he built the fire up and they sat together talking as they had when they walked the forest apron of the park on Throenark. Grey thought he'd never seen anything more lovely than the firelight from his own hearth reflected on Luna's smooth pearlescent skin. Luna found it a little disturbing that she felt so at home, perhaps more than she ever had at the Temple complex.

Everything about Stalkson Grey was addictive. His voice. His touch. His mesmerizing blue-gray eyes that seemed to change color depending on his surroundings. He was strong, calm and effortlessly self-assured and he made her feel safe. That was also strange because she had never before felt unsafe, except when he had grabbed her and run away.

"What did you think about the ride to town today?"

"I think this place is beautiful. I think riding in a

car is scary. And fun. I think supermarkets are marvelous. And I would like to say I understand money, but I'd be lying."

"You're smart. You'll get it."

"You think I'm smart?"

"Yes. Don't you think you're smart?"

"I'm not sure I ever thought about it really. And, even if I did think so, it wouldn't be very humble to say so out loud."

"Humility is overrated. I'm smart and don't mind saying so."

"That's because you're an arrogant son-of-a-bitch."

"Was that a racial slur?" His eyes twinkled with teasing.

"What if it was?"

"Then you'd have to be punished."

"Punished?"

He didn't like the fact that she sounded a tiny bit alarmed, as if she thought there was a chance he might hurt her. "Yes. Take it back or you will suffer more unwanted kisses."

"I take it back," she said without hesitation. He had hoped she would refuse and opt for punishment instead. "Do you have a TV?"

He looked at her as if her head had turned around on her shoulders and faced backward.

"I do not have a television and never thought I needed one. Do you need one?"

"I wouldn't say I need it, but it can be fun to watch once in a while."

They fell into silence with Grey contemplating how much he loved his life with minimal electronics. He looked over his shelves of books that he'd spent a lifetime collecting and was supremely grateful that his tantrum hadn't resulted in damage to them.

"Tomorrow is the full moon."

"Okay."

"I take it by your lack of enthusiasm that you're not a fan?"

"A fan of the full moon? I like it as much as the next person."

"Well, werewolves like it more than that. It's one of our favorite things."

"Why? You're werewolves *and* witches?"

He laughed. "You know, you say the most bizarre things. I can never guess what may come out of you next." He shook his head. "Werewolves are affected by the moon's cycle even more than humans. We feel more powerful, more... driven." He looked at her meaningfully. "And more feral."

"What am I missing? Am I supposed to read something into that?"

"For one thing, I have to shift tomorrow. Well, I don't have to, but staying in human form would be almost painful. Going out on a full moon... It's joyful." Looking at his face, it wasn't at all hard to believe that was true. "And I want you to come with me."

"You mean I have a choice?"

"Well. No. Not really."

She nodded. "It was nice of you to ask though."

He nodded in return. "We'll dress you up so warm. You'll have a good time."

They turned their heads in unison when they heard a timid knock. Grey opened the door for Cloud, who was laden with shopping bags and holding his credit card between her teeth. He took the card out of her mouth.

"Looks like you were thorough." He eyed the packages while wiping the card on his jeans leg.

"No need to thank me. I was happy to do it." She looked at Grey pointedly. "As a favor. For family."

Okay. Message received.

Cloud looked at Luna and grinned as she held up the bags. "Stuff for you."

Luna practically squeed in that semi-irritating way that women do, as she accompanied Cloud to the bedroom and closed the door. Stalkson realized it was not nearly as irritating when it was *your* woman doing the squeeing.

He drew up short when he realized that was the first time he'd dared to use a possessive pronoun when thinking about the lovely alien from Throenark dimension. *My woman*. He tested the feel of that, saying it again in his mind. With each silent repetition he was more convinced that he'd do anything to keep her. Anything.

CHAPTER_16

After Luna drank a cup of mulled wine, Grey entertained himself watching her eyelids grow heavier and heavier. *Who needs TV?* When she was drowsy enough to nod, he picked her up to take her to bed. She didn't resist. On the contrary, she nestled her nose into his neck and breathed him in. When he laid her down on the bed, she sat up.

"I want to change into one of my new nightshirts."

Grey didn't know she had new nightshirts, but was eager for her to have any pleasurable distraction that would keep her from thinking about the life she had left and missing it. He took a step back.

"Can I have some privacy so I can change?"

"Why? You've seen me without clothes."

"It's for your own good, werewolf. I don't want you to lie awake all night feverishly fretting over what you can't have."

He briefly considered teasing her about the phrase 'feverishly fretting', but concluded that it was only funny if not true.

"Very well, healer. Two minutes."

When he closed the door she sprang into action, grabbing the red satin nightshirt from the hanger where Cloud had put it. She ripped her clothes away as fast as she could, but she was still a novice at fasteners and she was still pushing the jeans down her legs when he came back in.

"Here. Let me help you with that." He helped her sit on the edge of the bed without falling over and began unlacing her boots. "You look beautiful in red, Luna."

She'd been watching him unlace the boots, but her eyes flew up to meet his when she heard the compliment. "Thank you," she whispered.

He cocked his head. "I'll bet you're tired of hearing how beautiful you are." She shook her head vigorously. "No? Well, I will make a note to remind you until you do grow tired of hearing it."

He saw her throat move when she swallowed and had to remind himself that he was supposed to be untying laces. He pulled the boots from her feet.

"Do you want to sleep in your socks?"

She smiled and said no, but made no move to take them off. He took that to mean that she was enjoying having him undress her. He hid a smile, rose, and pulled back the covers.

"Do you usually sleep alone?"

"Always. You're the first person I've ever slept with."

That simple and innocent-sounding admission made his heart swell in his chest. He removed his clothes, switched off the lamp, and got under the covers to find that she'd turned on her side facing him. Her face was bathed in the light of the nearly full moon coming through the window.

"Luna. Would you show me how you like to be kissed?"

Her eyes dropped to his mouth and stayed there for a couple of heartbeats before returning to his eyes.

"No. I'm mad at you for taking me without asking."

He reached over and traced the line at the ridge of her bottom lip with his thumb, making the sensitive area tingle in response.

"But I got you fruit."

"That's true."

"And nuts."

"Also true."

"And breads."

"Yes," she breathed.

He scooted an inch closer. "And a red hat."

"And hot chocolate. You're a good provider." Her eyes returned to his lips. "And I've always thought your mouth is... kissable."

His responding slow smile gave her shivers from stem to stern.

"All the better to kiss you with."

"A goodnight kiss then. Just one. No more."

He took her hand and placed it on his bare chest, over his heart. She allowed it and didn't pull back. "I want you to feel the way my heart speeds up when you come closer to me."

She surprised him by rising above him and urging him to his back. He'd never been in a submissive position before, except once, and that time was neither pleasant nor by choice. He thought he wouldn't be able to tolerate submitting, but found that he wasn't bothered at all. The only thing he cared about was the agony of waiting for her touch. The anticipation made him groan as she slowly lowered her mouth to his. It was as if she wanted to prolong the moment and savor it for herself.

Luna's lips brushed his. She smiled when he jerked slightly as his nerve endings came alive, readying for a proper plundering. Her soft mouth descended taking his sweetly at first, inviting his tongue to push between her lips and join them together in a delicious imitation of copulation. The pressure she applied gradually became more insistent, as did the throbbing in his engorged cock which was trapped between their bodies. The nightshirt had ridden up just enough to give him the heavenly sensation of skin on skin where her bare thigh pressed against him.

She whispered against his mouth. "Your heart is beating faster."

"Stay with me."

"Are you giving me a choice?"

"If I say yes, what will you do?"

"Go home." The fact that she didn't hesitate at all broke his heart.

"Why?"

"My work. With herbs. Knowing that I make medicines that heal... It's important."

"You could do that here." She lay back on the pillow and looked at him, but said nothing more. "Stay, Luna. Heal me."

Those two words ripped the last remnant of her resolve away. When she had met the werewolf in the forest on Tuesdays and Saturdays, she must have known - on some level - that it could only end one of two ways. Either they would part and not see each other again or she would leave with him and begin a new life. She never could have imagined that new life would be another world or that the beautiful stranger was a man who could turn into a wolf, but, in the grand scheme of things, perhaps those details were minor.

Long after her breathing had evened out into heavy sleep, he lay watching the moon on its path across the window until it was almost out of sight.

That was when flakes began to fall, the kind that were so big and fluffy you could almost see the unique kaleidoscope pattern in each one. There was no wind so they fell straight down, so fast and heavy that everything would soon be covered in white. There was still enough moonlight coming through the window to illuminate the beauty of it.

He rolled over and gently shook her shoulder. "Luna."

"Hmmm?" She sounded sleepy, but opened her eyes.

"Look."

She followed his line of sight to the window.

"What is it?" she whispered.

He smiled to himself. Just as he had thought. He knew she came from a place where the only footwear she'd ever worn was sandals, which gave him cause for suspicion that she might never have seen snow.

"Snow."

"I've never seen snow." She scrambled out of bed, complained about how cold the floor was, grabbed her discarded socks, put them back on her feet, and went to stand in front of the window wrapping her arms around herself. Even so, she was shivering.

He chuckled at her unsuccessful effort to be warm. Throwing the covers back he came to stand behind her, wrapped his arms around her and pulled her into his big, warm body. She sank back against him like she belonged there.

"Beautiful." She said it in such a reverent tone that he tried to view it through her eyes.

He'd lived through thousands of snowfalls, but seeing her respond to it like it was a miracle made it seem like one.

"Let's go out in it." She sounded as excited as a child.

"Tomorrow. Definitely."

Just then his acute nakedness began to demand attention. It was evident that he wasn't cold at all.

"How can you manage to stand here in this cold without clothes?"

He bent and nuzzled her ear, laughing softly. "You make me warm."

She couldn't be sure if it was the deep rasp of his voice, or the sexiness of his laugh, or the warm breath at her ear, or the feel of lips nibbling her earlobe, but one of those things made her lower body clench with desire. She understood why Cloud insisted that she needed panties. Because werewolf males made feminine juices flow like a river.

"Luna," he growled. "I smell your need. It's overpowering."

She turned in his arms to face him. He slipped his hands under her red nightshirt so that he could cup her ass with his big hands and lift her up. Her legs wrapped around his waist like they had a mind of their own, then she closed the distance between her mouth and his. Grey was far too exciting a lover to kiss sweetly, so she gave in to the passion she'd held at bay and kissed him with a demand that surprised as much as delighted him.

"Show me what to do, Luna," he breathed her name in a way that made her want to hear it again and again. "Show me what you want."

"You're doing fine, werewolf. Just don't stop."

He backed toward the bed until the backs of his knees touched the mattress then sat down with her straddling his lap. She released his mouth and alternated trailing kisses and licks along his neck from one ear to the other before coming back to lose herself in another kiss so deep it felt like she was trying to possess him. With one arm around her waist to hold her to him, he allowed the other hand to wander freely underneath her nightshirt, tracing her curves up the small of her back and around her side. When his warm hand cupped her breast she moaned. When his thumb ran slowly over her sensitized nipple and began circling, she pulled her mouth from his and gasped. The sound of her panting and the feel of her hands in his hair and on his bare shoulders was ratcheting his need higher. He had never had an erection that size, ever, and he was sure he couldn't get bigger.

That certainty lasted only until she reached between them and encircled the velvety flesh with her hand. She eased herself back far enough so that she could look down and watch her hand stroke his cock. While she was fascinated with watching the movement she created, he undid the nightshirt buttons and pushed it off her shoulders. He hissed in a big shuddering breath as he triumphed in the fact that the woman was with him, skin to skin, willingly asking for a coupling that he would never get over if he lived to be three hundred.

He pulled her with him as he lay back on the bed and then rolled them both so that she was on her back. She protested the deprivation of no longer having his cock in her hand until he dragged his tongue slowly and leisurely over her nipple and repeatedly circled her areola before nibbling with his lips and sucking deep enough that she felt the response all the way to her womb. While he gave the other breast equal attention, she pulled the thong from his hair and let it loose. When he rose to look down on her, his hair fell around them like a curtain. She ran her hands through it marveling at the sensual juxtaposition of the soft silkiness with the hard-as-a-rock body.

When he slowly ran his fingertips in a line from her throat, between her breasts, past her belly button, not stopping until he brushed the lips of her entrance, she cried out wantonly.

"Like this?" he asked.

She'd made him doubt himself by talking about sex with the demon. She flushed with shame knowing that it had been a lie and, worse, a taunt. Of course she preferred him in every way. That was why she'd been walking and talking with him on Tuesdays and Saturdays instead of waiting her turn with Deliverance.

"Yes. Like that. It's you I want, Grey. No one else. Only you."

Her words stung his eyes and sent a flood of emotion through his system. He stilled long enough to allow the power of it to subside so that he could breathe normally again. The woman made him feel things in places he hadn't known existed before.

He changed the angle of his hand and spread her so that he could sink two fingers into the haven of her sheath. When his thumb lightly brushed her clit, she gasped as her body arched toward him. "So responsive," he rasped. "Luna." He said her name like it was a prayer.

She caressed his upper body, exploring the chest and abs that were sculpted and well-defined as a work of art.

"Your body is so strong, wolf."

"Strong enough to hold you and protect you. Are you mine, Luna?"

The woman's body knew her heart before her mind did. She was ready to join with him physically, but not ready to say she belonged to him. The idea of saying those words made her throat close off so that she couldn't speak.

He pulled back and saw distress on her features. "You can't say you're mine?" She shook her head. "That's alright," he smiled and lovingly brushed the hair away from her cheek. "Maybe tomorrow."

"Are...?" She couldn't finish that question. It wasn't fair to ask and she knew it.

"What? Am I yours?" She gave a small nod as she searched his face in the moonlight. He smiled his wolfish smile that made her will turn liquid, and spoke softly. "I think I've been yours since the moment I saw you. I watched from the forest and saw you on the walkway in your red garment. Your hood blew away from your beautiful face in the wind. I saw you laugh. I lost my breath. And my heart. And any foolish notion that I might be able to live without you."

His words were such perfection. And it was such a very long speech for her wolf. She felt tears slip from her eyes.

"Now. Now. What's this? You're not happy to learn you own a werewolf? Too much responsibility?"

"Make love to me, Grey. I want to feel you moving inside me."

He captured her mouth with a vengeance and shifted his body. She felt his thick cock poised at her entrance. Its delectable rigidity was a testament to the passion he held for the woman. When he surged forward she cried out, which shocked her to the core because she had never been an overly vocal lover. He wasn't sure that the extreme pleasure didn't cause his consciousness to wink for a second, but he was sure that the woman beneath him was a perfect fit in every way, as if she had been custom designed for him.

Grey was so thoroughly engaged he almost forgot one of the demon's most important lessons - clitoris stimulation. As he rocked forward and back, encouraged by Luna's moans and murmurs, he reached between them and lightly tapped her swollen bud. She responded with a shout so loud he jerked his hand away, sure he had hurt her, but her shout was quickly followed by a series of pleas featuring the word, "please", and the phrase, "don't stop".

Luna's orgasm spiked quickly. It was so massive in length and intensity, that she had Grey silently chanting thanks to the incubus for his lessons on sexing a human. When he surrendered to his own convulsive release, he came hard and long. He collapsed, half on, half off a smiling Luna and reveled in the feel of her hands skimming across his back. When her fingers lazily trailed their way to his buttocks, he jerked involuntarily and they both laughed.

The king didn't sleep. Too many thoughts ran through his head, one right on top of another. Did this mean she would stay? Did it mean she had feelings for him? Could he make her happy? Because he couldn't give her up. He could not give her up.

One question was settled. Committing to sex while only in human form wouldn't be a problem. No.

Not a problem at all.

Stalkson Grey had never particularly enjoyed sex in wolf form anyway. Beyond the compulsion to release when his female was in heat, he didn't see the point.

Before Luna, he had believed that his inside matched the crusty exterior of an intractable lupine leader. Luna reached deep inside him and pulled out a tender heart with the desires and feelings of a romantic. A night in the arms of the healer had left him addicted to sex in human form because only then was lovemaking possible. He liked the options of fingertips for light touches on smooth skin, watching expressions change face to face, not to mention using and hearing vocalizations of love accompanying both tender and torrid passions.

Whereas there was no point to wolf sex for reasons other than procreation, he was on the way to learning that sex as a man was another thing entirely. He would never get enough of Luna.

When light started to filter through the window, he turned his head on the pillow. As if she knew she was being watched in her sleep, Luna opened her eyes after a few seconds. Staring into her eyes so close, Grey could see that they looked copper-colored because they were light brown with a starburst pattern of gold and yellow flecks.

"What are you looking at?" He smiled and kissed her on the nose which made her giggle. She started to stretch, but her relaxed expression was suddenly replaced with excitement. She sat up and grabbed for her nightshirt that had been haphazardly thrown at the foot of the bed. "It's tomorrow!"

He chuckled. "I think you mean it's today."

"You know what I mean. I'm going out in the snow!"

She jumped up and ran for the front door. Grey settled back, putting his hands behind his head, simply luxuriating in the way his body felt on the morning after the best sex any male had ever had.

His eyes flew open. She probably didn't know that snow stung bare skin. When he tried to scramble after her, his feet got tangled in the covers and he almost didn't get there in time. He had to put on a supernatural burst of speed to snatch her out of a mid air leap by grabbing her around the waist. Setting her down just inside the threshold of the open door, he reached out and got a handful of snow.

"It's so beautiful. Gimme."

She held out her hands reaching for it.

"Are you sure?"

"Yes!"

He laughed. "Don't ever say you didn't ask for it." He lifted her nightshirt and plastered the snow against her warm, bare tummy. Her eyes bulged as she sucked up most of the oxygen in the Pacific Northwest. He tried to keep a straight face as he said in a perfectly calm voice, "I was saving you from stepping in it barefoot by showing you how horrible it feels against bare skin."

When she was able to breathe normally again, she narrowed her eyes and simply said, "Thank you. That was very kind." Having spent her entire life in a dormitory, she knew everything there was to know about how to manage being the target of a prank, and how to play the prankster. For starters, she would not put on a big show of being distressed. That would only feed the satisfaction factor and tempt him to make a habit of practical jokes.

"You're welcome. I'm making breakfast." He turned away grinning and headed to the hearth to get a fire started.

Without another word Luna walked to the bathroom. She showered and brushed her teeth. She towel dried her hair, combed it out and braided it wet knowing that it would form sensual waves if it dried that way. She put on a black sports bra and black cotton high cut panties under her stretch jeans and a plaid, flannel shirt. After lacing up her boots exactly the way Grey did it, she walked toward the front door.

On the way she heard the werewolf call out to her. "Do you want bacon this morning?"

"Of course not!" she replied without breaking her stride. She glanced his direction with appreciation of the fact that he hadn't gotten dressed yet.

A minute later he heard her come up behind him. "I guess you'll be having fruit again."

"Yes. I'd like a kiss first."

Smiling he turned around, but instead of a kiss he got a fist full of snow pressed to his groin. His gasp was even bigger than hers had been and, for a minute, he thought perhaps he was going to expire. Through it all he knew he would never forget the look of mischief on her face, or the all-consuming wickedness of her laugh as she watched him try to recover from having his male parts withdraw into his body like a turtle into its shell.

When he was finally able to breathe again, he gave her a deceptive look of calm, switched off the gas flame underneath the frying bacon, and slowly turned to face her. She took one look at his expression and squealed as she pivoted to run. He caught her in two steps and carried her to the bedroom while she kicked and squirmed and giggled.

Holding her with one arm he grabbed two bandannas out of a dresser drawer and tied each wrist to a rung in the headboard.

She fought until she was breathless and heaved, "What are you doing?"

It was his turn to give her an evil smile. He lifted one foot. She tried to draw it back to kick, but he held on. "I'm going to give you a chance to show me how sorry you are."

"Why should I be sorry? You started it."

"Because life is not fair."

He removed her boots, socks, jeans, and panties so painfully slowly that she was tempted to kick him in the face about a hundred times. When he finally had her bare from the waist down, he grasped her ankles gently, but firmly, and pulled her legs apart. She watched his eyes darken even further as he stared at her exposed.

"What are you doing, werewolf?"

His eyes flicked up to her face for just a second. "I'm trying something I learned in a class."

He placed his big hands on her thighs and nuzzled all around her opening which made her undulate in a way that almost broke his resolve. She felt his hot breath on her core and tried to raise her hips. When he ran his long, wolf's tongue up her channel and over her clit, she bucked hard enough to throw him backward. He got up laughing.

"That really works, huh?"

Thinking he was laughing at her, she jerked on the bandannas securing her wrists which made the head board thump against the wall, and pulled her foot back with every intention of kicking him in the face. His wolf reflexes, being fast and powerful as they were, enabled him to catch her foot easily. Then watching her face, he turned his head and licked up the arch of her foot. Her eyes darkened as she licked her bottom lip.

Sometimes his eyes momentarily turned a breathtaking shade of yellow gold and made him look not quite human. She was lost in the exotic experience of a lover who barely clung to humanity. He was a sexual predator and she was the female lucky enough to be his prey.

Holding her legs down, he slowly kissed his way back up her inner thigh, stopping now and then to draw lazy wet circles with the tip of his tongue. By the time he'd made it back to his target, she was writhing and begging to be touched. He petted and licked and nibbled all around her clit until she was panting and cursing his name.

Abruptly he stood and said, "How about that bacon now?"

It was impossible to really pull off nonchalance when his cock was stiff as a well pump.

"Wolf, I'm warning you. Untie me now. If you leave me like this, you'll be sorry."

He grinned and leaped at her. As he hovered over her, he said, "Tell me you're sorry." She pressed her lips together. He looked down between them and gently traced a pattern on her mound with a light touch. "Tell me you're sorry."

When he looked at her face, he watched a tear slide out of her eye and realized she was never going to say she was sorry. By the time he understood that his game had taken a wrong turn and turned serious, he was ready to throw himself at her feet and volunteer for a lashing.

"Luna, I was playing. I'm not trying to break your spirit."

"You're a monster, Stalkson Grey."

"I am. And I'm sorry. I'm *so* sorry."

"Ha!" She grinned. "You said it first. Now untie me so I can punish you properly."

He gaped at her for a couple of beats and then started laughing. "Luna. I'm out of my depth."

"You want me to like it here?"

"You know I do."

"Then make me come or untie me so I can do it myself."

He heard and obeyed. His mouth captured hers in a desperate kiss at the same time his touch found its way home. He kissed and stroked until she screamed and shuddered. While her body continued to convulse from the aftershocks, he reached up and pulled the ties free.

She wound her fingers into his hair and embraced his body with her legs in open invitation. He plunged into her in one thrust, grateful that she wasn't either hurt or angry. She rolled him over so that she was on top and began to ride him slowly. He was looking at her like she was a miracle. Luna wouldn't have guessed that was because it was his first time to experience that position.

While she moved to a captivating rhythm, he unbuttoned her shirt and pushed it off her shoulders. She withdrew her arms from the sleeves and pulled the sports bra over her head, without ever stopping the friction that was winding Grey tight. He reached up and cupped her breasts with both hands, then lightly pinched her nipples. She cried out.

"You like that, Luna."

She bent at the waist and kissed him like she was desperate for his taste. "I like *you*, werewolf."

After breakfast, Grey made sure she was bundled up. They headed out to see some of the scenery and experience snow. The wolf and the woman. They walked to one of his favorite lookout spots, the one overlooking the lake.

"It's so beautiful," she said. "What does it feel like to fall down in the snow?"

Grey looked around and saw a deep drift. He bounded toward it, leaped into the air and dived in. When he came up, he had snow all over his muzzle. She laughed and he wagged his tail. At first he wasn't sure what was happening. He felt something different going on at the end of his spine. It took a few seconds for him to put together that it must have been...

No. No. No, he thought. *Stalkson Grey does not wag his tail.*

The woman was taking him apart bit by bit. That was four firsts in one day. He'd taken a snowball to the groin, submitted to the pleasure of being ridden by a female, apologized, *and* wagged his tail. How did he feel about that? He examined his feelings and concluded that his life had taken a decided turn for the better. What tribe needed a king with a twig up his sphincter?

They spent a couple of hours hiking. From time to time Grey ran here and there showing off how fast and flexible he was.

At one point she asked about the lack of people.

"Aren't you afraid to be out here alone? What if there were bad animals or something?" He ran around in front, whirled and leaped into her path baring his teeth and snarling with a ferocity she was glad wasn't turned on her in earnest. "So you're saying you're the baddest animal of all?"

His ears pointed straight up while he gave her a doggy-style grin and wagged his tail. She laughed again and kissed him on the snout.

When they returned to the lodge, Luna opened the door and let him in.

She turned around just in time to see him shift into a gloriously naked, indescribably beautiful man. Following her line of sight, he looked down and then grinned at her.

"Admit it. You are *fascinated* by my penis."

She raised her eyes to his. "It's magic. I've learned that I can make it grow just by staring at it."

She gasped when he rushed her without warning and gathered her into his arms. His tone dropped to low and raspy. "Is that the only reason it's magic?"

She giggled, but felt silly about it. She just couldn't seem to stop. "You want me to list the ways?"

"Oh, I don't think you've seen *all* the ways yet."

"Can we start a fire before you show me more magic tricks?"

They spent the afternoon lazing together in front of the fire with mulled wine, talking and touching the way lovers do. When Grey's stomach rumbled, they got up and went to the kitchen to make an early dinner together.

CHAPTER_17

When Pandora learned that Rejuvenata was missing, presumed taken by force, she was furious. For a light Abraxas, anger was a state that was as unusual as an unselfish act by a dark Abraxas.

Deliverance didn't age like humans and his body didn't suffer stress like humans either. He didn't breathe harder if he exerted himself and his heart didn't speed up either. It maintained a strong, slow, steady beat no matter what, even if he was pounding a court clerk on the desk of a judge's chambers. The woman's back was on the desk that had been cleared by the sweep of a powerful forearm. Her rump was pulled to the edge of the desk and her legs rested on the bronzed shoulders of the demon who stood over her.

The incubus didn't enjoy sex the way humanoids did. He took sustenance from the pleasure his partners took from having sex with him. Some might call that a subtle distinction, but there is a difference between enjoying succulent lobster dipped in pure melted Irish butter and having an orgasm. Anyone who has experienced both will testify to that fact.

When Pandora popped in next to them, Deliverance grinned and said, "Auntie! S'up?" without compromising the rhythm of his stroke. He continued to grin while she fumed, as if he got an extra thrill out of performance exhibitionism taken to the extreme.

"Are you quite done?" She was livid.

"Hold on."

The woman on the desk with her skirt bunched around her waist might have been modest enough to want to be embarrassed. She probably wanted to stop the loud and open-mouthed moaning and various other guttural, somewhat unattractive noises. Between that and the squishing, suction, and slapping noises that tend to accompany fucking in that position, it was a pornographic symphony. She may or may not have been able to think clearly enough to have processed the fact that the recent arrival, the one who had appeared out of nowhere and was then standing two feet away glaring, appeared to be in her mid to late twenties and was as flawlessly perfect as a goddess. All of that was pure conjecture, because all that could be known for sure was that the clerk was too caught up in the moment to stop the crest she was riding.

"Wait for it." Deliverance continued to hold his aunt's gaze and grin as he thrust his impressive cock like a piston. She had hands on hips and looked ready to strangle him. "Wait for it."

When the random snack reached her orgasm, Deliverance closed his eyes as the pleasure of filling up his energy stores washed over him. An incubus demon didn't experience ejaculation unless coitus was performed with a partner who carried sufficient demonic genetics. The end was entirely established by the orgasm of the female being engaged. Without a doubt he could have brought the court clerk to multiple orgasms, but he decided it would probably be disrespectful to make his aunt wait for more than one.

"Sorry to keep you waiting."

He didn't look the least sorry.

"Deliverance, you idiot. Do you have something you want to tell me?"

"Wow. Nice to see you too." Her color was starting to darken. "Alright. Alright. I did it."

"Needless to say..."

"You want her back."

She exploded. "Of course I want her back, you miscreant! Where did you take her?"

Deliverance had the decency to look a little sheepish. "I let the werewolf have her."

The color that had been building in Pandora's face disappeared all at once and left her looking pale. She opened her mouth to speak, but was so stunned that she simply gaped while willing the earth to open up at her nephew's feet and swallow him whole. *After* he had returned her property.

"You gave her to a werewolf?"

"Well, first, I didn't give her. I just facilitated the transportation. And, he's not just any werewolf. He's one of the Loti Dimension kings."

Her shock and outrage were so complete that she couldn't seem to stop shaking her head back and forth.

"Why would you do something so utterly bizarre?"

"I think he loves her."

"Loves her? That's impossible. When would one of my thirteen have an opportunity to court love?"

He looked at his cuticles. "I'd rather not say."

"This isn't over. She had better be back in the annex by tonight."

"Whatever."

"Ugh! You are *such* a child."

And with that she was gone.

Grey was slicing cheese at his kitchen counter. It was one of the few things they would both eat.

"Luna."

"Yes?"

"Will you stay?"

She sighed. "What would I do if I stayed?"

"You'd be free to pursue your own interests. What would you want to do?"

"I would want to do what I'm trained to do - work with herbs."

"We have herbs. You could do that here." He opened a cabinet to reveal rows of glass apothecary jars.

"Grey! Bring these down and let me see what you have!"

"Okay." He started setting the jars on the counter.

"This is wonderful. Did all of these come from around here? They're wildcrafted?"

"Most of them. Some of them are from other places."

She took the lids off the jars one at a time and examined each herb. Then she froze, holding a pinch of an herb that looked like dried mushroom. "What do you use this one for?"

"Which one?" He looked over. "Oh. That's frenalwort. We use it for celebrations." She looked so serious he knew something was wrong. "What is it, Luna?"

"This herb is psychotropic. It's an hallucinogen."

"Okay," he said cautiously.

"Do all your, um, werewolves use this herb?"

He shrugged. "Sure. Yeah. Now and then." He

didn't know how to interpret the look on her face. "What's wrong?"

"I don't know how to tell you this." She shook her head. "The properties in this herb stay in your system a long time." He nodded for her to continue. "And, if even a tiny residue of this was in the system of a female when she became pregnant, it could influence the gender of her baby and prejudice development toward male."

She watched various emotions cross his face without him ever moving a muscle.

"That can't be right. My people have been using frenalwort for generations."

"Does it grow here?"

His brows drew together in a frown. "No."

"So you get it from somewhere else."

"We trade for it. It grows in the southwest desert lands. There are tribes there who live off the sale of it."

"At some point, you began getting a supply from a different strain. Or the plant mutated because of changes in the environment.

"We call it drayweed. It has a very bad reputation and it's against the law in most places for women of child-bearing age to use it. There was a region in my world with a culture that valued males over females. In that culture the males had privilege, authority, power, respect, entitlement, everything. Every family wanted boys because it gave the family more prestige.

"You can probably guess what happened. They were not forward thinking enough to realize that females are necessary to survival of a race, actually *more* necessary to be precise.

"They discovered that drayweed, what you call

frenalwort, adds something to the advancing pregnancy so that the fetus proceeds on a path to express masculinity. In one generation an entire culture was threatened with extinction."

She let the pinch she held between her fingers drop back into the jar and put the lid back on. "You know what this means?"

"It doesn't mean anything." He went back to putting slices of cheese on plates.

She looked at him like he'd gone mad. "What do you mean? Didn't you just move half your people off world because of this?"

He shrugged. "It's done now. Do you want pears?"

"Grey!" Her voice was raised and he ignored her. "Grey!"

She was yelling at him? Yelling? He didn't have a problem with her looking him straight in the eye like she was an equal. He submitted to her during sex when she wanted to be on top - even liked it. He even tolerated having her put her arms around his neck when he was in wolf form. But scolding? No. That would not be tolerated.

"Grey! You have to tell them!"

He slammed the knife into the cutting board and wheeled on her.

"You seem to have mistaken me for someone who is not the king of this tribe. I don't *have* to do anything, human. I'm alpha." He was breathing heavy. "Alpha!" She took a step back, a little scared and a lot surprised. "Rain never argued with me like this."

Grey saw hurt in her eyes.

"Rain. Your mate who died?" she whispered.

He immediately regretted what he'd said and started to reach for her, intending to pull her close and smother her with kisses and tell her how sorry he was. But, just as a huge tear spilled out of her eye, Deliverance popped in next to her.

The demon grabbed her arm. "Sorry, dude. Auntie wants her girl back. Ho's before bro's. You know how it is."

Grey lunged for Luna as his mouth tried to form the word, "No,", but she was gone. He was certain he'd seen shock and sadness mixing with the hurt on her beautiful face before she disappeared.

She was sure she'd seen him soften and relent just before she was ripped away.

CHAPTER_18

Stalkson Grey sat facing the window that had bathed his bed in filtered moonlight for the only two nights of his life that were worth reliving. It was the night of the full moon, which meant that it was painful to stay in human form, but that pain didn't even have a chance to make an impression on his consciousness next to the loss of Luna, the human who was his true mate.

For three days he sat on the side of the bed. Sometimes he would lose consciousness to sleep, but then he would raise himself up only to stare at the window again. He divided his time between grieving her absence and yearning for her presence. He simply had no motivation to move. His desire to function had left with Luna and dissolved into despondency.

At the end of the third day there was a knock on the door. He willed whoever it was to go away, but they persisted.

He opened the door and Cloud was standing on the porch with a package. She looked at him strangely. He said nothing.

"Alpha. I brought something for Luna."

"She's not here."

"Not here?" Cloud repeated, trying to peer around where his body blocked the doorway.

"Anything else?"

"Um, no, I..."

He shut the door in her face.

A half hour later there was more knocking, louder, demanding. Something about the insistence of the knocking aggravated Grey.

VICTORIA DANANN

He flung the door open. It was Win.
"What!"
"I came to check on you, Dad. You look really...
awful." His nose twitched. "Have you bathed lately?"
The alpha just stared at him with hollow eyes. "Or
eaten?"
Win stepped inside. His father allowed it.
Grudgingly.
"It's cold in here. Even for one of us. I'm going to
build a fire and put some venison ribs on a plate."
Grey didn't reply. He didn't move, either. He
simply stood unmoving by the front door while Win
built up a fire and heated meat for his father.
"Dad. Come sit by the fire and eat a little
something. I'm worried about you." Grey shuffled to
his chair by the fire and sat without looking at Win or
the food that was set in front of him. "Is this all about
the human woman?
"I don't know what happened, but it's probably
for the best. You know she could never be a real mate
to you. You could never have offspring with her."
Grey's face slowly formed in a scowl and his
eyes cleared a little as he looked at Win. "Why not?"
Win gaped like he was flabbergasted to be asked
that question. "Because your young would be part
human."
The lines formed by Grey's scowl grew deeper as
those words sunk in. How would he feel if Luna was
pregnant? She might already be pregnant. He hadn't
used protection and she hadn't insisted on it. Why
hadn't she insisted on it? He didn't dare let himself
read anything into that. What difference did it make
anyway? She was gone. Yet he was still thinking
about it.

He searched his heart and his mind and saw imaginary pictures of what a child of theirs might look like. His heart responded with an eager, steady thumping, not regret. How could he have been so insensitive to the role love plays in assigning parentage? Because he hadn't known one thing about love.

He looked at his son and felt shame for teaching Win that hybrids were inferior - less than pure weres, not *real* werewolves. And he remembered the young hybrid from Black Swan who had easily dominated a pack of his young males and brought them to submission. He and Luna might have had a child like that. If he'd been willing to look closer and open his mind to new ideas, he might have learned that cross-breeds had something uniquely special that transcended being either pure human or pure were.

He spoke quietly.

"If I had offspring with the woman, I would cherish them just as I do you."

Grey's heart told him he might love them even more, but he would never suggest such a thing to his heir. Win was aghast.

"You're not yourself. We need to get you fed and cleaned up. You look like you haven't slept in days."

The king wasn't motivated to think of a good reason to say no. So he allowed his boy to fuss over him and treat him like he needed assisted living. When Windwalker was satisfied that his father was clean and that food was prepared for him, he built up the fire, handed him a warm cup of mulled wine and hoped it would lull his father into a badly needed sleep.

"I'll be over in the morning, Dad. If you need

anything, take your phone out of the cabinet and call me."

The alpha simply sighed. He was relieved when his son had gone. He just wanted to be alone in the lodge with his memories. If he was human, he knew they would say he had fallen into a depression. Well, of course he was depressed. There was an impenetrable wall between him and the woman he loved.

If she was going to be taken from him forever, he wished that last memory would have been any of a hundred different times when he'd said or done something to make her laugh. He loved it when her eyes danced with sparkles like tiny firecrackers.

Over and over in his mind he saw the look on her face when he had thoughtlessly, senselessly compared her to his mate who had passed over so long ago, and led Luna to believe that she didn't fare well in the comparison.

He hated himself for having done that and would give anything to take back the fact that it was the last thing that would ever pass between them. The last thing shouldn't have been a lie, and implying that he preferred anything about his first wife was a lie. He didn't want to speak ill of her. As mates go, LapsRain had been nice enough.

His breath caught on that last sentence. When he realized what he'd said, he didn't know whether to laugh or cry. That's what the old ShuShu, BlueClaw, had tried to tell him - that he was going to get a chance for *real* love, to be looking out for it, and to grab hold if he found it. At the time Grey couldn't hear BlueClaw because he thought that the only thing big enough to satisfy his large appetite was the power of being king. He was so wrong.

He'd always had a sense that there was a hole in his middle that begged to be filled and he could never feed it enough to be satisfied. Until Luna. When she was there, he had never had the uneasy feeling of needing something more. He wished he had told her that ten times every hour.

She was a miracle to him and his people. Luna solved the mystery of what had gone wrong and he chose his pride over telling his people the truth and keeping faith with the woman he loved. He didn't want to admit that it was a mistake to split the tribe in two, separate families, create hardships.

He set his cup down. He looked into the fire and looked into his soul. Such a king did not deserve the trust of his people. Such a man did not deserve the love of a woman like Luna.

Through the night he continued to sit in front of the fire and ponder.

He asked himself if he would give up being alpha to be with Luna and the answer was yes. He asked himself if he would give up Elk Mountain to be with Luna and the answer was yes. He even went so far as to ask himself if he would give up shifting to be with Luna. Could he really deny half of his nature and never again feel the joy and freedom of running in his wolf form? The answer was still yes.

Then he asked himself what was the point of that exercise. It wasn't like he could get a ticket to her world. "Hello. AAA Travel? I'd like to know the fastest way to Throenark Dimension."

Sometime before morning, weariness finally overcame the werewolf and he slept. In his dream he saw the park where the Temple of the Cult of Vervain housed Luna. He saw a young woman emerge from the temple wearing red silk. He waited at the forest edge as she approached. When she drew near enough, she pulled her hood back from her face, but it wasn't Luna. It was Litha, the demon's daughter.

He sat up when he woke and pulled a hand down over his face thinking that the image in the dream would vanish like smoke as dreams most often do. But it remained clear as a photograph, which meant that it was a message from Spirits. Fortunately for him, he knew someone who could help him find the way into the dream world and hear that message.

Stalkson Grey changed his clothes and stepped outside. After walking a few feet he spied a pup and motioned him over.

"Go find LongPaw and say that the king would like to meet with him at Drift's lodge."

The young one was ecstatic to be given an errand for the king and ran away, knowing he would have something to brag about to his friends.

LongPaw reached Drift's current encampment just minutes after Grey. The three sat on skins on the ground around a small fire. The design of the lodging was perfection. The space left at the apex of the hides created a draft that pulled the smoke straight up and away.

"I'm going on Vision Quest and, as alpha, I require that the tribe elders guard my body."

Drift and LongPaw glanced at each other.

"Did you receive a message from Spirit?" Drift asked.

"Yes."

"And the message was that you need to seek the

dream world?" LongPaw asked.

"Yes."

"Who will guide you on the journey?" Drift sounded concerned.

"I plan to ask the ShuShu, BlueClaw."

Drift said, "Ah. BlueClaw is a good man. We will accompany you, Alpha. Your body will be safe if you choose to return to it." Grey nodded. "When shall we seek out BlueClaw and ask for his help?"

Grey looked between them. "Now. If you're hungry, eat. If you're thirsty, drink. Then gather what you need and go with me."

The two old ones didn't try to hide their surprise. Drift offered jerky to LongPaw and Grey. LongPaw took it and ate. Grey didn't.

Before mid-day, the three werewolves walked into the camp BlueClaw had made that day. His lodging was the same type and style as Drift's, as their ancestors had shared the design. As they neared they could see by the smoke rising from the lodge that there was a fire burning inside.

BlueClaw stood outside looking in the direction of their approach. He raised his hand in greeting. "Stalkson Grey. Old ones."

Grey smiled. "You've been waiting for us."

"Yes. The stones are warm and ready."

Drift said, "He is not prepared."

BlueClaw looked at Drift. "He has prepared himself even if he didn't realize that's what he was doing, old wolf. He has spent three days alone - fasting, searching his heart and mind, looking for the way back to his true path. Stalkson Grey is ready."

He raised the flap to his lodge and stood aside in welcome and invitation.

Inside the lodge, Stalkson stripped out of his clothes and sat to the west of the fire. He didn't need to be told where to find west. Each of the four present was always aware of where they were in relationship to the directional pull of the earth's magnetism.

Grey sat in the west because that was where the spirit and dream worlds converged, or some would say, collided. The intersection created a gap in the fabric that separated the living from the dead.

The tribe elders were alarmed when Grey disrobed and they saw how much weight their alpha had lost, but they knew it was a necessary component of the quest. The old werewolves and the ShuShu removed their shirts. BlueClaw would sit in the east where he could give or withhold air to the other elements depending on what was needed during the journey. Drift sat in the north and LongPaw in the south.

BlueClaw had laid the fire inside a circle of large black river rock stones that had been polished smooth by eons beneath water rushing to the sea. Outside the ring of large black stones, being heated by the touch of flame and embers was another ring of smaller stones warming to a temperature appropriate for touch. On the ShuShu's left was a stack of wood for the fire. On his right was a bucket with a long-handled, dipper style ladle.

He took a leather pouch from around his neck, loosened the latigo lace tie, and withdrew a small quantity of something dark brown that resembled moss. He handed it to Grey who put the whole mess in his mouth at once and began to chew. When the alpha finished swallowing he lay down on his back with his left side to the fire.

BlueClaw took one of the smaller stones and placed it over Grey's heart. Another went over his solar plexus and a third covered the center of his forehead. BlueClaw took his place and began to chant while he poured a dipper of water over the large stones, enough to make steam rise, but not enough to put out the fire.

The air in the lodge immediately became close, filled with warm moisture. Blue Claw stoked the fire, added wood, and sat as he sang another chant in ShuShu language. After a few moments, the alpha's eyes drifted closed. From time to time BlueClaw ladled more water onto the stones. They hissed and sizzled and the air became heavier with steam.

After a time Grey began to sweat profusely, further dehydrating his body, partly from the heat of the room and partly from the fungus-induced fever. His skin was flushed all over. Now and then those who watched over his body observed minor convulsions or tremors rippling through his muscles.

Stalkson Grey emerged from a thick gray mist to find himself in a place unlike anywhere he'd been in his present incarnation as a werewolf. Treeless hills in varying shades of green undulated underneath a cloudy sky. There was not a single blemish on the land, no buildings, no machinery. There was, however, a person.

A woman stood with her back to him. Her long auburn hair was loosely bound by a ribbon and was being whipped about by a strong, uneven, and noisy wind. She was wearing a long dress made of the same scarlet silk that Luna wore on Throenark and it billowed in the wind. From her vantage point at the top of a hill, hands on her waist resting at the flare of her hips, she gave the impression that she owned the land as far as the eye could see.

Grey walked toward her. When he was within a few feet, she turned and gave him a smile of welcome. He knew she was a relative of Litha's because of her features. She looked very much the same except that she was fair-skinned and had red hair. Same lips. Same green eyes. Same air and expression.

"Stalkson Grey."

"Yes."

"My name is Lapis." She smiled. "I'm Litha's grandmother."

She waved her hand across the landscape. "I spent my childhood here on the moors. It was the best time of my life. So when I died I made a point of recreating it from memory so that I could come here from time to time." She looked him over. "There used to be wolves here, but like the forests, they were all gone by the time I was born." She laughed. "The stories lingered though. Nothing works so well to keep children in line as stories about being gotten by wolves."

She stopped, as if she was waiting for him to say something.

"It's... beautiful. In a way. I'm very partial to trees."

"Yes. Well, it seems you've wandered off your path."

"Have I?"

"Why else would you be here?"

"I don't know. For information?"

Lapis smiled like she knew something he didn't. "Alright. What kind of information would you like?"

"I want to know if it's possible for me to reach Luna."

"By that, do you mean to go to her physically?"

"Yes. Forgive me, but that's the best way."

She laughed. "Debatable, but I can see why you'd think so. What you ask is easy, Stalkson Grey. My granddaughter can help you. If that is what you wish, I will visit her in her dreams and request that she do so as a favor to me."

"Thank you." The words were simple, but filled with relief and emotion. It was a heartfelt utterance of gratitude and she knew that his appreciation was sincere.

"I said, 'if that is what you wish'."

He frowned. "It is."

She laughed. "Rash. I suspect that's how you got into your bit of trouble in the first place." He frowned. "Before you were born into the lifetime you are now experiencing, you agreed that you would take on a challenge - one that would require a great sacrifice from you physically and emotionally. The circumstances are now in place for you to fulfill that self-determined destiny. But there is an optional exit. You can decline."

"I don't understand."

"You can return to Elk Mountain and live out your life as king of your people who remained behind. You will keep the wealth, power, and authority you have earned. Those who serve you will respect you and some will even admire or honor you. These are the things you have always believed to be worth pursuing. And they are yours already.

"If you choose a different way, your future will not be so certain. The only thing that is sure is that the alternate way, wherever it leads, will not be easy. Are you willing to gamble everything you have for an unknown?"

He started to respond, but she held up her hand. "Do you not want to think it over?"

"I don't need to think it over. Yes. I am willing to gamble everything I have for an unknown."

"Very well, then. I have already spoken to Litha in her dream and asked her to help you. When you speak to her, tell her that her grandmother, Lapis, loves her and is often with her and that her daughter will be the most gifted witch ever born to our line.

"There's just one more thing you need to do."

"What is it?"

Lapis waved her hand and a wall of fire appeared behind her. Grey took a step back. The human part of his personality had great respect for fire. The fear of fire in his wolf was soul deep.

"Are you willing to run into the fire for her?"

He stared at the fire, horrified by the idea. The roar was louder even than the wind. The pops sounded like gunfire. He could feel the heat and knew that the fire was real and not illusion.

Desire must be powerfully consuming to override survival instinct. For whatever reason, his desire for the human woman, Luna, was more powerful than aversion to pain, more powerful even than his wish to continue living in a body. So he summoned his courage and made a commitment in his heart to meet the witch's challenge, even if it resulted in death or disfigurement.

All of his muscles tensed and he ran headlong into the fire wall.

Just as the flames touched his skin, Grey sat up with a shout that was followed by a gasp that looked painful. The river stones fell into his lap. He felt groggy, disoriented, and looked worse. His body was heavy, cumbersome.

BlueClaw handed him a liter of bottled water which was gulped down without stopping. The ShuShu then opened the flap of the lodge to let the steam escape.

When cool air came in contact with sweaty bodies, the elders put their shirts back on and contemplated shifting so that fur could insulate and warm old bones.

Looking at Grey, BluClaw said, "Did you find your answer, Alpha?"

Stalkson looked at him with steely blue eyes that looked brighter than usual because his spirit had just returned from a place of greater clarity than the physical world. "I did. You've done me a service."

BlueClaw smiled. "So tell me. Was it *nice*?"

Stalkson sneered. "I would have thought you above I-told-you-so moments. Yes. I get it. It would be better to have a woman who spits and claws at your eyes than to have one who gives you a *nice* life."

BlueClaw laughed softly. "You're not as dumb as you look, wolf."

"The fire wall was way over the top though."

"Fire wall?"

BlueClaw looked confused. Maybe he only pretended to know everything.

As they neared the edge of the tribe settlement, Grey thanked the elders and hurried home. When he stepped inside his personal sanctuary and closed the door, he realized that he was ravenous. He ate almost enough food to make up for his three-day fast without regard to table manners then retrieved his cell phone from the cabinet where he kept it plugged into a charge.

He called Simon Tvelgar for Litha's phone number, not thinking about the fact that it was the middle of the night in Edinburgh.

Simon sometimes felt that nights when he wasn't awakened by someone who had forgotten about the time difference were more the exception than the rule. He wanted to ask why the Elk Mountain king requested Litha's number, but decided to forego curiosity in the interest of courtesy.

The wave of a little victory settled over Grey when he procured Litha's number and another followed that when she answered.

"This is Stalkson Grey. We met at Jefferson Unit."

"Of course I remember you."

"I don't know any way to approach this other than to just say outright that I need a favor."

"I see. Would you rather talk in person?"

"Ah. Yes. If it's soon."

"If you're decent then, I'll pop in."

"I am dressed." Humans were so strange about clothing.

"Okay. Keep the phone connection open so I can track you."

Two minutes later she was standing in his living room. He invited her to sit and offered mulled wine.

"I can't. No alcohol right now." She pointed to her tummy as she said it.

He nodded and offered water or coffee which she

also declined. "Thank you for coming so soon."

"Not at all. What can I do for you?"

"Let me start at the beginning."

He told her the entire story, omitting only the most intimate parts, from how he'd courted Luna on the days when Deliverance was scheduled to be there until the moment when Deliverance had reclaimed her.

At that point he stopped to refresh his drink and asked again if Litha would like water or coffee.

"I had a strange dream in which you appeared at Luna's Temple complex on Throenark. I believed it was a message from the spirit world so I journeyed there to learn what it meant.

"While I was out of my body, I met your grandmother, Lapis. She said you would help me, that she would ask you in a dream to do it as a favor, and to tell you that your daughter will be the most talented witch ever to be born to your line."

Litha blinked several times. "Can you describe the way she looked?"

"She actually looks very much like you, but her coloring is different. She has fair skin and red hair."

Litha looked a little misty-eyed and a laugh gushed out of her. "My grandmother! What did she say her name was?"

"Lapis. Oh, one other thing I left out. She said to say that she loves you and is often with you."

Litha nodded, looking more teary-eyed, but she didn't cry.

"I did see her in a dream, but I wouldn't have known she was my grandmother if you hadn't told me. So it seems I owe you a favor. How do you see me helping in this situation?"

"I want to go to Throenark. Do you know how to get there?"

"I don't know how to get there, but I could find out. If I have a great-aunt there, my other grandmother is sure to know. But if I bring her back here for you, won't Dad just come for her again?"

"Yes. I suspect he would, which is why that wouldn't be a good plan. Besides I'm not ever going to force her to do anything against her will again."

"A wise choice if you want the lady to love you."

He nodded thoughtfully as he glanced at the fire. "I plan to go there."

"You mean for a visit?"

"No. I mean permanently."

"I thought you said it's urban. High rises surrounding the park where the temple is."

"Yes. It is."

"Look, I'm no expert on werewolves, but that doesn't sound like a viable change in lifestyle."

"Yeah. It's not ideal. But it's not as bad as being where I know for a fact I will *never* see her again."

Litha's features softened in sympathy. "You *really* love her.

"Okay. What's your plan?"

"If you can find your way to Throenark, I need you to help me figure out what I need to live there. Can I trade gold for their money? How much would I need? Will I need ID? What kind of clothes do they wear? What do I need to know about their customs? Stuff like that. Try to help me anticipate what could go wrong, because I know I only get one shot at this relocation."

"You think you're going to make an adjustment to city life."

"I'll be as adaptable as I need to be."

"Please think about this. You won't know anybody and everything will be alien to you. Wolves are pack animals, right? Really social? How are you going to adapt to being alone?"

He took a deep breath. He didn't want to sound like he was pleading. "I'm alone now."

She studied him for a minute, then stood up. "I'll call you when I have more info."

"Thank you."

And she was gone.

He kept his phone close by where he would know if she called.

Three days worth of pacing later, Litha's name appeared on the Caller ID.

"Are you decent?"

"All clear."

She arrived carrying a stack of paper products.

"I brought stuff."

"I see that. What is it?"

"A to Z. This has got to be what the witness protection program is like.

"Found Throenark, but that was just the beginning. The country you're interested in is Greenland only, unlike here, it's actually green. The region is Grand Lakes. The city is New Bay. They call it an island because it's practically surrounded by water, but it's actually a peninsula.

"Brought you maps and magazines to give you some insight into culture. There's a *Xenophile's Guide to Greenland* and a *Xenophobe's Guide to Greenland*. If you study both you should be able to pass as a visiting foreigner. As you've already figured out, they speak Anglish.

"I got an angel to help me with some of the details 'cause he's a sucker for love. Don't tell my father. He's not crazy about angels.

"Anyway, he got you an apartment and the ID you need and he's done the calculations on how much gold you should bring to trade for currency. There's also info in there on where to put your assets to keep them safe.

"I hope you don't feel like this is too personal, but I need measurements so my friend can get you some starter clothes."

Stalkson was overwhelmed with the amount of work to do to prepare for blending in with an alien human culture and with gratitude for everything Litha had done for him.

"I don't know where to start with thanks."

"Start with the *Xenophile's Guide*. When you think you're ready for the next step, call me. I should have your clothes by then."

"Thank you and thank your, um, angel friend."

"Kellareal."

"Yes. Can I offer you...?"

"No. No. I'm on my way somewhere. But, listen, you can change your mind at any time and, if you're having second thoughts at all, I think you should. You've spent forty-eight hours with this woman. Forty-eight hours isn't much of a test of getting to know each other."

He smiled. "So I take it you don't believe in love at first sight?"

Litha's hands flew to her distended tummy of their own accord. Then she laughed quietly. "As a matter of fact, I *do* believe in love at first sight. But I know somebody who works at Headquarters. She's a past life therapist. She says it's not really first sight, but the soul part of our natures recognizing each other from another time of being together. Or not being together."

CHAPTER_19

Grey undertook preparation for his move to a new world by studying everything Litha had brought. She continually admonished him to rethink his plan and was so insistent about it, that he found himself searching his own feelings. Daily.

He did a checklist of the worst anticipated hardships. He would be a wolf alone. A wolf alone in a high rise apartment. A wolf alone in a high rise apartment with no way to shift or run again. Ever.

Every day he went through the list and every day he came to the same conclusion, that, even if she never spoke to him again, even if he never touched her again, if there was a chance he might see her again - even from a distance, he had to take that chance. Even though he knew it could be a death sentence to his sanity, because werewolves have been known to go mad if they couldn't release their wolves from time to time.

So he studied everything from maps to architecture to fashion to tipping. It was a lot to take in. The saving grace was that so much was similar to his own world. All he had to do was find the differences and concentrate on those.

Luna was an instant celebrity among her sisters. What she wanted was to crawl into her bed, pull the covers up, and be left alone to cry and sort out her feelings until such time as that was no longer the only thing she wanted to do. Unfortunately, the other girls were titillated by the phenomenon of being taken and wanted to hear every detail.

Who was he?
What did he look like?
Did he force himself on her?
Did he try and win her?
What was it like where he took her?
What was she expected to do?

The questions were endless and she didn't want to answer any of them. Her time with Stalkson Grey was something that she wanted to keep private, locked away in her heart forever like a treasure.

Grannie had called her in and asked if she would like to see the abductor punished. She had said no, that everything that occurred was consensual. Grannie found that answer troubling, but let it pass.

Luna went back to work, but she wasn't the same. Whereas she'd been happy with her life and her work beforehand, she found her thoughts were always on Elk Mountain instead of Temple Park. The worst part was going to bed at night. It had only taken two nights to learn to love sleeping with someone else, whether that someone was wearing a luxurious fur coat or skin over tantalizingly sexy muscle.

She had seen the look on Grey's face when Deliverance took her away and knew in that instant that he had spoken hastily and regretted what he'd said. If they had been left alone, they would have worked it out. She knew it. Perhaps he would have said he didn't mean it. Perhaps he would have said he was sorry for comparing her to another female, especially one who had been his mate.

A couple of tears accidentally slipped from her eyes and slid to her pillow. She knew there was no point in asking Deliverance to take her back. But she wondered what Grey was doing. She wondered if he was thinking about her as she was thinking about him.

She even went so far as to lie awake and ask herself if, knowing everything she knew now, would she have gone with him willingly? Would she have chosen that if he had asked her? And the answer was yes. She wanted to be his.

CHAPTER_20

Litha's friend, Kellareal, calculated how much gold Stalkson would need to bring to Throenark based on the rate of inflation in the value of gold for the past two hundred years, the cost of the lifestyle he had outlined with cost of living increases, and factored in that he could, conceivably, live for another hundred years. They then determined that it would take all three of them carrying to transport that much gold through the passes.

When moving day came, he packed the few sentimental mementos he wanted to keep with him along with the maps and cultural guides Litha had supplied. He sorted gold into three containers, looked around the lodge that had been his home for a very long time, and sighed.

Grey walked to Win's lodge and knocked. His son answered the door.

"Dad. It's good to see you looking so much better."

Grey nodded. "Come go for a run with me. Can I leave my clothes inside?"

Win stood back and opened the door wider then told Cloud he was going out for a run. The two shifted to wolf form. Grey took the lead. They alternately trotted and jogged to the king's favorite lookout from where he could see so much of his beloved valley. Now and then he playfully nipped at Win's ears or at his heels. Win would respond with a fake growl and take off so that Grey had to give chase. For some reason, and he didn't know why, it was easier to show Windwalker affection in wolf form.

The outing served two purposes. He would be able to see his valley one more time and burn the picture into his memory and he would be sure that he didn't leave without letting Win know he was loved. When they reached the outcropping where Grey had spent so much time surveying his dominion, he shifted into human form. Win did the same.

"I've come here often when there was something on my mind that needed to be sorted out. You're going to find that you need such a place where there is enough silence and peace to hear your own thoughts and keep your own counsel."

"Dad." Win sounded a little confused and a little concerned. "What do you...?"

Grey held up his hand. "This is the day, the morning, when you're named alpha. When we go back down, you will be king."

"No. Well, first, I'm not ready and, second, you're king."

"Only for a few minutes more. I'm going away to one of the other worlds and it's permanent."

"That's impossible. The tribe needs leadership more than ever. With the fed bypassing the Jefferson liaison and issuing a permit for gas drilling? So close to the reservation? They may even do that thing where they drill sideways under our land and take our resources without asking or paying! This is no time for you to leave and it's certainly not a good time for a change in alpha."

Grey put his hand on top of his boy's trapezius letting his thumb curl lovingly around the curve of his neck. "See, Win, the very fact that you're concerned about these things, coupled with the fact that you're reluctant, tells me that you *are* ready. You're going to be a great king. Much better than I have been."

Win was shaking his head no. "Cloud is whelping in the spring. You're going to miss being a grandfather."

The king smiled, but did look saddened by that. "I will miss not seeing the young ones, but the tribe will make sure there is enough love and guidance to make up for my absence."

Win narrowed his eyes. "This isn't about that human woman, is it?"

"I don't expect you to understand. There's no way you could. But I don't want to live without her."

Windwalker's eyes widened and he hissed in a breath. "You mated with her!"

Grey hadn't thought about that. He looked downward toward the ground so that he could contemplate that without the distraction of Win and the scenery. But his eyes found his penis on the way and it made him chuckle, remembering how Luna had regarded it as her personal prize.

"What in Fenrir's name could possibly be funny?" Win thought his father wasn't taking the subject at hand seriously enough, and was getting agitated.

Looking him straight in the eye so that he would know the decision had been made and was no longer up for discussion, Grey said, "This is our last run together. The elders will help you as they've helped me. And BlueClaw is a conduit to the spirit world if you lose your way altogether. He's been a good friend to me. He'll be a good friend to you.

"I have left a short list of phone numbers in my lodge. If you decide you want to follow those who have migrated, The Order of the Black Swan will help you. If you need their help, call Glendennon Catch. He's the future of The Order, a quarter werewolf, very dominant like you, but my advice is that you cease feeling superior to human hybrids *before* you ask him for help.

"If, at some point, you are challenged for position as alpha, your response is easy. Decide how badly you want it. The job always goes to the werewolf who wants it most. If you don't want it at all, there's no shame in that. And please hear me when I say that those are not just words."

Stalkson grinned. "Sometimes the Fates have surprises in store. We may see each other again and, if we do, you may be my alpha."

Win sighed deeply and looked out over the valley. Grey could see that the heavy shroud of kingship was settling around his son like an aura. It was evident in the change in his posture and expression. It made Grey proud that his progeny was up to the task. It made him sad that Win would experience no more carefree moments until someone else took the mantel of responsibility from him.

At the appointed hour, Litha arrived with Kellareal. He was ridiculously tall, perhaps six six, and ridiculously well built, with eyes almost as black as Deliverance or Storm, and short spiky hair so pale it was almost white. The look was so exotic that it assured he would never be able to appear in that form anywhere in the human world. Unless he was masquerading as a professional wrestler.

Even with his intimidating physical presence, there was no sense of threat or danger. He exuded amiability and his smiles were infectious.

Litha just had to ask one more time. "I just have to ask one more time. Are. You. Sure? As in really, really, really, really sure? If it doesn't work out, you won't be able to reach me by cell phone."

"Look, Litha. I owe you debts I'm never going to be able to repay. I want you to know that I'm grateful. I appreciate every single thing that you've done for me. You and your friend." He nodded at Kellareal and Kellareal returned his nod in kind. "More than I can express.

"So please don't take this the wrong way, but, if you're that worried about what will become of me and about me being stranded, then maybe you could check in on me. Stop by and say hello once a month or so."

Litha looked stunned. "Wow. How stupid do I feel?"

She looked at the angel who shrugged and smiled as if to say, "I don't know. How stupid are you?"

"Of course I can do that. Why not? I can make it every few days in the beginning. If all is well, taper off to once a week, then once a month, and so on. What do you think?"

Grey grinned and his eyes twinkled. "Takes all the risk right out of the gamble."

"Yeah." She frowned. "Of course it also takes all the romance out of giving up everything for love."

Kellareal spoke up. "What's important is that he was *willing* to give up everything for love."

"I still say it's not as tragically romantic, but it does take a load off my mind."

Grey had put on a Greenland outfit that Litha had supplied. It was a sleeveless, belted tunic over pants that looked like linen or hemp.

"That looks good on you, werewolf." Litha noticed that he seemed self-conscious.

Stalkson Grey rolled his eyes. "It feels silly."

"Why? Because you look like an extra from a Robin Hood movie?" asked the angel.

Litha gave the angel a warning look, which made him shrug and chuckle, "Truth telling. Just can't help it. Not always popular, but it's always real."

Litha ignored that and turned back to Grey. "That's just because you aren't used to it. When you're surrounded by people wearing similar clothes you'll be glad."

"If you say so."

"Is this the gold?"

Kellareal was pointing to the three containers that were designed to be used as tool kits, but Grey thought they'd work for his purpose because they were sturdy enough to carry heavy tools and they had handles.

"Yes. The one on the end is lighter."

Litha went to the one on the end and started to lift it, but it didn't move. "Come on! Is this a joke? You know I'm pregnant. You could cause me to deliver early with a prank like that."

Grey blinked. "Is that too heavy for you?"

Kellareal laughed and handed the lightest container to Grey. "You take this one and your bag. I'll take these two and Litha can take you."

Three minutes later they were standing inside an impressive vault, steel walls lined with safety deposit boxes.

"I got you one of these big ones down here." He pointed to one of the large boxes near the end and handed Grey the key. "Your ID is inside, along with the lease to your apartment, and some currency to get you started. You can sell gold in the lobby during their business hours."

"Thank you." Grey opened the box, took out the currency and ID, and loaded the gold inside. Then he turned, "Now what?"

They gathered the empty containers and transported Grey to the elevator in the holdings building where his vault was located. The three exited onto the sidewalk at street level looking like they were emerging from a bank transaction rather than an interdimensional event.

Grey's two guides spent the next half hour helping him get his bearings. They showed him where he was in relationship to his apartment building and where that was in relationship to Temple Park. They had also staked out the closest grocery complete with butcher shop and pointed that out on the way.

His apartment was the sort of place that would make sophisticated urbanites feel like they'd won the lucky-in-life lottery. It was located on the thirty-second floor, but that wasn't a concern. He estimated that he could descend the stairs in less than six minutes in case of fire. Since it was a corner unit, it featured views of the cityscape with water beyond on two sides. He had to admit that the sunlight sparkling on the pale blue expanse of liquid motion was hypnotic.

The best part, by far, was that he was high enough above the trees to see Temple Park below. He smiled at Litha and her angelic friend.

She laughed. "Based on what you told me, I thought you'd like it. Best of a bad situation and all that."

It seemed there was nothing left to do. Between the three of them, they'd thought of everything. "Is there anything else we can do before we go?"

Grey shook his head. "Thank you. Again."

Kellareal stuck out his hand. "Good luck, wolf."

Litha surprised him by stretching up to give him a kiss on the cheek. "See you in three days."

And they were gone.

Grey didn't waste any more time. He hid his key to the security vault inside the small wall safe and pocketed his apartment key. He walked to the elevator thinking that he had committed to living in a spiraling tower, high above the earth, in the most anti-organic nightmare possible, amid throngs of smelly loud humans and pastel-colored vehicles with nasty exhaust. And, in spite of all that, he was excited about the possibility of getting a glimpse of Luna. All he could think about was getting to that park where he could begin a vigil of hope.

He found a vantage point in the forest apron, a good place from which to watch. And wait.

The first two days he saw women in red silk come and go, but Luna was not among them. He didn't need to see her face to recognize her. The graceful movement and subtle nuances of her unique curves were burned into his memory. As the hours wore on, his excitement over the possibility of catching sight of her began to wane and at the end of the second day he went back to the metal and glass building feeling sad and wilted.

On the morning of the third day, however, he saw

her as she traversed the breezeway between the temple and the residences, walking with several others. She said something, but even with wolf ears, he was too far away to hear what it was. She broke away from the others and stepped out into the park gardens carrying a basket. It looked as though she was interested in harvesting limited quantities of herbs grown by the cult for use in salves and potions. Since the plants in Temple Park were sacred, it was against the law for anyone but the Vergins to touch them.

Luna's eyes were on the ground as she meandered toward a healthy patch of blithemoss, but movement caught in the corner of her eye jerked her attention toward the forest. Her heart leapt when she thought she saw a familiar shape in the trees. Her mind knew it couldn't possibly be the cause of her despondency, a werewolf who occupied her waking thoughts and her nighttime fantasies. But her feet didn't ask permission when she veered off the path that led back to the temple and started into the forest.

She wondered if her separation from Stalkson Grey might have been distressing enough to cause hallucinations. There was no point denying that the werewolf had captured her heart when he took her body. As she mused, she asked herself if a person suffering a psychotic episode would be likely to consider that as a possible explanation for the unfolding of unlikely events. She concluded that, either her subconscious mind found sport in torturing her with images of the werewolf she longed to claim as lover or it was a trickster spirit intent on taking advantage of her vulnerable state of mind.

Regardless, she determined to scorn timidity and

investigate. If her experience with Grey had taught her anything, it was that willingness to face the unknown without fear can render the sweetest rewards imaginable.

Stalkson hoped to use quick glimpses of himself to pique her curiosity and draw her deeper into the forest than usual. When he was ready to reveal himself fully, he stepped out from behind a tree close enough to startle her. Still not ready to believe it could be Grey in the flesh, she reasoned that she would force the doppelganger to speak.

"What is it that you want here, likeness of a werewolf?"

"I want to see you and touch you." He cocked his head and his eyes darkened. "Perhaps taste you."

"I will rephrase. What are you doing in this dimension?"

"I live here. In an apartment in one of those tall buildings."

"Really. What was it you called them?"

He tried to remember the exact word he had used to describe then. "Monstrosities."

"Say your name," she challenged.

"Stalkson Grey."

"You *cannot* be Stalkson Grey. He told me that he would rather be cast into an eternal pit of fire than live in one of those buildings in the middle of a city."

"At the time I didn't understand that there are worse things."

"You seemed quite sure about it."

"Living away from my tribe, high above the earth, those things cause me distress, but not nearly as much as the prospect of not seeing you."

She didn't look convinced.

"Why are you wearing Greenlander clothes?"

"I live here now."

"How did you get here?"

"I asked people who can move between worlds to bring me."

"Who?"

"Deliverance's daughter, Litha, and her friend, the angel."

"An angel," she smirked.

"Yes."

"I don't believe in angels."

"But you do believe in werewolves."

She ignored that. "And I don't think Deliverance has a daughter. He's never said so."

"Well, how odd that he doesn't talk about his daughter while fucking girls her same age."

She narrowed her eyes and studied him. "You are very skilled at deceit, Spirit. Clever enough to add sarcasm to your impatience which is *exactly* what Stalkson Grey would do.

"You are a poor imitation, here to torment me, for what reason I don't know, but I do know that such things happen. When I was a child, my older sisters in the temple told us stories about spirits who pretend to be someone you know."

"Luna. I'm not a spirit and not an imitation. Actually it's a little disturbing to be called a 'poor' imitation of myself. And the last thing I'm here to do is torment you."

"Again, what is it that you want?"

"You."

"For the sake of argument, let's assume I believe that you are Stalkson Grey who has traveled from another world to lurk in my forest and stalk me. The last time I saw you, I was told that you prefer a mate who doesn't argue."

She noticed that his shoulders slumped a little.

"That was a stupid thing for me to say. Stupid and untrue. I want *you*. If that means arguing, then I want that, too."

The look on his face was so sincere that, whatever tenuous restraint she had on her impulse to throw herself at him dissolved. He was in the middle of making a case for belief in his existence when he found himself suddenly holding armfuls of lush woman. Her body molded to his as she melted into the kiss that she craved far more than air and water.

She was breathless when she finally pulled back. "It's really you, wolf."

He smiled a wolfish smile.

"It is."

"Did you come to take me home?"

He held her tight with one arm and pushed her hood back from her hair with the other hand.

"Home?"

"Elk Mountain."

"I can't. I'm stranded here. At least until tomorrow."

"What happens tomorrow?"

"Litha, the demon's daughter, is going to check on me."

"And she can take us away then."

"No."

"What?"

"She could, but then your overseer would just send Deliverance to bring you back again. It seems that you're a slave."

"I'm a slave," she repeated it like it had never occurred to her. Her eyes went slightly out of focus for a few heartbeats while she tried to organize that thought within her reality. "If that means that I can't choose what I do and can't choose to leave if I want, then, yes, I guess I am a slave. And, if I am, then all my sisters are slaves as well."

"We have to find a way to get them to release you."

"Why should I let you go?" Pandora stood behind her massive, ornate desk with her hands on her hips and looked Stalkson Grey up and down before returning her attention to Luna.

"Because, if you don't, I'm going to give the others an education on what's wrong with taking baby girls from their families and making slaves of them."

Pandora looked shocked, and spluttered, "That is *not* what we do here!"

"No? I have two questions for you. Did anybody ever ask any of us what we wanted? And, am I free to go? If the answer to either one of those questions is no, then we are innocents who have been enslaved and had our lives stolen from us."

Pandora narrowed her eyes and pressed her lips together so tightly her mouth turned white.

"Go." She waved her hand. "If you speak to any of the others on the way out or in the future, the deal is off."

Grey was so relieved he thought his knees might give out from under him.

Luna grabbed his hand and led him through an alcove and a side door where they were unlikely to encounter anyone.

"Wait." He pulled her to a stop. "Is there nothing you want to bring with you?"

She shook her head and pulled him along. "Everything I want and need is right here."

Without letting go of each other's hands, they ran through the park, through the forest, through the city streets and didn't stop until they were inside Grey's apartment with the door closed and locked.

Luna looked at him, her chest heaving, and started to laugh. "We did it! I'm free."

He laughed with her. "No. *You* did it. And *we're* free."

They decided to stay in the apartment until Litha returned because they didn't want to miss her. Grey had been told to call the building concierge if he needed anything. He placed an order for fruit and vegetables and nuts and cheese and had it delivered.

Luna had never seen her island from a vantage of height and was fascinated to see how things looked from the other side of the forest. She really couldn't have imagined the sparkling lakes that surrounded the city or what that much water looked like.

Grey could think of at least five different things he'd like to do to her body, but didn't want to be in a compromising position when Litha came. So he pacified himself with assurance that soon he'd be free to love his human with abandon and indulge her every fantasy.

"Before Litha comes, we need to decide what we want to do."

"What we want to do about what?"

"Where we're going to live."

"Don't we want to go to your home at Elk Mountain?"

"I want you to hear the options and then we'll decide. Together."

"You know I don't have any experience making choices, wolf. I'm not sure I'd be very good at it."

"When you were with me at Elk Mountain and I asked you to stay, that was a choice and you knew what you wanted."

"That's exactly my point. I didn't know what I wanted. I knew what I was *supposed* to want, but now I don't think that's the same thing."

"It's not complicated. It's easy. I'll tell you something about this and something about that and then you say how you feel about it. Like a game."

She looked uncertain, but said, "Okay. Let's try it."

"Choice number one. We could go back to Elk Mountain and there are some good things to be said about that. But I passed leadership on to my son and they are not expecting me back. They may have already moved into my lodge."

Luna looked disappointed.

"That's not all about choice number one. That world is getting more and more populated. One day the humans are going to become envious of our land and break their agreements. It's already started. In the future there won't be anywhere safe for werewolves to go and hide our nature."

Her mouth formed an "oh" and she looked pensive.

"Choice number two. You remember me telling you that half my people migrated to a new world to start over? Well, there's more to it than that. Many of the young males from my tribe have taken human mates. If we went there and joined with them, you'd have lots of human company. You could be instrumental in forming new traditions. And it's beautiful, Luna. Clean air. Clean water. There's so much land and the resources are untouched.

"We'd be surrounded by other tribes of werewolves so it would be safe. It would be a wonderful place to raise little ones. A wonderful, safe place."

Luna had never personally experienced a sales pitch before, but she would have had to be very dim not to recognize which option made Grey animated and excited.

"Little ones?" she smiled.

"Yes. If you want. But we don't have to. For me, the only constant in this equation is you. You're the beginning and the end, the requirement and the deal breaker. So what do you say?"

"Am I making a choice about babies or about where we're going to live?"

"Where to live. The other might have been too much information."

"Alright. I pick choice number two."

It was evident that he was suppressing a grin. "Are you sure? I don't want to influence you one way or the other."

She laughed at that. "Yes. I'm sure."

He grabbed her up and twirled her around.

CHAPTER_21

It was Storm's night to get dinner. Litha was due back from an errand any minute. She didn't say what exactly. Something about relocating that werewolf again.

He drove the Aston Martin to town for take-away Chinese and spent the time mapping out his life as far as he could conceivably plan, which was the next hour. He returned with Litha's favorite, which was shrimp with Chinese greens and his, which was General Tso's chicken. He tossed the keys on the kitchen counter, set the bag down, and started to set the table with plates, napkins, and real utensils. Litha didn't mind that he got take-out on his nights, but she did mind cartons and plastic forks.

He had expected her to be sitting at the table by then. Shrimp with Chinese greens usually brought her running. He ducked his head into the den then started down the hallway toward their bedroom. When he got to the doorway he heard a sharp hissing intake of breath. He hurried to the bath and found her there on a wet floor and clearly in a lot of pain.

He sank down next to her. "Baby. Is it time?" She couldn't even get out a decipherable answer and her eyes looked a little scared. "Can you take us to the clinic?"

Her reply was a scream that was stifled by a sob.

Storm's mind was racing. If she couldn't get them to Edinburgh and going to a regular hospital was out of the question, for obvious reasons, then what in the name of Hades could he do? He was near panic, when he saw the black diamond pendant roll across the v-neckline of her shirt. Bracing her upper body against his, he took her hand, curled it into a fist around the pendant, and squeezed gently.

In a heartbeat, Deliverance responded to the charm he had given his daughter and was standing over them. Storm gathered Litha into his arms. As he struggled to get to his feet, holding her without slipping on the wet floor, he was overcome with the déjà vu of reliving performance of a similar feat when Elora Laiken arrived in their world.

The demon looked every bit as scared as Storm was feeling. He carefully placed Litha in her father's arms saying, "Get her to the headquarters clinic in Edinburgh. Ask for Doc Lange. And come back for me before you do anything else."

Without another word, they were gone.

Standing there in pants that were wet, he realized he was shaking. Not from the cold. Deliverance was back in under three minutes, but it had felt like so much longer to Storm. When they popped into the clinic, he was already yelling, "Where is she?"

The nurse attendant on floor duty pointed toward the end of the hall. They asked him to wait outside the door while they changed her clothes and prepared her for delivery. Apparently they had awakened the doctor and he still hadn't arrived. Litha's moans were getting louder.

Storm turned to Deliverance. "Find that worthless medic and get him here now even if he's not wearing pants." The demon vanished and Storm decided he'd waited in the hall long enough.

They didn't try to stop him from entering. They'd already cleaned her up and gotten her into a hospital gown.

He brushed the damp hair back from her face. She looked up at him and tried to say his name, but the only sound that came out was a cry of pain. The door opened a second later and the doctor hurried in, as he was more or less pushed from behind by the anxious grandemon.

They had discussed the use of drugs with Doc Lange ahead of time and concluded that they couldn't risk it because they had no idea how Litha and the baby, with their unusual genetics, would handle various chemicals. Or even if they could. That left Litha facing what sounded like a difficult delivery with no help.

"What can I do?" Storm asked her helplessly. She was trying to say something, but she was clenching her teeth so hard he couldn't understand her. She tried again. He thought he understood, but couldn't believe she had asked for Elora. "You want Elora?" Litha nodded, at the same time she gripped his hand hard enough to break the bones.

Storm turned to Deliverance. "She wants Elora. I'm going to call Ram. You go get her."

Ram and Elora were curled up on the couch watching a movie and Helm was in bed for the night, gods willing. Ram heard his phone on the kitchen counter.

He reached over the bar and grabbed the phone. Looking at the caller ID, he said, "Stormy."

Elora grabbed the remote and paused the video. "Storm."

"Ram. She's in labor. I think it's bad. She wants

Elora."

He sounded scared to Rammel.

"Where are you?"

"Edinburgh. The demon is coming for Elora."

There was a loud knock on the door.

"I think he's here. She'll be there in a minute. I'll follow as soon as I can."

"Ram..."

Ram waited, but Storm didn't finish that thought. "I know. We're on the way." Elora started to open the door, but Ram got there in time to put his hand on it. "Wait! That demon is on the other side of the door. He's goin' to take you to Edinburgh. Litha's in labor and askin' for you." He opened the door and looked at Deliverance. "I have to get the nanny for my boy. Will you come back for me in fifteen minutes?"

Deliverance nodded, gripped Elora's forearm, and was gone. It was Elora's first ride through passes and she wouldn't say she was the least bit fond of the experience or any of the associated sensations. They walked through a wall of mist into Litha's hospital room and Elora didn't waste any time getting to her side.

She took Litha's hand. Looking down into her eyes the fear was so potent she could swear she smelled it, but she managed a little smile. "Hey there. We're gonna have a baby tonight. It's the most marvelous thing in the universe and, when you get on the other side of this, you'll say it was worth it. I promise."

Without looking away from Litha, she asked Storm, "What's going on?"

"She went straight into hard labor. She can't have any drugs because we don't know what they would do in her system. Or the baby's."

Doc Lange was on a rolling stool with a miner's light on his head trying to see what was going on.

Storm looked at his cell phone. "Yeah?" He turned to Deliverance. "Ram says he's ready. Would you go get him, please?"

Elora hissed at Doc Lange. "Tell me something. Now."

"We have a baby on the way." He said it nonchalantly, as only a person who has never given birth can do.

Elora wanted to throttle him and, in fact, made a mental note to do so when the crisis was over. "Idiot. Tell me something useful." Litha's shouts were starting to sound more like screams and Storm looked like he was about to lose it. "The baby is big and we can't give the mother any assistance of a pharmaceutical nature. The combination of those two things makes for a rough ride."

The next time Litha screamed, Storm grabbed the doc and shook him. "Do something!"

Elora couldn't have let go of Litha's hand if she'd wanted to. The witch's grip was like a vise and it crossed Elora's mind that she was lucky Litha had good control on the burn impulse or her hand could end up charcoal broiled.

She yelled for Ram and hoped that he was in the hall where he could hear her. He opened the door and looked in.

"Can you get the dad out of here and get him under control? Sedate him if you have to. That moron may be a quack, but he's the only quack we've got."

Hearing that, Deliverance assisted Rammel in pulling Storm off Doc Lange and dragging him out into the hall by force where he continued to fight them both. Ram was going to have a prize black eye to show for his trouble.

"Storm! Listen to me!" With the demon's assistance, Ram got behind Storm and got him into a throat lock. This wasn't the first time he'd been in this situation. Storm didn't respond well when people he loved were in trouble and he felt helpless to do anything about it. "If you do no' pull it together, we're goin' to have to sedate you. You do no' want to be conked out when your little girl makes her debut into this world." Ram gave him a little jerk. "You can no' help your wife this way."

Storm grew still.

"That's right." Ram took in a deep breath of relief and relaxed his hold a little bit. "'Tis no' easy to wait, but I'll be stayin' right here and Elora has your girl."

Slowly Storm sat up with his back against the hallway wall and Ram did the same. They stayed that way for the next half hour while Deliverance paced the hallway. Just as Storm said, "I hate this," everything went quiet in the room beyond the door. Too quiet.

Storm struggled to get to his feet. He had once told Glen that he had experienced fear. It was a lie. He hadn't experienced *real* fear until that moment. He reached out to open the door, but his hand was shaking badly. Rammel stood behind. Close. Just in case.

When Storm opened the door, the first thing he saw was Elora covered in blood with a shocked look on her face. The white bedding next to her was also drenched in fresh blood. He started to crumple, but Rammel grabbed him around the waist and held him up.

"Litha," Storm's voice broke into a whisper.

Elora smiled. "She's good. Or she will be. Just as soon as we show her that plump baby with all the black hair. Why don't you come take my place here? Hold your wife's hand, give her a kiss, and tell her she's the most beautiful woman who ever lived."

Storm started toward Litha, but one of the nurses stepped in front of him. Before he knew what was happening the woman had thrust a pink bundle into his hands, saying, "Mr. Storm. Would you like to hold your baby?"

She wasn't cleaned off yet, but that didn't matter. He looked from the baby to Litha with the characteristic shocked look of new fatherhood. The new mom was weak, but managed to smile, partly from the joy of knowing all was well with her little girl and partly from seeing that awestruck expression on her husband's face.

"Let me see."

He put the baby on Litha's chest where the new mom could feel the weight and warmth of that precious, pliant brand new little person. Storm kissed his wife and said, "Gods Almighty, Litha. You *are* the most beautiful woman who ever lived."

"Tired."

"Sleep then. We'll be here when you wake up."

Storm carefully retrieved the little one from Litha's chest like she was made of glass, then went with the nurse to clean the afterbirth off the baby, weigh her, measure her, brush her hair with a feather-soft baby brush, and wrap her in a clean pink blanket. Then he got to hold her on his shoulder and breathe in the heavenly aroma of brand new infant with Deliverance practically glued to his side. The demon had been visibly moved, but was strangely silent.

Litha didn't get to rest for long. While Storm and the baby were down the hall, the nurses got busy cleaning the blood away from Litha and changing her linens so that she could rest comfortably.

They also showed Elora where she could have access to a shower and gave her a clean set of scrubs to change into. Twenty minutes later she returned, looking clean but tired. She did a double take when she saw that Ram's eye was swelling closed, red on the way to black.

"You did good," he said.

She reached toward his eye instinctively, but stopped her hand before she touched it. "You too. Let's have a nurse take a look at that."

"'Tis fine."

"No. 'Tis no' fine." After mocking his accent lovingly, she left the room, but returned a few minutes later with ice. "I insist." She placed it in his hand. He smiled and nodded. Who doesn't love to be fussed over?

Litha roused from sleep when she heard voices in the room. A nurse was asking for the baby's name and the clipboard indicated that the question was official.

Storm said, "Liberty Rose Brandywine Storm."

"No." Litha's voice sounded so rough from all the screaming and she sounded like she might be drugged as well, even though she hadn't been. "Her name is Elora Rose Brandywine Storm."

Storm blinked. He could not have been more surprised if Litha had said the baby's name was

Clarence the Clown. After all the teasing about naming the baby Elora and Litha alternating between threats of burning him or leaving him in a pass if he continued talking about naming the baby Elora, which was never his idea in the first place, he really couldn't believe that she had done the very thing she had sworn would never happen in a thousand years.

Elora had been sitting on the radiator ledge under the window. When she heard the announcement, her hand flew to her mouth and she came to the side of the bed closest to the new mom.

"Litha. That's the loveliest thing I can think of."

"We're still calling her Rosie."

"It's a great honor."

Litha took Elora's hand. "I'm a demon, Elora. It's not an honor. It's a deal. If anything happens to you, we will take care of Helm and love him like he's our own. If anything happens to us, you'll do the same with Rosie."

Elora swallowed hard and looked over her shoulder at Ram. He took the ice away from his eye and nodded. "Ram says yes, we will. You know we would love her like she's our own and take care of her even without the contract."

"I know. But this way it's official."

"Don't burn me to seal the deal."

Litha smiled and let go of Elora's hand. "Okay. Sleepy."

Elora walked straight to Storm, gave him a one-armed hug, and gave Rosie a tender kiss on the cheek.

"That was scary," Storm said looking down at Elora. "You haven't looked that gory since the day you arrived at Jefferson Unit."

"Well, I guess that's what happens when a little

demon decides to skip the birth."

Storm looked confused. "What do you mean?"

Elora glanced at Ram who was leaning against a far wall. "You don't know?"

"Know what?"

"Rosie didn't come into the world like most babies. Litha was in so much distress... I guess Rosie just decided to put an end to it. So this little infant girl simply appeared in the air above her mother, still attached to the placenta. I reached out and caught her before she fell onto Litha's stomach. The afterbirth broke all over me, which is where all the blood came from.

"Doc Lange and the nurses got it together pretty quickly, cut the cord and tied it off. I asked if they were going to make her cry. They said they had already cleaned out her mouth and that she was breathing normally so there was no need to traumatize her. It's the first thing that quack has ever done that sounded right to me."

Storm looked stunned. "You're saying my baby wasn't really born."

"Well, obviously she was born. She just exercised an option that's not available to most of us. It made things a lot easier on her mama and that's for sure."

Elora chuckled. "Good luck trying to ground her."

She exchanged grins with Ram who was shaking his head and thanking Paddy it wasn't going to be his parenting problem.

Storm turned to Deliverance. "Have you heard of this before?"

"Not exactly, but we knew that the only thing we

knew was that we didn't know what to expect."

Elora smiled. "The main thing is Litha's fine and she'll be back to normal so much faster this way. It's probably the closest thing to a virgin birth that's ever happened.

"The baby's fine and she looks really happy where she is right now. I'm thinking daddy's girl." Storm couldn't help but look a little delighted at that possibility. He tucked his chin so he could look down at his baby sleeping on his shoulder, as if to confirm whether she was as happy as Elora said.

"No. She's not just fine. She's *so* beautiful," Elora gushed as she ran the back of a finger over her little pink cheek.

Turning to Ram she said, "Her first name is Elora. Did you know that?"

"Got a feelin' you'll not be lettin' any of us forget it."

At home in their apartment at Jefferson Unit, Elora gently swayed back and forth with Helm falling asleep on her shoulder. "Wasn't she beautiful, Ram? She looked more like a two-month-old baby than a newborn. Her cheeks. Her lips. All that black hair. It's so funny about her name being Rosie, because she makes me think of Rose Red from..."

"I know what you're goin' to say. That she's so pretty she's like a character from one of those stupid stories."

"I'm on to you, Ram. You call my fai... elftales stupid stories because you like getting a rise out of me."

His eyes twinkled. "Aye. Gettin' a rise out of you is the second most entertainin' thin' I can think of."

EPILOGUE

Baka's Log.

I have moved to Paris and settled into the temporary facility. Naturally I hope to be here for a short time, not because of any personal opinion about the location, but because the length of our stay directly corresponds to the success of our mission, which is to locate those infected with the vampire virus, administer the curative vaccine, and offer rehabilitation.

With each passing day, The Vampire Inversion, which is the informal name referencing the overall mission, becomes more sophisticated and better able to address the entirety of the problem, including what to do with the lost when they are recovered. Hiring personnel is a painfully slow and laborious process because of The Order's need for secrecy. Nonetheless, we have taken on some badly-needed psychologists and social workers who are in a position to follow our operation, like a carnival or circus, from place to place as needed.

We have also employed a master aromatherapist because we have learned, quite by accident, that some combinations of herbs or essential oils relieve the stress symptoms that mimic withdrawal. That speeds physical recovery of the victims, but psychological or emotional healing will require time. Therefore, we are going to need to leave our "halfway houses" operational after we have concluded the hunter phase of the operation. The biggest problem I anticipate with that is oversight of the mid level administrators left in charge.

The scope of that, in terms of resources and administration, is daunting. It's a good thing that The Order of the Black Swan is well-heeled because my projections of potential costs are staggering. My projections are based on fantasy numbers as we have no way of estimating how many virus victims remain at large in the world.

Of course costs could be reined in, considerably, if The Order took the same just-turn-them-loose approach as prison systems. But, because The Order adheres to its own doctrine which involves a far stricter code of morality than most religions, it has pledged rehabilitation of the cured regardless of expense. Naturally, I am more than proud to work for this organization.

We are like fishermen who go out every day and cast our nets. Perhaps we will be rewarded with a big haul. Perhaps we will return with a few of the lost who may be restored to the living. Perhaps we will be frustrated and have nothing to show for our time and energy.

At the close of each day, I collect and analyze reports of how many victims were recovered. I then coordinate with the local heads of operations on where to take them and how to transport them. I wish this task force had an organizational wizard as capable as Farnsworth from Jefferson Unit. How that would simplify my life.

One of the bright lights in this undertaking is the fact that I am able to work with my wife, who happens to have a unique and supremely useful ability to call vampire to her. The scientific operations that explain her talent are beyond us at this point in time and, therefore, seem quite magical. There are, in fact, many things about her that seem magical to me, but those thoughts shall be reserved for my personal journal. Let it suffice to say that I feel blessed to have her with me.

Speaking of my wife, one of the tricky things about her involvement is the irritant caused by the fact that the vampire juveniles do not even try to disguise their interest in her. They may be the emotional equivalent of human teens, but they are dangerous predators in every sense, meaning their interest in taking blood is inextricably entangled with their sexual urges. We have managed this problem, to the best of our ability, by making sure that Jean Etienne is always present when Heaven is called to play.

The vampire were, if anything, encouraged to pursue boorish standards by their early super-Americanization. Their view of what might be acceptable behavior toward a man's wife was severely tainted by the videos they watched both at Jefferson Unit and when they were guests of the somewhat quirky demon, Deliverance.

Realistically there may never have been a chance of them expressing anything resembling a civilized manner. For example, one of the biggest hurdles we've encountered is that none of them can maintain any focus if there is a woman in the area experiencing menses. From what Jean Etienne tells me, only mature vampire with a measure of self-discipline can remain focused with such a distraction.

Apparently menstrual blood is irresistible to them. Jean Etienne unabashedly describes the ecstasy of burying their faces in blood-covered pussy and rolling around in a state of euphoria. It sounds quite similar to the reaction that might be observed when one gives catnip to a feline.

Unfortunately, since there is no way to control for the presence of menstruating women, this is an issue that will probably persist.

The thing that weighs upon my mind most fervently is the persistent thought that we can never say job well done until the last vampire in existence is either dead or cured. It worries me that the possibility of that seems unlikely and yet I know that the other choice, to do nothing, is not a choice at all. ✺

POSTSCRIPT

Torn Finngarick called for a Guinness Extra Stout to be served to Glen, who wasn't used to alcohol at all and certainly wasn't ready for Irish black beer. He took a manly mouthful, thinking he had arrived, and promptly spewed it all over Torn in a spectacular demonstration of human fountain power. The other three members of Z Team laughed so hard they had to wipe tears.

"That was almost as funny as the night that Chokarzi stripper puked half a gallon of half-digested Cuervo in your face in the middle of a lap dance."

For reasons that defied logic, or perhaps because he had given them a much needed laugh, Z Team took a liking to Glen and accepted the news that they were reassigned to Jefferson Unit without any discernible reaction, violent or otherwise. When he informed them that they were to accompany him to Fort Dixon after the funeral, they simply shrugged as if they could care less. Glyphs said, "New York's no worse than any other place."

For all Glen could tell, that may have been Z Team's highest, most enthusiastic recommendation.

Excerpt from Book 5, *Gathering Storm,* Chapter One

"'Tis a good thing that Stormy and I are the bad asses that put the bad in Bad Company, else the two of us might be intimidated by unhappy wives standin' over us with mean faces and hands on delectably curvy hips."

"I concur," added Storm.

"You can *concur* until the cows come home *Sir* Storm, but you are still NOT playing in the Jefferson Unit Annual Rugby Match." Litha's voice was loud enough to make the babies get quiet and listen.

"Yeah. What she said." Elora couldn't really see what more could be added.

"We're playin'."

"We are."

"You. Are. Retired!" Elora countered.

"Retired is no' dead."

"*And* I'd like to add that we retired *early*. Lots of active duty hunters are older than we are and they'll be playing. There's *never* been a match that didn't have B Team represented and there's not going to be one this year either."

Elora huffed. "Since they retired B Team as a commendation to you..."

"*And* you," Storm added.

"Thank you for the thought, but not really and I don't think any of you would enjoy having me play. Stop trying to distract me. I'm in the middle of asking if you plan to still be repping for B Team when you're ninety."

The husbands looked at each other. They both sat on the sofa in Ram's and Elora's Jefferson Unit apartment with their arms crossed and looking like they had dug in to be stubborn.

"She might have a point," Storm said to Ram.

"We're no' givin' any points or any ground. With them 'tis always a slippery slope slidin' toward capitulation."

Storm looked at Elora. "We're not ninety now. We'll torch that bridge when we come to it. We're not even nearing thirty. And we're playing."

"Aye. We are."

Ram and Storm uncrossed their arms long enough to give each other a fist bump.

"Look," Elora began, "you're both young, strong, still in your prime and tough as they come."

"We're no' fallin' for the flattery approach."

"I'm just saying that you're also husbands and fathers with bones that can be broken and organs that can be ruptured." Elora left out the part about how she also hated overhearing the female spectators objectifying her husband. She already knew that he was the stuff of nocturnal fantasy and didn't need to have that driven home by listening to women talk about imagining him when they're with somebody else. Ugh!

They were silent and resolute. Resolutely silent.

Litha whispered something in Elora's ear and they withdrew to the bedroom, closing the door behind them.

"What do you think they're doin' in there?"

"I think they are saying that they will have better luck with a divide-and-conquer strategy."

"Aye. 'Tis my thought as well."

"Pact?"

"Indeed."

"Lust to dust."

"Sperm to worm."

"Womb to tomb."

Elora whispered to Litha. "Quiet. Ram's ears are amazing."

"Then let's duck out for a coffee. Or cocoa," she corrected.

When Elora nodded, Litha closed her fingers around her fellow conspirator's wrist and they popped into the lounge downstairs. The trip wasn't far enough to disturb equilibrium. It was no worse than a fast elevator drop.

"It won't hurt them to watch the babies for a little while."

Elora chuckled. "Neat trick."

They picked out two of the comfiest chairs, the

ones that made sitting feel like a hug, and sat facing each other.

"Hmmm. Well, I'm thinking that we're not going to get anywhere as long as they're together. They're feeding off of each other and ratcheting up the resolve. We need to interrupt that feed."

"Brilliant. Let us have yummy drinks and then go to our separate bedrooms to see if we can't get their arms uncrossed."

Litha smiled and initiated a soft five.

"Does it strike you that they're bein' *too* quiet?"

"It's your bedroom. You go check."

Ram opened the door and said. "Great Paddy loves a fuck. They're gone."

"What?" Storm got up.

"Gone. G.O.N.E. As in your wife always brin's an unknown factor to the mix. Great Paddy, I'm glad we were never assigned to hunt somebody like her." Ram ran a hand through his hair and looked at Storm. "So. Guess who's babysittin'?"

To all of you who have helped make this serial saga a success, I am so humbled and so grateful to be able to spend my days spinning tales.

The Witch in the Woods,
Victoria Danann

CPSIA information can be obtained
at www.ICGtesting.com
Printed in the USA
LVOW13s1015211117
557162LV00012B/215/P